GW01398771

The Vanishing Light

J.D Rivers

Published by J.D Rivers, 2024.

This is a work of fiction. Similarities to real people, places, or events are entirely coincidental.

THE VANISHING LIGHT

First edition. November 24, 2024.

Copyright © 2024 J.D Rivers.

ISBN: 979-8230075448

Written by J.D Rivers.

Table of Contents

The Echoes of Truth

Six months later, the world was a different place.

The streets, once filled with the hollow hum of indifference, were now alive with a kind of fervor that hadn't existed before. People had changed—woken up, as Evelyn liked to think of it. The world was slowly but steadily recovering from the shadow that Samuel Corvus had cast over it for years. Governments were forced to confront the corruption he'd sewn into their systems. Corporations had begun to clean house, some of them dismantling entirely, unable to survive the exposure of their complicity. The ripple effects of the revelations Evelyn, Victor, and Luke had brought to light had sent shockwaves through every corner of the globe.

And through it all, Evelyn stood at the forefront of that change, a quiet witness to the transformation.

She sat in the corner of a café, the steam from her coffee swirling up into the air as the sun filtered through the window, casting long rays across the table. She was alone—something she'd grown accustomed to. Her friends, her allies, had gone their separate ways. Victor had returned to his home country, taking up a position within a nonprofit organization dedicated to reforming the justice system, his once unflinching dedication to the cause now redirected to rebuilding what had been broken. Luke had slipped away quietly after the dust had settled, though he still kept in touch. He'd found a place working as an investigator for a human rights organization, the same fire in his eyes that had once burned for revenge now focused on using his skills for good.

And Evelyn? She had done what she had always done: she kept moving forward. The files, the truth, were out there. Samuel Corvus was in prison, though there were still whispers that he had friends, powerful ones, working on a way to release him. But Evelyn wasn't worried. The truth had always had a way of finding its way to the surface, no matter how deeply it was buried.

In the months since Corvus' fall, the world had seen uprisings, protests, and a cascade of revelations. But it wasn't just the destruction of the powerful that was important—it was the building of something new. People were waking up to the idea that the system, as it was, wasn't unbreakable. It was fragile, just like everything else.

Evelyn had become something of a symbol, though she hadn't asked for it. She had been interviewed by every major news outlet, her face plastered across magazines, but she hadn't allowed it to change her. She had spoken on the need for transparency, accountability, and the importance of never losing sight of what truly mattered—justice for those who had been oppressed by the very systems meant to protect them. She'd even taken a small position in a public accountability organization, one that ensured that the people who held power could no longer hide their secrets behind closed doors.

She was happy, or at least as happy as someone could be who had spent years in the dark, fighting for a future they couldn't fully grasp. There were moments of peace, of quiet satisfaction, but they were fleeting. The work was never done.

Her phone buzzed, pulling her from her thoughts. She glanced at the screen, a soft smile tugging at her lips when she saw the name.

Luke Bennett.

She hadn't heard from him in a few weeks. Her finger swiped across the screen to answer.

"Hey," she said, the smile still in her voice. "What's up?"

"Just checking in," Luke replied, his voice calm and steady. "How are you?"

"I'm good," she said. "Busy. But... good."

She could hear the subtle shift in his tone, as if he was about to say something important. "I've been thinking. About everything. And I think it's time we meet."

Evelyn's heart skipped a beat. *Meet?*

"Where?" she asked, her curiosity piqued.

"There's a place. I think you'll like it," Luke said cryptically. "It's in the mountains. Somewhere quiet."

Evelyn hesitated for a moment, the weight of the past months on her shoulders. It had been a long time since she'd seen Luke, since they'd stood together in that final confrontation with Corvus. The years had changed them, but it hadn't erased the bond they shared, the shared determination that had driven them through the hardest parts of their journey.

"Okay," she said, the words surprising even her. "I'll meet you there."

After hanging up, Evelyn sat in the quiet for a long while. The café was full of chatter, but the noise seemed distant, muffled. She thought about everything that had happened, all they had accomplished. But she also thought about the future—the one that was just beginning to take shape. A future that no longer seemed hopeless, but full of possibilities.

Chapter 1: The Vanishing Light

Evelyn Chase squinted into the rearview mirror as the last flicker of sunlight vanished behind the jagged peaks of the mountains. The sky above had turned a bruised purple, the kind of color that felt both ominous and beautiful—too beautiful for a place that had never fully accepted her. She ran a hand through her dark hair, pulling it back into a messy ponytail as the car rumbled over the winding roads. The faint hum of the engine was the only sound accompanying her as the night began to descend like a heavy curtain.

Brookhaven, she thought. It was just a small town, nestled deep in the Appalachian foothills, but there was something about the name that always made her uneasy. The kind of place where the air was thick with secrets, and the residents wore their smiles like armor.

The town had been quiet for years—or so she'd been told. But as soon as she'd heard the word "disappearance," Evelyn couldn't stay away.

Her fingers tightened around the steering wheel. She wasn't just a journalist anymore; she was a woman on a mission. And that mission had led her here, to this isolated pocket of the world where people still whispered behind closed doors, and the past refused to stay buried.

The car bounced over another pothole, jolting her back into the present. A few more miles and she would be there. She had arrived just before dusk, and now the town was coming into view—its crooked houses and overgrown yards framed against the silhouettes of the mountains.

There it was, just ahead, on the horizon like a black-and-white photograph slowly being soaked in ink. Brookhaven.

Evelyn exhaled slowly, more out of habit than necessity, and checked her watch. She was cutting it close. The last thing she needed was to arrive late and miss the chance to speak with the people who could finally help her answer the questions she'd been asking for far too long.

She rolled down the window, letting the cool air sweep in and ruffle the pages of her notebook, her only companion on this journey. The smell of pine and damp earth flooded her senses, sharp and fresh. It was the kind of scent that made her want to take deep breaths, even if the air itself felt like it was hiding something beneath its layers.

Brookhaven's main street looked like something out of a forgotten postcard. The stores were mostly shuttered, and the sidewalks were cracked in places where the trees had pushed their roots through the concrete. The few lights still glowing from shop windows cast faint pools of yellow on the empty street, as if they were trying, and failing, to keep the darkness at bay. It was the kind of town where the clocks seemed to run slower, where the passage of time couldn't be trusted to be anything but an illusion.

Evelyn parked the car in front of a small, rundown diner that looked as though it hadn't seen a remodel in decades. The windows were smudged, the neon sign flickering above the door spelling out "Open" in a tired, yellow glow. She took a moment to sit back in the driver's seat, closing her eyes briefly and allowing the quiet to settle in.

The vanishing of Natalie Harris had been a story that had caught her attention months ago. The headline had been simple, almost unremarkable: *Teacher Missing in Small Town, Police Suspect Foul Play.* But when the name "Brookhaven" had appeared under the headline, Evelyn's instincts had kicked into gear. She knew that name.

There was no mention of foul play. No mention of the whispers. But Evelyn had been trained to see what others didn't, to hear what others couldn't. The small towns she'd investigated over the years always had their undercurrents—places where the past ran deeper than anyone could imagine. And that was the kind of place Brookhaven was shaping up to be.

She grabbed her bag and stepped out of the car, the sound of gravel crunching beneath her boots loud in the stillness. The diner door creaked as she pushed it open, a gust of warm air hitting her face. The scent of fried food and stale coffee lingered in the space. There were a few patrons scattered around, sitting at booths, their hushed conversations drifting in and out of her hearing. Everyone stopped talking when she entered, and for a moment, Evelyn was certain the town was sizing her up.

A man behind the counter, graying at the temples and wearing a faded red apron, looked up from his coffee. His eyes were dark, with deep bags beneath them, like someone who had spent too many sleepless nights thinking about things he couldn't change. He didn't smile, but there was something in the way he regarded her—an almost imperceptible shift in his expression.

"You lookin' for someone?" he asked, his voice rough, like gravel scraping against metal.

Evelyn stood her ground, her hand resting casually on the edge of the counter. She met his gaze with steady eyes, careful not to reveal the weight of her questions too quickly. "Actually, I'm looking for a story."

The man raised an eyebrow, his gaze narrowing slightly. "You're not from around here."

"No," she replied. "I'm from out of state. But I'm here to do some research on Natalie Harris. I'm a reporter."

For a moment, the man didn't say anything. His eyes flickered to the other patrons in the diner, who had all returned to their meals, though there was an air of discomfort hanging in the room. Evelyn could feel it, too. The silence. The weight of being an outsider.

"You might want to talk to Ray," the man finally said, his voice low. "The sheriff. He's the one who's been handling all this."

Evelyn's pulse quickened. "Ray Donovan?"

The man nodded once. "That's the one. He'll be at the station. But don't expect him to be too friendly. He don't take too kindly to strangers."

"Thanks," Evelyn said, her hand already reaching for her wallet.

He waved it off, his eyes still not meeting hers fully. "Don't mention it."

Outside, the air felt colder than before. The street was quieter now, the fading light casting long shadows across the uneven sidewalks. The sheriff's station wasn't far, just a few blocks up the road. Evelyn made her way there, her mind racing with questions. What had happened to Natalie Harris? Was she just another victim of some tragic accident? Or had she vanished into thin air for reasons that ran much deeper than anyone was willing to admit?

The station was small, the windows lined with bars, giving the building a fortress-like feel. Evelyn pushed open the door, the bell above it jingling with an unsettling cheer. The room was sparse, with old wood paneling that looked like it hadn't been touched in years. A woman sat behind a desk near the back, flipping through a file. She didn't look up as Evelyn approached.

"I'm looking for Ray Donovan," Evelyn said, trying to keep her voice steady.

The woman's eyes flicked up, but her face remained neutral. "He's in the back. You'll have to wait."

"Is he available?"

The woman didn't answer right away. She just stared at Evelyn, as if assessing whether she belonged in this place. Finally, she nodded toward the door behind her. "He'll be with you in a minute."

Evelyn took a seat in one of the chairs along the wall. The station was eerily quiet, as though it had been left behind in time. The faint scent of coffee lingered in the air, and the distant ticking of a clock on the wall was the only sound in the room. She wondered how long it would take for her to get any answers—or if she would get any at all.

A door at the back of the room opened, and a tall man stepped into the main area. He was wearing a dark jacket, his face shadowed by the brim of his hat. His eyes were sharp, like those of a man who had seen too much, and his jaw was set in a firm line. He had the air of someone who was both approachable and entirely unapproachable all at once.

"You Evelyn Chase?" he asked, his voice gruff.

She stood, extending her hand. "Yes. I'm here to talk about Natalie Harris."

Ray Donovan looked her up and down, his gaze lingering on her with the subtle scrutiny of a man who didn't trust easily. Finally, he shook her hand, but it was a perfunctory gesture—more out of obligation than warmth.

"Come on back," he said, turning on his heel without waiting for a response.

Evelyn followed him down a narrow hallway to an office that was as dimly lit as the rest of the station. The air inside smelled of old paper and tobacco, and there were files stacked in haphazard piles on every surface. Donovan gestured for her to sit.

"You want answers?" he asked, his voice low. "So do I. But you're gonna have to understand something: this isn't a place where people talk. And I don't plan on making it any easier for you."

Evelyn sat down slowly, trying to read the sheriff's face, but it was as unreadable as the cluttered office around her. The only light in the room came from a dim desk lamp casting long shadows over piles of paperwork and a vintage fan that rattled quietly in the corner. The room smelled faintly of coffee and cigarettes, like a place that hadn't seen a thorough cleaning in years. It was a far cry from the modern, sterile offices she was used to, but something about the disarray made her feel even more out of place.

Donovan leaned back against his desk, crossing his arms over his chest. His eyes narrowed, scanning her with a kind of cold detachment that made her feel like she was on trial. Evelyn had learned early in her career that this was how seasoned investigators operated—no niceties, no wasted time. They sized you up first, gauging your resolve before they revealed anything.

"I'm guessing you're here because of the article," he said, his tone clipped.

Evelyn took a breath and nodded, her fingers resting on the edge of her notebook. "That's right. I've been following the case for a while. The disappearance of Natalie Harris... It's... it's unusual. There's something about it that doesn't add up. I want to get to the truth, Sheriff. For Natalie. For her family."

Donovan's lips twitched, but he didn't smile. "Everyone wants the truth," he muttered. "Some truths are better left buried."

Evelyn fought to keep her expression neutral, but she could feel the weight of his words pressing on her. He was trying to warn her. She had no intention of backing down now.

"I don't think it's something that can be buried," she replied. "Not when there's a pattern here. People don't just disappear, Sheriff. Not without a reason."

The sheriff's eyes hardened, and for a moment, Evelyn thought he might snap. He was tired—she could see it in the slump of his shoulders, the deep lines etched into his face. But there was more to it than that. Something about him screamed that he was carrying more than just the weight of this case. It was as if this town itself had taken a piece of him, slowly worn him down, until he had little left to give.

He exhaled sharply through his nose, his gaze never leaving hers. "You think you're going to get the answers you're looking for here? People in this town don't talk. They don't trust outsiders. And you're a stranger to them. Hell, you're a stranger to me."

Evelyn didn't flinch. She had dealt with hostile law enforcement before. "I don't need them to trust me," she said calmly. "I need them to be honest. And if you're not going to help me, Sheriff, then I'll find another way."

He stared at her, his expression unreadable. After a long silence, Donovan stood up abruptly and walked over to the window, his back to her. The heavy curtains were drawn, blocking out any remaining daylight. The only light came from a flickering streetlamp outside, casting jagged shadows on the floor. It was almost as if the town itself was drawing back into darkness, retreating into some hidden, forgotten place.

"The thing about this town is, people have long memories," Donovan said, his voice quieter now. "They remember everything. And they know things they won't say, even when they should. You might be able to crack that shell for a while, but I don't think you'll like what you find inside."

Evelyn felt a flicker of unease, but she pushed it aside. She had to stay focused. "I don't care what they remember," she said, her voice steady. "I care about what they're hiding."

Donovan turned to face her, his eyes dark with something that could have been suspicion—or maybe it was just exhaustion. He didn't answer immediately. Instead, he dropped into the chair behind his desk and stared at her for a long moment. Finally, he spoke again, his voice low.

"Brookhaven's always been a place of quiet," he said. "But quiet doesn't mean innocent. There's a reason why people come here and disappear. The town has a history. Not a proud one, either. And if you dig too deep, you might not like what you find."

Evelyn felt a chill slide down her spine. History. That word was like a warning, one that had been left unspoken but still hung heavy in the air. She'd known this wasn't going to be easy, but something about his tone—something about his warning—made her second-guess her decision to come here alone. The hairs on the back of her neck stood on end, but she refused to let him see that.

"I don't care about the past, Sheriff," she said. "I care about finding Natalie. She deserves to be found. People deserve to know what happened to her."

Donovan's eyes flickered, and for a brief moment, she thought he might actually relent. But then his gaze hardened once again, like a stone wall being built between them.

"If you're set on this, fine. But I won't help you," he said, his voice sharp. "If you want to look around, do it on your own time. But don't come crying to me when you get too close to the wrong people. Because in this town, there are people who can make you disappear just like the rest."

Evelyn could feel the weight of his words hanging in the air, but she didn't back down. She'd heard threats before. She was used to it.

"I'll take my chances," she said, standing up. "But if you change your mind, Sheriff, I'll be here."

Donovan didn't respond. He didn't need to. His silence was just as telling as anything he might have said. As Evelyn turned to leave, she caught a glimpse of something in his eyes—something like regret or maybe even fear. But it was gone before she could be sure.

Outside, the air was cooler now, the last remnants of daylight slipping away as the evening settled over the town. Evelyn walked briskly back to her car, her mind racing. She had come here expecting resistance, but Donovan's warning unsettled her. There was something more to this town, something darker than she had anticipated. And it was clear that she had only scratched the surface.

The streets of Brookhaven were quieter now, the sounds of the diner fading as the night took over. Her footsteps echoed in the empty space, and the streetlamps flickered above her. She had no idea where to go next, but she knew one thing for sure: she couldn't let fear or intimidation stop her. Natalie's disappearance was more than just another case. It was a thread that, if pulled, might unravel everything.

Evelyn reached her car, unlocked the door, and slid into the driver's seat. Her fingers hesitated over the keys for a moment before starting the engine. She couldn't afford to second-guess herself now.

The road ahead was still long, both literally and figuratively. And Evelyn Chase had never been one to back away from a challenge. The mystery of Brookhaven, with its shadows and secrets, had only just begun.

As the car pulled away from the sheriff's station, Evelyn couldn't shake the feeling that something was watching her from the shadows. The road twisted ahead, dark and winding, with nothing but the occasional glow of a far-off streetlamp to guide her way. She had come to Brookhaven to find the truth. But now, with every turn she took, she felt the weight of the town's past closing in on her, like a thousand eyes watching from the darkness, waiting for her to make a mistake.

And she knew—whether she was ready or not—the past of this town would soon come rushing to the surface.

Evelyn's mind was whirling as she drove away from the sheriff's station. She could feel the weight of Donovan's words still hanging in the air, an unspoken promise that things in Brookhaven were more complicated than they appeared. As she maneuvered the car through the twisting streets, the dim glow of the streetlights stretched long across the asphalt, casting eerie shadows that seemed to follow her every move.

The town felt different at night. It wasn't just the silence—it was the way the buildings loomed over the streets like forgotten ghosts. There was an unsettling stillness, a kind of quiet that made her feel as if the entire place was holding its breath. The kind of silence that didn't belong in a living town. It was the silence of a place with secrets, secrets it would rather keep hidden. Evelyn had been in small towns before, but this one felt different. Too quiet. Too watchful.

She glanced in the rearview mirror, her eyes scanning the empty road behind her, the dark corners of the town stretching out like a web. She knew the feeling well—the sensation of being followed, of being observed from the shadows. It was the kind of gut instinct every investigative journalist learned to trust.

But as she drove further into the heart of Brookhaven, the sensation didn't fade. Instead, it deepened, as if the entire town was alive and waiting to see what she would do next.

Evelyn slowed down, her eyes drifting over the darkened storefronts, the empty parking lots. The occasional flicker of a light in a window—maybe someone inside was watching her as she passed. She couldn't tell. The windows were too high, too far from the street. But she had the unsettling feeling that she was being sized up. That they were all watching her, waiting to see how far she would go before she understood that some things were better left alone.

Her fingers drummed lightly on the steering wheel. She needed to focus. She couldn't let her paranoia cloud her judgment—not yet.

She turned onto another road, the narrow, winding streets snaking deeper into the town. Her headlights swept over the houses—small, dilapidated buildings that looked as though they hadn't been touched in decades. The lawns were overgrown, weeds pushing up through the cracks in the sidewalks. There was a sadness in the air, an overwhelming sense of neglect.

Her gaze flickered to one house in particular—a large, two-story Victorian at the end of the block. Its windows were dark, but there was something about the way the house stood there, looming, as though it had seen too much. Evelyn's breath caught for a moment, and she instinctively slowed the car. She had no reason to feel uneasy about it, but she couldn't shake the sensation that the house was... waiting.

She wasn't sure why, but something in her gut told her that the answers she was looking for were closer than she thought. She had to see this house up close.

Parking the car just past the corner, she sat for a moment, watching the old house from behind the wheel. Its windows seemed to peer down at her like vacant eyes, dark and hollow. The air around it felt thick—like a warning, though she couldn't put her finger on why. After a beat, she grabbed her notebook, locked the car, and started walking toward the house.

The grass was high and unkempt here, as though no one had bothered to care for it in years. Evelyn's footsteps barely made a sound as she walked toward the front yard, the crunch of gravel and leaves beneath her feet the only noise in the otherwise still night. She hesitated before stepping onto the porch, glancing back over her shoulder as if expecting someone to be watching from behind the curtains of a nearby house. But there was nothing. Just silence.

The front door was ajar. A thin sliver of light leaked out from inside, illuminating the porch in a faint yellow glow. It wasn't much, but it was enough to make her heart rate quicken. Evelyn approached cautiously, her instincts alert. Her hand reached out for the door, but as her fingers brushed the handle, she froze.

A noise—soft at first—came from inside the house.

It was the sound of a chair scraping across the floor, a dragging sound, followed by a low murmur of voices. They were too muffled for her to make out what was being said, but the air shifted, thickened, and Evelyn's pulse raced.

She should leave. This was foolish. She wasn't supposed to be here.

But something—something deeper than logic or caution—pulled her forward.

Evelyn took a step inside, just enough to peer into the dim hallway. She couldn't see much, but she felt the presence of something in the room beyond. Another sound—someone moving across the floor—then a voice, clearer now, but still not enough to make out.

It was a man's voice.

"Not yet," the voice said, low and gruff. "We'll wait. She'll come to us. She always does."

Evelyn's breath caught in her throat. Her pulse quickened. Was this about Natalie Harris? Was this some kind of clue? She had no idea, but the hairs on her neck stood up as a sense of dread crept over her. She shouldn't be here.

Before she could retreat, a door creaked open further inside the house. She jerked her head back in alarm, but the shadow of a figure appeared in the doorway—a tall man, his silhouette barely visible against the dim light.

Evelyn froze. Her heart hammered in her chest as the figure stepped closer, the outline of his face just visible in the soft glow. He was older, with a strong jawline and sharp features. His eyes, though, were what caught her attention—too sharp, too intent.

He didn't seem surprised to see her, but he didn't smile either. Instead, he raised an eyebrow and looked her over, his expression unreadable.

"Didn't think anyone would be interested in this old place," he said, his voice rough and gravelly.

Evelyn's mouth went dry, but she forced herself to speak. "I was just—" She cut herself off, unsure of how to explain.

The man stepped back, gesturing toward the door. "If you're looking for answers, you won't find them here. Not tonight."

Evelyn hesitated. Her instinct was telling her to turn around, to leave and never look back. But there was something in the way he spoke, something in the quiet authority of his voice, that made her want to stay.

"I'm not looking for trouble," she said carefully. "I'm looking for Natalie Harris. She disappeared a few weeks ago. The sheriff—"

"The sheriff doesn't know anything," the man interrupted, his voice low. "He's been trying to put together the pieces for years, but he'll never see the whole picture."

Evelyn blinked, caught off guard by his bluntness. "What do you mean?"

The man's eyes hardened. "The past has a way of catching up to us here. And when it does, there's nowhere to hide. Especially not in this town."

Before Evelyn could respond, the man gave her a look—a look that seemed to weigh her down, making her feel like an intruder in a place she didn't belong. "You've been warned," he said, his tone final. "Don't dig too deep, Miss Chase. Some things are better left buried."

Evelyn's stomach turned. The warning felt like a curse, one that might follow her through every step of her investigation. But she was in too deep now. She had no choice but to continue.

With one last look at the mysterious man, Evelyn backed away, heart racing, and turned back toward the street. The house loomed behind her, its dark windows now reflecting the glow of her headlights.

As she walked back to her car, she couldn't shake the feeling that she had just crossed a line. A line that, once crossed, couldn't be uncrossed.

She started the engine and pulled away from the curb, the town's oppressive silence closing in around her once again.

The investigation was just beginning, but Evelyn knew one thing for sure: whatever she uncovered in Brookhaven would change everything.

Chapter 2: Beneath the Surface

Evelyn woke the next morning to the quiet hum of a town that seemed to hold its breath, waiting. The darkness outside her window had given way to pale gray light, and the cold air that filtered through the cracks in the old building made her pull the covers tighter around her shoulders. She hadn't expected to feel unsettled, but the night had left its mark. She had spent most of the early hours staring at the ceiling, replaying the strange encounter with the man from the old house over and over in her mind.

"Don't dig too deep, Miss Chase. Some things are better left buried."

His words lingered in her mind like a poison, and the more she thought about them, the more they gnawed at her. What did he know that she didn't? Why had he warned her so specifically? Was it because of Natalie Harris? Or was it something deeper? She had never been one to back away from danger, but she wasn't naïve either. The people in Brookhaven were hiding something, and she was determined to find out what it was.

Evelyn swung her legs over the side of the bed and rubbed her eyes. She had been staying at the only motel in town—the one that smelled faintly of mildew and where the walls were thin enough to hear the faint hum of the radio from the neighboring room. It wasn't much, but it was all she could afford for now.

There was no denying it: something in Brookhaven had her on edge. The air was thick, like it was hiding something that wanted to be left in the past, something dark, something that might have to do with the vanishing of Natalie Harris, or the strange warning she had received last night.

As Evelyn made her way to the small bathroom, the mirror above the sink reflected the tiredness in her eyes. She had bags under them, her face pale from a restless night. The weight of the investigation was already starting to settle on her shoulders.

She splashed cold water on her face and leaned closer to the mirror, trying to shake off the nagging sense of unease.

She needed answers.

After a quick shower, Evelyn grabbed a notepad, tucking it into her bag alongside her camera. The town had already begun to stir outside, and the morning light, weak but persistent, bathed the streets in a cool glow. Brookhaven was quiet, yes, but there was a rhythm to it—small town life that persisted despite the whispers that hung in the air.

She pulled on a jacket and stepped outside, the air sharp and crisp. The day felt like a clean slate, but as she walked down the main street toward the diner, she couldn't shake the feeling that something was off. She wasn't sure if it was the way the locals looked at her—or the way they didn't look at her—that bothered her more. People avoided eye contact here, as though even a simple glance might uncover something they didn't want to acknowledge.

The diner was just as empty as it had been the night before. The same old man with the graying hair sat behind the counter, his eyes cast downward as he sipped a coffee. The flickering neon sign outside buzzed sporadically, casting a dim, almost sickly light through the windows.

"Morning," Evelyn said as she walked in, forcing herself to ignore the gnawing tension in her chest.

The man behind the counter grunted in acknowledgment but didn't look up. Evelyn took a seat at the counter, setting her bag beside her and flipping open her notebook.

There was a waitress, a younger woman with a dark ponytail, who came over to refill the old man's coffee. She glanced at Evelyn with a look that seemed half curiosity, half caution, but said nothing. Evelyn knew she had to make the first move. She didn't have time to play games.

"Can I get a coffee?" Evelyn asked, her voice steady.

The waitress nodded and walked off without a word.

Evelyn pulled out her pen, scanning her notes from yesterday. Donovan had been no help—he had barely said anything useful. The sheriff had been adamant that the townsfolk weren't going to talk, and his cryptic warnings had done little to ease her concerns. Still, she couldn't let fear rule her. She had a job to do. A story to uncover.

She'd learned over the years that people didn't just vanish. There were always signs, always clues, even if they were buried deep. Evelyn had learned how to find them. It was a skill she had honed over a decade of reporting—tuning into the small, telling details, reading between the lines of what people said and didn't say. She was good at getting people to talk, but Brookhaven seemed different. They weren't just ignoring her. They were avoiding her.

She jotted down a few notes, the ink scratching against the page in the quiet diner. The silence was oppressive, but Evelyn didn't mind. It gave her space to think.

Her coffee arrived with a soft thud on the counter, and she looked up to find the waitress standing there, her arms crossed, her face unreadable.

"Is it true?" the waitress asked suddenly, her voice low.

Evelyn raised an eyebrow, caught off guard. "Is what true?"

"About Natalie Harris," the waitress said, her voice barely above a whisper. "That she... that she didn't just disappear. That something happened to her."

Evelyn felt her heart race, but she kept her composure. This was the first real lead she'd gotten in days.

"What do you mean?" Evelyn asked carefully, leaning forward just a bit.

The waitress hesitated, then looked over her shoulder, as if making sure no one else was listening. "There are people in this town who think she ran off on her own. That she just... left. But there are others who say something much worse happened to her. People talk about strange things, you know? Things that don't make sense." She swallowed, her eyes darting nervously. "It's just... it's hard to explain. But people around here—they're scared."

Evelyn's mind raced. This was what she had been waiting for, the first real crack in the silence.

"Who's scared?" she pressed.

But the waitress didn't answer. She glanced at the door, as if something—or someone—was making her anxious. Then, without another word, she turned and walked away, leaving Evelyn to stare at her coffee.

Evelyn sat back in her seat, her fingers gripping the edge of the table. She had been given a taste, a hint of something larger, but now the trail was cold again. She needed to find more, but the walls around this town were closing in, thick with the kind of fear that made people silent.

She finished her coffee and paid the bill, walking out into the crisp morning air. The town felt heavier now, like a weight pressing down on her chest, and the road stretched before her in a way that felt both promising and foreboding.

She needed to speak to more people. But who could she trust in a town where no one seemed to trust anyone else?

Evelyn spent the rest of the day canvassing the town. She walked down the small streets, passing a few lonely shops and houses with boarded-up windows. There was a palpable sense of abandonment here, a feeling that something had been lost and no one was willing to acknowledge it. Even the locals she approached for answers seemed more interested in getting away from her than in offering any information.

At one point, she came across an elderly woman sitting on a porch swing, her eyes squinting against the sun. Evelyn thought this might be a good chance to ask her about Natalie Harris. She approached with a polite smile, trying to seem as non-threatening as possible.

"Excuse me, ma'am," Evelyn said, standing at the foot of the steps. "I'm a reporter. I'm looking into the disappearance of Natalie Harris. Do you know anything about it?"

The woman didn't look at her directly. Instead, her gaze was fixed on something far off in the distance. After a long pause, she replied, "I don't know anything about that girl. People go missing here all the time. Nothing to be done about it."

Evelyn felt a chill run through her. "What do you mean? People go missing?"

The woman didn't respond. She just continued rocking in her chair, her face expressionless. Evelyn felt the weight of her words sink in. This wasn't a town where people disappeared accidentally. This wasn't a place where things happened without cause.

As she left the woman's porch, Evelyn's thoughts were heavy with uncertainty. What kind of place was Brookhaven? And what exactly had happened to Natalie Harris?

The rest of the day passed in a blur of fruitless attempts to speak with locals. No one seemed willing to help her—no one except for the waitress at the diner, who had offered just enough to make Evelyn believe there was something sinister lurking beneath the surface of the town.

By late afternoon, Evelyn was back at the motel, sitting at the small desk with her notebook open in front of her. The sun had begun to dip behind the mountains, casting long shadows across the room. The lights in the motel flickered once, then dimmed.

Evelyn rubbed her temples, her mind still racing. She couldn't shake the feeling that she was missing something—something important. She had to find out what happened to Natalie. She couldn't leave until she did.

There was something dark here, something buried deep in the town's past, and Evelyn Chase would be the one to uncover it—no matter what it took.

As the sun began to set, casting long shadows across the quiet streets of Brookhaven, Evelyn sat at her desk in the motel room, the dim light of the lamp beside her casting an uncomfortable glow on her notes. She had spent the better part of the afternoon canvassing the town, trying to find any lead—any shred of information—that might help her make sense of the disappearance of Natalie Harris.

Nothing.

People were tight-lipped, unwilling to engage with her beyond polite, dismissive answers. It was like the town had closed itself off from the outside world, as if everything about it was hidden beneath layers of dust, never to be disturbed.

But Evelyn was persistent, and despite the town's cold shoulder, she refused to give up. She had uncovered enough to know that something wasn't right, but she still couldn't put her finger on what that something was. The atmosphere in Brookhaven was suffocating, like a thick fog that clouded every corner of her investigation.

Her phone buzzed on the desk, breaking the silence. Evelyn glanced at it. The message was from her editor, a terse reminder to check in and provide a progress update. She sighed, feeling the weight of her job pressing down on her. She wasn't sure what she had to report yet, but she couldn't afford to leave with nothing.

She texted back, a simple reply: *"Still investigating. No real leads yet, but I'm digging."*

With a sigh, Evelyn turned her attention back to her notes. She reviewed the scribbles on the page—pieces of conversations, observations, anything that might reveal a clue. The more she thought about the waitress's cryptic words about people being "scared" and the warning she had received from the man in the old house, the more she felt the oppressive weight of the mystery pressing down on her.

The one thing that kept circling in her mind was the idea that Brookhaven had secrets—deep ones—and that whatever had happened to Natalie Harris was tied to those secrets. The sheriff's disinterest, the way the locals avoided eye contact, the cryptic warning from the man in the house—it was all adding up to something far darker than she had anticipated.

Evelyn leaned back in her chair, rubbing her temples as she let her mind wander. She couldn't help but think of the town's history. She knew that every place had its skeletons, and the more she uncovered about Brookhaven, the more it felt like those skeletons had been carefully buried, forgotten by time. But someone—or something—was still watching.

Just then, a knock at the door startled her. She jumped in her seat, her heart racing, and quickly stood up to answer it.

She opened the door to find a man standing there, his face partially obscured by a baseball cap pulled low. He looked like a man in his mid-thirties, his features hardened by time, though there was something oddly familiar about him.

"Can I help you?" Evelyn asked, already feeling the tension rise in her chest. Was he here to warn her away from the story? Was this another dead end?

The man looked past her into the room, and Evelyn could see the way his eyes darted nervously, scanning the space behind her. His hands were shoved deep into his pockets, and he stood with his shoulders hunched, almost as if he were trying to make himself smaller.

"I... I saw you asking around today," he said, his voice low and hesitant. "About Natalie Harris."

Evelyn's pulse quickened. "Yes, I'm a reporter. I'm looking into her disappearance. Do you know anything about it?"

The man hesitated again, his lips pressing into a thin line. He glanced down the hallway, as if to make sure no one was listening. When he spoke again, his voice was barely a whisper.

"You need to be careful," he warned, his eyes darting back to her. "People around here—they don't like strangers digging into their past."

Evelyn frowned. "Who's 'they'?"

"The ones who... who know what happened," the man said, his voice growing more urgent. "People who've been here long enough. Some things are better left forgotten."

He paused, as though considering whether to say more, but then he shifted his weight uncomfortably, clearly uncertain. "You should talk to Mr. Ward, the historian. He's lived here for decades. If anyone knows what happened to Natalie, it's him. But..." He trailed off, swallowing hard.

"Is he a reliable source?" Evelyn asked, her tone skeptical. "Because everyone I've talked to so far hasn't exactly been forthcoming with information."

The man nodded slowly, but there was something dark in his eyes, something that made Evelyn feel as though she was on the edge of uncovering something too dangerous to know.

"I don't know if I'd call him reliable," he said finally, glancing over his shoulder one more time. "But if you want to know the truth... he's your best bet. Just don't push him too hard. There are people in this town who don't want things brought up from the past."

With that, the man turned and walked away, his steps quick and deliberate. Evelyn stood in the doorway for a long moment, her mind racing. She had no idea who this man was or what his motivations were, but there was something about him that felt sincere, even if his warning was wrapped in ambiguity.

The name *Mr. Ward* stuck with her, gnawing at her thoughts. If he was the town's historian, he might know something—anything—that could help her unravel the mystery surrounding Natalie's disappearance.

Evelyn closed the door and grabbed her jacket. She wasn't going to let the night slip away without following up on this lead. She had to see Mr. Ward, no matter how reluctant he might be to talk.

By the time Evelyn reached Mr. Ward's house, the town was shrouded in twilight, the air cooler and more still than it had been all day. Brookhaven was different at night—empty, almost suffocating, as if the town was holding its breath, waiting for something to happen.

Mr. Ward's house was at the far end of a narrow street, nestled between overgrown trees. The house itself was old, a two-story Victorian with peeling paint and a sagging porch that looked like it had seen better days. The windows were dark, but there was a faint light coming from the upper floor.

Evelyn approached cautiously, her footsteps muffled by the thick carpet of fallen leaves. As she reached the door, she paused for a moment, wondering if she should turn back. Her instincts screamed at her to be careful—this was a small town, and Mr. Ward might not appreciate being disturbed, especially not by a reporter. But she had come this far, and there was no turning back now.

She knocked, and after a moment, the door creaked open. Mr. Ward stood there, his features sharp and angular, his eyes tired but alert. He was tall, with a graying beard and thinning hair. His clothes were old-fashioned, a tweed jacket and brown slacks, as though he were living in a different era.

"Can I help you?" he asked, his voice quiet but direct.

"Mr. Ward?" Evelyn said, offering a polite smile. "My name is Evelyn Chase. I'm a reporter. I'm investigating the disappearance of Natalie Harris."

At the mention of the name, Mr. Ward's expression shifted—just slightly—but it was enough for Evelyn to catch the change. His eyes narrowed, and he stepped back, looking her up and down.

"I'm not sure I can help you with that," he said slowly, his voice low. "It's a painful subject for many of us here in Brookhaven."

Evelyn's heart skipped a beat. She had expected some resistance, but the way Mr. Ward had reacted—it felt different. He wasn't just avoiding the topic. He was afraid of it.

"I understand," Evelyn said carefully, trying not to push too hard. "But if you know anything—anything at all—it could help me understand what happened."

Mr. Ward hesitated, his gaze flickering to the darkness beyond his porch. He looked as though he was considering something, weighing the decision in his mind. After what felt like an eternity, he nodded and stepped aside.

"Come in," he said quietly. "But we'll need to be careful what we say."

Evelyn entered the house, the air inside thick with the scent of old books and wood. The walls were lined with shelves, filled with dusty volumes on local history. The room felt like a museum, each object a piece of a forgotten past.

"Sit," Mr. Ward said, motioning toward an old armchair by the fireplace. "I'll get us some tea."

As he disappeared into the back of the house, Evelyn sat down, her mind racing. She knew she was on the verge of uncovering something important, something that might finally bring her closer to the truth about Natalie Harris and whatever had happened in this strange, secretive town.

The clock on the wall ticked loudly in the silence, the sound echoing through the room as she waited for Mr. Ward to return.

Chapter 3: The Historian's Secrets

Evelyn sat in the old armchair, the fabric worn and threadbare from decades of use. The fire in the hearth crackled softly, its warm glow casting long shadows on the walls, which were lined with shelves of dusty books and old photographs. The air smelled of must and aged paper, thick with the weight of history, as if the house itself were a relic of a bygone era.

Mr. Ward had disappeared into the back of the house to prepare tea, leaving Evelyn to her thoughts. She glanced around the room, trying to piece together what she had learned so far. The man who had warned her to speak to Mr. Ward had seemed sincere, but Evelyn wasn't sure what to make of the historian. He seemed too cautious, too reluctant to talk about what had happened to Natalie. What was he hiding?

The faint ticking of a clock on the wall was the only sound in the room, and Evelyn found herself growing impatient. She had come here for answers, and she wasn't going to leave without them.

A door creaked open, and Mr. Ward returned, carrying a small tray with two cups of tea. He set the tray on the table in front of Evelyn and sat down across from her. His eyes were intense, but there was a guardedness to them, a reluctance that made Evelyn feel like she was about to hear something she wasn't supposed to.

"I assume you've heard about the history of this town," Mr. Ward said, his voice low and steady. "Brookhaven is not just any small town. It has a past—a dark one. People here know things, but they don't like to talk about them."

Evelyn nodded, her curiosity piqued. "I'm aware that something happened here. That Natalie's disappearance isn't the first of its kind."

Mr. Ward's eyes darkened. "No, it's not the first. But it may be the most recent." He paused, sipping his tea before continuing. "You're right to suspect that something is off about this town. But you're also right to be cautious. If you dig too deep, you may unearth more than you bargained for."

Evelyn leaned forward, her voice steady but insistent. "What do you mean by that?"

Mr. Ward set his cup down and folded his hands in his lap. "There are things in Brookhaven that we've tried to forget. Things that some people wish had stayed buried. I've lived here my entire life, and I've seen things, heard things, that would make your skin crawl. The town has a long history of—" He hesitated, searching for the right words. "Of disappearances, of people vanishing without a trace. And it's not just a coincidence. It's a pattern."

Evelyn's heart skipped a beat. "What kind of pattern?"

Mr. Ward's face grew grim. "Brookhaven has always had a dark side, a side that most people prefer to ignore. There are forces at work here, things that go beyond the normal understanding of reality. We've lived with them for so long that we've learned to accept them, to pretend they don't exist. But every few years, something happens—a disappearance, a tragedy—and we're forced to face what we've been avoiding. That's what happened with Natalie."

Evelyn's mind raced as she tried to process what Mr. Ward was saying. A dark side to the town? Forces beyond normal understanding? What could he mean?

"I'm not sure I understand," she said cautiously. "Are you suggesting that there's something supernatural going on here? Something otherworldly?"

Mr. Ward's expression remained unreadable. "I'm not saying it's supernatural, but there are forces—call them what you will—that have influenced this town's history. People have tried to ignore them, to push them aside, but they've always been there, lurking beneath the surface. It's as if the town itself has been built on top of something—something ancient. And sometimes, it wakes up."

Evelyn's skepticism flared, but she kept her tone neutral. "What do you mean by 'wakes up'?"

"Look at the history of this place," Mr. Ward replied. "Brookhaven wasn't always the quiet, sleepy town it appears to be now. It was founded over a hundred years ago, during the late 1800s, and its founding coincided with a series of strange occurrences. People started disappearing, sometimes in pairs, sometimes in groups. No one could explain it. But it was never random. There was always a pattern."

Evelyn's brow furrowed. "A pattern? What kind of pattern?"

"Look at the disappearances," Mr. Ward continued, his voice growing more intense. "The first major disappearance was back in 1883. A family—the Hendersons—disappeared without a trace. The father, the mother, and their two children. No one knows what happened to them, but their house was found abandoned, their belongings left behind. Then, in 1910, another family—the Carvers—disappeared in much the same way. Over the years, it kept happening, every few decades. But it wasn't until the 1950s that people started to notice a disturbing trend. The disappearances were always tied to certain dates—usually around the full moon, or the solstices. Some people started to believe that there was a curse on the town, that it was being haunted by something ancient."

Evelyn felt a chill creep up her spine. A curse? Haunted? It sounded like something out of a horror novel, not a legitimate investigation. But there was something in Mr. Ward's eyes that made her hesitate. He wasn't lying. He believed what he was saying.

"And what about Natalie Harris?" she asked. "How does she fit into all of this?"

Mr. Ward sighed, rubbing his temples. "That's the part that doesn't make sense. Natalie's disappearance is the first one in over twenty years. But this time, it's different. She was seen talking to someone—someone who shouldn't have been here."

"Who?" Evelyn asked, her voice barely above a whisper.

Mr. Ward looked around the room, as if ensuring they weren't being overheard, before leaning forward. "There are rumors about a man who's been seen around town recently. He's been staying at the old house on the outskirts—the one you've probably seen. The one with the broken windows and the overgrown yard."

Evelyn nodded, the image of the house flashing in her mind. "I've seen it."

"Most people avoid it," Mr. Ward continued. "It's been abandoned for years, but recently, there have been reports of someone moving in. Some say it's the same man who was seen with Natalie just before she disappeared. But no one knows for sure. Whoever he is, he's not someone you want to get involved with. There's something wrong about him, Evelyn. Something... unsettling."

Evelyn's heart raced. "Who is he? Do you know?"

Mr. Ward shook his head. "I don't know his name. But I can tell you this: he's not like anyone else in Brookhaven. He doesn't belong here."

A heavy silence hung in the air as Evelyn processed the information. A mysterious man. A pattern of disappearances. The town haunted by something ancient. It was all starting to feel like pieces of a puzzle she couldn't quite put together.

Mr. Ward cleared his throat, pulling Evelyn back to the present. "I've said too much already. If you want to continue your investigation, I'd advise you to be careful. Some things are best left alone."

Evelyn stood up, her mind buzzing with questions. "Thank you, Mr. Ward," she said, her voice firm. "I'll be careful. But I need to find out the truth about Natalie Harris. I can't stop now."

Mr. Ward's gaze lingered on her for a moment before he nodded, a weary expression on his face. "You've been warned."

As Evelyn turned to leave, she felt the weight of his words settle heavily on her shoulders. She was no closer to understanding what had happened to Natalie, but the pieces of the puzzle were beginning to fall into place, one unsettling fragment at a time.

Evelyn left Mr. Ward's house feeling both more informed and more uncertain than ever. The fire in the hearth had burned low, and the night air felt even colder as she stepped back into the quiet streets of Brookhaven. The town seemed different now, as if it were hiding something just beneath the surface, something ancient and dangerous. She couldn't shake the feeling that she was getting too close to something, and that made her uneasy.

She had learned a lot tonight, but the questions only deepened. Who was the man living in the abandoned house? What was the connection between the disappearances and the full moon? And why had Natalie Harris vanished? Was she another victim of whatever force had haunted Brookhaven for over a century?

Evelyn's thoughts were interrupted by the sound of footsteps behind her. She turned, her heart racing, only to find a figure emerging from the shadows. A man, his face hidden in the darkness, was approaching her.

Before she could react, the man stepped into the light, revealing his face. It was the same man she had seen earlier—the one who had warned her about the town's secrets.

He was back.

The man who had stepped from the shadows had the same unsettling presence Evelyn had noticed earlier. His appearance was startlingly ordinary—too ordinary. His jeans and hoodie were worn, nothing out of the ordinary for someone passing through a small town like Brookhaven, but there was an intensity in the way he moved, a quiet urgency that made Evelyn feel on edge.

For a moment, neither of them spoke. The wind had picked up, stirring the leaves that cluttered the edges of the street, and the faint rustling seemed to intensify the silence between them. Evelyn's instincts screamed at her to be cautious. She had been warned about getting too close to the truth, and here she was, standing face-to-face with a man who had already shown an interest in her investigation. Was he trying to deter her, or did he know something she needed to hear?

The man's eyes were shadowed by the hood of his sweatshirt, but she could still make out his sharp features—dark, angular, with a hint of something hardened in his expression. There was no warmth in his gaze, only a cold intensity, as though he was studying her, evaluating whether or not she posed a threat.

"I thought I'd find you here," he said, his voice low, barely above a whisper.

Evelyn narrowed her eyes. She was used to encountering wary locals who eyed her suspiciously when she inquired about the missing persons, but this man was different. There was something about the way he spoke—measured, careful—that suggested he knew more than he was willing to say.

"What do you want?" Evelyn asked, keeping her tone even, but alert.

He looked over his shoulder, scanning the street as though making sure no one was watching. Then, with a slight nod toward the darkened streets of Brookhaven, he spoke again.

"You're digging too deep. It's dangerous."

Evelyn didn't flinch, though her pulse quickened. "You've already warned me once. What is it you want from me?"

The man's lips twisted into a faint, almost imperceptible smirk. "I'm not here to stop you. But I've been watching you. I know what you're looking for. You won't find it the way you think you will."

Evelyn took a slow, measured step back, studying him carefully. She had already learned that Brookhaven was a place where people hid their true motives, often behind layers of false pleasantries or subtle threats. This man, however, seemed to speak in riddles—an unsettling pattern that suggested he knew more about the town's hidden history than he was willing to admit.

"Who are you?" Evelyn asked, crossing her arms.

For a long moment, the man didn't answer. Instead, he glanced once more down the street, then seemed to make a decision. He looked at Evelyn, his eyes narrowing.

"I'm someone who's seen this happen before. Someone who knows what happens to people who try to uncover the truth here. You'll find out soon enough, but I can't stop it for you. No one can."

"Why not?" Evelyn demanded. Her voice betrayed a hint of frustration. "What are you so afraid of?"

The man tilted his head slightly, as if amused by her persistence. "Because the truth isn't something you can just walk into, and it's not something that can be explained easily. It's more than the town's past. It's something older than that. Something that doesn't want to be found."

Evelyn's mind raced. This wasn't just a warning. It felt like a challenge. Something about the way he spoke, the darkness in his voice, made her wonder if this man was connected to whatever had been haunting Brookhaven for so long.

"So what exactly is it you're afraid of?" she pressed. "What are you trying to protect?"

The man didn't answer right away. Instead, he took a deep breath, glancing away, as if grappling with something deep within. Finally, he spoke.

"I don't know if you're ready for the answers," he said, his voice quiet but heavy. "But I'll tell you this: the town wasn't always like this. There was a time when it was... different. It was founded on something—something that people don't talk about anymore."

Evelyn's heart skipped a beat. She had heard Mr. Ward mention the town's strange history, the disappearances, but this man seemed to be hinting at something far more sinister. She could feel the pull of his words, an urgency in his tone that seemed to deepen the mystery of Brookhaven.

"What happened here?" she asked, her voice low, almost reverent as the weight of his words settled on her.

He looked up, his eyes now locking onto hers. "You're not going to like the answer. But it's all connected. The disappearances, the town's history—every person who has vanished from Brookhaven was taken by something. Something that isn't human."

Evelyn's breath caught in her throat. A chill ran down her spine. She wanted to dismiss his words as the ramblings of a man who had become consumed by fear, but there was something about his intensity, something that felt real.

"What do you mean, 'taken by something that isn't human'?" she asked, her voice barely a whisper.

The man hesitated, then spoke again, his voice barely audible.

"Something ancient, something that lives beneath the earth. It's not a myth. It's real. And it's waiting. The disappearances are part of it—an offering, if you will. The town was built on top of it, and every so often, the price must be paid."

Evelyn felt a coldness seep into her bones. "You're telling me this town has been built on top of something... ancient?"

The man nodded slowly, his eyes never leaving hers. "Yes. And every time someone like you comes looking for answers, it wakes up. It senses curiosity, and it feeds on it. And every time it does, it takes someone—someone connected to the search for the truth. You're already too deep. If you keep going, you'll be next."

A heavy silence fell between them, the weight of his words pressing on Evelyn's chest. She wanted to reject them outright, to laugh them off as the delusions of a paranoid mind, but something in his eyes told her that he wasn't lying. He believed every word.

"Who are you?" she asked again, her voice firmer now. "And why are you telling me this?"

The man's expression hardened. "I'm trying to save you," he said. "But it's already too late for me."

Evelyn was about to press him further when a car's headlights appeared in the distance, cutting through the night's darkness. The man stiffened and glanced over his shoulder, his gaze scanning the approaching vehicle. Without a word, he turned abruptly and melted into the shadows, disappearing before Evelyn could react.

For a moment, she stood there, stunned, as the car passed by. She looked around, but the street was empty, the man now gone as if he had never been there at all. The air was still, the quiet punctuated only by the sound of her own breath.

Her mind raced, the chilling words of the mysterious stranger echoing in her head. *Something ancient. It feeds on curiosity. You'll be next.*

Evelyn couldn't shake the feeling that she had just glimpsed the edge of something much larger than a missing person's case. The town of Brookhaven was hiding something—something deep, dark, and old. And whatever it was, it didn't want to be found.

She shook her head, trying to clear the fog of doubt that had settled over her. She needed answers. The man's warning, as unsettling as it was, only deepened her resolve. She had come this far, and she wasn't going to back down now. But as she walked back to her motel, the weight of his words pressed on her like a shadow, and she couldn't shake the feeling that her investigation was about to take a much darker turn.

Chapter 4: The Shadow in the Woods

The morning sun barely pierced the fog that clung to the streets of Brookhaven, casting the town in a gray, oppressive light. Evelyn walked to her car, her mind still whirling from the cryptic encounter with the mysterious man. She had never believed in things like curses or supernatural forces, but the way he spoke... it felt real. The desperation in his eyes, the weight of his warning—it was enough to shake even her skepticism.

But no matter how unsettling his words were, Evelyn was resolute. She had a job to do. She was here to uncover the truth about Natalie Harris's disappearance, and she wasn't going to back down. The town was hiding something, and she intended to find out what it was.

After spending most of the previous day reviewing old newspapers and town records at the local library, Evelyn had pieced together a few more details. The disappearances had started with the Henderson family in 1883, but there were others—smaller incidents, rumors of people vanishing without a trace, often linked to certain locations in the town, or specific times of the year. The reports were vague, usually filed away in dusty archives or dismissed as coincidence.

It was clear that the town had a long history of keeping secrets. What struck Evelyn the most, however, was the pattern: the disappearances seemed to coincide with certain times, the full moon, the solstices, even specific weather patterns. She couldn't ignore the chilling thought that these were more than just coincidences.

Evelyn drove toward the outskirts of town, her eyes scanning the landscape. The trees that lined the roads seemed to grow thicker the further she went, their twisted branches reaching out like fingers, clawing at the sky. It was a part of Brookhaven that few people spoke about—no businesses, no tourist attractions, just dense woods and

the occasional dilapidated house. The abandoned house Mr. Ward
had mentioned was nearby. She had to see it for herself.

Her car rumbled down the overgrown road, the tires crunching
over loose gravel as the fog thickened. A sense of unease gnawed at
her, but she pressed forward, determined to follow the trail wherever
it led. There was no turning back now.

As she neared the property, the house came into view. It was a
faded Victorian mansion, its once-ornate features now broken and
decayed. The windows were shattered, and the roof sagged in places,
as though it had been abandoned for decades. The yard was
overgrown with weeds, and the trees around the house loomed tall
and imposing, casting long, eerie shadows across the ground. It was
as if the house itself had been swallowed by the forest.

Evelyn parked her car at the edge of the road and stepped out,
her boots crunching against the gravel. The air smelled damp and
musty, thick with the scent of earth and decay. She paused for a
moment, looking up at the house. Something about it felt wrong,
like it was watching her, waiting for her to make the next move.

Taking a deep breath, she approached the front steps, which
were cracked and uneven. The house seemed to pulse with a strange
energy, as though it had absorbed the sorrow and secrets of the
many years it had stood empty. Evelyn reached out and touched the
doorframe, her fingers brushing against the cold, weathered wood.
The door was ajar, and she hesitated for a moment before pushing it
open.

The inside of the house was even darker than she had imagined.
Dust motes floated in the stale air, and the faint creak of the
floorboards beneath her feet made her jump. The walls were lined
with old wallpaper, peeling and faded, with strange, twisted patterns
that seemed to move in the corner of her vision. The air felt thick, as
though the house itself was holding its breath.

Evelyn took another step, her hand resting on the railing of a staircase that spiraled upward, its wooden banister smooth but worn. The house was eerily quiet, but she couldn't shake the feeling that something—someone—was watching her. She swallowed hard, her pulse quickening.

The back of her neck prickled with a sudden chill, and she spun around. Nothing. Just the empty, dust-choked air of the abandoned house. But she couldn't shake the sensation that she was being drawn into something much larger than herself.

As she explored the first floor, Evelyn found signs of life—faint remnants of the past. An overturned chair in the corner. A stack of old newspapers, their edges yellowed and brittle with age. A photograph, framed and slightly askew, of a family—two parents with their children standing in front of the house, smiling. She picked it up and examined it. The family looked happy, almost carefree. But there was something about their eyes—something vacant and distant, as though they were all hiding a secret. Evelyn turned the photograph over, but the back was blank.

She continued moving deeper into the house, pushing open doors that creaked loudly, as if protesting her presence. She passed a dusty library and what appeared to be a dining room, the once-grand table now covered in a thick layer of dust. The farther she went, the more oppressive the air became, thick with the weight of years of neglect.

It wasn't until she reached the back of the house that she saw it—a narrow door leading into what appeared to be a basement. The wooden steps were broken, and the door itself was partially ajar, just wide enough for her to slip through.

Against her better judgment, Evelyn descended into the darkened basement. The air down here was cold, musty, and smelled of earth. She fumbled for her phone, using the flashlight to cut through the darkness. The beam revealed shelves of old boxes, crates, and stacks of paper, most of which had long been abandoned to rot. But what caught her attention was a large wooden trunk in the far corner of the room. It was locked, the metal hinges rusted, and it seemed oddly out of place, as though someone had deliberately left it there.

Her curiosity piqued, Evelyn approached the trunk and knelt beside it. She examined it for a moment, the hairs on the back of her neck rising. Something about the trunk felt wrong—too deliberate, too hidden. She tried to lift it, but it was heavy, as though weighed down by more than just the rust and dust.

As she reached down to inspect the lock, her flashlight beam flickered and died, plunging her into darkness.

Her breath caught in her throat. The silence in the basement was deafening, and for a long moment, she couldn't move. Her phone buzzed in her pocket, and she jumped, startled. Pulling it out, she saw that it was a message from Mr. Ward.

Be careful. Don't trust the house.

Evelyn's heart hammered in her chest. Her instincts screamed at her to leave, but she couldn't—*wouldn't*—back down. She needed answers. And she was close.

But before she could reach for her phone to respond, a sound came from the corner of the room—a faint rustling, as though something was moving in the darkness.

Evelyn froze.

Her heart pounded, and she slowly turned her head toward the noise. The flashlight flickered back on, casting its weak beam toward the source of the sound.

A figure stood at the edge of the shadows.

Evelyn's pulse thundered in her ears as she stood frozen in the darkened basement. Her flashlight flickered again, casting weak shadows across the room. For a moment, she could barely make out the figure standing in the corner, just outside the range of the dim beam. It was tall, unnaturally still, and its presence felt like a weight in the air, pressing down on her chest.

Her heart pounded louder, almost drowning out the sound of her breath as she slowly raised the flashlight, trying to focus on the shadow. The beam of light shuddered with each movement, as though it, too, were uncertain about what it was illuminating.

Then the light fell on the figure, and Evelyn gasped.

The person standing before her was dressed in dark clothes—nondescript, but his posture was rigid, almost unnatural. His face was hidden by a hood, but Evelyn could make out the faint glint of pale skin beneath. It was the same man—the one who had warned her. The one who had appeared from the shadows on the street the night before.

He was standing just out of reach, his gaze fixed on her with an unnerving calmness, his eyes glowing faintly in the dark.

Evelyn's breath caught in her throat. "You..."

He didn't answer immediately. Instead, he took a single step forward, and the floorboards groaned beneath his weight. He was taller than she had realized, and his movements were slow, deliberate, as if he was calculating his next step, measuring her response.

"You shouldn't be here," he said, his voice low and almost hypnotic, with an edge of something... darker. "I warned you."

Evelyn's hand tightened around the flashlight. "I didn't come here to be warned. I'm here to find the truth about what's happening in this town." Her voice was steady, though the fear gnawing at her insides threatened to make it crack.

The man tilted his head slightly, studying her with an expression that was impossible to read. He took another step closer, and Evelyn instinctively took a step back, her foot brushing against the rusted trunk she had been investigating earlier. The sound seemed to break the stillness, and the man's gaze flickered toward it for the briefest of moments.

"That trunk..." he began, his voice trailing off as though he hadn't intended to say it aloud. He quickly recovered, his attention returning to Evelyn. "It's not for you to open."

Evelyn narrowed her eyes, her curiosity piqued. "What's inside it? Why is it so important?"

The man's jaw clenched, his eyes hardening. "You don't understand. You're meddling with things that have been buried for a reason. There's a price to be paid for what you're looking for."

Evelyn's resolve hardened. She wasn't about to back down, not now. Not when she was so close.

"I don't believe in curses," she said, her voice firm. "I'm not afraid of some 'price' you keep talking about. What I want to know is what happened to Natalie Harris. What happened to all the others?"

The man stiffened at the mention of Natalie's name, his eyes flashing with something Evelyn couldn't quite place—guilt? Fear? But it was gone in an instant, replaced by an implacable calm.

"You're asking the wrong questions," he said softly. "But you'll learn soon enough."

Evelyn didn't know whether to be frustrated or intrigued. She took a breath, steadying herself. "Then help me. If you know what's going on, help me."

The man's lips curled into a faint, bitter smile, but his eyes remained cold. "Helping you won't change anything. It won't stop what's coming."

A chill ran down Evelyn's spine. The air around them felt heavier, thick with tension. It was as though the house itself was alive, responding to the exchange. The oppressive darkness pressed in, and she suddenly had the overwhelming sensation that they were no longer alone in the basement.

She glanced around, but the room was still as silent and empty as it had been moments before.

"What is it that you're so afraid of?" Evelyn pressed, her voice stronger now. "What is so dangerous about opening that trunk?"

The man hesitated, his eyes briefly flickering toward the trunk once more. But instead of answering, he seemed to withdraw further into the shadows, his presence fading like a memory. For a moment, Evelyn wasn't sure if he would speak again.

"You think you can handle the truth?" he finally said, his voice distant, almost hollow. "There are things buried here—things that are older than this town. Older than the people who built it. You're standing on the edge of something that you don't fully understand."

Evelyn's heart raced. "What does that mean? What's buried here?"

The man didn't respond. Instead, his shadow seemed to melt into the darkness, his presence becoming less and less tangible, as if he were fading into the very air itself.

Evelyn stood there for a long moment, the silence in the basement feeling almost suffocating. She didn't know whether the man had left or if he was still watching her from the shadows. The chill in the air seemed to grow colder, and the sense of unease intensified. But she couldn't leave now—not without answers.

She turned her focus back to the trunk. With a deep breath, Evelyn crouched down and examined it more closely. The rusted lock was old, but it wasn't beyond her ability to open. She had tools in her car—things she had picked up in case she needed to get into places that weren't meant to be opened. The thought of what might be inside the trunk both terrified and fascinated her.

Something about it—the way the man had reacted to it—told her it was important. It was the key to unlocking whatever dark secret the town had buried for so long.

Without hesitation, Evelyn stood up and made her way back up the stairs to the main floor, the floor creaking beneath her weight.

She moved quickly, gathering her things and rushing back to the car. She didn't stop to question her decision—she couldn't afford to.

As she drove back toward town, her mind churned with what she had learned so far. The man's warnings echoed in her head, but she couldn't ignore the pull of the mystery. The man had been right about one thing—she was already too deep into this to turn back.

Later that Evening...

Back at her motel room, Evelyn sat in front of her laptop, her fingers dancing across the keys as she typed out her notes. She had driven around the outskirts of Brookhaven for hours, thinking through everything she had learned. But the town still had its secrets, and the man's warning lingered in the back of her mind.

She scrolled through the local newspaper archives again, reading about the disappearances that had plagued the town for over a century. The Hendersons in 1883. The Carvers in 1910. And then, more recently, people like Natalie Harris. Each time, the articles were sparse—nothing concrete, nothing that tied the cases together beyond the vague mention of "unexplained disappearances."

The hairs on the back of her neck stood up as she found something new. A passage from a book on Brookhaven's history caught her eye. It was an old account of the town's founding, dating back to the late 1800s. The author, a historian from the university, had written about the unusual number of disappearances in Brookhaven's early years. But there was something else—something that made her blood run cold.

The town's founders, according to the text, had been deeply involved in occult practices. They had arrived from a place called "The Hollow," a remote area that was said to be haunted. The settlers, the book claimed, had been looking for a place to build a new life, but they had unknowingly built the town atop a site that had once been a sacred ground. A place where ancient rituals had been performed. Rituals that, according to the text, required "sacrifices" to appease the forces beneath the earth.

The pieces were beginning to come together. The ancient rituals, the disappearances—each time, a sacrifice was made, and the town's history was stained by the need for these dark offerings.

Evelyn stared at the screen, feeling her stomach turn. This was no coincidence. The man had been right. Brookhaven wasn't just haunted by its past—it was built on something that demanded to be fed.

But the most disturbing part came next: The book mentioned a "key" to unlocking the truth about the town's curse. A key that was said to be hidden in plain sight, somewhere in Brookhaven. And only by finding it could the town's darkness be lifted—or allowed to consume everything.

She closed the laptop with a trembling hand. The key. The trunk. The man's cryptic warnings.

The answers were out there. But the deeper she dug, the more she realized she might be getting too close to the truth—closer than anyone had ever dared to go.

Chapter 5: Beneath the Surface

Evelyn couldn't shake the feeling that Brookhaven was more than just a sleepy town. It wasn't the quiet, picturesque streets or the looming presence of the woods that unsettled her—it was the pulse beneath it all. The secret heartbeat that the town had hidden for decades, possibly longer. The more she uncovered, the more she realized that everything, every piece of this puzzle, led her down a darker and more dangerous path.

She sat in her motel room late into the night, the only sound the rhythmic tapping of her fingers on the keyboard as she pieced together her findings. The book she'd found, the one that detailed the occult history of Brookhaven, had unsettled her more than she cared to admit. The idea of a town built on an ancient ritual—a town that demanded a "sacrifice" to keep its dark forces at bay—was enough to make anyone question their own sanity. But the more Evelyn thought about it, the more the pieces began to fall into place. And with each piece, a new question emerged.

The rituals, the disappearances, the strange man who had appeared in the shadows—what if they were all part of something much larger? Something that had been waiting for the right moment to reveal itself?

She rubbed her eyes, staring at the glowing screen. Her fingers hovered over the keyboard, but she hesitated. She had seen something in the old book, something that had struck her as odd. A reference to a "key," something hidden in the town, something that could unlock the truth behind the town's curse. She hadn't found any mention of the key in the archives or in the town's historical records, but there was a line in the book that mentioned it in passing: *The key rests beneath the surface, bound by blood and time.*

Evelyn felt a chill crawl down her spine. Beneath the surface. Blood and time. It felt like a riddle, one that she had to solve.

Her phone buzzed, interrupting her thoughts. She glanced at the screen and saw a message from Mr. Ward.

You're asking the wrong questions. Leave it alone.

Evelyn's heart sank. She had expected a warning, but the urgency in his message made her pulse quicken. He had been right about the danger before. But she couldn't back down now. She needed to know the truth.

She typed a quick reply.

I'm not stopping. I'm getting closer.

She stared at the message for a moment before putting the phone down. Something was calling her. Something was pulling her toward Brookhaven's secrets, and she couldn't turn back.

The Next Morning

The fog was thick when Evelyn left the motel early the next morning. It clung to the streets like a shroud, muffling the sound of her footsteps as she walked toward her car. The town seemed different today—more oppressive, as if the weight of the past was pressing down harder than ever before.

Her mind was focused on one thing: the key. The hidden truth beneath the surface. She had a feeling that it was tied to the town's past, to the founding families, and to whatever was buried deep in the woods surrounding Brookhaven.

As she drove through the fog, the streets seemed empty, the houses too quiet. The town felt abandoned, as though it were holding its breath, waiting for something to happen. Evelyn couldn't shake the feeling that she was being watched, though she couldn't pinpoint why. She glanced in the rearview mirror, but the road behind her was empty.

She turned onto the old road that led to the woods, the same road she had driven the day before to reach the abandoned house. This time, she drove further into the forest, past the dilapidated structures and overgrown paths. The trees grew denser the farther she went, their twisted branches stretching out like claws, their shadows thick against the gray morning light.

Eventually, she reached a clearing—a small, secluded area that seemed to be untouched by time. In the center of the clearing stood a large, weathered stone. It was round, about six feet in diameter, with strange symbols carved into its surface. Evelyn's heart raced as she pulled over and stepped out of the car. There was something about the stone, something that felt ancient, as if it had been waiting for her.

She moved closer, carefully inspecting the markings. The symbols were unlike anything she had ever seen—circular patterns with intersecting lines, as though they were part of some complex, otherworldly language. It felt like a puzzle, but Evelyn couldn't make sense of it. The stone seemed to pulse with an energy she couldn't explain, as if it were alive, breathing in sync with her own heartbeat.

She ran her fingers over the symbols, feeling the grooves and indentations in the stone. There was a low hum, almost imperceptible, but it was there. As her fingers brushed over one of the symbols, something happened—a shift, a crack, as if the stone was responding to her touch.

Suddenly, the ground beneath her feet trembled.

Evelyn stumbled back, her heart hammering in her chest as the earth shook beneath her. The trees around her groaned, their branches swaying violently as if something deep within the ground was awakening. The stone seemed to glow faintly, its symbols now illuminated by a strange, otherworldly light.

Her breath caught in her throat. This was it. This was what the man had warned her about. The ancient force that had been lying dormant, waiting for someone to disturb the surface. She could feel it now—its presence, its power, drawing closer with every second.

Then, just as suddenly as it had begun, the tremors stopped. The stone was still. The forest was quiet again, as though nothing had happened.

Evelyn stood frozen, unsure of what to do next. She had felt it—whatever had stirred beneath the ground—but now it was gone. Or was it? Was this just the beginning?

She took a cautious step forward, but before she could reach the stone again, a voice from behind her made her freeze.

"*I told you to leave it alone.*"

Evelyn turned slowly, her heart racing in her chest. The man—*the one from the shadows*—was standing in the clearing, his face hidden beneath the hood. His voice was cold, his words laced with an edge of desperation.

"You shouldn't have come here," he continued, stepping closer. "You don't know what you're dealing with. The key... it's not something you can control. It's something that controls you."

Evelyn's mind raced. The key. This was it, wasn't it? This stone, these symbols—this was the key to unlocking everything.

"*What is this?*" she asked, her voice trembling with both fear and curiosity. "*What is the key? What does it do?*"

The man shook his head, his gaze filled with something dark—guilt, fear, perhaps even regret. "You don't understand. The key isn't just an object. It's the beginning. It awakens things, things that have been buried for centuries. And once you open the door, there's no going back."

Evelyn's mind raced. "*What happens when the door opens?*" she asked, almost desperate for answers.

The man's eyes darkened. "*It feeds.*"

He said no more. The forest was silent once again, the air thick with tension. The man turned, as if to leave, but Evelyn took a step toward him, unwilling to let him go without more answers.

"Wait!" she called out. "Please! You know what this is! What happened to the people who disappeared? What's behind all of this?"

The man paused but didn't turn around. "*It's already too late.*"

Evelyn's stomach churned as the man melted into the shadows, disappearing into the dense woods. She stood alone, surrounded by the silent trees and the mysterious stone.

Her mind was reeling with everything she had just learned, but one thing was clear—there was no turning back now. The truth was buried here, in Brookhaven, and she had just unlocked the first layer.

But there was still so much she didn't understand. And the more she uncovered, the more dangerous it would become.

Back in Town

Evelyn returned to Brookhaven, her mind overwhelmed with everything that had transpired. The stone, the symbols, the man's cryptic warnings—it was all too much to process. But one thing was certain: she had to keep going. The town had secrets, and now she was getting closer to uncovering them.

Back in her motel room, she sat down at the desk, her fingers trembling as she typed her notes. The key wasn't just a literal object—it was part of something much larger. She could feel it now, as if the town itself was alive, its ancient heartbeat pulsing beneath the surface.

Evelyn knew that whatever she had found in the woods was just the beginning. The truth was out there, hidden beneath layers of time, blood, and fear. But there was one thing that gnawed at her: the man's words. *It feeds.*

She didn't know what *it* was, but she had a feeling that the answer was closer than she thought. She couldn't stop now, no matter what.

Evelyn woke the next morning with a sense of unease settling deep within her bones. Her dreams had been fragmented and full of strange images—flashes of faces she didn't recognize, shadows moving beneath the earth, and the echo of her own voice calling out into an endless void. She could still hear the man's warning in her mind. *It feeds.*

There was no denying that Brookhaven's history, its rituals, and the stone in the woods were all connected. She could feel it in her gut. The more she learned, the less she understood. But the one thing she was certain of now was that whatever this *thing* was, it had been feeding on Brookhaven for generations. And she was getting closer to the truth.

As she got dressed, Evelyn stared out the window of her motel room. The fog had lifted, but the town still felt heavy, as if the weight of centuries was pressing down on it. The woods loomed in the distance, just beyond the outskirts of town. She knew she had to go back there—she couldn't let what had happened in the clearing remain unanswered.

Evelyn grabbed her notebook and jotted down her thoughts as she tried to make sense of the information she had. The symbols on the stone. The strange energy she had felt. The man's cryptic words. What did they all mean? Was the key tied to some sort of ancient pact? Was it a relic from the town's early settlers, or was it something older—something that had always been there, buried deep in the land itself?

She closed her eyes for a moment, trying to calm the storm of thoughts swirling in her mind. The sound of her phone vibrating on the table broke her concentration. She picked it up, expecting it to be another message from Mr. Ward, but instead it was an email from an anonymous address. Her heart skipped a beat as she opened it.

The subject line was simple: *"You're getting too close."*

Evelyn stared at the email, the blood draining from her face as she read the message. It was short and direct.

"Stop digging. Leave Brookhaven. You're in over your head. The truth will destroy you."

The email was unsigned, but it didn't take much to figure out who it was from. The tone, the urgency—it was unmistakable. The man from the woods. She wasn't sure how he had gotten her email, but she wasn't going to let that stop her. This only confirmed one thing: She was on the right track.

She deleted the email and stood up, her hands shaking with a mix of fear and adrenaline. There was no going back now.

The Drive Back to the Woods

The drive back to the woods was even more oppressive than before. As Evelyn made her way toward the clearing, she couldn't shake the feeling that she was being watched. The trees seemed to close in on her as she approached, their gnarled branches twisting like dark hands reaching out for her. The road grew narrower, the air thicker, and the deeper she went, the more isolated she felt.

As she parked the car and stepped out, the silence in the woods was almost deafening. There was no sound of birds, no rustling of leaves, just an eerie stillness that seemed to stretch on forever.

The clearing was just as she had left it—ominous and silent. The stone was still there, its surface smooth and dark, the strange symbols faintly glowing in the dim light of the afternoon. She stepped forward cautiously, feeling the familiar hum of energy in the air.

Her fingers brushed against the stone once more, and she felt a cold shiver run down her spine. The stone was warm to the touch now, as if it had absorbed something—a presence, maybe, or a force she didn't understand. But as her fingers traced over the markings, something else happened. The ground beneath her feet trembled again, and the trees seemed to groan with a low, unnatural sound.

Evelyn's heart pounded in her chest as she stepped back, but this time, she didn't turn away. The tremors escalated, and then, in the distance, she heard a faint whisper—a voice, barely audible but unmistakable.

"*You should have listened to me.*"

Evelyn's breath caught in her throat. She turned quickly, but there was no one there. The clearing was empty, the air thick with a strange tension.

She looked back at the stone, feeling drawn to it despite her fear. There was something she had to do—something she couldn't explain. As if on instinct, her hands moved to the base of the stone, searching for something—anything—that might trigger a reaction.

Her fingers brushed against a small indentation at the bottom. She hesitated for a moment, then pressed harder. The stone shifted beneath her touch, and with a low grinding sound, it slid open, revealing a small compartment inside.

Evelyn's heart raced as she peered inside, half-expecting something to leap out at her. But what she found was far worse. It was a collection of old papers—maps, journals, and faded photographs. She picked up the first piece of paper she saw, a journal entry written in a hand so shaky it was almost illegible.

She squinted at the words, trying to make sense of the hurried scrawl.

"*The pact is made. The ritual is complete. The key will open the door, but it must be fed first. We cannot stop what we have started.*"

Evelyn's stomach twisted. She grabbed more pages, each one more disturbing than the last. The journal was filled with references to a "door" and "the key" that would open it—references to an ancient force that had been awakened by the town's founders. It spoke of sacrifices, of blood offerings to keep the entity at bay.

The deeper she read, the more she realized that the entity—the one they had bargained with—was something far older than anything she could have imagined. It wasn't just a creature or a demon; it was something far worse. A force that existed beyond time, beyond space. And now, the time had come to feed it again.

Her fingers trembled as she flipped through the remaining pages. Each one was more fragmented than the last, as though the journal's owner had been driven mad in the process. But the last page, scrawled hastily, was the most chilling of all.

"It's coming. The door is open. The blood must flow. The key... the key will bind it forever."

Evelyn's hands went cold as she stared at the words. *The blood must flow.* The key... it had always been about the blood. The sacrifices.

A sudden realization struck her like a bolt of lightning. The disappearances in Brookhaven weren't random. They weren't just victims—they were offerings. The town had been feeding the force for generations. And now, she had opened the door.

She felt something behind her, a cold presence that seemed to permeate the air. Slowly, she turned around, her breath catching in her throat.

Standing at the edge of the clearing was the man. The one who had warned her. His face was still hidden beneath the hood, but his eyes glinted in the dim light—eyes that seemed to know everything, that had seen the horrors she was only now beginning to understand.

"You shouldn't have come back," he said, his voice a low rasp.

Evelyn took a step toward him, her heart pounding. "*It's not over, is it?*" she whispered. "*The key—it's a trap, isn't it?*"

The man didn't answer right away. He stepped forward, and the ground seemed to shift with him, as if the earth itself was reacting to his presence.

"The truth," he said softly, "is that you're already too late."

Evelyn's breath hitched as the air around them seemed to grow colder, the shadows deepening. "What do you mean? What's going to happen?"

His eyes flickered toward the stone, and then back to her. "The force you've unleashed—it's already feeding. And now that you've opened the door, there's no closing it. Not anymore."

Evelyn's mind reeled as the pieces fell into place. The key, the sacrifices, the dark presence in the town—it had all been building toward this moment. And now, it was too late to stop it.

"*What happens now?*" she asked, her voice trembling.

The man looked at her, his expression unreadable. "Now," he said, his voice heavy with finality, "it's your turn."

Chapter 6: The Price of Truth

The silence in the clearing was oppressive, the shadows cast by the trees stretching like dark fingers over the ground. Evelyn's heart raced as she faced the man. His words echoed in her mind—*Now, it's your turn.* She hadn't expected him to say anything else, and for a moment, there was only the eerie stillness of the forest around them. The air seemed to hold its breath, as though the entire woods were waiting for something to happen.

Evelyn didn't move, her eyes locked on the hooded figure. His words hung between them, chilling and cryptic, and she felt a rising tide of fear grip her chest. What did he mean by "your turn"? Was he talking about her? Had she somehow triggered the ritual? Or was this all just part of the town's long-standing nightmare?

The man didn't speak again. Instead, he stepped back into the shadows, his movements slow and deliberate, as though he were waiting for something. Evelyn's gaze flickered to the stone, still humming with an otherworldly energy. She could feel it now, pulsing beneath the surface like a living thing, as though it were calling to her.

Without thinking, she stepped toward the stone. Her fingers reached out, brushing lightly against its surface. The moment she touched it, the ground trembled again, more violently than before. The trees around her groaned, their branches rattling in a strange wind that didn't belong to the woods. A deep, guttural sound reverberated through the air, a sound that felt like it was coming from the earth itself.

Evelyn's pulse quickened as the shadows seemed to deepen, closing in around her. She took a step back, her breath shallow, but she couldn't look away. The stone—it was more than just a relic. It was the epicenter of something ancient, something dark. A presence, ancient and hungry, had been bound to it for generations, and she had just set it free.

"*What have you done?*" The man's voice was low, filled with a kind of resigned bitterness. He stepped out of the shadows, his eyes locking onto hers. "*You've opened the door, Evelyn.*"

His words hung in the air like an accusation, and for a moment, she couldn't move. She was paralyzed by the weight of what she had just unleashed. The key—the stone—had been the catalyst, and now the forces tied to it were beginning to stir.

"*I didn't mean to,*" she said quietly, the words tasting like ash in her mouth. "*I didn't know what it was... What this town... What it's been hiding.*"

The man's expression softened for a brief moment, as if the weight of the past had taken its toll on him. "No one ever does. No one understands until it's too late."

Evelyn's mind spun, trying to make sense of everything. "*What is it? What's behind all of this? What's been feeding all these years?*" She swallowed, her throat dry. "*I need to know. Please. You have to tell me.*"

The man looked at her for a long time, his gaze unreadable, as though he were weighing the cost of his words. Finally, he sighed, a sound that seemed to carry the weight of years.

"*You think you're the first to ask that question?*" He shook his head, his voice dropping to a whisper. "*You think you're the first to try and understand? There are things in this town that have been buried for centuries. Things that no one should ever know.*"

Evelyn's hands trembled, but she stepped closer to him. "*Then why are you telling me? Why are you warning me?*"

He looked down at her, his face still hidden in shadow. "Because, for all its horrors, you still don't understand. This isn't just about the town. It's about you. You're part of it now. And once you're in, there's no getting out."

Evelyn felt a chill grip her heart, but she couldn't back away now. She had already seen too much, uncovered too many dark truths. She had to know what had happened to the people of Brookhaven—the missing residents, the disappearances, the rituals.

"*What happens to me now?*" she asked, her voice barely above a whisper.

The man stepped back, his expression hardening. "*What happens to you? You're the one who opened the door. Now, you'll have to pay the price.*"

Before Evelyn could respond, the ground beneath them trembled again. The stone began to glow, faint but unmistakable, the symbols carved into its surface lighting up like veins of fire running through the rock. The hum that had been pulsing beneath the earth grew louder, a low, vibrating sound that seemed to penetrate her bones.

Then, from the depths of the forest, came a sound—a voice, a chorus of whispers, too faint to make out, but unmistakably growing louder. A low, guttural chant, as though the earth itself was speaking. Evelyn felt it in her chest, the vibrations of the voices resonating deep within her.

She turned to the man, her eyes wide. "*What is that? What's happening?*"

He didn't answer at first. Instead, he seemed to be listening, his eyes scanning the woods as if waiting for something to emerge. Slowly, he turned back to her.

"*It's starting,*" he said, his voice hoarse. "*The door has been opened, and the thing you've released... it's awake now. And it's hungry.*"

Evelyn's blood ran cold. She took a step back, but the man's eyes locked onto hers with a sudden intensity.

"*You can't leave now,*" he said urgently. "*It's too late. You need to finish what you started.*"

She opened her mouth to protest, but before she could speak, a figure stepped from the shadows. It was tall and thin, its movements jerky and unnatural, as if its very form was being held together by forces not meant for this world. The figure was draped in tattered black robes, its face hidden beneath a hood, though Evelyn could sense something ancient and malevolent in its presence.

The man stiffened. "*It's here.*"

Evelyn felt the air grow colder, a rush of icy wind cutting through the clearing. The figure raised its head, revealing eyes—glowing, blood-red, like burning embers—fixed on her. Evelyn's breath hitched, and she took an instinctual step back, but the figure moved toward her with unnerving speed.

"*Who... What is that?*" she gasped, her heart hammering.

The man didn't answer immediately. Instead, he stepped in front of her, blocking her path. "*That,*" he said softly, his voice trembling with a kind of reverence and terror, "*is the keeper.*"

"*The keeper of what?*" Evelyn whispered, her mind struggling to comprehend the horror before her.

The figure did not speak. It simply extended its hand toward her, the motion slow and deliberate. The air thickened as it drew closer, an overwhelming sense of dread pressing down on Evelyn's chest. She felt herself being pulled toward it, as though invisible threads were binding her to the creature.

She struggled against the unseen force, but it was no use. The closer the keeper came, the more she felt her own strength fading, her limbs growing heavy and weak. The whispers grew louder, almost deafening, and for a moment, she thought she could hear words—dark, foreign words that made her head spin.

No, this can't be happening. Evelyn's mind screamed, but her body refused to obey.

The keeper's hand reached her, and for an instant, she thought she could see its face beneath the hood—pale, gaunt, with hollow eyes and a mouth that seemed to stretch impossibly wide, as though it had never known the bounds of human form.

"*You have come too far,*" it said, its voice like a rasping wind. "*Now, you will become part of us.*"

Evelyn's mind raced. The key. The stone. The blood. This... this was what the town had been feeding for generations. The keeper, the creature bound to the stone, was the force that had been sustained by the rituals, the disappearances, the sacrifices. And now it was awake.

The man's voice broke through the chaos. "*You have to finish it, Evelyn. You have to—*"

But before he could finish, the keeper's hand reached her chest, and in that moment, Evelyn felt the weight of the darkness consume her.

Evelyn's breath quickened as the Keeper's hand pressed against her chest. The cold was unbearable, like an icy void that sought to consume her from the inside out. She could feel the very marrow of her bones freeze as the force, whatever it was, wrapped itself around her, choking her thoughts, clouding her mind. The whispers grew louder, but now they weren't just whispers—they were commands, insistent, demanding. *Join us. Become one. Give yourself to the darkness.*

For a brief, fleeting moment, Evelyn struggled to hold on to her own thoughts, to resist. She could feel her will slipping away, like sand through her fingers. The Keeper's touch, cold and deathly, was like an anchor, pulling her further into the depths of a world she didn't understand. She tried to scream, but her mouth was dry, her voice drowned by the oppressive, suffocating silence.

"*No...*" she gasped, her throat raw, her eyes wide with terror. "*I didn't mean to—*"

The Keeper's lips stretched into a horrifying, grin-like expression. Its eyes, glowing with that blood-red fire, seemed to burn into her soul. It leaned in closer, its breath chilling, as if it could taste her fear. "*It is too late. You have crossed the threshold, Evelyn. You cannot turn back now.*"

A surge of panic coursed through Evelyn as the memories of everything she had uncovered rushed back in a torrent—*the key, the stone, the pact.* The journal, the whispers, the disappearances. She had unlocked something that had been kept sealed for centuries. She had opened the door that had kept this thing contained.

Her knees buckled, and she fell to the ground, trembling. The Keeper's hand pressed harder into her chest, and the force seemed to swell around her like an ocean pulling her under. *This is how it ends,* she thought. *This is how they all end.*

But then, through the fog of her fear and the suffocating darkness, a faint voice cut through the chaos—urgent, desperate.

"*Evelyn!*"

The voice was familiar. The man from the woods.

"*You can still stop it! You can still make it right!*"

With everything in her, Evelyn focused on the voice, the single thread of hope in the nightmare she had unwittingly woven. She didn't understand how, but she had to hold on. She had to fight.

The Keeper's eyes flashed as it sensed her resistance, and a violent shudder rippled through its form. It snarled, the shadows around it shifting, coiling like smoke. "*You cannot escape it. It is your fate. You are bound to it now.*"

But Evelyn, despite her terror, pushed back. She struggled to lift her arms, her hands grasping at the cold air, fighting the heavy presence that pressed down on her like a physical weight. She didn't know what she was doing—she only knew she couldn't let it take her completely. She had to understand. She had to finish what she started.

"*Please...*" she begged, her voice weak. "*What is it? What do you want?*"

The Keeper's voice was a low rasp, a growl that seemed to come from the depths of the earth. *"What do I want? What I want is what has always been. I am the keeper of the gate. I guard the threshold. You opened it. Now, you will serve me, as they all have before you."*

The darkness pressed in further, and for a moment, Evelyn thought she might lose herself in it, swallowed whole. But then—something inside her snapped. A flicker of realization, like a candle in the dark, ignited her will to fight back. The Keeper was not invincible. There was a way to stop it.

It wasn't the Keeper that was controlling this world. It wasn't the Keeper that had created the pact—it was the stone, the key. The stone was what had held the force at bay. The Keeper was merely a servant, a guardian of the door. If the stone could be closed again, if the key could be locked back in place, the balance might be restored.

She gasped for breath, her vision clearing for just a moment. She had to make a choice. She had to fight.

And in that instant, she understood: **The stone was the answer.**

Her heart pounded as she reached toward it, her hand trembling with the effort. The Keeper's form twisted and writhed as it sensed her intentions. It tried to stop her, pushing harder, but she wasn't going to let it. She wasn't going to become another lost soul to feed its endless hunger.

With every ounce of strength she had left, Evelyn reached out and touched the stone.

The world exploded.

The Unleashing of the Past

The ground trembled violently beneath her, and for a split second, Evelyn felt as though she were being torn from the earth itself. There was a deep, resonant *crack*—louder than anything she had ever heard—and the stone pulsed with an intense, searing light. She gasped, shielding her eyes, but the light was blinding, and she could feel the pressure in her chest as if the very air was pressing against her skin.

The Keeper howled in fury, its form dissolving into shadows that swirled around the clearing, trying to reach her, to pull her away from the stone. But Evelyn held fast, her fingers wrapped around the symbols carved into its surface. She closed her eyes, her mind racing with the fragments of knowledge she had pieced together over the past few days. She remembered the journals, the words of the settlers, the sacrifices, the blood that had been spilled.

The key was not just an object—it was a conduit. A connection to the entity, to the force that had been bound for centuries.

As the stone's light intensified, Evelyn could feel a pulse in the air, like the heartbeat of the world itself. The Keeper's influence began to recede, the whispers fading into silence. But she knew the battle wasn't over—not yet.

She gritted her teeth, her whole body trembling with the exertion of forcing the stone back, pushing against the dark force that was trying to reclaim her. She had to finish it. She had to sever the connection for good.

"*No!*" she cried out, her voice breaking as she fought to maintain her grip. "*You won't control me! You won't control anyone anymore!*"

The stone began to respond, its glow shifting from a sickly red to a brilliant, blinding white. The earth beneath her feet shuddered, and then—there was silence.

A complete, oppressive silence.

Evelyn dared to open her eyes, blinking against the afterglow. The clearing was still. The Keeper was gone, its presence entirely erased, like a shadow that had never existed. The wind had stopped, the trees no longer groaned under the weight of something unnatural. Everything was still, as if the world was holding its breath.

Her chest heaved with the effort, her body weak from the strain. The stone was now dull and lifeless in her hands, no longer humming with the strange energy it had once held. The power she had felt, the force that had nearly consumed her, was gone. And yet, Evelyn knew that the danger was far from over.

As she pulled herself away from the stone, her legs shaking beneath her, she glanced around the clearing. It was still and quiet, but she didn't trust it. She didn't trust that this was over.

The man from the woods had disappeared, leaving nothing but a faint imprint in the dirt where he had stood. Evelyn couldn't be sure if he had ever truly been there or if he was simply another part of the town's strange web of secrets. Had he helped her? Had he been a part of the town's curse all along?

There were too many questions, too many things left unresolved. She had broken the cycle of sacrifice, but in doing so, had she merely created a new one? And was the town truly free, or had she only delayed the inevitable?

Evelyn stood alone in the clearing, her heart pounding, the weight of everything she had learned pressing down on her like a stone. She couldn't shake the feeling that the battle was only just beginning. That even now, in the silence, the thing she had awakened was waiting... waiting for her to make the next move.

Evelyn stood alone in the clearing, her chest heaving with exhaustion. The stone in her hand now lay dormant, its once-blazing light extinguished, its power seemingly snuffed out like a candle in the wind. But even in the eerie silence that followed, Evelyn felt the weight of something—something unfinished, something lurking beneath the surface of this unnatural calm.

Her legs wobbled as she moved back toward the edge of the clearing, her mind still reeling from the power that had just coursed through her. Her fingertips tingled with the residual energy of the stone, as though a part of that dark power had seeped into her very being. She wiped the back of her hand across her forehead, trying to push away the dizziness that clouded her senses.

What have I done? she thought, the question swirling in her mind like a whisper she couldn't escape. She had felt it—the moment when the Keeper's presence began to fade, when the pressure of its influence released its hold on her. It had felt like a victory, but it also felt... incomplete. She didn't feel free. She didn't feel *safe.*

She turned around, scanning the clearing, looking for any sign of the Keeper or its influence. The shadows that had once been thick with dread and malice were now just that—shadows. The woods, once alive with whispers and unseen movement, were still, almost unnaturally so. Nothing stirred. No wind, no rustling leaves, no creaking branches. The oppressive atmosphere had lifted, but Evelyn knew it couldn't be this easy.

She walked back toward the stone, kneeling beside it, her fingers brushing over the cold surface one last time. There was no longer any pulse, no heartbeat beneath her hand. It had gone quiet. But Evelyn knew that quiet could be a trap. The stone, its dark energy, and the forces behind it were not easily dismissed.

Suddenly, the faintest sound broke the silence. A twig snapped behind her, the crunch so sharp it seemed to reverberate through the forest. Evelyn's heart skipped a beat, and she instinctively spun around, her breath catching in her throat.

Standing at the edge of the clearing was a figure—a silhouette shrouded in the dim light of the fading evening. Her breath hitched in her throat. The shape was too familiar, too unsettling.

It was the man from the woods.

His features were still mostly hidden by the hood of his tattered cloak, but Evelyn could make out the sharpness of his jaw, the intensity of his gaze. He hadn't been there when the Keeper had disappeared. He hadn't been anywhere. But now, here he was, as if he had been standing at the edge of her vision all along.

"*You're still here,*" Evelyn said, her voice hoarse. "*I thought... I thought it was over.*"

The man didn't respond at first. He simply watched her, his eyes flickering to the stone in her hand, then back to her. There was a long, charged silence before he spoke, his voice calm but edged with something Evelyn couldn't quite place.

"*It's never over,*" he said softly, his voice almost lost in the rustling of the windless trees. "*You've done something—something irreversible. But there are... consequences.*"

Evelyn felt a chill creep down her spine, her stomach tightening. *Consequences? What did he mean?*

"*What did I do?*" she asked, the question tumbling out before she could stop it. "*I stopped it, didn't I? I sealed it away—whatever it was.*"

The man shook his head slowly, his face unreadable beneath the cloak's shadow. "*No. You haven't sealed anything. You've only... postponed it.*"

Evelyn's blood ran cold. The stone in her hand felt heavier suddenly, as though it were pulling her toward the earth. She tightened her grip around it, unwilling to let it slip from her fingers.

"*What does that mean?*" she demanded. "*What did I release? What have I done?*"

The man sighed, taking a slow step forward, the faintest glimmer of pity in his eyes. "*You released an ancient force. A force that was never meant to be contained in the first place.*"

"*I don't understand.*" Evelyn's voice broke, frustration and fear mixing. She wanted to scream at him—*why hadn't he told her sooner? Why hadn't he warned her of what she was about to awaken?*

He looked down at her, his eyes dark with an unreadable emotion. "*No one could warn you, Evelyn. Not truly. You had to discover it on your own, just like everyone before you.*"

Her heart pounded in her chest as she processed his words. "*Everyone before me?*" She stepped closer to him, feeling the distance between them grow more unbearable with every second. "*What do you mean by that? Who are you? And why do you keep saying it's too late?"*

The man's expression softened for the briefest of moments before hardening again. *"I am... part of the town, part of this cycle. I've watched over Brookhaven for years. I've seen it all."*

Evelyn frowned, her mind racing. *"Seen what? The disappearances? The people who vanished? The strange rituals?"*

"Yes," the man replied, his voice low and almost regretful. *"And I've tried, all these years, to stop it. To end it. But it always comes back. It always finds a way to resurface. And now—now you've given it new life."*

Evelyn took a step back, confusion clouding her thoughts. *"But I thought I stopped it."*

The man shook his head again. *"You didn't stop it. You've just given it a new vessel. A new host."* His eyes met hers, and she saw something in them—an ancient sorrow, a deep, resigned pain. *"The key, the stone... it's not just a doorway. It's a vessel, a prison. And now, you're tied to it."*

Evelyn's mind reeled. *"Tied to it? What do you mean?"*

He didn't answer immediately. Instead, he glanced toward the horizon, where the last vestiges of light were slipping away, the night creeping in.

"You are part of the curse now," he said quietly, his voice heavy with a kind of finality. *"You didn't just release the Keeper. You released something worse. And now, you're part of it. You always were."*

The words cut through Evelyn like a blade, the implications of them sharp and cruel. Her thoughts spun wildly, trying to process everything he was saying, but nothing seemed to make sense. She was part of it? How was that even possible? She had only stumbled into this town weeks ago. She wasn't from Brookhaven. She wasn't tied to the curse. Was she?

Before she could ask more questions, a low rumble echoed through the forest, sending a shiver of dread through her spine. She turned her head, scanning the woods, and in the growing darkness, she saw something—a flicker of movement. And then, another. And another.

Shapes.

Shadows.

Figures, emerging from the trees.

"*What is that?*" she whispered, a wave of panic sweeping through her. The figures were growing closer, but there was something strange about them—*unnatural.* They moved too fast, too fluid, like phantoms, like things that didn't belong to this world.

The man stepped in front of her, his posture protective. "*You've released them,*" he said, his voice colder now. "*The others. The souls bound to the curse. The ones who fed it. And now they're free.*"

Evelyn's mind raced, but before she could react, the figures were upon them. The clearing was filled with the sound of footsteps, the unmistakable feeling of something terrible approaching. Evelyn's heart hammered against her ribs, her breath caught in her throat.

They weren't human.

Not anymore.

The shadows were alive—each one more distorted, more monstrous than the last. As they stepped forward, they revealed grotesque features, faces twisted in agony, their forms half human and half something... something else. Each one was connected to the curse, to the stone, to the thing Evelyn had inadvertently awakened.

And they were coming for her.

Chapter 7: Shadows of the Past

The air had gone still again, but this time it felt thicker, like a suffocating blanket closing in around her. Evelyn's breath came in shallow gasps, her pulse drumming in her ears as the creatures from the shadows closed in. The figures, dark and distorted, moved with unnatural grace, their movements a strange mix of human and something far darker—something older.

They were unlike anything Evelyn had ever seen. Twisted, grotesque things, their faces half-formed, their limbs bent at impossible angles, all of them bearing the same maddening, hollow stare. Eyes devoid of humanity, eyes that seemed to be searching for something—her. *No, not just me*, she realized, her stomach sinking. *They're looking for more than just me. They're looking for the key.*

The man from the woods, who had stood so protectively in front of her moments ago, now took a slow step backward, his face hardening. His eyes flicked to Evelyn for a split second, then back to the figures. The movement was subtle, but it was enough for Evelyn to realize that he was preparing for something—something that would not end well.

He didn't look afraid, not exactly, but his expression was one of grim determination. *So, he's seen this before.*

Evelyn's throat tightened, the weight of her previous actions crashing down on her with full force. *The Keeper, the curse, the stone... it wasn't over. It had only just begun.*

"*What are they?*" she whispered, her voice trembling.

"*They are the souls bound to the curse,*" the man replied, his voice quiet but firm. "*The ones who fed it, who kept it alive over the years. Their pain, their anger—they are what keeps this place in chains.*"

The creatures didn't move closer immediately. Instead, they swarmed the perimeter of the clearing, circling them slowly, as if savoring the moment before the inevitable confrontation. Their eyes—those hollow, dead eyes—never left Evelyn. They were fixated on her, as though she was the source of all their torment.

One of them—a particularly grotesque figure, its limbs contorted at unnatural angles—took a step forward. Its mouth opened, and a guttural rasp emerged, like the sound of old leather tearing. "*You've... freed us.*"

The voice was low, wet, as though the thing had not spoken in centuries. Evelyn shuddered at the sound, her body instinctively moving closer to the man for protection, though she knew he might not be able to save her.

The man didn't flinch. His face remained expressionless, as though this moment had long been foreseen, long been expected.

"*What do you want?*" Evelyn managed to ask, her voice barely above a whisper. Her mind raced, trying to piece together the meaning of the figure's words. *Freed them? But they're not human anymore... are they?*

The creature, with its broken face and contorted body, stepped closer, its jagged teeth glistening in the dim light. "*You think you've ended it. You think you've sealed the door.*" It hissed, its voice rasping like metal against stone. "*But the door was never locked. It was waiting. Waiting for you.*"

Evelyn's blood ran cold. She had thought that by stopping the Keeper, by taking the stone in her hands and severing the connection, she had been putting an end to whatever ancient evil had plagued this town. But this... this was something else. The Keeper wasn't the only entity tied to the stone, wasn't the only force that had been sealed away. It was a much larger, more insidious force, a force that had been waiting for the right moment to rise again.

"No..." Evelyn whispered, her heart sinking. "*No, this can't be possible.*"

"*Oh, but it is,*" the creature crooned, its jagged grin widening. "*You are the key, Evelyn. You and the stone. Together, you opened the door. And now... you must pay the price.*"

The world seemed to tilt, the ground beneath her feet suddenly unsteady. She staggered back, her vision swimming. *Pay the price? What does that mean?*

Another figure, this one smaller but no less twisted, advanced on her. It had the face of a child—though the eyes were empty, lifeless—and its limbs were unnaturally long, elongated like a spider's. The thing's movements were quick, too fast for comfort, its gaze never leaving Evelyn.

"*You've taken our suffering,*" it whispered, its voice like a thin thread of sound. "*You've become a part of it. Now you must endure what we have endured.*"

The creature's voice echoed in her head, its words burrowing deep into her mind. Evelyn recoiled, fighting the wave of dizziness threatening to overwhelm her.

The man moved with a sudden speed, his arm outstretched as he stepped between her and the creatures. His gaze was cold, his face set in a hard, resolute expression. "*Enough,*" he said firmly, his voice cutting through the night air like a blade. "*This isn't her fault.*"

The creatures halted, their forms flickering for a moment, as if uncertain. The child-like figure hissed, its face distorting further. "*Not her fault? She opened the door! She brought us back!*"

The man's jaw clenched, his fists tightening at his sides. "*You don't understand. She's part of the cycle now, just like you were. And unless you want to remain trapped in this place forever, you'll back off.*"

Evelyn's heart pounded, her eyes darting between the man and the creatures. Her mind was racing—*cycle? Trapped?* What was he talking about? What was this cycle? And why did he seem so calm, like he was the one in control of the situation?

The child-creature hissed again, but there was a moment of hesitation in its movements, as if it were weighing the man's words. The air grew thick with tension, as though even the forest itself was holding its breath.

Finally, the creature stepped back, its face twisting with rage. "*This isn't over, mortal,*" it spat. "*The stone has chosen her. The curse cannot be broken. Not now. Not ever.*"

With that, the creatures began to retreat, their forms dissolving back into the shadows. The last figure, the one with the broken face, lingered for a moment longer, its hollow eyes still fixed on Evelyn. "*You will suffer for what you've done,*" it murmured. "*You will learn... too late... that there is no escaping the price of truth.*"

The clearing fell silent again, the air still heavy with the aftertaste of their words. The man remained standing, his posture tense but unbroken. Evelyn was frozen in place, her mind racing as she processed everything that had just happened.

"*What was that?*" she finally managed to ask, her voice shaky. "*Who were they? And what do you mean, I'm part of the cycle?*"

The man didn't answer immediately. Instead, he turned slowly, his eyes scanning the forest around them as if expecting something more to emerge from the dark. "*They were the ones who kept the curse alive. Their souls were bound to the stone, to the ritual. They were sacrifices, trapped here for eternity. Until you came.*"

Evelyn's head was spinning. "*I— I didn't mean to open anything! I just... I wanted to stop it. I thought I was ending it!*"

The man gave her a hard look, his eyes unreadable. "*You didn't end it, Evelyn. You only prolonged it. The curse was never truly sealed. It was waiting for someone like you to come along, someone with the power to release it again. And now you've done exactly that.*"

Evelyn felt her chest tighten with fear. "*What do you mean, 'someone like me'?*"

He finally turned to face her fully, his expression softening just slightly. "*The curse has always been tied to this town. To the stone. To the blood of those who came before you. And now... to yours.*"

A chill ran down her spine. "*My blood?*"

"*Yes.*" The man took a step toward her, his gaze steady. "*Your ancestors were the ones who first made the pact. They gave their blood to the stone, to keep the darkness at bay. And now, that blood runs in you. The stone chose you.*"

Evelyn's breath caught in her throat as the pieces began to fall into place. Her family. Her father's strange obsession with the town, the journals, the stories—*it was all connected.* Her bloodline had been tied to this curse long before she ever set foot in Brookhaven.

But why hadn't anyone told her? Why had no one warned her that she was walking into this... this trap?

"*But... what does that mean?*" Evelyn's voice was barely a whisper. "*What do I do now?*"

The man's eyes softened, just for a moment, and he seemed to hesitate. Then, in a voice that held more weight than she could ever have imagined, he said, "*Now, you survive.*"

The forest had gone eerily silent again. The creatures, the shadowed souls that had circled her moments ago, had melted back into the darkness. Evelyn's heart hammered in her chest, and she could still feel the oppressive weight of their eyes upon her. The hollow gazes, the twisted mouths—they were still with her, their whispers lingering in her mind like the echo of a nightmare she couldn't shake.

The man—the only one who had dared to stand against the creatures—now turned away, moving toward the edge of the clearing. His cloak rustled in the windless night, the shadows clinging to him like a second skin. Evelyn remained frozen, her mind racing. What had just happened? The creatures had retreated, but the words they'd spoken... *The price of truth.* What was that supposed to mean?

For a long moment, she stood still, feeling like a weight had descended on her chest. The stone, still in her hand, had grown cold. She glanced down at it, as if expecting it to suddenly come to life again. But it was just a stone. Nothing special. Nothing magical. Or was it? Evelyn's fingers tightened around it, the smooth surface cool against her skin. The moment she'd picked it up, everything had changed. Her entire reality had shattered, and now, she was entangled in something ancient and malevolent. Something that had been waiting for her.

She couldn't stay here in this clearing forever. The man—whoever he was—seemed to be waiting for her to gather her thoughts, but the silence between them felt heavy, as though some unspoken understanding had passed between them. The weight of his words pressed down on her like a physical force.

"How do I stop this?" Evelyn finally asked, her voice barely above a whisper. She felt like she was asking the impossible—*How do you stop something that has already been set in motion for centuries?*

The man, who had been staring at the dark horizon, slowly turned back to face her. His expression was unreadable, but there was something more than resignation in his eyes—something that bordered on sympathy. Sympathy for what she had unknowingly brought upon herself.

"Stop it?" he repeated, his voice calm, but there was a hardness there. *"You don't stop it. Not now. It's too late for that. The cycle... has already begun."*

Evelyn blinked in disbelief. Her mind reeled from the finality in his words. Too late? She had barely begun to understand what she had unleashed, and now he was telling her it was already beyond her control?

"I... I can't just let this happen. I can't let them destroy everything," she said, her voice trembling with frustration and fear. "There has to be a way to stop it. You said... you said I was part of it. Part of the curse. But that means I can end it too, right?"

The man shook his head, his face hardening once more. "You can't undo what's been done, Evelyn. The curse has been here long before you came to Brookhaven. Long before you even knew the truth about your family."

Her heart skipped a beat. *Family?* Was he talking about her father? The strange journals he'd left behind? The stories he'd told her when she was young? They had always sounded like fairy tales—wild, impossible tales about a dark history that had plagued Brookhaven for generations.

The man took a step toward her, his expression growing more intense. "You are part of this, Evelyn. Your family... they made the pact with the stone long ago. Your bloodline is what ties it all together. Without you, the curse would have died. But you came here. You found the stone. And now, it's bound to you."

Evelyn recoiled. She felt a rush of cold panic as the pieces of the puzzle started to fall into place. Her father had known something. Something he hadn't shared with her. But why hadn't he told her the truth? Why hadn't he warned her about the legacy of her family? The curse that had bound the town to suffering for generations?

"My family?" Evelyn said, her voice barely audible. "My father—he knew?"

The man nodded slowly, his eyes filled with a sorrowful understanding. "He knew. He tried to keep you away from it. That's why he never wanted you to come back here. He wanted to protect you. But you couldn't stay away, could you? You're like them. Like all of them. Drawn to the stone, drawn to the power it holds."

Evelyn took a step back, feeling the ground beneath her feet shift. She could barely breathe. Her father had been trying to protect her from something he knew was inevitable, something that had been ingrained in her bloodline. But why hadn't he told her more? Why hadn't he prepared her for this?

"*I don't understand,*" she whispered. "*If the curse is tied to my blood, then... I can't escape it, can I?*"

The man's gaze softened, but there was no pity in it, only the kind of understanding that came from years of experience. "*There's no escaping it. But that doesn't mean you're helpless. You still have choices. You can fight the curse. You can resist it. But you can never run from it.*"

Evelyn shook her head, her mind racing. *Fight it? How?* She had no idea what she was supposed to do. No plan, no weapons, no allies. And yet the weight of the stone in her hand felt heavier, like a reminder that this was now her burden to carry.

"*What happens now?*" she asked, her voice steady despite the storm of emotions swirling inside her.

The man stared at her for a long moment before speaking, his voice low. "*Now... you survive. And you learn. You'll have to uncover the truth of your family's pact. The only way to end this cycle is to understand it. To go back to the beginning.*"

Evelyn felt a chill run down her spine. *Back to the beginning?*

"*The beginning?*" she asked, trying to make sense of his cryptic words. "*What does that mean?*"

"*It means the town, the stone, the curse—it all started long before your father. It goes back centuries. Your family's bloodline is part of that story. The pact, the price of it, the truth of what they did to keep the darkness at bay... you need to uncover it. You need to find out what your ancestors did—and what they left behind.*"

Evelyn nodded slowly, though her mind was a storm of confusion. *Centuries?* She couldn't even wrap her mind around what he was saying. How could she uncover the truth when the very foundation of it was buried in the past? Buried by her family, no less?

But she knew one thing for certain: the man wasn't lying. She could feel it in the pit of her stomach. She had no choice but to follow this path, no choice but to uncover the secrets her family had hidden. The curse was real. It was here. And she was at the center of it.

"*Where do I start?*" she asked, her voice quiet but resolute.

The man paused, glancing at the darkened sky above them. His expression shifted, becoming more distant, as if he were seeing something far beyond the present moment. "*You start at the heart of it. The town. There's a place—the old church. The one they tore down a hundred years ago. It's still there, buried beneath the ground.*"

Evelyn's heart skipped a beat. "*The church?* What does that have to do with anything?"

The man's eyes met hers, his gaze unwavering. "*That's where it all began. That's where your ancestors made the pact. And that's where you'll find the answers you need.*"

Evelyn felt a shiver crawl up her spine. The old church. It had always been a part of the town's dark history, the one place everyone whispered about but never spoke of aloud. Her father's journals had mentioned it only in passing, as if it were something too dangerous to acknowledge.

"*The church…*" she murmured, her thoughts racing. "*I'll find it. I'll go there.*"

The man nodded. "*Good. But be careful. The deeper you go into this, the harder it will be to escape. The curse is strong. Stronger than you think. And it won't just let you walk away.*"

Evelyn's breath caught in her throat. She knew he was right. Whatever path lay ahead, it was one she would have to walk alone. She was tied to the curse now—tied to the stone, tied to her bloodline, tied to the dark history of Brookhaven.

She had no choice but to uncover the truth.

And she had no idea what she would find.

Chapter 8: The Heart of the Curse

The sky had taken on an ominous hue, thick clouds gathering overhead as if they, too, were complicit in the looming darkness that had descended upon Brookhaven. Evelyn's mind was a maelstrom, the weight of the man's words pressing down on her with every step she took. She couldn't stop thinking about the old church. She had to go there. She had no other choice.

The man—who had yet to offer his name—had given her little more than a cryptic warning and a direction. "*The church.*" Those words echoed in her mind as she walked through the forest, her boots crunching on the leaves beneath her feet.

Her thoughts flickered back to her father's journals—the way they had described Brookhaven's past, the strange happenings, the missing pieces of history. She hadn't fully understood them at the time. Now, she knew better. The truth was darker, more twisted than she could have imagined. The town itself had been built upon blood. The blood of her ancestors.

Evelyn had lived in this town her entire life, but she had never truly *known* it. She had never seen it for what it truly was. The people, the places—everything had been shrouded in an eerie calm, a veneer of normalcy. But now that she was awake to the curse, she saw the cracks in the facade everywhere. The air tasted different, colder. The trees seemed to watch her as she passed by, their gnarled branches reaching for the sky like skeletal hands.

The church was the key. She could feel it deep in her bones. But what had happened there? What had her ancestors done to bind this curse to the land?

Her feet carried her deeper into the woods, toward the old part of town, a place she had never ventured. The streets here were desolate, the buildings worn down by time and neglect. They looked like ruins, standing as a testimony to something forgotten—or deliberately erased.

She could hear the soft murmurs of the wind, but it didn't offer any comfort. It was as if the very air itself was haunted, alive with the whispers of the past. Evelyn felt it—the weight of the town's secrets pressing in on her.

As she walked past an abandoned house, the windows dark and empty, a flash of movement caught her eye. Her heart lurched, and she quickly turned, but there was nothing there. Nothing but the wind playing with the long, dry grass.

Her breathing quickened, but she forced herself to stay calm. It was just her mind playing tricks on her. She was alone out here, and she had a job to do. She had to reach the church.

But when she reached the clearing where the church had once stood, she stopped dead in her tracks. The ground was overgrown with weeds, and the foundation was long gone. All that remained was a patch of earth, marked only by the remnants of crumbled stone walls.

Evelyn's stomach tightened as she surveyed the area. *This is it?* She had expected something more, something substantial. But the church had been destroyed long ago, the foundations of the structure buried beneath the weight of time. Still, there was an unsettling presence here—an aura of decay, of something ancient that refused to be forgotten.

Her eyes scanned the clearing. There had to be something. The man had said this was the starting point, the place where it all began. But all she could see were overgrown plants, broken remnants of stone, and dirt. The place felt... wrong. Like the earth itself was poisoned.

She crouched down, her fingers brushing the dirt, and that was when she felt it—a subtle shift, a strange vibration beneath her fingertips. She froze, listening. There it was again, a hum, deep and resonant, coming from the very earth.

Evelyn's heart raced. This was no ordinary vibration. This was something powerful. The curse was alive here, buried beneath the ground. And she had just touched it.

A low growl echoed in the distance, and Evelyn's head snapped up. Her pulse quickened as she strained her ears, but the sound faded as quickly as it had come. The forest around her was unnervingly still, too quiet. She stood slowly, her fingers still tingling from the sensation beneath the soil.

She had to dig.

With trembling hands, she pulled a small trowel from her bag and knelt by the ruins. It wasn't much, but it was enough to begin. She scraped away at the earth, her breath shallow as the minutes turned into hours. The sun had dipped below the horizon, and the forest was bathed in the eerie glow of twilight, casting long shadows over the land.

The earth resisted, as if it were pushing her back, reluctant to give up its secrets. But Evelyn pressed on, her determination growing with each scrape of the trowel. She had to find something. Anything.

Finally, after what felt like an eternity, her trowel struck something solid. Her heart skipped a beat as she cleared away the dirt, revealing the edge of a stone slab. It was ancient, covered in moss and grime, but it was unmistakable—a part of the church's foundation.

She wiped away the dirt with her hands, her fingers numb from the cold. The stone was inscribed with strange symbols, their meanings lost to time. But there was no mistaking what it was. This was a part of the church—something that had been buried for centuries.

Her mind raced. *Was this a marker? A doorway? A seal?*

Evelyn could feel it now. The curse was alive here, pulsing beneath the earth, waiting to be unleashed.

Before she could act, the ground trembled beneath her. The slab shifted slightly, as if it were awakening, responding to her presence. She took a step back, her breath catching in her throat. The air around her seemed to crackle with energy, and the hum from the earth grew louder, more insistent.

And then, with a sound like thunder, the earth split open.

A deep fissure appeared before her, and from it, a cloud of dust and smoke billowed up, obscuring her vision. Evelyn staggered back, her hands raised to protect her face, as the ground trembled again, louder this time. A figure emerged from the cloud—tall, thin, its body cloaked in darkness. Its form was indistinct, a shadow within a shadow, but its eyes—its eyes glowed with an unnatural light.

Evelyn froze, her heart thundering in her chest. The figure stood motionless for a moment, its eyes locked on hers. It tilted its head, almost as if curious.

This was no ordinary ghost, Evelyn realized. *This was something much worse.*

The figure stepped forward, its movements unnaturally smooth, its footsteps making no sound on the ground. Evelyn's body tensed, every instinct screaming at her to run, but she couldn't. She was rooted to the spot, trapped by some invisible force.

"You should not have come here," the figure said, its voice like the rustling of dry leaves, a whisper carried on the wind.

Evelyn's throat tightened. *"Who are you?"* she managed to say, her voice barely a whisper.

The figure did not answer immediately. Instead, it seemed to study her, its glowing eyes flicking over her, as if assessing her very soul. *"I am the Keeper of the Gate,"* it said finally. *"And you, child of the bloodline, have opened it."*

Evelyn's heart skipped a beat. *The Keeper of the Gate?*

"I... I didn't mean to. I didn't know." Her voice trembled, the weight of the situation sinking in. The man had warned her that the curse was tied to her bloodline, but she had never imagined it would manifest like this.

The Keeper's form shimmered, flickering like a reflection in water. "*It does not matter whether you meant to or not. The blood runs through you. And the curse follows where it leads.*"

Evelyn swallowed hard, trying to steady herself. "*What do you want from me?*" she demanded. "*What are you?*"

The Keeper's eyes narrowed, and its form seemed to become even darker, its presence suffocating. "*I do not want anything from you, child. But the curse demands payment. It demands suffering. And now, you will pay the price for awakening it.*"

Before Evelyn could react, the ground trembled again. The earth split wider, and more figures began to rise from the fissure, their forms emerging like shadows from the depths. Their eyes glowed with the same unnatural light, and their presence filled the air with an overwhelming sense of doom.

Evelyn's pulse raced. She was surrounded, and the Keeper's words echoed in her mind. *The curse demands payment.*

But how could she fight something like this? How could she possibly face the darkness that had been waiting for centuries?

The Keeper stepped closer, its dark form towering over her. "*You cannot fight what you do not understand,*" it said, its voice cold. "*But you will learn. And when you do, the curse will claim you... as it has claimed so many before.*"

Evelyn's breath caught in her throat. Her body screamed for her to flee, but she stood her ground, her mind racing. She wasn't alone anymore. The man, the one who had warned her, had to have known this was coming. She needed answers—*the truth.*

And with that, she made a silent vow. She would uncover the full extent of her family's dark past. She would learn the truth about the curse. And she would find a way to stop it—no matter what the cost.

The ground beneath Evelyn's feet continued to tremble, and the figures emerging from the fissure grew larger, their forms more defined as they materialized from the very earth itself. She could hear the scraping of their feet, a sound like broken glass skittering across the ground. The Keeper of the Gate towered over her, its presence a suffocating weight on her chest, its glowing eyes fixed with unnatural intensity.

Evelyn's breath came in shallow gasps as she stood frozen in place. Her heart pounded in her chest, the sound nearly drowning out the strange hum that still vibrated through the air. *This can't be happening,* she thought desperately. *This is all too much. I can't—*

The Keeper's voice broke through her panic, its tone cold, yet strangely hollow, like the whisper of a forgotten memory. "*You think you understand, but you are still blind to the truth.*"

She swallowed hard, forcing her feet to move. Her instincts screamed at her to run, but her legs felt rooted to the earth, as if some invisible force was holding her in place. She had to fight. She had no choice but to understand—this was all connected. The curse. The stone. The town's dark past. And now these... creatures, these figures from the depths of the earth. They were the consequences of her bloodline. Of her actions.

"What do you want from me?" she asked, her voice shaky but louder now, more defiant. "What is this curse? Why am I the one it's seeking?"

The Keeper's hollow laugh echoed in the clearing, sending a chill through Evelyn's spine. "*You are not the first to awaken the curse. Your bloodline has been a vessel for the darkness for generations. The price you pay for your ancestors' sins is not one you can avoid. It is yours to bear, whether you wish it or not.*"

Evelyn's mind raced. *Her bloodline.* Her ancestors. This had been set in motion long before she'd arrived in Brookhaven. She had known, deep down, that her family's history held more than the innocuous stories of lost inheritance or a tarnished legacy. There was something darker buried beneath it all, something that linked her to the stone, to the cursed town, to this very moment.

But what was the curse? What had her ancestors done?

Her fingers trembled as she reached into her coat pocket and pulled out her father's journal. The tattered pages felt cold against her skin, like they too had been waiting for this moment. She flipped it open to a page she had studied many times—her father's last entry before he had disappeared.

They will come for you, Evelyn. The bloodline always pays the price. The curse cannot be stopped. You must leave before it claims you.

That's all it said. A warning, a plea.

She could feel the weight of her father's words now more than ever. But the Keeper of the Gate wasn't done speaking. It stepped closer, its dark form casting a shadow over Evelyn, its glowing eyes never leaving hers. The air grew colder, biting at her skin like icy needles.

"*Your father was a fool,*" the Keeper said, its voice like gravel grinding underfoot. "*He thought he could protect you. He thought he could run from the curse. But it follows. It always follows. And now you have returned. The bloodline calls, and the darkness answers.*"

The creatures that had risen from the fissure—shadowy, indistinct forms—shifted around Evelyn, their movements unnaturally fluid. There were no features, only faint outlines, but their eyes were unmistakable—glowing, void-like, pulling her gaze in with an irresistible force.

Evelyn's heart pounded harder, her pulse a drumbeat in her ears. She was surrounded. There was no way out. And even though every instinct screamed at her to flee, she knew it would be futile. The curse was inevitable. The Keeper was right: it had always followed her family.

But Evelyn wasn't about to let it claim her without a fight. She clenched her fists around the journal, its worn pages crinkling under her grip. There had to be something she could do. Some way to stop it, or at least survive long enough to understand the true depth of this curse.

"You don't know me," she said, her voice suddenly clear, her fear giving way to a surge of determination. "You don't know what I'm capable of."

The Keeper's eyes narrowed. "*I know you.*" It stepped closer, its form flickering like a dark flame. "*I know your blood. I know your history. And I know the price you will pay.*"

Evelyn's hands shook, but she didn't lower her gaze. "*I don't care about my history,*" she said, her voice steady now. "*I care about ending this. About stopping it from spreading. Whatever curse you think you can impose on me, I will find a way to break it.*"

A dark, twisted smile curled across the Keeper's lips, if it even had lips. "*You cannot break what is already broken,*" it whispered. "*But you will try. And in doing so, you will understand the true cost of your blood.*"

The ground beneath them began to tremble again, the fissure widening. The earth seemed to crack open further, as if to swallow them whole. Evelyn's breath caught in her throat, and she instinctively stepped back. The Keeper's dark form moved with her, always at her heels, its presence more suffocating by the second.

A voice echoed in her mind—the man who had warned her earlier. "*You will have to uncover the truth,*" he had said. *The truth.* Evelyn's mind grasped for the words, the meaning, as if trying to piece together the scattered fragments of knowledge she'd gathered in the short time since she'd arrived in Brookhaven.

The truth was here, buried beneath the earth. But it wasn't just in the journal. It wasn't just in her father's warnings. It was in the very stone that had cursed this town. It was in her blood.

"You're wrong," Evelyn said suddenly, the words coming to her with force. "*I know I can break it.*"

The Keeper stopped, its glowing eyes focusing on her. "*Do you?*" it asked, the words dripping with malice. "*Then show me. Show me how you will break the curse that has bound your family for centuries.*"

Evelyn's eyes widened. The air around her seemed to still, the sound of her breathing growing louder in the silence. Show it? How could she show it something that she didn't even fully understand?

But as the Keeper's words echoed in her mind, something clicked. It was as if the pieces of a long-forgotten puzzle were falling into place. Her father's journals, the stone, the cursed bloodline—it was all connected.

And if she was going to end it, she would need to understand the origins of the curse. She would need to trace it all the way back to the source.

Evelyn steadied herself, gripping the journal tightly. Her father had hidden the truth in these pages—hidden something that could undo everything. There was something in this journal, something she had missed before. A final clue. She was certain of it.

As she opened the journal again, the Keeper's eyes followed her every movement, its presence pressing in on her like an unrelenting storm.

"*You cannot escape the curse,*" the Keeper whispered again, its voice full of disdain. "*It will claim you, just as it claimed your father, your ancestors... and every soul that dared to oppose it.*"

But Evelyn didn't hear it. She was too focused on the pages before her. The words she had read countless times before now made sense in a way they never had.

The stone is the key. The stone binds us all, and it is in the blood that the curse is kept alive. To break it, one must sever the bond. One must find the root—the heart of the curse—and destroy it.

She could feel the weight of those words sink deep into her heart. *The root.* She had to destroy the root of the curse.

And the root was buried beneath this town. Beneath the church. Beneath everything her family had tried to bury.

The Keeper of the Gate's laugh echoed again, harsh and grating. "*You will fail, child. You will never understand the price of what you seek. The cost of defying the curse.*"

Evelyn closed the journal with a snap, her resolve hardening. "*We'll see about that.*"

With a final, steadying breath, she turned and walked toward the fissure—the heart of the curse.

She was going to find the truth. And she was going to end it.

Chapter 9: The Root Beneath

The night was thick with shadows as Evelyn stood before the fissure in the ground, its edges jagged and sharp, like the teeth of some ancient beast rising from the earth. Her hands were clammy, her heart hammering in her chest, but her resolve had hardened like steel. There was no turning back now. She had come too far.

The Keeper's warning echoed in her mind—*The cost of defying the curse*—but Evelyn was no longer listening to the threats. She couldn't afford to. Not when the truth was within reach. Her family's bloodline, the curse, the town of Brookhaven—they were all intricately connected, and she was the key to unraveling it all.

But how?

She had no answers yet, no clear path forward, but the journal had given her something. A starting point. The stone. The curse was bound to her ancestors, to the land. The root was buried here, in the very earth that had been poisoned by centuries of dark history. And Evelyn was the one to unearth it. The one to destroy it.

She took a deep breath, clutching the journal tightly in her hands. She glanced back toward the Keeper, whose presence loomed behind her like a dark cloud. The Keeper had warned her that she would fail. That the curse could not be undone. But Evelyn refused to believe that.

There has to be a way.

She squatted down at the edge of the fissure, brushing her fingertips against the cold stone. Her body trembled slightly, not from fear but from anticipation. There was something here. Something ancient. And if she could find it—if she could understand it—maybe she could break the cycle. She just needed to figure out what the stone was. What it meant.

A low, guttural voice interrupted her thoughts, and Evelyn turned quickly, her eyes narrowing. The Keeper had moved closer, its form flickering in the dim light, almost as if it were made of smoke.

"*You cannot undo what has been done,*" the Keeper hissed, its voice like dry leaves scraping across the ground. "*The blood will always claim you. You cannot escape your fate.*"

Evelyn met its gaze, her jaw clenched tight. "*I'm not trying to escape anything. I'm here to end it. You don't own me. You don't own this town.*"

The Keeper's eyes glowed brighter, its form flickering as if it were no longer tethered to the physical world. It leaned in, its voice cold as winter. "*The curse is a part of you. It is woven into your soul, into every drop of blood that runs through your veins. You are bound to it. And when it comes for you, it will not let go.*"

Evelyn's chest tightened, but she refused to flinch. She turned her attention back to the fissure, ignoring the Keeper's warning. Whatever it was saying—whatever its dark promises—it couldn't be true. She refused to believe it.

There was a whisper in the back of her mind, a growing pull to the earth, to the stone. She closed her eyes and placed her palm against the cracked ground, feeling the pulse of something beneath her fingers. It wasn't just the hum she had sensed earlier. This felt different. More solid. More real.

Her breath hitched as the earth beneath her hand shifted. The fissure widened, and with it, the stone emerged. At first, it was just a fragment, dark and cracked, but as she pressed down harder, it began to rise. More stone. More history. More power. It was as if the earth itself was yielding to her touch, as if the stone were calling to her.

Evelyn's pulse quickened, the air around her thickening with an unearthly pressure. It was then that she noticed the symbols etched into the stone—symbols she recognized from her father's journal.

The binding sigils.

Her stomach lurched as she traced her fingers over the markings. The sigils were ancient, but they weren't just decorative. They were part of the curse. Part of what held it in place. And if she could break these marks—if she could shatter the symbols—the curse might be destroyed with them.

But the Keeper was watching. She could feel its eyes boring into her back. There was no time to hesitate.

Taking a deep breath, Evelyn pressed harder against the stone. The ground shook beneath her, and for a moment, it felt as though the earth itself was fighting her. But Evelyn wouldn't stop. She couldn't.

Suddenly, a crack split the air, sharp and deafening. The stone shifted violently, and Evelyn was thrown back, her body slamming into the cold, hard ground. She gasped, her breath stolen from her as she fought to regain her bearings. Her hands shook as she pushed herself up, but it was too late. The Keeper had already moved forward.

"*You fool,*" it spat, its voice full of fury. "*You think you can break the curse by disturbing what was set in motion centuries ago? You cannot. You are nothing but a child trying to play at power.*"

Evelyn struggled to her feet, but the Keeper was upon her in an instant. She could feel its cold, oppressive presence closing in, threatening to suffocate her. There was no room to breathe, no space to think.

But as the Keeper reached out toward her, something inside Evelyn snapped.

She reached down to her side and grabbed the journal, clutching it tightly in her hands. With the Keeper bearing down on her, she opened it once more, her eyes scanning the pages in desperation. There had to be something—*anything*—that could stop this.

Her finger traced the final entry her father had made, the one she had barely understood before. It was written in a scrawl, as though he had been in a hurry.

The stone is not the root of the curse. The blood is. Find the bloodline. Find the source. Only by severing the blood that binds it can the curse be undone.

Evelyn's heart raced as she read the words again, and then it hit her—the bloodline. It wasn't just about breaking the stone, or the sigils. It was about confronting the curse where it began.

Her father hadn't just hidden the key to breaking the curse in the stone. He had hidden it in his bloodline. Her bloodline.

Suddenly, the ground around her seemed to come alive. The earth beneath her feet began to rumble, the fissure widening. And then, the Keeper's voice filled the air, a low growl that seemed to shake the very bones of the earth.

"You cannot escape. You cannot outrun what is already inside you. Your bloodline will always call to the darkness. Always."

Evelyn's blood ran cold. She realized, too late, that the Keeper wasn't just warning her. It was telling her the truth. She couldn't escape the curse. It was woven into her very soul.

But she still had one choice left.

With trembling hands, Evelyn tore out the page from the journal—the page her father had written his last cryptic words on. The ink was fading, but she could still make out the sigils her father had drawn around the passage. The last instructions.

With a deep breath, Evelyn pressed the torn page into the stone, the symbols aligning as she forced them together. The ground shook again, but this time, it wasn't an earthquake. It was something much more primal. The stone began to glow, the symbols igniting with a brilliant, eerie light that filled the clearing.

The Keeper let out a shriek, a sound like metal scraping against stone, as the light from the stone grew brighter, blinding Evelyn. She closed her eyes, feeling the heat of it searing her skin. But she couldn't stop. She had to finish this. She had to break it.

Then, everything went silent.

The light faded, and Evelyn slowly opened her eyes.

The Keeper was gone.

For a moment, she thought she had been hallucinating. That it had all been a dream, a nightmare brought on by stress and fear. But when she looked down at the stone, now cracked and broken in her hands, she knew the truth.

The curse had been broken.

At least, for now.

But Evelyn knew that this was only the beginning. The darkness that had plagued her family for generations would not be so easily silenced. The curse had been broken, but the root of the evil remained. She had only taken the first step.

And there would be more steps to follow.

The earth beneath Evelyn's feet still trembled, a low, ominous hum that vibrated in her chest. She stared at the shattered stone in her hands, its glow dimming with each passing second. The air was thick with the smell of burnt earth and something else, something that she couldn't quite place, but it clung to the atmosphere like smoke from a fire that had burned too long.

For a moment, everything was silent, as though the world had stopped breathing.

Then, slowly, Evelyn's legs buckled, and she sank to her knees. Her hands trembled as she clutched the fragments of the stone. The Keeper was gone—its malevolent presence evaporated as quickly as it had come—but the weight of what she had just done settled over her like a shroud.

Had she really done it?

She looked around the clearing, half-expecting the dark form of the Keeper to materialize again, or for the ground beneath her to crack open once more. But there was nothing. No shadows creeping toward her. No distant howls or shrieks.

For a fleeting moment, it seemed as though she might have succeeded. But deep in her gut, Evelyn knew better. She had only broken the surface of the curse. The root was still buried somewhere, somewhere far deeper than this. And while the stone had been a powerful symbol, a key to unlocking the deeper mysteries, it was only a piece of the puzzle.

Her breath came in sharp bursts as she staggered to her feet, the journal still clutched tightly in her hands. The pages had begun to curl at the edges, worn from the countless times she had read them, studied them, searched for some way to understand what was happening to her.

The words her father had written, the instructions for breaking the curse, had been both a curse and a blessing in themselves. *Find the bloodline. Find the source.* What did that mean? Was the source the root of the curse? Or was it something far more sinister—something she had yet to uncover?

Her thoughts were interrupted by a sudden rustling behind her. She spun around, but all she saw were the dense trees surrounding the clearing, their branches creaking in the wind. There was nothing. No figure stepping out from the shadows. No whisper in the night.

Yet Evelyn couldn't shake the feeling that she wasn't alone.

The sensation of being watched prickled at the back of her neck, sending a chill down her spine. *Was it the Keeper's lingering influence?* The thought made her shiver. Or was it something else? Something more... insidious?

She forced herself to focus, forcing the doubts from her mind. She had to be strong. She had to keep moving forward. There was no time for hesitation. If she was going to undo this curse, she couldn't waste another second.

Taking a deep breath, she turned away from the fissure and began walking toward the town. The stone may have been broken, but the battle wasn't over. Not by a long shot. Evelyn's mind raced with possibilities, trying to piece together the fragments of the mystery that had been haunting her since she arrived in Brookhaven.

She had come here to escape the shadows of her past, but now she realized that her family's past was more of a prison than she had ever imagined. The curse wasn't just a remnant of the past—it was alive, and it was *alive in her*. The blood that coursed through her veins was the very thing that bound the curse to this land. But how? Why?

And what exactly was she supposed to do now?

The Hollow Man

As Evelyn neared the outskirts of Brookhaven, the familiar streets, once so ordinary, now felt alien. The air tasted different—charged with something darker. She wasn't sure if it was the result of her encounter in the woods or something deeper, a shift in the town's very fabric.

But something was wrong. Something had changed.

She hurried past the rows of empty houses, their windows dark and lifeless, and finally came to the main square. The heart of Brookhaven was eerily quiet, save for the soft flutter of leaves being blown across the cobbled streets. It was as though the town itself was holding its breath, waiting for something to happen.

Evelyn was almost to the library when she heard the soft scrape of footsteps behind her. Her body tensed, her senses alert. She turned quickly, but there was no one there. Just the wind pushing a stray piece of paper across the pavement.

For a moment, Evelyn's heart raced. *Was it the Keeper? Had it come back?*

But no. There was something else—something different.

She turned back around, just as a man appeared at the far end of the street.

He was tall and thin, his silhouette stark against the dimming light of dusk. His features were gaunt, his face pale, as if he hadn't seen the sun in years. His eyes, however, were the strangest thing. They gleamed unnaturally in the low light, like pools of black ink, and for a moment, Evelyn couldn't look away.

The man took a slow step forward, his footsteps eerily quiet against the cobblestones.

"*Evelyn,*" he said, his voice a rasp, like sandpaper against wood. "*You've made a mistake.*"

The sound of her name on his lips sent a chill down her spine. She had never seen this man before, but there was something... familiar about him. Something that tugged at the corners of her memory.

"Who are you?" Evelyn demanded, taking a step back, but her feet felt rooted to the ground.

The man smiled—a slow, cold smile that didn't reach his eyes. "*You don't remember me, do you? I suppose that's understandable. Not many do.*"

Evelyn's pulse quickened. There was something about his presence that felt wrong. She had to get away. But before she could turn, the man took another step forward, his eyes narrowing.

"*You've awakened the curse,*" he continued, his voice rising slightly, as though the words themselves had weight. "*And now, there is no going back.*"

Evelyn felt her breath catch in her throat. "What do you mean? What curse?"

The man tilted his head, his smile widening ever so slightly. "*You think you've broken the stone. You think you've done something monumental, something that will change everything. But you haven't. Not yet.*"

Evelyn's heart sank as she realized the gravity of his words. He knew about the stone. He knew about the curse.

He was part of it. *Part of the bloodline.*

She stiffened, backing up another step. "You're one of them, aren't you?" she asked, her voice steady despite the terror clawing at her throat. "One of the ones who cursed this town."

The man's smile flickered, but he didn't answer right away. Instead, he took a step closer. "*I am older than you think, Evelyn. I was there when it all began. When the curse was first sealed. And I have watched as your bloodline failed time and time again.*"

Evelyn's mind raced. *The Keeper's words... "the bloodline calls, and the darkness answers."*

"I don't care about your past," Evelyn said, her voice growing firm. "You and whatever curse you represent—*it ends now.*"

The man's smile twisted into something cruel. "*You don't understand, do you?*" His voice dropped to a near-whisper. "*There is no end. The curse is not something you can simply end. It's not just about the stone, or the blood, or the land. It's a part of you. It always has been. And it always will be.*"

Evelyn's chest tightened as the weight of his words sank in. Her hands trembled. "*You're lying.*"

But she wasn't so sure. She wasn't so sure anymore.

The man's eyes gleamed, his mouth opening in a soundless laugh. "*You'll learn soon enough.*"

Before Evelyn could respond, he turned and disappeared into the shadows, his footsteps vanishing as if he had never been there.

For a long time, Evelyn stood frozen in place, the echoes of his words swirling around her like a dark storm. She wanted to run. She wanted to scream. But all she could do was stand there, feeling as though something vast and cold had just shifted in her very soul.

The curse wasn't just on her family. It was inside her.

The stone had been a key, but it wasn't the *source* of the curse. The root—the true root—was *her bloodline*.

Chapter 10: The Hollow Echo

Evelyn's footsteps echoed through the empty streets of Brookhaven, the air around her heavy with an oppressive stillness. The encounter with the Hollow Man lingered in her mind, a puzzle piece that refused to fit anywhere. She had tried to dismiss it at first, but something in his cold, knowing eyes told her that whatever game was being played, she was an unwilling player—and worse, she was far from the final move.

Her chest still felt tight, as though a phantom hand had closed around her heart and hadn't let go. The chilling words he had spoken repeated over and over in her mind, each one digging deeper. The curse was not just tied to her family, not just to the stone or the land. It was *her*. Her blood. Her *very being* was tied to it. The Hollow Man had been right about one thing: Evelyn could no longer escape it.

"*It ends now.*" She had said those words to him. But they felt hollow. How could she end something that was woven into her very soul?

Her breath came in sharp bursts as she walked faster, moving toward the one place that had always felt like a sanctuary in the midst of all this madness—the Brookhaven Library. The stone fragments she still held in her hand burned against her palm, almost as if the power within them was calling out to her, urging her to finish what she had started. To find the *root* of the curse.

When she reached the library's entrance, she hesitated for only a moment. The air inside the library always smelled like dust and old paper, like time itself had been preserved within the walls. It had been the one place where she felt even remotely safe since her arrival. But now, with every step she took, that safety seemed less certain.

Inside, the library was as quiet as ever. The faint hum of the ceiling lights and the rustling of the old books on their shelves were the only sounds. Evelyn barely noticed the rows of books that lined the walls as she moved past them. She had one destination in mind—her father's desk.

Her father's study had always been a place of mystery for her, even when she was younger. She would spend hours sifting through his things, trying to decipher his notes, looking for some understanding of the strange legacy he had left her.

She approached the back of the library, where the study was hidden behind a heavy curtain. As she stepped into the small, dimly lit room, a sense of unease washed over her. The desk sat before her as it always had, cluttered with papers, books, and journals. The worn leather chair, still slightly tilted back from her father's last use, creaked under her touch.

Evelyn closed her eyes for a moment, breathing in deeply. She had always felt his presence in this room, even after his death. But now, as she touched the surface of his desk, it felt... different. There was a heaviness, an anticipation in the air. It was as if the room itself were holding its breath.

She set the fragments of the stone down beside the journal, her hands trembling. Opening the journal, she quickly skimmed through the pages, trying to focus, trying to make sense of the clues her father had left behind. His handwriting was nearly illegible in some places, but the same symbols that had appeared on the stone—those same sigils—were scattered throughout. The symbols were *woven* into the words, as though the words themselves were part of the spell that held the curse in place.

Her eyes landed on one entry that stopped her cold. It was near the end of the journal, written in a rushed, frantic scrawl.

The source is not just in the blood. It's in the heart of the curse itself. The heart lies beneath, hidden in plain sight, where the roots of the earth intertwine with the bloodline. The stone is not the vessel—it is the key. And the key will lead you to the truth. But be careful, Evelyn, for the truth is darker than you can imagine. The Hollow Man was not just a keeper of the curse. He was the one who started it. The one who bound it to our family.

Evelyn's throat tightened as she read those words again. *The Hollow Man?* The same man who had appeared on the street? The same man who had spoken of the curse as though it were a part of her? He was the origin of it?

She swallowed hard, feeling her heartbeat in her ears. It was as if the weight of her father's revelation was pressing down on her, suffocating her. The Hollow Man had started the curse. And now he was here, in Brookhaven, still pulling the strings from the shadows.

Evelyn took a step back, the journal trembling in her hands. She couldn't—no, *she wouldn't*—let the curse continue to control her. She had to stop it. But how?

Her gaze drifted to the fragments of the stone on the desk, its jagged edges catching the light. It wasn't the stone itself that was important—it was the *key* it represented. But to unlock that key, she needed to understand *where* to go next.

Her father's words hung in the air: *The heart lies beneath, hidden in plain sight.* Beneath? Beneath what? Where?

The answer came to her in a flash—a memory she had buried deep in her mind, from when she was just a child. She and her father had once visited the old church on the edge of Brookhaven. It had been abandoned for as long as Evelyn could remember, its crumbling walls overgrown with vines, its stained-glass windows cracked and dusty.

Her father had taken her there for a reason. But what?

Could the church be the heart of the curse? Was it possible that the source of the evil that had plagued her family for generations was hidden there?

Without thinking, Evelyn grabbed the journal and the stone fragments and made for the door. There was no more time to waste. She couldn't wait for answers to find her. She had to go to the source.

The Forgotten Church

The church loomed ahead like a forgotten monument, its twisted spire jutting into the sky. The evening sky had turned a deep, bruised purple, and the wind had picked up, whipping around her as if the air itself was trying to keep her away.

Evelyn stood at the gate, staring at the church for a long moment. There was something profoundly unsettling about it—the air around the building felt thick, as if the very ground was resisting her presence. Every step she took forward felt like an intrusion.

She pushed open the rusted iron gate with a groan, the sound sharp in the still night. As she crossed the threshold of the overgrown yard, the air shifted again. A wave of nausea rose in her throat, and she fought to keep herself steady. The feeling that something was *wrong* here grew stronger with every passing second.

The church doors were wide open, as if waiting for her. She hesitated just outside the entrance, gathering her courage, before stepping over the threshold.

Inside, the air was colder. The space was suffused with shadows, the faintest light filtering through the broken windows. Her footsteps echoed off the cracked stone floors as she moved further into the church, the remnants of old pews and rotting wood scattered throughout. The scent of decay was overwhelming, and the stained-glass windows, once vibrant with color, now only offered fragments of broken light.

But it was the altar that drew her attention. It was unlike anything she had expected. The altar was *new*. Too new. The wood gleamed in the dim light, the surface unmarred by age or dust, and there were strange, arcane symbols carved into its surface. The same symbols she had seen in her father's journal. The same ones on the stone.

Her heart pounded in her chest as she approached it, her hand instinctively reaching for the stone fragments in her pocket. As her fingers brushed the cold surface of the altar, a deep, resonating hum filled the air.

Evelyn gasped, stumbling back. The hum wasn't just in her ears—it was in her bones. The altar *was* the heart her father had mentioned. And now, she was standing at its center. The source of the curse was here, beneath her feet, in this cursed place.

But how? What now?

Before she could process the feeling, the ground beneath her shifted. A low growl rumbled from somewhere deep within the earth, and the walls of the church seemed to close in around her.

It had begun.

The air inside the church grew thicker, heavier. It felt as though the walls themselves were closing in, pressing down on Evelyn's chest with every breath she took. The strange hum that had filled the room wasn't just in her ears anymore—it seemed to reverberate through the very bones of the building, echoing in the hollows of the old stone walls, in the shattered windows, in the hollow spaces beneath her feet. It was as if the church itself were alive, breathing with her.

Her heart beat faster, the cold stone floor beneath her feet seeming to tilt and shift, just a little, as if the building were moving. Or perhaps it was just the overwhelming weight of what she was standing on—the heart of the curse itself.

The altar in front of her loomed larger now, its intricate carvings seeming to pulse with an energy she couldn't quite understand. The symbols were no longer just markings—they were *alive*, their lines flowing like dark rivers across the polished wood. As her hand hovered over them, a flicker of something passed through her—a flash of memory, a vision.

She saw her father's face, twisted in anguish, his hands pressed against the altar's surface. She saw him whispering, chanting words she didn't understand, words that made the very air seem to vibrate in response. The ground beneath him had cracked open, and from the fissures, dark tendrils had reached up, curling around his arms, around his neck, pulling him into the earth. He had screamed, and in that moment, Evelyn felt his terror as though it were her own.

A sharp intake of breath escaped her lips, and she pulled her hand back. She stumbled away from the altar, her mind reeling from the vision. What had just happened? Was that a memory of her father—or was it a *warning*?

The hum intensified.

"*Stop!*" Evelyn cried, her voice echoing through the church. But there was no response. The symbols on the altar had begun to glow, faint at first, and then brighter, like dying embers igniting once again. The tendrils from the vision—those dark forces—were real. They were here. They had always been here, buried beneath the church, waiting for someone to unlock the gate.

Evelyn's pulse raced as she backed toward the door. Her body screamed for her to leave—to escape before whatever dark force had been awakened consumed her. But then, she stopped. Her fingers tightened around the fragments of the stone she had brought with her. She had come too far to turn back now.

A voice, soft and slithering like smoke, seemed to drift from every corner of the room.

"*You cannot run, Evelyn. The heart is yours now. And you will bring it to life, or you will die trying.*"

Evelyn's breath caught in her throat, but she wasn't sure if the voice was real or just a product of her own fear. The shadows in the church seemed to deepen, curling around the edges of the room, like the darkness itself was moving toward her.

Suddenly, the floor beneath her feet cracked with a loud *bang*, and Evelyn stumbled back, barely keeping her footing as the ground split open in front of the altar. She could feel the earth shifting, the tremors deep beneath the church, and a cold gust of wind swept through the open door, as though some great force was rushing in.

From the gaping crack in the floor, something rose—slowly, impossibly slow, as though it had been waiting for centuries to be freed. A shape, dark and indistinct at first, began to take form, rising from the blackness below. As it emerged, it grew clearer, solidifying into the shape of a man.

Evelyn's eyes widened in horror. The figure before her was tall, clad in tattered robes, its skin a strange ashen gray. But it was not the figure itself that froze her in place—it was the face.

It was the Hollow Man.

But this time, he was different. This time, he was... *real.*

He stepped forward, his every movement deliberate, his feet barely making a sound as they touched the ground. His eyes, still those hollow, jet-black pits, locked onto hers. There was no emotion there—only a cold, infinite emptiness.

"You came," he said, his voice like the rustle of dead leaves, brittle and sharp. *"I wondered when you would finally arrive. Your bloodline has always been drawn to this place. To me."*

Evelyn's stomach twisted with a surge of dread. *"What do you want from me?"* she demanded, trying to steady her voice. But the words felt weak, as though the very air was pressing down on her.

The Hollow Man smiled—a slow, chilling twist of his lips. *"What I want? What I have always wanted, Evelyn. You."*

His words were a blade, sharp and deep, cutting through the very core of her being. Her blood ran cold.

"You... want me?" Evelyn's voice was almost a whisper, disbelief filling her chest.

He nodded. *"Yes. Your blood is tied to the curse. You are the last of the line, the last piece of the puzzle. You are the key that will either end this, or ensure it continues for eternity."*

Evelyn stumbled back a step, her mind racing. Her father had known this. He had known the price, the cost of trying to break the curse. She hadn't just inherited the curse—*she was the curse.*

Suddenly, a thought pierced her mind like a lightning bolt: the journal. Her father had written about the source of the curse being tied to her bloodline. The *heart* of it. And now, standing before her, the Hollow Man was claiming her as the one who would bring it all to fruition.

She felt her hands tremble as she gripped the stone fragments tighter, the sharp edges digging into her palm. She could hear the hollow whispers in her mind, urging her to give in—to accept the role she had been born into. *It was always meant to be you,* the voice seemed to say. *You can't escape it, Evelyn.*

"No!" Evelyn shouted, shaking her head violently. "I *won't* do this! I won't let you win!"

The Hollow Man tilted his head, as if studying her reaction. *"You have no choice, Evelyn. The power is within you, always has been. You can try to resist, but it will only make the inevitable more painful."*

Before Evelyn could respond, the ground beneath her feet trembled again. The hum returned, louder this time, resonating deep in her chest. The symbols on the altar burned with a ferocity that made her eyes water. The church, the very earth, seemed to groan under the weight of the curse. It was happening. The curse was awakening.

And Evelyn was at the center of it all.

Suddenly, the air around her seemed to crackle, and the Hollow Man raised his hand, his long, thin fingers stretching toward her like the tendrils of some terrible vine.

"Come to me, Evelyn. Accept your fate. Let it be done."

Evelyn's heart pounded in her ears. Her body screamed in protest, every fiber of her being telling her to run, to flee, to get away from this place. But she couldn't. The stone fragments in her hand were burning now, the heat so intense it almost felt like they were about to incinerate her skin. She could hear her father's voice in her mind, as clear as if he were standing beside her.

"The heart lies beneath. The truth is buried. You have to find it. Only then can you break the curse."

With a cry of desperation, Evelyn dropped to her knees, her fingers searching the ground beneath her. She could feel the tremors intensify, as if something—*something terrible*—was awakening beneath her. She had to find it. She had to find the truth. The *root* of it all.

Her fingers brushed against something cold, hard, and smooth. At first, she thought it was just another stone, but then she realized—it was different. She dug deeper, her fingers trembling as she unearthed an object, an old, rusted key.

The key to the curse.

With the key in her hand, Evelyn stood, facing the Hollow Man. His smile had faded, and his dark eyes narrowed as he saw the key in her grasp. For the first time, there was a flicker of something—fear?—in his eyes.

"You..." He stepped back, his voice a hiss. "*You cannot—*"

But Evelyn was already moving. With the key in her hand, she felt something shift in the air. The hum of the curse, the oppressive force that had filled the room, began to waver, to weaken. She wasn't sure how—*or why*—but in that moment, she knew that she had found the source.

And with that knowledge, she could *end* it.

Chapter 11: The Unraveling

The air was thick with anticipation as Evelyn clutched the key in her trembling hands. The faint hum that had pulsed through the church's stone walls now seemed to fade, replaced by an eerie silence, broken only by the erratic rhythm of her breath. Her mind raced as she stared at the key—the ancient, rusted object that now felt like the anchor of her fate. She had found it, but what did it unlock? The Hollow Man's reaction—the fear in his eyes—only deepened her confusion.

His smile had vanished, and his entire form seemed to contract, as if the very essence of his being was threatened by the key she held. Evelyn had never seen him react like that before. The powerful, predatory figure that had haunted her every step was now a shadow, retreating in the face of something she couldn't fully understand. For a moment, she allowed herself a breath of relief, but that moment was fleeting. She was still trapped. The curse was still pressing in on her, its weight heavier than ever.

The Hollow Man's dark eyes flashed with an intensity that sent a shiver down her spine. He took a step forward, but his movements were slower, more cautious now. "*You don't know what you've done, Evelyn,*" he hissed, his voice low, yet laden with venom.

Evelyn's fingers tightened around the key. "*I know exactly what I've done,*" she said, her voice unwavering despite the fear gnawing at her insides. "*I've found the heart of this curse. And I will destroy it.*"

The Hollow Man let out a low, throaty laugh—an unsettling sound that echoed in the cavernous, crumbling church. "*You are not the one who will destroy it, child. The curse does not die with you.*"

Her heart sank. She had hoped, so desperately, that this key—this discovery—would be the answer. But the Hollow Man's words sent a jolt of panic through her chest. Could it be that this was all a trap? A way to bring her closer to her own destruction?

Evelyn didn't have time to entertain the thought. The air around her was thickening again. The oppressive weight of the curse was returning, pressing down on her with a suffocating force. The ground beneath her feet rumbled, and the church seemed to groan in response, as if the very earth was stirring, awakening to the presence of the key.

Before she could react, the floor in front of the altar cracked open again, wider this time. The dark tendrils from the vision she'd seen earlier began to emerge from the fissures in the stone, twisting and reaching toward her. She had no time to question their nature—she simply knew they were *wrong*—unnatural. They were a part of the curse, part of the force that had been binding her family for generations.

Without thinking, Evelyn raised the key above her head. "*I won't let you win,*" she shouted, her voice defiant. She brought the key down toward the altar.

The moment it made contact, the entire church seemed to shudder. The ground beneath her feet cracked wider, and the tendrils recoiled, as though in pain. The key thrummed with a strange, powerful energy, its surface glowing with an eerie, otherworldly light. Evelyn felt the pulse of it deep inside her, a connection to the heart of the curse, something primal and ancient that she couldn't fully comprehend. But she could feel it—she could feel the power coursing through her veins, through the key, through the very air around her.

The Hollow Man's expression twisted with fury. "*No!*" he screamed, his voice carrying an unnatural distortion. "*You cannot stop it. The curse will never be undone!*"

Evelyn's fingers burned with the force of the key as it pressed harder against the altar. Her heart raced, and for a moment, she feared the pressure would overwhelm her. But then—nothing. The key stopped glowing. The tendrils recoiled, retracting back into the earth.

The church fell silent.

Evelyn stood frozen for several long seconds, her breath shallow, her pulse pounding in her ears. The key was still in her hand, but it no longer felt like a tool of destruction. It felt... empty. The energy she had sensed had vanished, leaving only a faint, lingering hum that reverberated through the air.

She glanced toward the Hollow Man. He stood motionless, his expression one of disbelief.

For a moment, neither of them moved.

Then, the church groaned, a deep, resonant sound that made the very walls tremble. And in that instant, the ground beneath Evelyn's feet gave way.

Evelyn fell.

Her body plummeted into the darkness, a black void that seemed to swallow her whole. She gasped for air, her hands flailing as she tried to grasp onto something—anything—to stop her descent. The ground, once solid and unyielding, had vanished beneath her, replaced by an endless fall into a chasm that seemed to stretch forever.

There was no sound. No light. Just the suffocating darkness closing in around her.

In the distance, she thought she heard the Hollow Man's voice—his laughter, warped and distorted—echoing through the void. *"You cannot escape, Evelyn. You never could."*

The words stung, a cruel reminder of how powerless she had felt, how trapped she had always been. She had hoped that the key, the very thing that had held her family's curse in place for generations, would be the key to her freedom. But now, as she fell through the void, she realized that she had made a grave mistake.

She had underestimated the curse. She had underestimated *him*.

As her descent continued, she braced herself for the inevitable impact, knowing that there was nothing she could do to stop it. The world had become a blur, spinning faster and faster as the darkness pressed in. Her thoughts were fragmented, each one disjointed and fleeting as she struggled to hold onto some semblance of clarity.

Then, finally, there was a jolt. The ground beneath her feet reappeared, not solid, but strange—like wet clay, soft and unyielding, and then—nothing. Her body slammed into the earth, knocking the wind from her lungs.

Evelyn awoke with a start.

She gasped for breath, her eyes snapping open as she tried to make sense of her surroundings. Her body ached, her limbs heavy, as though the fall had drained every ounce of strength from her. The air was thick with dampness, the scent of earth and decay filling her nostrils.

She was no longer in the church. No longer in the place where the Hollow Man had confronted her.

She was somewhere else.

The room—or what appeared to be a room—was vast, cavernous, and dark. Only the faintest light seemed to seep in from above, illuminating the walls around her in sickly hues. The ground beneath her was damp and uneven, covered in thick, twisting roots that seemed to pulse with an unnatural energy. The air was heavy, as though it were alive with a presence that she couldn't understand.

And then she saw it.

In the center of the room, a large stone pedestal rose from the earth, and atop it, a familiar sight—a gleaming, pulsing object, a stone that radiated with the same dark energy she had felt earlier.

It was the other half of the stone she had been carrying. The one she had thought was lost. The other half of the curse.

Her breath caught in her throat as she realized where she was.

She wasn't in the church anymore. She was *beneath* it.

The Heart of the Curse.

Evelyn stood shakily, her limbs unsteady as she took her first steps toward the pedestal. Her mind raced as the weight of her discovery settled in. This was it—the place her father had warned her about. The place where the curse had originated. Where it had been anchored. And now, as she approached the stone, she could feel it—the pulse of power beneath her feet, beneath her skin.

The stone on the pedestal seemed to call to her, its surface shimmering with dark energy. This was where it all began. The very root of the curse, bound to her bloodline, to her family.

And Evelyn knew, with a certainty she couldn't deny, that this was where it would end.

Evelyn's breath was shallow as she approached the stone pedestal, the pulse of the dark energy beneath her feet growing stronger with each step. It was almost as if the ground itself was alive—alive with the curse, with the malevolent force that had haunted her bloodline for generations. The stone, now only a few feet away, gleamed with an unnatural light. Its surface seemed to ripple, distorting the shadows around it, casting long, twisted shapes on the walls.

Her heart hammered in her chest as she took another step forward, her fingers tightening around the key that had brought her here. She could feel its heat in her hand, the same pulsating energy that had surged through her when she had touched it earlier. It wasn't just a key—it was a conduit. A key to something much bigger, much darker than she had ever imagined.

The stone on the pedestal began to glow more brightly, casting an eerie light over the chamber. Evelyn's pulse quickened. She was so close now. She could feel the weight of her father's words in her mind, the warnings he had left behind. *"The curse is bound to your bloodline. You are the last of the line. You have to destroy it, or it will destroy you."*

But how? How was she supposed to destroy something this old, this powerful? And was it even possible? Or had she already made a fatal mistake by coming here, by confronting the very heart of the curse?

As her hand reached for the stone, the shadows around her seemed to stir. The air grew thick, oppressive, pressing in on her from all sides. She could feel the presence, the force, the *thing* that had been pulling the strings behind the curse, watching her every move.

A voice—low, guttural, and familiar—drifted through the air, breaking the silence.

"You cannot destroy me, Evelyn. You are a part of me. You always have been."

Her heart lurched in her chest, and she spun around, searching the chamber for the source of the voice. But there was no one. The walls, the floor, the very air around her seemed to be vibrating with the power of the voice, as though the chamber itself was alive with it. It was as if the darkness had taken root in every corner, every crack, every crevice of the space.

The Hollow Man's laughter echoed through the room, distorted and cruel.

"You think you can undo what has been done? The curse is older than you can fathom. It has been waiting, Evelyn. Waiting for you. Your bloodline is the key. You are the key."

Evelyn's stomach twisted with dread. His words cut through her like a blade, carving deep into her sense of self, into the very core of her being. She could feel it now—the weight of the curse pressing down on her, as though it had been part of her all along. She could hear the voices of her ancestors, trapped in the same cycle, the same darkness. And she realized, with a sickening clarity, that her father had never been free of it. He had only been its *puppet*.

Tears pricked at her eyes as the truth settled in. The Hollow Man had been right. She wasn't just connected to the curse—she was *bound* to it. She was part of it. Her bloodline had always been a vessel for its power.

But that didn't mean she had to accept it.

With a fierce determination, Evelyn reached forward and gripped the stone. The moment her fingers made contact, a violent surge of energy coursed through her, so intense that it felt like her very soul was being torn apart. Her body convulsed, and the world around her began to warp and twist. The light from the stone pulsed, faster and faster, until it was blinding.

"You cannot escape me," the Hollow Man's voice boomed, now echoing from all directions, as if it were coming from within her own mind. *"You are me. I am you. We are bound together. You cannot destroy me. You will only bring me back stronger."*

Evelyn gritted her teeth, her fingers digging into the stone as she fought against the force trying to pull her under. She could feel the dark energy surging through her veins, trying to take control of her body, of her mind. But she wouldn't let it. She couldn't.

"No," she whispered, her voice hoarse but resolute. "I *won't* let you win."

With a final, desperate effort, Evelyn forced the key into the stone's surface. The moment the key made contact, there was an explosion of light, a blinding flash that filled the entire chamber, and for a moment, Evelyn thought she had gone blind. The force of it threw her back, slamming her into the stone floor.

The room around her seemed to shudder as if the very foundation of the earth had been shaken to its core. The energy from the stone pulsed once more, then faded. The light dimmed, leaving only an eerie silence in its wake.

Evelyn lay still for several moments, her body aching, her mind spinning. Had she done it? Had she destroyed the curse?

No.

The answer came to her with a sickening clarity. She hadn't destroyed it—she had *released* it. The force that had been bound to her bloodline, the curse that had haunted her family for generations, was no longer contained. It was free.

Evelyn scrambled to her feet, her heart pounding in her chest. The shadows in the chamber were shifting, moving as though they had a life of their own. The dark energy that had been bound to the stone was now swirling around her, closing in from all sides.

A voice—her father's voice—whispered in her ear.

"You have to finish what I started, Evelyn. You can't let it go any further. Destroy the heart. Destroy the stone. Or we will all be lost."

Evelyn's head spun, the weight of his words crashing down on her. He had known. He had always known what the curse was, what it would become. And now she was the one left to deal with it.

But how?

How could she destroy something that had existed for centuries, something that had become so deeply entrenched in her very being?

She glanced down at the key in her hand. It had stopped glowing, but the warmth still lingered in her fingers. The energy from the stone still pulsed through her, resonating deep inside her chest.

And then, she understood.

The key wasn't just the key to the curse—it was the key to her salvation. To her freedom.

With trembling hands, Evelyn placed the key into the stone pedestal, aligning it with a small slot she hadn't noticed before. The stone's surface hummed to life again, but this time, it wasn't a violent surge of power. It was a gentle pull, as though the stone were inviting her in, beckoning her to release whatever it was that had been trapped within.

Her heart pounded as she placed her hands on the stone. The curse—the Hollow Man, the darkness that had haunted her family for generations—was still here, but it was no longer an external force. It had become part of her, part of her blood. To destroy it, she would have to destroy *herself*.

But she couldn't let it continue. She couldn't let it consume the world, let it consume her family any longer.

With a final, resolute breath, Evelyn closed her eyes and pressed her hands into the stone. The moment she did, the world seemed to shift. The ground beneath her feet trembled again, and the light in the chamber flickered. She felt the pull of the curse deep within her, like a thousand hands reaching inside her chest, trying to tear her apart.

But she didn't let go. She couldn't.

Evelyn *fought*.

The energy of the stone surged through her, and for a brief moment, everything went dark. But then, as if in response to her will, the stone *shattered*—its energy fracturing, splintering into thousands of pieces that scattered into the air, evaporating into nothingness.

For a moment, there was silence. Complete, utter silence.

And then—she felt it.

The weight that had been pressing down on her, the darkness that had consumed her every thought, was gone. The stone had shattered, and with it, the curse had finally been broken.

Chapter 12: The Aftermath

Evelyn stood in the remnants of the underground chamber, the echoes of the shattering stone still reverberating in the air. The heavy silence that followed felt like a weight pressing down on her chest, suffocating in its finality. The curse—the darkness that had defined her family's bloodline for centuries—was no more. Or was it? She could still feel the residual energy in the air, the echoes of something ancient and powerful that lingered in the very stones of the chamber.

She looked down at her hands, trembling despite the stillness of the room. The key, which had once thrummed with power, now lay cold and inert in her palm. She had done it. She had broken the curse. But what had that truly cost her? What was the price for tearing apart something so ancient, so entwined with her own being?

The last remnants of the stone's glowing light had dissolved into the air, leaving only the dim glow of the chamber's natural phosphorescence to illuminate the room. The floor beneath her feet was cracked and torn, the walls marked by deep gouges where the stone had fractured. Yet there was no more darkness pressing in on her, no more twisting tendrils trying to consume her. The suffocating weight of the curse had lifted. For the first time in what felt like forever, Evelyn could breathe.

But even in the absence of the curse, something still felt wrong.

A distant hum filled the space around her, faint but insistent. She could feel it deep in her bones, like the hum of a distant earthquake, or the warning tremor of a storm on the horizon. The air tasted metallic, bitter in her mouth.

Is it over? she thought. *Did I do the right thing?*

For a long moment, she stood there, unable to move, her mind struggling to piece together what had just happened. The moment she had plunged the key into the stone and shattered it, everything had seemed to dissolve in an explosion of energy. She had thought she was freeing herself, freeing her family, freeing the world from the grip of the curse. But now, standing in the wreckage of the Heart of the Curse, Evelyn wondered if she had merely unleashed something darker, something far worse than she could have imagined.

A cold breeze stirred the air, snapping her out of her reverie. She looked up, her eyes scanning the edges of the chamber. Something was wrong. The silence had been too complete. Too final. And yet, as she stood in the center of the shattered stone and broken earth, she realized that the very air had changed. There was a subtle shift, something deeper than she could understand. The energy that had once held the curse in place had morphed, been redirected—she could feel it, pressing against her skin like the weight of a thousand invisible eyes.

She wasn't alone.

Evelyn's pulse quickened, a sudden wave of dread crashing over her. She turned in a slow circle, scanning the shadows. The room felt suffocating now, as though the walls themselves were closing in.

A voice, low and raspy, cut through the silence like a knife.

"You think you have won, Evelyn. But you have only begun to understand the true nature of the curse."

Evelyn froze. She recognized that voice. It was the Hollow Man.

"You are not free," the voice continued, *"You are a prisoner of something far older than your family's bloodline. Something far darker than you can comprehend."*

A chill washed over her as his words reverberated through the chamber. The ground beneath her feet trembled again, and she felt the sensation of being *watched*, as if the very stone around her were alive, shifting, closing in.

"No," Evelyn whispered, shaking her head, her voice trembling with disbelief. "It can't be. I broke it. It's gone."

"Gone?" The Hollow Man's voice was a dark chuckle, filled with malice. *"You broke the stone, yes. You broke the curse's physical*

manifestation. But the curse is not just a stone, Evelyn. It is an ancient force. A part of this world. And now you have released it."

The realization hit her like a bolt of lightning, and her stomach dropped. She hadn't destroyed the curse. She had *unleashed* it.

The ground rumbled beneath her feet, the chamber shaking as though a great beast was awakening. The walls seemed to pulse with energy, the very air becoming thick with a malevolent presence that she couldn't name. Evelyn's thoughts raced as the floor cracked open beneath her, deep fissures spreading outward like the roots of an ancient tree.

"You are mine now, Evelyn," the Hollow Man's voice said, full of dark satisfaction. *"You are bound to the curse. You can never escape."*

Fear constricted around her chest. The Hollow Man was right. She had freed something far worse than the curse itself. She had released the darkness that had been waiting—waiting for her to make that fatal mistake. And now that it was free, there was no going back.

Evelyn turned, desperate for an escape, but the walls of the chamber were closing in on her, the very ground shifting beneath her. She stumbled backward as the earth beneath her cracked, revealing a black pit that seemed to stretch into infinity.

A sharp, metallic taste filled her mouth as she felt a pull deep inside her chest. It was the key—the power from the shattered stone—drawing her in, binding her to whatever force had been unleashed. Her vision blurred, and she fought to maintain her balance, her body trembling with the weight of the energy flowing through her.

No. She couldn't let it take her. Not like this.

With a roar of defiance, Evelyn raised her hand and forced the energy back. It pushed against her, but she clung to her will, fighting the pull. The shadows seemed to reach for her, tendrils of darkness, but she refused to yield.

For the first time since this journey had begun, Evelyn realized that she wasn't just fighting for her life—she was fighting for the world.

The air around her crackled as she summoned every ounce of strength she had left. The Hollow Man's laugh echoed through the chamber, and for a moment, she thought she heard his voice in her head, mocking her. *"You cannot fight what you are, Evelyn. You cannot escape it."*

The darkness surged, pushing back against her, but Evelyn refused to falter. She gripped the key once more, her fingers burning with its power. It was her last chance, her only chance. She couldn't give in to it.

With a final scream of effort, Evelyn slammed the key into the center of the shattered stone.

A blinding light erupted from the ruins of the Heart of the Curse, and the ground beneath her feet cracked open. For a split second, everything went still. The darkness stilled, as though holding its breath.

And then—*nothing*.

The light faded.

The rumbling stopped.

For a moment, Evelyn wasn't sure if she had succeeded. The chamber was eerily silent again, and the oppressive weight in the air had lifted. She glanced around, but there was no sign of the Hollow Man, no sign of the darkness. The pit that had opened beneath her had closed, and the walls of the chamber seemed to have returned to their original form.

But Evelyn knew, deep in her gut, that this was far from over. The curse was not gone. It had only been *delayed*. The forces she had unleashed were far from defeated.

There was only one thing left for her to do.

Run.

Evelyn's breath came in shallow gasps as she stumbled backward, her hands pressed to the cracked stone floor for balance. The air had returned to its unnatural stillness, but her skin prickled with an unsettling sensation. The darkness was still there—lingering, like a presence just out of sight, watching her every movement. She could feel it in her veins, in the pit of her stomach, like a growing ache that wouldn't subside.

Her eyes darted around the chamber, the dim light of the phosphorescent walls casting long, eerie shadows. It was as if the room itself had become a part of the curse. The remnants of the shattered Heart of the Curse pulsed faintly in the center of the room, its fragments scattered like broken glass. The key she had used to unlock the stone lay beside it, cold and lifeless.

For a moment, Evelyn allowed herself to rest, her body trembling with exhaustion. Her thoughts were muddled, and she struggled to make sense of what had just transpired. She had shattered the Heart, but the darkness had not disappeared. It had not been destroyed—it had only *shifted*.

A distant rumble sounded in the distance, deep and ominous, causing the ground beneath her feet to shake. Her heart skipped a beat as she straightened up, her senses heightened. The chamber was no longer stable. The very earth beneath her felt as if it were unraveling. The walls began to groan, the stone shifting and cracking, as though something below was clawing its way up through the foundations.

Evelyn's eyes widened. She didn't have much time.

The light from the shattered Heart flickered one last time, casting jagged shadows along the walls. She could feel the pressure building again, a tidal wave of dark energy surging from the depths of the earth, converging on her. It was like a malevolent force gathering itself, about to pounce. But what had she truly released?

What have I done?

Her mind raced back to the Hollow Man's voice, the cryptic words he had spoken as the curse unraveled. *You are bound to the curse now, Evelyn.* What did that mean? Was the darkness tied to her in some irrevocable way? Had she truly broken free—or had she simply become its new vessel?

No. She couldn't accept that. Not after everything she had been through.

She had to find a way out.

With one last glance at the scattered remains of the stone pedestal and the Heart of the Curse, Evelyn turned and bolted toward the narrow passageway leading back up to the surface. The floor groaned beneath her feet, the rumbling growing louder as she pushed herself faster, her muscles burning with exertion. Every instinct screamed at her to run, to escape whatever had been unleashed.

As she reached the entrance of the passage, her foot struck something hard—a jagged shard of stone that had fallen from the ceiling. She stumbled, nearly losing her balance, but she caught herself just in time. Her pulse quickened, but she forced herself to keep moving, her footsteps echoing in the narrow tunnel.

The air here was thick with dust, and the dim light from the fissures in the stone cast long, crawling shadows along the walls. She could hear the distant rumble of the earth shaking beneath her, the tremors now a constant presence, threatening to collapse the very tunnel she was racing through.

Evelyn's breath came in ragged gasps as she ran, her legs aching, the muscles screaming with fatigue. She was almost to the surface. Almost free. But with every step, the unease gnawed at her. It was the Hollow Man's presence—she could feel him, even now, lingering in the recesses of her mind. His dark influence was still there, like a shadow she couldn't outrun.

"You think you can escape me, Evelyn? You are mine. You always have been." His voice echoed in her mind, cruel and mocking.

No. She wasn't his. She would *not* be his.

The tunnel ahead began to narrow, the walls closing in around her. She pushed through the claustrophobic passage, her breath ragged, her pulse thumping in her ears. But then, just as she thought she might make it to the surface, the tunnel ahead seemed to darken, the shadows deepening in unnatural ways. The air grew colder, heavier, and she felt a shiver run down her spine.

A whisper—a voice that was not her own—reached her ears.

"You can never outrun the curse, Evelyn. It is within you."

Evelyn froze, her heart racing. Her hands trembled as she wiped the sweat from her forehead. She had to keep moving. But the voice, that insistent whisper, wrapped around her mind like a vice, making it impossible to think clearly.

With shaking hands, she gripped the wall beside her, willing herself to keep going. *No. I won't be its prisoner.*

And yet, as she moved forward, something *felt* different. It was as though the walls were shifting with every step she took. The passage felt *alive*, responding to her presence, closing in, reshaping itself in ways she couldn't understand.

Her breath caught in her throat as she reached a dead end.

No. This wasn't possible. The tunnel had never ended here before. She had come through this way just hours ago, before she had descended into the depths.

She turned to look behind her, but the way she had come had already disappeared, swallowed up by the encroaching darkness.

A flash of light—a jagged pulse of energy—illuminated the passage for a split second. It was the Heart of the Curse, the shattered remnants still alive with a force she couldn't comprehend. The light flickered again, and Evelyn felt the darkness closing in, squeezing the air from her lungs.

"There is no escape, Evelyn," the voice of the Hollow Man whispered. *"You belong to me now."*

Her heart raced, and she felt the oppressive weight of the words in her chest. She was trapped, suffocating. The walls were closing in around her, and the shadows were coming for her. She could feel it. Something—*someone*—was pulling her back into the abyss.

Then, a sudden rush of wind filled the passage, like a violent gust of air. It slammed into Evelyn, knocking her back against the cold stone wall. She gasped, struggling to stay upright, but the wind had a force to it now, as though it was alive, tugging at her every move.

Before she could react, a figure appeared in the tunnel ahead of her, silhouetted against the faint light from the fractured stone.

"Evelyn," a deep voice called, sharp and commanding. "You're not alone."

Her breath caught in her throat as she recognized the figure standing before her. It was Victor. But how?

"Victor?" she gasped, her voice trembling. "How are you—?"

He raised a hand, cutting her off. His eyes were hard, focused, as though he had seen something she couldn't.

"You've done something... dangerous, Evelyn," Victor said, his voice low, almost gravely. "You've unleashed the curse. And now, it's not just bound to you—it's *hunting* you."

Evelyn's eyes widened in horror as the ground beneath her shook again, the rumbling now a deafening roar. The walls seemed to warp, the air growing thick with the presence of the curse, and the shadows—*the shadows*—were closing in faster.

"No!" she cried out, grabbing Victor's arm in desperation. "We have to get out of here. We need to stop it."

Victor's eyes softened, but there was a resigned sadness in them as he looked at her. "There's no stopping it now. We can only delay it. We need to *destroy* the source. The Heart—it's still alive, Evelyn. And now it's pulling us back."

Evelyn's stomach twisted. "What are you talking about? The Heart was shattered. It's gone."

Victor shook his head slowly, his jaw tight with resolve. "No. It was never just the stone. The Heart of the Curse was merely a manifestation of what you've truly released: a force that exists beyond time, beyond understanding. And now, you have to face it."

The rumbling grew louder, and the air began to crackle with energy. The wind howled, and the shadows surged forward with terrifying speed.

"We have to go," Victor said urgently, his grip on her arm tightening. "Before it's too late."

Evelyn's mind raced as they turned and fled down the now-twisting passage. The walls were closing in. The shadows were following. But this time, she wasn't running alone.

Chapter 13: A Reckoning Approaches

Evelyn's heart thundered in her chest as she raced down the twisting passage, her breath sharp and uneven. The walls around her seemed to shift and bend, as if the very earth had become alive, responding to her every movement. It was a feeling she couldn't shake—the air was thick with an oppressive energy, and the shadows clawed at the edges of her vision, always just out of reach but relentless in their pursuit. It was as if the world itself was closing in on her, and she could feel the weight of something ancient and hungry pressing against her mind.

Victor's grip on her arm was firm, pulling her through the narrowing tunnel with urgency. His face was set in a grim line, his jaw tight with resolve, but Evelyn could see the tension in his eyes. He was just as scared as she was, though he tried to hide it.

"Victor," she gasped, struggling to keep pace with him. "What is happening? Why is this tunnel changing?"

His eyes flicked over to her for a split second, the worry flashing briefly before he masked it. "The Heart was never just a stone. It was a manifestation of a force older than anything you can imagine. When you shattered it, Evelyn, you didn't just break the physical object—you released its essence. Its *power*."

Evelyn's mind reeled at the revelation. "But I thought the curse was contained. I thought the Heart was the key to stopping it."

Victor's face twisted in frustration. "It was only a part of the curse—a symbol, a representation of the force that controls everything. The Heart was a seal, a lock. And now that it's broken, the force is free to wreak havoc."

Her pulse quickened as she tried to process his words. "So, what is this 'force'? What are we dealing with?"

Victor's eyes grew dark, haunted. "It's something ancient, something that existed long before your family's curse, long before civilization as we know it. It's tied to the very fabric of the world—beyond time, beyond space. The curse was never really about your family's bloodline. It was always about *containing* this force."

Evelyn's mind was spinning. Every instinct screamed at her to keep moving, to get out of the tunnel and into the light. But the closer they got to the surface, the more she realized the darkness was following them—not just through the walls of the tunnel, but in the very air they breathed. It was inescapable.

"Where are we going?" she asked, her voice trembling with desperation.

"We need to get to the old temple," Victor said, his tone urgent. "There's something there that can help us. It's the only place where we might be able to stop this."

"The temple?" Evelyn echoed, a sense of dread tightening in her stomach. "Where is it?"

"Not far from here," Victor replied, his eyes scanning the passage ahead, his pace quickening. "But we'll need to hurry. The curse has already begun to spread, and if we don't stop it soon, it could consume everything."

Evelyn's mind raced. The temple. She'd heard whispers of it in the old family records, but nothing concrete. It was said to be a place of great power, hidden away for centuries, its true purpose lost to time. But now, it seemed to be their only hope.

They continued running through the twisting tunnel, the air growing heavier with each step. The walls seemed to close in on them, pressing against them as if they were being swallowed by the earth. It was the curse, she realized—its power had started to manifest in the very surroundings. She could feel it now: the darkness, the malevolent energy that had once been contained, now spreading like a sickness.

Then, just as she thought she might collapse from exhaustion, they reached the end of the tunnel. The walls gave way to an open space, and Evelyn's breath caught in her throat as she stepped into the sunlight.

They were outside—barely, but outside nonetheless. The clearing was surrounded by tall trees, their twisted branches arching overhead, casting dark shadows across the ground. But the light was a relief, the warmth of the sun a stark contrast to the suffocating coldness of the tunnel.

Evelyn could feel her pulse begin to slow, the tension in her body easing slightly as she took in the open air. But her relief was short-lived.

A sound—a low growl—reached her ears. She whirled around, her breath catching in her throat. The shadows in the trees were moving, shifting unnaturally. Something was out there.

Victor, too, had heard it. He gripped her arm tighter, his eyes scanning the surrounding forest. "It's already here," he muttered, more to himself than to her. "We're not safe yet."

Evelyn's gaze locked onto the shifting shadows, her senses on high alert. Whatever had been released with the breaking of the Heart was now hunting them, closing in with a relentless fury. The darkness wasn't just a force—it was a *presence*. A presence that had been waiting for this moment.

The ground trembled beneath their feet, a deep, resonating thrum that seemed to come from the very earth itself. Evelyn felt it in her bones, a warning, a signal that the worst was yet to come.

"Victor, what do we do?" she whispered, her voice shaking.

"We need to reach the temple," he replied, his voice grim. "The power inside it—if we can tap into it, we might be able to stop the curse from spreading any further."

"But the darkness..." Evelyn hesitated, fear rising in her chest. "It's coming for us."

"We have no choice," Victor said firmly, his grip on her arm tightening. "We need to move. Now."

They ran, weaving between the trees, the shadows closing in behind them. The sound of cracking branches and low growls grew louder, more insistent, as if the forest itself was alive with the curse's influence. Evelyn's heart hammered in her chest, her mind racing. What was this force that had been unleashed? And why had it chosen now to awaken?

After what felt like an eternity of running, the trees began to thin, and they emerged into a small clearing. In the center of the clearing stood a stone structure—an ancient temple, its walls overgrown with moss and vines. The air around it hummed with an almost palpable energy, as if the very ground beneath their feet was alive with power.

Victor slowed his pace as they approached the temple, his eyes scanning the surroundings. "This is it," he murmured. "The place where the curse was bound. If we're going to stop it, this is where it has to happen."

Evelyn's breath was ragged as she gazed at the temple. It was ancient—older than anything she had ever seen. The stones that made up its walls were worn and weathered, etched with symbols that seemed to pulse with energy, faintly glowing with a light that was both soothing and unnerving. There was something inside, something hidden within its depths that had the power to contain the curse.

But would it be enough?

The growls from behind them were growing louder, the presence of the curse closing in on them. Evelyn could feel the weight of its energy, like a physical force pressing down on her chest. She had no idea how much time they had before it was too late.

Victor moved quickly toward the entrance of the temple, pushing open a set of massive stone doors that groaned in protest. The air inside was thick, heavy with the power that had once contained the curse. Evelyn stepped inside, her heart racing. The interior was vast, its walls lined with old carvings and symbols that seemed to tell a story she couldn't quite understand. The floor was covered in dust, and the air was thick with the scent of ancient incense, still lingering from centuries past.

"This is it," Victor said again, his voice barely above a whisper. "This is where it all started."

Evelyn turned to him, her brow furrowing. "What do we do now?"

Victor stepped forward, his hands brushing against the walls, as if searching for something. "We need to find the heart of the temple," he said. "It's the only place where the power is still active. The only place where we can lock the curse away for good."

Evelyn nodded, her mind still racing. The shadows outside were closing in. They didn't have much time.

Victor led her deeper into the temple, and as they passed through a large archway, Evelyn saw what he had been searching for. At the center of the temple stood an altar—a massive stone slab, its surface covered in intricate carvings. At the center of the altar was a hollow depression, large enough to fit the shattered remains of the Heart of the Curse.

"This is where it all began," Victor murmured. "The Heart was created to keep the curse contained, but it's only a temporary solution. The true power lies within the temple itself."

Evelyn took a deep breath, steeling herself for whatever came next. She had no idea what would happen once they placed the remnants of the Heart on the altar, but she knew one thing for certain.

If they didn't act quickly, the curse would consume everything.

And they would be its first victims.

The air inside the temple was still, thick with ancient energy, and yet it felt alive—alive with the echoes of countless years, the pulse of a power that had been carefully hidden, forgotten, and now awakened. Evelyn could feel it in her bones, a low hum that resonated in the pit of her stomach, growing stronger as they moved deeper into the temple. It wasn't just a place of worship or old rituals. No, this was a place that had been designed to *hold* something, something far more dangerous than they could have imagined.

Victor didn't speak as he led her through the vast space. His face was tight with concentration, eyes scanning the walls, the floor, the ceiling. It was as if he were listening to something she couldn't hear, tuning into frequencies she could only vaguely sense. The walls themselves seemed to respond to his presence, the ancient symbols etched into them glowing faintly as they passed.

"I can feel it," he murmured after a few moments. "It's not just in the air here. It's in the stone, in the foundation of the temple itself. This is where the curse was *born*."

Evelyn swallowed, her throat dry, trying to calm the frantic thoughts spiraling in her head. She could feel the darkness now, thrumming at the edges of her mind. The shadows were no longer something she only saw. Now, they seemed to be creeping within her, as though they were part of her own thoughts. The curse had already begun to invade her in ways she didn't understand, and it was only a matter of time before it completely consumed her.

They reached the altar—a massive stone slab that dominated the center of the temple. It was both imposing and serene, an ancient monument to some long-forgotten deity. The symbols on its surface seemed to writhe, changing shape as the dim light from the temple's cracks and fissures flickered across them. The carvings were intricate, swirling in patterns that Evelyn could almost recognize, but not quite. They were foreign to her, yet somehow familiar, as if they were calling to her in a language she should have known long ago.

Victor knelt before the altar and motioned for Evelyn to join him. He placed his hands on the stone, his fingers tracing the symbols in a ritualistic pattern. She watched him with growing concern, but said nothing. It was clear to her that this was something deeply personal for him, something he had prepared for his entire life. She had no idea what he was doing, but for now, she had to trust him.

"This is the only way," Victor said softly, almost as if to himself. "This is where it all began, and it's where it must end."

Evelyn stood back, her mind still racing. She glanced around the temple once more, her eyes landing on the remnants of the Heart of the Curse scattered at the base of the altar. The pieces of stone shimmered in the low light, and she could feel them calling to her, the fragments like magnets pulling her in. The Heart, or what was left of it, was what had contained the curse—and now it was broken, shattered, scattered like a thousand shards of broken glass.

"Victor," she said, her voice barely above a whisper. "What if this doesn't work? What if we can't stop it?"

His gaze met hers, and she saw something there—a flash of doubt, quickly masked by resolve. "If this doesn't work, then it's over. For all of us."

Evelyn's heart skipped a beat. "What do you mean?"

Victor stood up and turned to face her, his expression grave. "The curse doesn't just want to be released. It wants to *consume* everything. It will spread through the world, unchecked. If we fail here, Evelyn, there will be no stopping it. No more light. Only darkness."

The weight of his words sank in. The world was teetering on the brink of something unimaginably dark. She had been a part of this, whether she wanted to admit it or not. She had broken the Heart. She had released the curse. And now she had to help stop it—before it consumed everything in its path.

Victor's voice was steady as he continued, "I've spent my whole life learning about the curse—studying the ways to control it. My family has been trying to find a way to stop it for centuries. But we were all wrong. The Heart wasn't the answer. The true power of the curse lies in this temple, in its heart. We need to use the energy here to seal the curse again."

Evelyn's head spun as she tried to make sense of his words. "But why me? Why am I the one who broke the Heart? Why not you?"

Victor's face tightened, and for a moment, Evelyn could see the strain in his eyes, the weight of something he hadn't told her. "Because you were always meant to be the one to break it. The curse is tied to your bloodline, Evelyn. It has always been tied to you. And breaking the Heart was the only way to unlock the true power of the temple."

Her stomach turned. "What are you saying? You're telling me this is all part of some grand plan?"

Victor turned away, his hand clenched at his side. "No. I'm telling you that your bloodline was never meant to destroy the curse. It was meant to *control* it. You were always meant to *contain* it. That's why your family was chosen—chosen to hold the power, to guard the curse, to ensure it never broke free."

Evelyn's mind reeled as she processed this new revelation. Her bloodline, her family—were they really the guardians of this curse all along? She'd never known the truth about her family's legacy, never known why they had been haunted by the shadows of the past. Now she understood, but it only made things worse.

"So... what now?" she asked, her voice strained.

Victor's eyes were hard with determination. "Now we finish what your ancestors started. We restore the Heart. We bind the curse, and we lock it away—again."

He turned back to the altar, his hands gently picking up the shards of the Heart, one by one. As he did, the air seemed to thrum with energy, each piece of the Heart resonating in unison with the temple's ancient magic. The stones began to glow softly, as if recognizing the pieces, as if acknowledging their importance. The room grew colder, the shadows deeper, as though the very essence of the curse was being drawn back into the Heart.

Evelyn stepped forward, her heart pounding in her chest. "Victor, we have to hurry. It's already—"

A low growl interrupted her. The sound seemed to reverberate through the temple, shaking the very foundation of the building. It was the darkness, she realized. It was coming for them.

The rumbling grew louder, the temple quaking beneath their feet. A flash of light exploded in the center of the altar, and Evelyn instinctively shielded her eyes. When she looked again, she saw something that made her heart freeze in her chest.

The shadows in the temple were moving.

They weren't just moving—they were *alive*. The darkness had taken form. It was a twisting mass of black tendrils, stretching from the corners of the room, wrapping themselves around the pillars, crawling up the walls. The darkness was no longer an abstract thing—it was a *creature*. And it was coming for them.

Victor cursed under his breath, his fingers still gripping the shards of the Heart. "It's too late," he muttered. "The curse is feeding on the temple's power. It's trying to stop us."

Evelyn's pulse raced. "What do we do now?"

"We finish the ritual," Victor said, his voice steely. "We have to complete the binding. It's the only way to stop it."

But the darkness was closing in. It was fast—too fast. The tendrils shot out, grasping at the walls, the altar, and then at them. The air around them grew thick with an unnatural coldness, like the breath of something ancient and predatory.

Without warning, the darkness surged forward. One of the tendrils lashed out at Evelyn, its touch like ice, sending a shock of fear through her body. She screamed, her hands instinctively reaching for the nearest thing to defend herself. But before she could react, Victor was there, his hands raised, his voice a chant that seemed to vibrate the very stones beneath them.

"No!" he shouted. "Stay back!"

But it was too late. The darkness had already begun to swallow the room.

Evelyn felt it then—something cold and suffocating. It wasn't just the darkness. It was *him*—the Hollow Man. His presence filled the room, surrounding them, choking the very air. His voice echoed in her mind, louder now, overpowering everything else.

"You can't stop me, Evelyn. You can't run. You can't hide. I am you, and you are mine. Forever."

The shadows pulsed, and Evelyn could feel them inside her, crawling under her skin, worming their way through her mind. The power of the curse was within her now, trying to break her, to consume her. Her head spun as the tendrils of darkness wrapped tighter around her thoughts, threatening to crush everything she had ever known, everything she had ever been.

But then, she remembered something—something Victor had said earlier. The Heart was the key. The Heart was what contained the curse, what held it at bay. And now, they had to restore it—before it was too late.

With every ounce of strength she had left, Evelyn reached out. She grabbed the pieces of the Heart, feeling the cold, ancient stone beneath her fingers. She could feel the power surging through her veins, the curse pushing back, but she *would not* let it win.

Victor's voice joined hers in the chant, their voices intertwining, calling on the temple's power, its ancient magic. Together, they placed the shards of the Heart back into the altar's center.

The room exploded with light.

Chapter 14: The Heart of Darkness

The world erupted in light.

Evelyn's body shook with the intensity of it, as if the very fabric of reality was tearing at the seams. The glow from the altar bathed the temple in an unnatural brilliance, casting long, twisting shadows that reached toward every corner of the room like gnarled hands. Her ears rang with a deafening hum, the sound of the curse—of the darkness—fighting to remain free.

She could feel it inside her. The tendrils of the curse had wormed their way into her veins, deeper than ever before, spreading like wildfire beneath her skin. Her breath caught in her throat as a sharp, icy sensation clawed at her mind, pulling her toward the edge of something dark and cold. She fought to hold on, but the darkness pushed harder, stronger, desperate to consume everything in its path.

Victor stood beside her, his hands raised to the heavens, chanting words that Evelyn couldn't quite make sense of. The language was old, older than time itself, and the power it carried was nearly overwhelming. His voice trembled with the weight of the ritual, and though he seemed calm on the surface, she could see the strain in his eyes.

"We have to finish it," Victor said, his voice barely audible over the cacophony of sound around them. "We have to close the rift before it consumes us all."

Evelyn nodded, her heart pounding in her chest. But even as she stepped forward, the shadows in the temple began to writhe again, dark tendrils snapping out from the walls, coiling toward them like serpents. The energy in the room felt *alive*, filled with a hunger that seemed to devour everything in its wake.

"Victor, we're running out of time!" Evelyn shouted, her voice breaking through the rising tumult of the dark energy.

"I know," he said, his voice tight with urgency. "But we can't rush it. If we don't complete the binding, it will all be for nothing. The curse will *destroy* us all."

Evelyn's hands trembled as she reached for the shattered remains of the Heart on the altar. She could feel the pieces, the cold stone, pulsing with power as if the Heart itself was drawing from her. Her pulse quickened. She felt as if the Heart was calling to her, begging her to finish what had been started, to restore the broken seal.

But the longer she stood there, the more she realized the Heart wasn't just calling to her—it was *controlling* her.

She fought the urge to let go, to succumb to the pull of the curse. She couldn't. Not now. Not after everything she had been through. But it was getting harder to resist. The power of the curse was inside her, and it was like nothing she had ever felt before. It was ancient. It was primal. It was everything that the world had tried to bury.

And now, it was free.

Evelyn's vision blurred, the shadows twisting into horrific shapes that seemed to float just at the edge of her sight. She blinked, trying to focus, but the darkness *squeezed* her mind, drowning her thoughts. It was like a suffocating fog, blotting out her will.

Victor's voice broke through, sharp and commanding. "Evelyn, *fight it*!"

She nodded, desperate to hold on to herself, but it was getting harder. She could feel the ancient power twisting inside her, the knowledge of it seeping into her every cell. It was as if the curse was *alive* inside her, wanting to merge with her, to claim her as its vessel. The Heart pulsed in her hands, resonating with the energy inside her, feeding the darkness.

But then—something clicked.

Evelyn remembered the truth about her bloodline, the legacy that had been passed down through the generations. She wasn't just a victim of the curse. She wasn't just someone who had shattered the

Heart by accident. She was the key. She had always been the key. And the curse, for all its power, could not control her unless she allowed it.

With a force of will she didn't know she had, Evelyn pushed back. The darkness recoiled, just for a moment, and in that moment, she felt the Heart's power surge through her once more. The shadows screamed in protest, and Evelyn felt her feet leave the ground as the energy of the temple and the curse collided.

Victor's words echoed in her ears: "Complete the ritual, Evelyn. Close the rift."

Her heart raced, her mind sharp despite the overwhelming energy flooding her senses. She gathered every last ounce of strength, channeling it into the Heart. The shards fit together with a resounding crack, and for a moment, everything froze.

The world seemed to hold its breath.

Then, the power of the curse *roared*.

The temple trembled, the stones rattling as if the entire structure were being torn apart from the inside. The light from the altar grew blinding, brighter than the sun, and the darkness pushed against it with all its fury. It was as if the forces of creation and destruction were locked in an eternal struggle, and Evelyn was at the heart of it.

Victor reached for her, his hands clutching hers as he whispered, "We're almost there. Hold on."

Evelyn's teeth clenched as she forced the Heart to pulse with all the power she had left. The curse fought her every step of the way, but this time, she had the strength to *resist* it. The shadows screeched in agony as the energy inside her coalesced into something more powerful—something that had been buried deep within the temple for centuries.

The Heart was the key.

And now it was whole.

A blinding flash of light erupted from the altar, and Evelyn felt herself *falling*, falling into the heart of the curse itself.

Evelyn awoke with a sharp gasp, her body trembling as if she had just surfaced from deep underwater. Her breath came in short, frantic bursts, and her heart pounded in her chest as if it were trying to escape her body. She blinked rapidly, trying to clear her vision, but the blinding light had left dark spots in her eyes.

Victor was beside her, his hand gripping her shoulder, shaking her gently. "Evelyn. Evelyn, wake up."

She sat up abruptly, her breath coming faster as she looked around. The temple—the altar—the Heart—it was all... gone. The dark energy that had filled the room was nowhere to be found. It was silent. Eerily silent.

"Did we do it?" she asked, her voice hoarse. She didn't know what to expect, but the absence of the curse was overwhelming in its own way.

Victor's face was pale, his eyes wide with disbelief. "I think we did," he said, his voice thick with emotion. "It's over."

But Evelyn didn't feel relief. There was still something nagging at the back of her mind. Something wasn't quite right.

"What about the curse?" she asked, her voice low. "Did we really stop it?"

Victor was silent for a long moment, his gaze distant. "I don't know. But we sealed it—contained it. I think the curse is bound for now, but the Heart—it's still out there. We can't let our guard down."

Evelyn nodded slowly, but her thoughts were already spinning. She had felt the power of the curse, and she knew that even though they had sealed it, the Heart had not been destroyed—it had been restored. And with it, the temptation of the darkness still lingered, a shadow at the edges of her mind.

She knew that their fight was far from over.

Evelyn's fingers twitched at her side, and for a moment, she thought she was still holding the pieces of the Heart. But when she looked down, her hands were empty, the shards gone, as if they had never existed in the first place. She swallowed hard and pushed herself to her feet, her legs weak beneath her. The temple, once a place of suffocating darkness and tension, now stood silent. The oppressive weight of the curse that had hung over them had lifted, but in its place, an unsettling emptiness lingered.

Victor was already standing, brushing the dust from his clothes with an almost mechanical precision. His eyes were distant, his thoughts clearly elsewhere. Evelyn watched him for a moment, noting the subtle tremor in his hands as he wiped the sweat from his brow.

"What now?" she asked, breaking the silence between them.

Victor glanced at her, his face pale but resolute. "Now we leave. We've done what we could. The curse is contained—at least for now." His voice faltered as he looked around the vast, empty temple. "I just... I don't know how long it will last."

Evelyn felt a pang of unease. "You're saying it's not over?"

Victor's jaw clenched. "I'm saying we've sealed the curse back into the Heart, but we haven't destroyed it. The Heart isn't just an object—it's a conduit. It's the vessel for an ancient force, and as long as it exists, the curse has the potential to come back. Maybe even stronger than before."

Evelyn's mind raced. They had contained the curse, yes, but for how long? She had no illusions about the power they were dealing with. She had seen it firsthand—the way the darkness had clawed at her, taking control, making her feel like she was losing herself. And if it had been inside her once, it could certainly find another way back in. She could never let her guard down. None of them could.

But that wasn't the worst part. What if the Heart wasn't just an object of containment? What if it was... something else?

"Victor, I need to know more," Evelyn said, her voice low but urgent. "How do you know the curse is truly sealed? What was that energy we just felt—the light? That wasn't just the Heart, was it?"

Victor's eyes widened, and for a moment, she saw a flicker of doubt in his expression. But it was gone as quickly as it had appeared. "The ritual should have worked," he said, more to himself than to her. "We used the Heart's energy to reverse the curse's flow, to close the rift. The power should have been neutralized."

"Should have?" Evelyn repeated, a chill running down her spine.

He took a deep breath, running a hand through his hair as if trying to gather his thoughts. "The Heart is ancient, Evelyn. Older than anything we understand. I don't know how it works exactly, but it *binds* the curse. It doesn't destroy it. It keeps it contained. That's all we can hope for."

Her pulse quickened as his words sank in. The realization that they hadn't destroyed the curse—only contained it—hung over her like a sword about to drop. She looked at the altar once more, the faint glow of the Heart's energy still flickering in the cracks of the stone. It was as if the Heart was breathing, alive with something dark and hungry.

"I can't shake this feeling," Evelyn said, her voice tense. "That there's something more we don't know. Something about the Heart we're missing."

Victor's gaze flicked to the altar, and then back to her. "I don't know, Evelyn. But if there's one thing I've learned in all these years, it's that we can't *control* it. We can't even begin to understand it. The Heart—this temple—everything here was built to hold the curse in place. It was never meant to be destroyed, only contained."

Her thoughts began to spiral. They had learned so much about the curse, about how it had been passed down through generations, how her bloodline had been tied to it. But it seemed that every answer they uncovered only led to more questions. If the curse was just contained, then what was keeping it from slipping through the cracks and taking over once more?

Evelyn turned to leave the altar, stepping cautiously through the temple's crumbling corridors. Her footsteps echoed through the hollow stone walls, the air thick with the remnants of dark energy. They were in the belly of the beast now, and even though the curse was locked away—for now—it felt as though they were standing at the precipice of something much larger. She couldn't quite explain why, but she knew they weren't done. Not yet.

Victor followed her, his eyes scanning the darkness ahead. "We need to get out of here," he said, his voice weary. "This place—these ruins—they're a trap. If the curse was able to escape, it'll find its way back here eventually. The Heart *will* find a way to break free. It always does."

"How do you know that?" Evelyn asked, her voice tinged with disbelief. "Have you seen it before?"

Victor hesitated. His eyes narrowed, and for a brief moment, Evelyn saw the weight of years of research, years of studying the curse, weighing down on him. "No. I've never seen it happen. But I've read the records, Evelyn. My family's records. They've been trying to contain the curse for generations. And every time they think they've succeeded, the curse comes back stronger than before. It's a cycle."

Evelyn's heart sank as she processed this new information. She had suspected as much, but hearing it from Victor confirmed her fears. There was no final solution to this—no simple way to rid the world of the curse. It would always find a way back. And the Heart, the object that had been designed to contain it, was a ticking time bomb.

"How long do we have before it comes back?" she asked.

Victor shook his head slowly. "I don't know. But the fact that we've sealed it once means we may have bought ourselves some time.

If we can find a way to truly destroy the Heart, we might have a chance of ending it for good. But until then..."

His voice trailed off, and Evelyn felt the weight of his words settle over her like a heavy cloak. The curse wasn't over. They had only *delayed* it. And without answers, without understanding what the Heart truly was, they were no closer to destroying it than they had been when they started.

The journey back through the temple felt endless. Every step was a reminder of how much was at stake, how close they had come to losing everything. The walls seemed to close in around them, the shadows growing heavier with each passing moment, as if the temple itself were trying to pull them back into its dark embrace. The echoes of their footsteps were the only sound, haunting and endless.

Evelyn felt the pull again, the tugging sensation that came from deep within her. She wasn't just feeling the lingering presence of the curse; she was *connected* to it now. She had broken the Heart. She had touched the darkness in a way no one else had. The weight of that knowledge was unbearable. No matter how hard she tried to resist, she could feel it pulling at her thoughts, crawling beneath her skin, reminding her that the Heart was not just an object—it was a part of her now.

She shook her head, trying to push the thoughts away. There was no time for this. They had to keep moving.

"Victor, we need to get back to the surface," she said, her voice sharp. "We need to find a way out of this place."

Victor nodded, but there was something distant in his gaze, something that made Evelyn pause. She looked at him, her concern growing.

"What is it?" she asked, her voice soft but urgent.

Victor stopped in his tracks and turned to face her. There was a shadow in his eyes, something that hinted at something he wasn't telling her.

"We can't go back the way we came," he said quietly.

Evelyn's stomach dropped. "What do you mean?"

"The curse... it doesn't just disappear," he explained. "It's still here, even if we've sealed it. We need to leave, but we can't retrace our steps. We need to find another way out."

Evelyn swallowed hard. The air seemed to grow even heavier around them, as if the very temple was reacting to the dark power that had been unleashed. She could feel it now, too—the weight of something pressing down on them, an invisible force tugging at their very souls.

"We're trapped," she said softly.

Victor nodded grimly. "Maybe. But we don't have a choice. We need to find a way out before the Heart finds a way to break free again."

The search for an exit felt endless. They wandered through the temple's labyrinthine halls, passing through crumbling doorways and beneath towering arches. The deeper they went, the stronger the sense of foreboding grew. The shadows seemed to shift and move, as though they had a mind of their own, watching, waiting. The air smelled of dust and ancient stone, but there was something else—something faint, almost imperceptible, like a whisper that Evelyn couldn't quite catch.

It was then that they found it.

A small, hidden door. Not much more than a crack in the wall, but just large enough for them to slip through. They hesitated for a moment, unsure of what lay beyond. But Evelyn felt something else, too—an instinct, a feeling that the door was their only way out.

Without a word, she stepped forward, her hand gripping the door's cold handle.

Victor followed closely behind.

The moment the door creaked open, the world around them shifted.

The darkness pressed in.

Chapter 15: The Hollow of the Heart

The door opened with a low groan, its ancient hinges protesting the intrusion. Evelyn stepped through first, her eyes scanning the narrow passage ahead. The air was thick with dust, and the temperature seemed to drop, as if the temple itself were exhaling the last remnants of its dark power. Victor followed closely, his face pale in the faint light that filtered through the cracked stone.

The corridor they entered was different from the others they had traversed. It was narrow, claustrophobic, and curved in strange, unpredictable angles. The walls were etched with symbols that Evelyn couldn't understand, markings that seemed to move as she stared at them, as though they were alive, watching her. The sensation was suffocating, a constant pressure that made her skin crawl.

"What is this place?" she whispered, her voice barely audible, though she wasn't sure if it was because of the eerie silence or the weight of the air pressing in on her.

Victor's expression was tight with concern. "I don't know. I've never seen anything like it."

The passage narrowed further, the walls closing in as they continued down the path. Evelyn had the unsettling feeling that they were being funneled into something, like prey being drawn toward a predator's lair. The darkness seemed thicker here, not just in the shadows but in the very fabric of the place. The Heart, she realized, had never been fully contained. It had merely been hidden, waiting, dormant for a time—but now it had stirred, and with it, the darkness.

As they moved deeper, the walls began to hum, a faint vibration that seemed to come from the very stones themselves. It was rhythmic, hypnotic, and Evelyn's mind started to drift, to wander in ways that unsettled her. She fought to stay focused. She couldn't

141

afford to let her guard down—not now. Not when they were so close
to the end.

Victor's hand shot out, grasping her arm gently but firmly.
"Evelyn, stop."

She froze, instinctively pulling away from him. "What is it?"

Victor's eyes were wide, and for the first time since they had
entered the temple, he seemed genuinely afraid. He pointed ahead,
toward the far end of the corridor. At first, Evelyn saw nothing—just
a wall of darkness, like the mouth of a cave. But then, as her eyes
adjusted, she saw it.

The air shimmered, vibrating with an energy that made the hairs
on the back of her neck stand up. A faint outline appeared in the
shadows, a figure—or something like a figure—suspended in midair.
It was tall, featureless, and moved with an unnatural fluidity, like
smoke being blown on a breeze. It flickered in and out of sight, its
shape constantly shifting, as if it were never truly there, just a trick of
the light—or perhaps a trick of the mind.

Evelyn took a step backward, her heart pounding in her chest.
"What is that?"

Victor's voice was tight, almost a whisper. "It's the Hollow Man."

The name sent a cold chill down Evelyn's spine. She had heard
the   legends,   the   stories   passed   down   through   the
generations—stories of a creature that hunted those who sought to
uncover the curse's secrets, a being born of the curse itself, neither
living nor dead. It was the Heart's guardian, its protector. And it was
something that Evelyn and Victor would now have to face if they
wanted to escape the temple.

The Hollow Man seemed to notice them, or perhaps it was the
presence of their souls that it detected. It twisted in the air, its form
becoming sharper, more defined, a vague outline of a man—tall,
gaunt, with hollow eyes that burned with an unnatural, otherworldly

fire. Its mouth stretched into a grotesque grin, revealing rows of teeth that were too sharp, too elongated, to be human.

"It's coming for us," Victor muttered, his voice thick with fear. "We have to move."

But as they turned to flee, the walls around them began to shift, groaning and scraping against each other, sealing off the way they had come. A low rumble vibrated through the stone, and the passage behind them began to close, trapping them in the narrow corridor. The Hollow Man advanced, its limbs stretching unnaturally, reaching for them with hands that seemed to dissolve into the very air.

Evelyn's breath caught in her throat. "We're trapped."

"We have no choice," Victor said, his voice firming as he grabbed her hand. "We have to keep moving. We can't let it catch us."

Together, they sprinted forward, the Hollow Man's presence growing stronger with each step. Its form flickered and shifted in the shadows, always just behind them, always just out of reach, but it was gaining on them. The air seemed to twist around them, pulling at their limbs, distorting their senses. Evelyn's mind felt as if it were being squeezed, each breath harder to take, each step heavier than the last.

Then, ahead, she saw it—another doorway, a thin sliver of light just barely visible through the thick darkness. They had to reach it. They *had* to.

"Come on!" she shouted, her voice hoarse, panicked.

Victor's hand tightened on hers, and they pushed forward with everything they had, ignoring the crushing weight of the air and the oppressive darkness that tried to swallow them whole. The Hollow Man shrieked behind them, a sound that was more felt than heard—a deep, resonating wail that seemed to vibrate through their bones.

With one final burst of energy, they reached the doorway, throwing themselves through it just as the Hollow Man lunged. The last thing Evelyn saw before the door slammed shut behind them was the creature's hollow eyes, burning with fury, its arms reaching toward them like the tendrils of some nightmarish plant.

The door clicked shut with a deafening thud, and for a moment, there was silence. Evelyn's body sagged with exhaustion, her chest heaving as she tried to catch her breath. She glanced at Victor, but his face was pale, his eyes wide with shock.

"What the hell was that?" she gasped, her voice shaking.

Victor didn't answer right away. He stood frozen, staring at the door, his hand still gripping the doorknob as though waiting for something to happen. Finally, he turned to her, his face drawn and haunted.

"The Hollow Man," he said, his voice strained. "It's an extension of the curse. It's... the guardian. The Heart's protector."

Evelyn swallowed hard, her throat dry. "The Heart... it's not just a vessel for the curse. It *creates* things like that. Like the Hollow Man."

Victor's eyes darkened. "Yes. The Heart is a source of power, but it's also a curse in itself. It doesn't just bind evil—it feeds it. It allows it to take shape. To *live*."

Evelyn took a step back, feeling the weight of his words settle in her chest like an anchor. "So everything that's happened—the darkness, the creatures, even the Heart itself—it's all connected. It's not just a curse, it's... a living entity. And we're trapped with it."

Victor nodded grimly. "We have to get out of here. We have to find a way to destroy the Heart before it spreads. If we don't..."

"If we don't," Evelyn finished for him, "it will consume everything."

Victor didn't respond, but the look in his eyes said everything she needed to know. The Hollow Man was just the beginning. The curse wasn't contained—it was evolving, growing stronger. And as long as the Heart existed, the darkness would never truly be defeated.

They moved through the doorway, into a new chamber that opened before them. The walls here were covered in strange, alien symbols, more intricate and twisted than anything they had seen before. There was a faint pulse of light emanating from the far side of the room, casting long shadows that seemed to stretch toward them.

Evelyn felt the pull again—the deep, unsettling tug of the Heart's power, stronger than before. She could feel it in her chest, in the back of her mind, as though it were calling to her, pulling her toward something she couldn't see but knew was there.

Victor seemed to sense it too. His face was drawn with tension, his movements more deliberate. "We need to find a way to stop it," he said. "Whatever happens next, we can't let the curse spread. We're the only ones who can stop it now."

Evelyn nodded, but in her heart, she feared they were too late.

Evelyn's heart raced in her chest as they moved deeper into the chamber. Every step she took seemed to bring them closer to something—the source of the curse, the Heart, or perhaps something far worse. The air was thick with an unnatural heaviness, as if the very walls were closing in on them. The pulse of light ahead grew brighter, but it wasn't the comforting glow of an exit—it was far more sinister, pulsing with the same eerie rhythm that had echoed through the temple.

She glanced at Victor, who was just ahead of her, his eyes fixed on the light. His expression was taut, his jaw clenched, and he didn't seem to notice her hesitation.

"Victor," she whispered urgently, but he didn't respond.

She reached out, grabbing his arm, her grip tight with fear. "Victor, wait. We don't know what that is. We don't know what's waiting for us."

Victor slowly turned, his eyes flickering toward her. For a moment, he seemed far away, lost in his thoughts. Then, as if snapping back to reality, he nodded sharply.

"I know," he said, his voice thick with tension. "But we don't have a choice. We need to find the Heart, destroy it, and get out. We're running out of time."

Evelyn felt a surge of panic, but she quickly suppressed it. She had seen the Hollow Man—felt its presence close behind them. There was no going back, not without risking everything they had fought for. Still, the uncertainty gnawed at her, and the ominous glow in front of them made the hairs on the back of her neck stand on end.

They approached the source of the light cautiously, the ground beneath them now slick with a strange, viscous substance. It wasn't blood—at least, not in the traditional sense—but it was dark and sticky, like tar, pooling in the cracks of the stone floor. Evelyn stepped over it, careful not to let the substance touch her skin.

When they reached the center of the chamber, the source of the light came into full view. It was not a lantern, as she had imagined, nor a simple artifact. What they were looking at was far more terrifying.

In the center of the room, suspended in midair by some unseen force, was a massive stone pedestal. Atop the pedestal rested the Heart itself, encased in a protective shell of what appeared to be glass—or crystal. The object was radiating light, though it was not the warm, comforting kind. It was harsh, cold, almost like a distant star that had lost its warmth.

The Heart, pulsating with light, was a thing of beauty and terror. It was both hypnotic and repellent. Evelyn's gaze was drawn to it, and she felt the pull again—the deep, magnetic force that tugged at her very soul.

"Is that... is that it?" she whispered, her voice trembling.

Victor nodded grimly, his eyes locked on the object. "That's the Heart. It's alive, Evelyn. It's more than just a curse; it's the source of everything."

Evelyn swallowed hard. The Heart, pulsing before them, seemed to resonate with something deep within her. It felt as though it was calling her name, a whisper that only she could hear. She wanted to look away, to resist it, but she couldn't. It was as though the Heart had some power over her—like a string pulling at her, drawing her closer to it.

She stepped forward against her will, her movements slow and deliberate, as though someone else were controlling her body. Her vision blurred, the room fading around her as the only thing that mattered was the Heart.

Victor's voice shattered the silence, thick with panic. "Evelyn! Don't!"

But it was too late. She had already crossed the threshold.

The moment her fingers brushed against the surface of the Heart's casing, a surge of energy blasted through her, knocking her back with the force of a thunderclap. She screamed, but the sound was swallowed by the deafening roar that filled the room. Her body convulsed with the force of the shock, and she was sent crashing to the ground.

Victor was beside her in an instant, his hand on her shoulder, shaking her. "Evelyn! Are you alright?"

She blinked rapidly, her vision swimming, her body shaking. "I—I'm fine," she gasped, though she could feel something inside her stirring—something that had been dormant, buried deep within her, stirring back to life.

She pushed herself up, unsteady, feeling lightheaded. Her skin was tingling as though the energy from the Heart was coursing through her veins, but it was a bitter sensation, a burning cold that made her heart race in terror.

"I felt it," she whispered. "It—it's alive, Victor. The Heart. It's more than just an object. It's *aware*."

Victor nodded grimly, his face pale. "I've seen this before. It's a reaction to the Heart's power. It's—"

"Victor!" Evelyn gasped, suddenly clutching her chest, her breathing quickening. "It's *inside* me again. It's—"

Before she could finish, the air around them seemed to bend, like the space itself was warping. Shadows twisted in the corners of the room, stretching out toward them, converging on the Heart. The pulse of light grew brighter, and Evelyn felt a sharp, sickening sensation in her stomach, like she was being drawn into the center of a vortex.

A low, guttural growl echoed through the chamber, reverberating off the walls. From the shadows emerged the Hollow Man, its ghastly form flickering in and out of existence, its hollow eyes burning with rage.

It was faster this time, its limbs distorting with unnatural speed, as though it was feeding on the Heart's energy. Its grin widened as it reached out, its fingers long and skeletal, nearly touching the surface of the pedestal.

"No!" Victor shouted, grabbing Evelyn's arm and yanking her back. "We can't let it reach the Heart!"

Evelyn was struggling to regain control over her body. The pull of the Heart was growing stronger, its presence suffocating, and the Hollow Man's proximity was pushing her toward the edge of panic. "Victor... we have to *destroy* it," she gasped, trying to break free from the suffocating pull.

"We will," Victor promised, his voice sharp with determination. "We just need to figure out how."

But even as he spoke, the Hollow Man was closing in. It had reached the pedestal, and its fingers were now just inches away from the crystal casing. With each step it took, the Heart's light flickered and dimmed, as though the creature was draining it, siphoning the energy it had been holding back for centuries.

"No!" Evelyn cried out again, this time managing to tear her arm free from Victor's grip. She rushed forward, stumbling, her mind clouded with the overwhelming energy radiating from the Heart.

Before she could stop herself, her hand shot out toward the pedestal, and as if guided by some unseen force, she pressed her palm against the crystal.

The moment her skin touched the surface, the room erupted in a violent explosion of light. The Heart shone brighter than it ever had before, and Evelyn's entire body was engulfed in its energy. She screamed, feeling her body being torn apart, her thoughts dissolving as the Heart's raw power flooded her senses.

Victor's voice broke through the roar. "Evelyn, stop!"

But she couldn't hear him. The Heart's energy was overwhelming, swallowing everything around her—her thoughts, her emotions, her very sense of self. And then, as quickly as it had come, the light collapsed, leaving behind only an aching emptiness.

She collapsed to her knees, gasping for air, her chest heaving as the dark energy receded, leaving her drained and weak. Her vision blurred, and the world spun around her.

Victor was kneeling beside her in an instant. His hand was on her shoulder, his voice filled with desperation. "Evelyn, what happened? Are you okay?"

She shook her head weakly, still trying to clear the fog from her mind. "I don't know. I touched it, and then everything... everything went *black*."

Victor's expression was filled with concern, but there was something else in his eyes now—something deeper. "You felt it, didn't you?" he asked softly. "The Heart's power. It's not just energy. It's connected to us. It's tied to you. And now... it's inside you. Even more than before."

Evelyn's stomach twisted at his words. "What do you mean?" she whispered, though she already knew the answer.

Victor's face hardened. "The Heart's power is binding you, Evelyn. It's trying to use you as a vessel. And if we don't destroy it soon, it'll take you completely."

Chapter 16: The Heart's Grip

The cold, oppressive weight of the temple seemed to press in on them from all sides. Evelyn's breath was ragged as she sat on the stone floor, her body trembling from the force of the energy that had coursed through her. Her vision was still blurry, her head spinning, but she could feel the lingering presence of the Heart within her—its power, its pull, its hunger.

Victor remained beside her, his hand on her shoulder, but his eyes were fixed on the glowing crystal in the center of the room. He didn't speak immediately, his gaze distant, as though lost in his thoughts, or perhaps trying to process what had just happened.

Evelyn tried to steady her breath, to regain control of her body. She could still feel the Heart's presence, as if it were an echo in her mind, a whisper just beneath the surface of her thoughts. It was subtle, but unmistakable—the energy it had unleashed was not something she could easily forget. It wasn't just a physical sensation; it was a part of her now, like a seed planted deep inside her, waiting to grow.

"Victor..." Her voice was hoarse, and her throat felt raw, but she forced herself to speak. "We have to destroy it. Now. Before it takes over completely."

Victor turned to her, his eyes clouded with something close to fear. He opened his mouth to respond, but then paused, his brow furrowing as if he were considering something very carefully.

He reached out and gently touched the side of her face, his fingers brushing against her skin. Evelyn flinched, instinctively pulling away, but he only watched her, his expression pained.

"You don't understand," he said softly, his voice barely above a whisper. "The Heart isn't just something we can destroy. It's alive, Evelyn. It's more than an object or a curse. It's a force that's been here for centuries. A force that has shaped this place, this entire temple. And it's already inside you."

The words hit Evelyn like a punch to the gut. She wanted to pull away from him, to shut him out, but she couldn't. The truth was too clear, too undeniable. The Heart had marked her, and there was no going back now. She could feel it, pulsing within her chest, like a second heartbeat, one that didn't belong to her.

She closed her eyes, trying to steady her breathing, but it was impossible to ignore the deep sense of dread creeping up from her core. She didn't just feel connected to the Heart. She felt it inside her—pressing on her thoughts, whispering to her in a language she couldn't understand.

Victor sat down beside her, his face solemn. "I thought I could contain it. I thought I could stop the curse from taking over, but I was wrong. The Heart chooses who it binds itself to. And once you're chosen... it doesn't let go."

Evelyn's chest tightened at his words, but she didn't want to believe him. She couldn't. She refused to. "There has to be a way to destroy it," she insisted, her voice rising with desperation. "We can't just let it take control. We can't..."

Victor turned to face her fully now, his eyes serious, his jaw set with determination. "We need to understand how the Heart works—how it draws its power, how it controls its victims. Only then can we even begin to figure out how to destroy it. But that's going to mean going deeper. And that means confronting everything the Heart has touched. The temple. The curse. The Hollow Man. It's all connected."

Evelyn shook her head, a cold sweat breaking out across her forehead. She could still feel the lingering sensation of the Heart's power in her chest, tugging at her with a kind of malicious intent. It was still inside her, and with each passing second, it seemed to be growing stronger.

"We don't have time for that," she snapped, her voice sharper than she intended. "We have to act now. Before it's too late."

Victor didn't argue, but the look on his face said it all. He knew as well as she did that they were running out of time. The Hollow Man was still out there, and the curse was far from defeated. But Evelyn's mind was made up. They had no choice but to act, and to do it now.

She stood up, her legs unsteady beneath her, and made her way toward the pedestal where the Heart lay suspended. Every step felt like a weight dragging her down, but she pushed through it, her resolve hardening with each passing moment.

Victor was at her side immediately, his hand reaching for her arm. "Evelyn, stop. You don't understand what you're dealing with. It's not just an artifact. It's a consciousness, a living thing. If you try to destroy it without understanding how it works, you could—"

"I don't care," Evelyn interrupted, her voice steady despite the turmoil raging inside her. "We have to destroy it, Victor. Now."

Victor looked at her, his expression torn. He could see the determination in her eyes, but he also saw the fear—the fear of what the Heart might do to her if they didn't act quickly. It was a fight they couldn't afford to lose.

"Alright," he said quietly. "If we're going to do this, we need to be careful. The Heart feeds on fear, on emotion. It's not just a physical entity. It's a part of everything here, and it will fight back with everything it has."

Evelyn nodded, though she didn't fully understand. She wasn't sure she cared anymore. All she knew was that the Heart's grip on her was getting stronger by the second, and she had to break free. Whatever it took.

Victor hesitated, then reached into his pack and pulled out a small, silver dagger—an ancient relic, its blade engraved with symbols she didn't recognize. He held it out to her, the weapon gleaming in the dim light.

"This is the only thing that might work," he said. "It's imbued with a kind of magic—an old kind, one that's connected to the very essence of the Heart. It might be able to sever the connection between you and the Heart. But we don't know what will happen after that."

Evelyn took the dagger, feeling its weight in her hand. She didn't know if it would work, if it was the answer they were searching for, but it was the only option they had. She couldn't back down now.

With a deep breath, she stepped forward, moving toward the glowing pedestal where the Heart rested. She could feel the pulse of its energy in the air, vibrating in her chest like the beat of a drum. It was waiting for her, watching her with a silent, knowing gaze.

For a moment, everything went still. The world around them seemed to hold its breath, as if the very air was waiting for her next move. Evelyn raised the dagger, her hand trembling slightly, and without hesitation, she drove it into the crystal casing of the Heart.

The impact was immediate. There was a sharp, cracking sound, followed by a low, guttural rumble that seemed to shake the very foundation of the temple. The Heart shuddered, its pulse of light flickering erratically, its once steady rhythm now disturbed.

Evelyn's heart pounded in her chest as the energy surged through her body once more. This time, however, it was different. It was violent, raw, like fire and ice battling inside her, tearing at her insides. She gasped for breath, her vision swimming, but she refused to pull away. She had to hold on.

"Evelyn!" Victor's voice cut through the chaos, but it felt distant, muffled. "You need to let go! The Heart will destroy you if you don't—"

But Evelyn couldn't hear him. All she could hear was the sound of her own heartbeat, pounding in her ears, growing louder and faster with each passing second. The dagger was lodged deep in the Heart, its energy now flowing freely, and she could feel the connection snapping—ripping apart the bond that had formed between her and the Heart.

Suddenly, there was a deafening explosion of light, blinding her. The temple around her shook violently, and the floor cracked beneath her feet. The Heart shrieked in a sound that was beyond human comprehension, its light flashing brighter than the sun itself, its energy thrumming through the stone like an earthquake.

And then—silence.

The world around Evelyn was a blinding blur, a maelstrom of light and sound, as if the very temple were being torn apart. Her body felt as if it were being pulled in every direction at once, her limbs heavy and unresponsive. The pulse of the Heart—the energy that had been inside her and now raged violently outside—surged through the air, vibrating every stone, every inch of space. It was unbearable, like the force of a hurricane ripping apart the very fabric of reality.

For a moment, everything seemed to freeze. The world stopped spinning, the light halted, suspended in the air as though the very laws of time had momentarily broken down. Evelyn blinked rapidly, trying to clear the spots from her vision, but nothing changed. The air was thick with a strange electric charge, like a storm cloud gathering just overhead, waiting to explode.

She felt Victor's presence beside her, his hand gripping her arm tightly, and she was vaguely aware of his voice, though it seemed muffled, distant.

"Evelyn, you have to stay focused!" Victor shouted, but his voice sounded far away, as if coming through water. "This isn't over! You have to pull away from the Heart!"

But how? How could she pull away when the Heart was so deeply embedded inside her? It was everywhere. The moment she had touched the crystal, it had burrowed its way into her mind, into her very soul, and now, its influence was unyielding. The presence inside her was overwhelming—like an internal storm, swirling in her chest, in her head.

The agony was unlike anything she had ever known. It felt as if every inch of her skin were on fire, every bone in her body being slowly crushed under the weight of something ancient and insidious. The Heart was feeding on her, drawing its power from her fear, from her pain, and it was growing stronger with every second that passed.

She gasped for air, but the atmosphere felt thick, almost gelatinous, and she could hardly breathe. The air was charged with raw energy, crackling with static that made the hairs on her arms stand on end.

"Victor... I can't..." Evelyn gasped, her voice barely audible. "It's... it's in me. I can't stop it."

Victor's grip tightened. She could feel the heat of his hand, but it was distant, as if it were underwater. His face came into focus, pale and stricken with worry. He was saying something, but she couldn't make out the words. His lips moved in a frantic rhythm, but they seemed muffled by the roar of the energy all around them.

In the distance, she could hear the Hollow Man's guttural laugh, echoing through the temple like a death rattle. It was as if the creature had been awakened, drawn to the chaos, feeding on the fear that had been unleashed. The air grew colder, the shadows lengthened, and the very walls of the temple seemed to be bending and warping, as if they were alive.

Victor's voice finally pierced through the haze. "Evelyn! Listen to me! You have to fight it! Focus! Think about the dagger—think about the connection between you and the Heart. If you can sever it..."

But the words barely registered. Evelyn's mind was no longer her own. The Heart's influence had grown so powerful, so pervasive, that it had started to drown out everything else. It was everywhere—inside her, around her, above her—whispering to her in a language she didn't understand, a language that felt older than time itself.

The walls of the chamber began to pulse in time with the Heart's energy, its rhythmic throbbing sending shockwaves through the air, vibrating the very stone beneath her feet. A strange warmth spread through her chest as if something deep inside her were stirring, something ancient and dormant, now awakening in response to the Heart's call.

No, no, no, she thought frantically. *I won't let it take me. I won't.*

But the Heart's pull was like a tidal wave, and her resistance was becoming weaker by the second. Her thoughts began to blur, and she could feel herself being pulled deeper into the abyss. The world around her seemed to dissolve into shadows, and the temple was now nothing but a haze of darkness, pierced only by the cold, harsh light of the Heart.

Suddenly, something cold and sharp pierced through the fog of her mind. It was Victor's voice—clearer this time, more insistent.

"Evelyn! You're not alone! You *can* fight this! You're stronger than it! Focus on *us*—on what's real!"

Evelyn blinked, her vision slowly coming into focus, and for the first time since the explosion of light, she felt something shift in her chest. The Heart's pull weakened, just slightly, as though it had momentarily been distracted by the presence of something else. She was still tethered to it, but now, she could see the thin line that connected them, the thread of light that bound her to the source of the curse.

Victor was standing beside her now, his face taut with determination. "You've already survived worse than this, Evelyn," he said, his voice steady, unwavering. "Don't let it control you. You *are* in control. You've *always* been."

Evelyn clung to his words like a lifeline. She closed her eyes, pushing away the whispers, the pull of the Heart. She focused on Victor, on the warmth of his touch, on the sound of his voice. *This is real,* she thought. *Not the Heart. Not the darkness. Victor is real.*

The connection between them, the bond they shared, was stronger than the Heart's influence. She could feel it, pulsing in her chest, and with it, the overwhelming urge to fight.

She took a deep breath and, with all her strength, willed herself to break the connection. The pressure inside her chest grew even stronger as the Heart fought back, sending waves of disorienting energy through her body. But Evelyn held firm, fighting back the urge to give in, focusing all of her willpower on severing the connection.

The dagger in her hand trembled, but she could feel its power—its ancient magic, its resonance with the Heart. She gripped it tightly, focusing on the way it hummed in her palm. She could feel the Heart weakening, its hold on her body and mind slipping, but it wasn't enough. Not yet.

The Hollow Man's voice echoed through the chamber again, low and mocking, as if it were laughing at her efforts. "You can't escape it, Evelyn. You *belong* to it now."

His voice was like ice in her veins, but she didn't flinch. She had to keep fighting. She had to finish this.

With every ounce of strength she had left, she raised the dagger and drove it deeper into the Heart's crystal casing. There was a loud crack as the surface of the crystal shattered, sending a shockwave of energy through the room. The force of the impact knocked her back, and she was sent sprawling across the floor, the dagger slipping from her hand.

The temple shook violently, and the walls groaned as if they were alive, fighting to hold themselves together. The very ground beneath her feet seemed to crack open, dark fissures appearing in the stone, leaking a thick, black ooze. The Hollow Man was moving toward them now, its form distorted and blurred, its eyes gleaming with hunger.

Victor was at her side again, his hand on her arm, pulling her up. "Evelyn, we need to go. Now."

But Evelyn didn't move. She couldn't. She was staring at the Heart, now exposed in the center of the pedestal. The crystal had cracked open, revealing the true nature of the Heart within.

It was not what she had expected. What lay inside was not a jewel or a stone but something alive. A pulsing, beating mass of light and shadow, like the core of some ancient creature, its energy swirling and undulating in patterns that defied comprehension. It was a heart—yes—but not of flesh. It was a thing of darkness and power, a nexus of life and death that resonated with the very essence of the curse.

And then, as if sensing her thoughts, the Heart pulsed again, its light flaring up, brighter than before. But now, Evelyn felt something shift—something had changed. The energy that had been feeding on her was no longer pulling at her. Instead, it was... retreating.

The Heart was weakening.

Victor's voice broke through the haze. "Evelyn, it's not over! The Hollow Man is coming—"

But it was too late. The Heart's light exploded in one final, blinding burst, a shockwave of energy that sent them both flying back. The chamber crumbled around them, and for one brief, deafening moment, the entire temple seemed to collapse inward, as if the very heart of the curse had imploded, consuming everything in its path.

Then, as quickly as it had started, everything went still.

The world around them was quiet. The walls of the temple were crumbling, the dark ooze slowly receding into the cracks in the stone. The echoes of the Hollow Man's laugh faded, and the oppressive energy that had filled the air was gone, leaving only the smell of dust and ruin in its wake.

Victor was on his feet, dusting himself off, his face grim but resolute. He looked down at Evelyn, his expression unreadable.

"It's over," he said quietly. "We did it."

But Evelyn could still feel the faint echo of the Heart's pulse within her. Its grip had loosened, but the damage had been done. She had survived, but she knew the Heart would never be entirely gone from her.

The curse had been broken, but its mark would remain.

And so, as they left the ruins of the temple behind them, Evelyn couldn't help but wonder: **Had they truly destroyed the Heart, or had they simply delayed its inevitable return?**

Evelyn stood shakily, her body still buzzing with residual energy from the Heart's final explosion. Her legs felt weak beneath her, as if the very ground had been pulled from under her feet, but she forced herself to take a step. And then another.

Victor was already moving toward the exit of the chamber, his steps swift and purposeful, though his expression remained grave. Evelyn couldn't blame him. They had just narrowly escaped an ancient curse, but the victory felt hollow. The Heart's destruction had shattered something in the temple, but whether it was the curse itself or merely the physical vessel of its power, she couldn't say. The air still felt thick with something she couldn't quite place—something dark and lingering, as though they had not erased the Heart, but only made it dormant.

They stepped over the shattered remnants of the stone floor, the cracks yawning like open wounds, swallowing the light from their torches. The deeper they ventured into the ruins, the more the oppressive silence weighed on them. The echoes of their footsteps reverberated off the walls, but there was no sound of pursuit. No more laughter from the Hollow Man. No ominous crackling of the Heart's pulse.

But Evelyn couldn't shake the feeling that they weren't truly free. She glanced at Victor, his face lit by the flickering flame, and saw a flicker of something in his eyes—something she had seen before, but couldn't quite place. Fear? Regret? Or was it just the weariness of someone who had been too close to an ancient, unspeakable power for far too long?

"Victor," she said, her voice hoarse. She could feel the weight of the question on the tip of her tongue, but when it finally left her lips, it came out softer than she intended. "Do you think it's really over?"

Victor paused, his hand still resting on the stone doorframe as he surveyed the broken temple. The once-mighty structure now felt like a hollowed-out shell, its grandeur reduced to rubble.

"I don't know," he said after a long pause, turning to meet her gaze. "But I don't think we'll ever be free of its influence, not entirely."

Her heart sank at the finality in his voice. **Not entirely.** She had known, deep down, that there would be no clear resolution, no easy conclusion to this battle. The Heart's power was ancient and unfathomable—it couldn't just be destroyed with a single strike. It could take years to fully understand the extent of its reach, or worse, it could awaken again when they least expected it. The curse might be dormant, but the damage it had done to them—specifically to her—would leave scars.

Victor took a deep breath, his eyes narrowing as if he, too, was wrestling with the enormity of their actions. "We might have delayed it. But we both know there's more to the Heart than just what's left in this temple. It's tied to something bigger—something older."

Evelyn nodded, though the words tasted like ash in her mouth. "And if it comes back?"

"Then we'll be ready," Victor said, his tone resolute, though there was a flicker of uncertainty beneath it. "We'll face it together."

She forced herself to believe him, but the image of the Heart's final, pulsing light haunted her. The creature inside it, that terrible, dark presence, was something beyond their understanding. And though they had survived this trial, Evelyn couldn't shake the feeling that they had only just begun to unravel the true consequences of their actions.

As they walked out of the ruined temple, leaving the broken stones behind, Evelyn felt the weight of what was yet to come settling upon her shoulders. The Heart might be silenced for now, but its shadow would follow them, lingering in the corners of their lives, waiting for the right moment to return.

The journey was far from over.

Chapter 17: Echoes of the Heart

The journey back to the city felt longer than it had any right to be. The sky was streaked with the dying colors of the setting sun, painting the clouds in hues of orange and purple that seemed too beautiful for the dark weight hanging over Evelyn's mind. The air was thick with the promise of rain, but there was no release—just the oppressive humidity pressing down on her like a physical force.

Evelyn's steps were slow, her body heavy with exhaustion. She had felt drained before, but nothing like this. It was as if the Heart's energy had not just been within her, but had intertwined with her very soul, leaving an imprint that would never fade. She could still feel it, an echo deep in her chest, like the soft beat of a distant drum. It was silent now, almost imperceptible, but it was there, lurking beneath the surface, waiting to surge again when the time was right.

Victor walked beside her, his face hard, set in a grim line. He had barely spoken since they had left the temple, his thoughts lost somewhere in the depths of their shared ordeal. Evelyn didn't know what he was thinking—whether he had the same unsettling sense of dread or if he was simply processing the weight of everything they had just faced.

The dense forest that had surrounded the temple now gave way to a narrow dirt road leading back to the nearest village. The familiar sights of civilization felt like an illusion—like stepping into a dream from which they could not wake. The distant rumble of thunder echoed across the sky, and Evelyn's pulse quickened. Every step felt too loud, too heavy, as if something in the world had shifted and she had missed the warning.

When they reached the village, the streets were strangely quiet. Most of the townspeople had retreated inside their homes, seeking shelter from the impending storm. The few that remained on the streets glanced at them with wary eyes, as if sensing something off about the pair. Evelyn couldn't blame them. She felt just as out of place.

"We need to find a place to rest," Victor finally spoke, his voice rough, his eyes scanning the dimly lit street. "We'll figure out what to do next."

Evelyn nodded, but the words didn't sit well with her. What *was* next? She had gone into the temple with a singular goal—destroy the Heart, end the curse. But now that it was over, now that they had done what they thought they needed to do, Evelyn felt as if she was stumbling through the dark, trying to find her way forward.

The storm was getting closer, the wind picking up as the first drops of rain began to fall. The village, though quiet, was not entirely without life. The sound of a door creaking open ahead of them caught her attention. A figure emerged from the shadows, a tall man with a hunched posture and a long, ragged cloak.

At first, Evelyn thought it was just another weary traveler. But as the man stepped closer, she felt a cold shiver race down her spine. Something about him was wrong. It wasn't the way he walked, or the fact that he was alone in such weather—it was the dark energy that seemed to radiate from him, like a shadow that clung to his every step.

Victor tensed beside her, his hand subtly moving toward the dagger at his belt. "Stay alert," he muttered under his breath, but Evelyn didn't need his warning. She felt it too—the unmistakable feeling of danger, the cold presence that stirred something deep inside her.

The man stopped a few feet from them, his pale eyes gleaming from beneath his hood. His face was obscured in shadows, but his voice, when he spoke, was smooth and cold.

"You've done it," the man said. His tone was almost congratulatory, though there was no warmth in it. "You've awakened the Heart."

Evelyn's heart skipped a beat. "What do you mean?" she demanded, taking a step back. "We destroyed it. It's over."

The man's lips curled into a thin, almost amused smile. "Destroyed it?" He chuckled, but there was no humor in the sound. "No, child. You have merely *delayed* its inevitable return."

Victor stepped in front of her, his stance protective, his eyes narrowing. "Who are you?"

The man didn't answer immediately. Instead, he reached up and lowered his hood, revealing his face. It was pale, too pale, with sharp features that seemed unnaturally angular. His hair was dark, almost black, but it was streaked with something that looked like ash. His eyes—they were the worst of it. Black as coal, but with a faint, flickering light deep within them. As if they had seen something no human should ever witness.

"I am someone who knows what you've done," the man replied finally. "And I'm here to make sure it doesn't destroy you."

Evelyn felt a chill run through her. "What do you want from us?"

The man studied her for a long moment, his gaze unsettling in its intensity. Then, with a slow and deliberate motion, he reached into the folds of his cloak and pulled out a small, intricately carved wooden box. He held it out to her.

"I came to offer you a choice," he said, his voice soft, almost coaxing. "Take this, and you may yet survive what you've unleashed."

Victor moved forward, his eyes locked on the box. "What's inside?" he asked, his voice low and wary.

The man didn't answer directly. Instead, he nodded toward Evelyn, as if waiting for her to make the decision.

Evelyn hesitated, her pulse quickening as she looked from the box to the man's inscrutable face. There was something about him—something deeply unsettling—that made her want to refuse. But a part of her, the part still haunted by the echoes of the Heart, felt an undeniable pull toward the box.

"What's in it?" she asked again, her voice steadier than she felt.

"The Heart's legacy," the man replied cryptically. "A way to ensure that it does not consume you, that it does not control you. A means of *sealing* the curse."

The word "seal" sent a cold shiver through her. "And if we don't take it?" she asked, already knowing the answer but needing to hear it.

"Then the Heart will rise again," he said simply. "And everything you've fought for will be lost. You will be lost."

Victor's hand tightened on the hilt of his dagger, but he said nothing. Evelyn knew what he was thinking—how could they trust this man? How could they trust anyone after everything they'd been through?

But the fear, the uncertainty, gnawed at her. Could they risk turning away from the only option they had? Could they bear the consequences if the Heart truly wasn't gone?

"Take it," the man said, his voice insistent now. "And you may yet live to see the end of this. Refuse, and you will regret it."

Evelyn reached for the box before she could think better of it. The moment her fingers brushed against the smooth surface of the wood, a shock of cold raced up her arm, and the sensation of the Heart's pulse—faint but unmistakable—surged through her once more.

With a heavy heart and a mind full of questions, Evelyn opened the box.

Inside was a simple, unassuming black stone, no larger than the palm of her hand. It seemed ordinary, even mundane, but there was something about it—something that felt deeply ancient. The stone thrummed with an energy that resonated deep within her bones, a familiar energy, the same that had surged through her in the temple.

The man's voice broke the silence again. "This is the only way to bind the Heart's curse to you permanently. To ensure it never rises again."

Evelyn closed her fingers around the stone, feeling its coldness seep into her skin. Her mind screamed in warning, but there was no turning back. Whatever this man was offering, it was the only choice they had left.

"Will it work?" she asked, her voice barely above a whisper.

The man's gaze softened, just for a moment. "That, my dear, is the question you will need to answer yourself."

Evelyn's fingers tightened around the stone. The sensation of its cold, smooth surface sent a shiver up her spine, its pulse reverberating through her fingertips. For a moment, she stood frozen, unsure whether to pull her hand away or clutch it even harder. The man who stood before them, his black eyes gleaming like dark mirrors, seemed to be waiting for her reaction, as though he knew something she didn't—something she desperately needed to understand.

Victor's hand twitched near his dagger, but he made no move to draw it. His eyes were fixed on the stone, then flicked back to the man with an intensity that bordered on dangerous. His jaw was clenched tight, and there was a coldness to his gaze that Evelyn rarely saw. He was always the pragmatic one, calculating, weighing the consequences. But now... now, he seemed lost, just as she was.

"I don't trust him," Victor muttered under his breath, but the words weren't for Evelyn—they were meant more for himself. He took a step back, clearly on edge. "Whatever's in that box, Evelyn, it's not something we should accept without knowing what we're dealing with."

Evelyn didn't answer immediately. Her mind was racing, flooded with conflicting thoughts. The stone was powerful, she could feel it. But there was something unsettling about the way the man spoke, the way he had appeared out of nowhere at exactly the right moment—*too* conveniently. Was he truly offering them a chance to end this nightmare, or was this just another layer of the curse, a new trap they were walking into?

"Victor..." she began, but her voice faltered. The storm was closer now, the wind picking up, the clouds swirling in ominous patterns overhead. The air felt alive with tension, as if the very earth was holding its breath. "What if he's right? What if the Heart will come back if we don't do this?"

Victor was silent for a moment, his gaze hardening. "What if he's lying to us? What if this is exactly what the Heart *wants* us to do?"

There was a long pause as the two of them stood there, caught between fear and the impossible weight of the choice before them. The man, who had not spoken again, seemed to sense their hesitation. His lips curled into a thin, knowing smile, and he stepped forward, closer to them. His presence felt like a chill settling over the very ground they stood on, a force that seemed to draw the warmth from the air.

"I don't have the luxury of time," he said softly, his voice an unsettling calm amidst the rising storm. "The Heart has already marked you. You will feel its influence, its hunger, until you accept what I offer. It will never let you go, not without this."

Evelyn swallowed, looking down at the stone in her hand once more. It felt like a weight that threatened to drag her under, but she couldn't bring herself to let go. It had a power that resonated with the Heart's, and it felt like the only lifeline in a sea of uncertainty.

She wanted to ask him more. To demand answers. Who was he? What did he know about the Heart? How could he be so sure that this stone was the key to ending it? But the man wasn't going to give her any clear answers. She could see it in his eyes—he was not here to explain things, but to offer an ultimatum. To force her hand.

She glanced at Victor, whose face had gone pale, but his eyes were sharp. There was a flicker of something in them—a flash of determination. He had made his mind up.

"No," he said, voice low but firm. "We don't know what that stone does. We don't know who you are, and we certainly don't know what you want from us. But I'll tell you this—*no one* controls us. Not you, and not the Heart."

The man's smile widened, but there was no humor in it—just cold amusement. "You misunderstand me," he said softly, almost pityingly. "I'm not here to control you. I'm here to offer you the chance to survive what you've unleashed. I'm here to ensure the Heart doesn't consume you, that it doesn't twist your minds and your bodies into something... far worse."

The words hung in the air, thick and heavy with implication. Evelyn's heart skipped a beat. She looked at Victor again, trying to read his expression. They were both scared—terrified, really—but Evelyn knew they had no choice. The Heart had already changed her, and if they didn't find a way to stop it, it would keep coming for her, for them, until nothing was left.

"What do we do?" she asked, her voice small but resolute. "What if we accept the stone? What happens then?"

The man's expression softened, just slightly, as if he had been expecting her to ask that very question. He took a step closer, lowering his voice. "The stone will bind the Heart's curse to you. It will absorb its power and lock it inside you. You will live, but you will be tethered to it, forever. It will be a part of you."

Evelyn's chest tightened at the thought. *Forever*. She had been so desperate to rid herself of the Heart's influence, to break free of its insidious power, and now she was being told that there was no escaping it—not really.

Victor's voice broke through her spiraling thoughts. "And if we don't accept it?"

"Then the Heart will return. It will reclaim what it's lost. And you will be destroyed. The curse will break free again, and this time, it will not be so easily contained."

"Destroy us?" Evelyn repeated, her throat tightening. "What does that mean?"

The man's eyes glittered with something unreadable. "It means you will become its vessel—its *host*—just as others before you have. You will be twisted and reshaped into something that is no longer human. The Heart will consume you from the inside out, until nothing remains of your former selves."

The words hit her like a physical blow. A host. A vessel. She could already feel the Heart's influence crawling through her veins, deep inside her, and the thought of it growing stronger, taking over every part of her, was unbearable.

"Why... why are you helping us?" Evelyn finally asked, her voice trembling. "What's in it for you?"

The man's smile returned, though it didn't reach his eyes. "I'm not helping you, child. I'm simply offering you a choice. It's not about me. It's about you and the Heart. *You* are the ones who awakened it. *You* are the ones who will face the consequences."

Victor moved closer, and Evelyn felt his hand on her arm, steadying her. She wanted to ask more, to pry deeper, but the storm was getting closer, and the oppressive weight of the moment was closing in around them. Every second they waited seemed to stretch longer than the last. Finally, she looked down at the stone again.

"This stone... If we take it... there's no turning back, is there?"

"No," the man replied softly. "There isn't."

Victor's face was hard, his expression unreadable. But Evelyn could see the conflict in his eyes. They both knew what had to be done, even if it felt wrong. There were no other options.

Taking a deep breath, Evelyn slowly placed the stone back into the man's outstretched hand. "We'll take it."

Victor's gaze flicked over to her in surprise, but he said nothing. The man nodded, his thin lips pulling into a satisfied smile as he took the stone from her hand.

"It is done," he said quietly. "But remember, Evelyn—*you* chose this. The Heart is not gone. It is simply *bound*. And if you ever break the bond, it will consume you without hesitation."

The man turned to leave, his cloak billowing behind him as he disappeared into the mist that had begun to creep along the road. The storm finally broke overhead, a flash of lightning lighting the sky, followed by the deafening roar of thunder.

Evelyn stood there for a moment, her mind spinning, the weight of the decision sinking in.

"What now?" she whispered, more to herself than to Victor.

Victor stepped up beside her, his hand brushing hers briefly. "We deal with what comes next. Together."

But Evelyn couldn't shake the feeling that the true test was only just beginning. The Heart may have been bound to her, but it was far from gone.

As the man disappeared into the darkening mist, Evelyn stood frozen for a moment, her gaze lingering on the spot where he had vanished. The air around her was thick with a strange, metallic scent—the storm was coming, but it felt like something more. The weight of the black stone in her hand seemed to grow heavier by the second. She had accepted it, but the implications of that decision were beginning to gnaw at her insides, a slow, creeping doubt.

Victor moved beside her, his steps quiet in the damp earth. The storm loomed just above them now, the clouds churning angrily overhead. The first crack of thunder sent a ripple through the air, as though nature itself was protesting the choice they had made. For a brief moment, the night seemed to hold its breath.

"Victor," Evelyn said, her voice hoarse, "do you think we did the right thing?"

The question hung in the air between them, unanswered. They both knew the truth—*no one* could know if it was the right thing. There were no guarantees, no clear path forward. All they had was the stone, and the man's cryptic words. The Heart was *bound*, not destroyed.

"I don't know," Victor finally replied, his voice strained with an edge of uncertainty. "But I can't help but feel like we've made a deal with something far worse than we imagined."

Evelyn nodded, the weight of his words settling like a stone in her stomach. She had hoped, when they entered the temple, that they would find a way to sever their connection to the Heart for good. That they could leave that place and never look back. But instead, they had just sealed their fate. The Heart's power might be dormant within them now, but its presence was still there, lingering like a shadow they couldn't shake.

A low rumble of thunder echoed in the distance, and the first few raindrops began to fall, tapping softly against the ground. Evelyn closed her hand around the stone once more, feeling its coldness seep into her skin. She could sense it now, the faintest tremor beneath her ribs, as though the Heart were waiting, still *alive*, even if it was bound.

"The Heart's still in us, isn't it?" she asked, her voice quiet but filled with a sense of finality. "Even with the stone, it hasn't gone away."

Victor met her gaze, his expression unreadable. "It's inside you," he said. "Inside both of us. The man wasn't lying about that. We've bound it, but not destroyed it."

Evelyn felt a sickening jolt in her chest at the truth of his words. For all their efforts, the Heart had not been eradicated. It had simply been trapped. And the thought of carrying it within her forever, like a parasite feeding off her life force, was unbearable. She squeezed her eyes shut for a moment, trying to block out the gnawing panic that threatened to rise in her throat.

"What happens now?" she whispered, almost to herself.

"We keep moving," Victor said, taking a step forward. His voice was steady, but there was something in his eyes—a flicker of doubt that he didn't want to acknowledge. "We find out what we need to do next. We find a way to keep it contained."

"And if we can't?" Evelyn asked, her voice cracking. She hated the question, but it was one they both had to face. What if the stone wasn't enough? What if they were just delaying the inevitable?

Victor didn't answer immediately. Instead, he walked a few paces, letting the sound of the rain fill the air around them. The storm was starting to intensify, the rain now falling in sheets, drenching everything in its path.

"I don't know," he said quietly, his voice strained. "But we can't afford to dwell on it. Not now."

Evelyn watched him for a moment, taking in the weariness in his face. He was right. They couldn't afford to break down now, not when they still had so much left to face. The Heart was still a threat, but they couldn't let it consume them—*not yet*. They had to keep moving. They had to figure out how to live with the curse, or they would both be lost.

"I'm sorry," she said, her voice barely audible. She hadn't meant to say it, but the words came out anyway. "For everything."

Victor stopped and turned back toward her, his expression softening. He shook his head slowly, as though dismissing her apology before she could say more. "None of this was your fault, Evelyn. We did what we had to do. The Heart's curse was already in motion before we even got to the temple."

She nodded, but the guilt still clung to her. She had started this—she had been the one to seek out the Heart, to find a way to destroy it. But in doing so, she had made things worse, far worse than she could have imagined.

"There has to be something we can do," she said, the words raw with desperation. "We can't just... live with this forever. We can't *let* it control us."

Victor looked down at her, his face unreadable in the dim light. "We'll figure it out," he said quietly. "We always do."

But Evelyn couldn't shake the feeling that they were running out of time. She had felt the pulse of the Heart within her, felt the way it stirred when she touched the stone. It wasn't gone, not by a long shot. And whatever it was, whatever *it* wanted, it would find a way to claim them both.

The storm had fully broken now. The rain fell in torrents, and the wind howled through the trees. The village was far behind them, and the road ahead stretched into a shadowy unknown. Evelyn could feel the pull of the Heart, faint but unmistakable, like a whisper in the back of her mind.

Victor pulled his cloak tighter around him, his jaw set with determination. "We can't stay here," he said. "We need to keep moving. We need to find answers. The longer we wait, the more dangerous this gets."

Evelyn nodded silently. The storm was only a backdrop to the storm inside her. The Heart was *bound*, but that didn't mean it was powerless. And she was beginning to understand that the true battle was only just beginning.

They traveled through the rain-soaked night, the world around them blurring into a wet, dark haze. The road ahead seemed endless, and the landscape unfamiliar, as if they had stepped into a different world altogether. The black stone rested heavily in Evelyn's hand, its cold surface a constant reminder of the curse that clung to her like a second skin. The man's warning echoed in her mind—*you are tethered to it now, and if you break the bond, it will consume you.*

Evelyn didn't know what breaking the bond would mean. But the thought of living with the Heart inside her, of being its vessel forever, was just as terrifying. She could feel it, pulsing faintly inside her—*alive*, waiting, biding its time.

But there was no turning back now.

They needed answers. They needed to understand the true nature of the Heart and how to *end* this once and for all. But in the quiet of the night, as the rain soaked through her cloak and the world seemed to close in around them, Evelyn couldn't shake the feeling that they were being watched. That the Heart—*or someone else*—was already moving against them.

And no matter how far they ran, she knew deep down that the Heart was never going to let them go.

Chapter 18: The Tethered Path

Evelyn's boots sank into the soft earth as they trekked through the dense, rain-drenched forest. The night was a murky swirl of shadows, mist, and the steady rhythm of the downpour. Every step she took felt heavier than the last, as though the very soil beneath her feet was trying to hold her in place, to stop her from moving forward. But she couldn't stop—not now, not when there was so much at stake.

The black stone was cold in her palm, an unsettling weight she couldn't shake, no matter how tightly she gripped it. The pulse of its energy had settled beneath her skin, a constant hum in the back of her mind. At times, it felt as though the stone was trying to reach out to the very heart of her soul, probing, testing, waiting. She tried to ignore it, but she could feel it growing stronger with every passing hour.

Victor walked a few paces ahead, his broad shoulders hunched against the storm. His cloak billowed behind him, though it barely shielded him from the downpour. He was always the more resilient of the two, the one who could weather the storm—both literal and metaphorical—with an unshaken resolve. But tonight, Evelyn could see the strain in his every movement. The heartache, the fatigue, the mounting pressure of their shared burden. He had always been the protector, the one who kept the darkness at bay, but she could feel the weight of his own doubts pressing on him now.

She had seen the change in him ever since they accepted the black stone. It wasn't just the curse—there was something else, something more primal, that had settled in his eyes. A coldness. A wariness. As though, deep down, he feared that they had made a terrible mistake.

"Victor," she called out, her voice barely audible over the crashing rain.

He stopped and turned, wiping the rain from his face, his eyes narrowing as they met hers. For a moment, he said nothing. Just stood there, a silent sentinel in the rain, his gaze unreadable.

"I feel it," she said, her voice faltering. "It's getting worse, isn't it?"

Victor let out a heavy sigh, looking away toward the darkened woods, as though seeking guidance from the towering trees. He didn't want to answer, but he couldn't hide it any longer. "Yes," he said quietly, "it's getting worse. The stone—it's changing you, Evelyn. It's changing us."

The weight of his words hung in the air, thicker than the damp fog surrounding them. The Heart, bound to them by the stone, was no longer a mere whisper in the back of their minds—it was becoming a presence. A constant, hungry pulse that resonated with every step they took, every breath they drew. It was there, in the way Evelyn felt the stone's power surging through her veins, in the way her thoughts sometimes grew distant and strange, as though the Heart was trying to take hold again.

"But what else can we do?" Evelyn asked, her voice breaking. "We can't undo it. We've already bound it to us."

Victor didn't respond at first, and for a long while, they simply stood there, drenched in the rain, the weight of their decision pressing on them both. The stone was a tether now, one they couldn't sever, not without risking everything. They had no choice but to continue, to search for answers, to understand what the stone meant and how they could keep it from consuming them completely.

"I don't know, Evelyn," Victor finally said, his voice rough with the unspoken fear he was hiding. "We're in uncharted territory now. We were supposed to destroy the Heart, not become part of it. And I don't think we're ready for whatever's coming next."

Evelyn's chest tightened. She wanted to argue, to tell him that they could figure it out, that they had to. But deep down, she knew he was right. Every step they took forward felt like a step deeper into unknown territory. The Heart wasn't just a curse anymore—it was part of them. It had become something they couldn't escape.

With a deep breath, she pressed her fingers to the stone, feeling its power thrumming in her palm. "We'll figure it out," she said, trying to convince herself as much as him. "We don't have any other choice."

Victor's expression softened for a moment, but it quickly hardened again. "We need to find a place to take shelter. There's no point in pushing forward in this storm. We'll be more vulnerable if we keep moving."

Evelyn nodded, reluctant to admit that he was right. As much as she wanted to press on, her body was screaming for rest, for a moment of calm. The storm was relentless, and the night seemed endless. The road they walked was treacherous, winding through dense forest that seemed to stretch on forever. The trees were ancient, their gnarled branches reaching toward the sky like skeletal arms, and the ground was slick with rain and mud.

Victor led the way, his instincts sharp as ever, despite the toll of the curse. After some time, they came across a small, half-dilapidated cabin hidden deep in the woods. It was isolated, a simple structure built of dark timber, its windows fogged from the inside. The door creaked as Victor pushed it open, and the stale air of the cabin greeted them, smelling faintly of mold and wood rot. But it was dry. And for the moment, that was all they needed.

Victor closed the door behind them, locking it with a quick, practiced motion. They stood for a moment in the dim light, listening to the rain pounding against the roof. Evelyn's muscles ached from the cold and the tension that had built up over the last few hours. She was grateful for the respite, but a new anxiety gnawed at her—*the stone was still with them.* It was only a matter of time before they faced the consequences of their decision.

Victor moved toward the hearth, quickly striking a match to light the dry wood he had gathered earlier. The fire crackled to life, casting flickering shadows across the walls of the cabin. He pulled off his wet cloak and shook it out, draping it over a nearby chair.

"Sit down," he said, his voice more firm than it had been outside. "You're exhausted. We both are."

Evelyn didn't argue. She sat, sinking into a chair by the fire, the warmth beginning to seep into her chilled bones. But even as the heat of the fire started to thaw her, the cold weight of the black stone never left her hand. It was always there, a constant reminder of what they had done.

Victor joined her, sitting on the other side of the fire. He looked at her for a long moment, his dark eyes studying her in a way that felt both comforting and unnerving at the same time.

"What's happening to you, Evelyn?" he asked softly, his voice tinged with concern. "I can see it—something's changing. You're not the same."

Evelyn swallowed, her throat tight with emotions she couldn't put into words. "I don't know," she whispered. "I don't know what's happening, Victor. But I can feel it. The stone... it's *pulling* me."

Victor leaned forward, his gaze sharp. "What do you mean, it's pulling you?"

Evelyn hesitated. Her mind was swirling with strange, fragmented thoughts—visions that weren't her own, whispers she couldn't quite understand. She closed her eyes, trying to block them out, but they were relentless. The stone *wanted something* from her.

"I'm hearing things," she said, her voice strained. "Voices... fragments. The Heart. It's calling me, Victor. It's not gone. It's inside me, and it wants... something. I don't know what. But it's getting stronger."

Victor's face hardened, but his eyes softened with a flicker of something like fear—fear for her, for both of them. He reached out and took her hand gently, squeezing it tightly.

"We'll get through this," he said, his voice firm, even though the doubt was still there in the way his fingers trembled ever so slightly against hers. "We'll figure out what's happening. Together."

The fire crackled between them, casting its warm glow, but it did little to dispel the chill that had settled in Evelyn's heart. The stone, the curse, the Heart—it was all part of them now, tethered to their very souls. And no matter how hard they tried to push it away, no matter how far they ran, Evelyn knew one undeniable truth.

The Heart was never truly gone.

It was just waiting.

The fire crackled in the hearth, the dancing flames casting long, shifting shadows on the walls of the cabin. Evelyn sat with her hands clasped tightly around her knees, her body drawn in on itself, as if trying to keep the world at bay. The stone, now resting in her lap, pulsed faintly beneath her fingers, as though alive—alive and waiting.

Victor sat across from her, his eyes fixed on the flames, but his mind was far from the comforting warmth they provided. His thoughts churned, restless. The silence between them had grown thick, the weight of their situation hanging heavily in the air. They had made their choice, accepted the stone, and yet the consequences were far more complicated than they could have imagined. Evelyn's face, pale in the flickering light, spoke volumes—*she was changing*.

Victor didn't want to admit it, but he could see the subtle shift in her. The way her eyes sometimes went distant, the faint tremor in her hands, the whispers that seemed to haunt her whenever she wasn't paying attention. He had heard her earlier, the strain in her voice when she spoke of the Heart calling to her, but he had hoped that it was just a passing thing. Now, he wasn't so sure.

He couldn't tell her how much it terrified him to see her like this—how the power of the stone seemed to be taking hold of her mind, her very essence. He wasn't sure how much longer he could protect her from the forces that had already begun to creep into their lives.

"Evelyn," he said softly, his voice cutting through the thick silence. "Tell me what you're feeling. Be honest. I need to know."

Her head snapped up at the sound of his voice, as if she had forgotten he was even there. The faintest flicker of fear passed over her face before she quickly masked it with a forced calmness.

"I told you, I'm fine," she said, her voice betraying her as it wavered, uncertain. "It's just... the stone. It's strange, Victor. It feels like it's alive, like it's trying to... communicate with me. And sometimes, I hear... things. Voices. But it's not clear. It's like a distant whisper, just beyond reach."

Victor's chest tightened at the admission, though he tried to hide it. He had seen the way the stone had affected them both, how their connection to it seemed to draw them deeper into a world they didn't understand. It was clear now—there was no simple solution to this. No easy way to rid themselves of the curse. If anything, they had just opened a door to something far darker.

"The Heart," he said, his voice low and heavy, "it's bound to you. And now to me. But if what you're hearing is true—if the stone is really reaching out to you—then we're not just carrying it. It's... it's trying to *take* you."

Evelyn's breath caught at his words, her grip tightening involuntarily on the stone. "What do you mean?"

Victor swallowed hard, leaning forward, his brow furrowed in deep thought. "It's not just dormant inside us. It's *feeding* off our emotions, our weaknesses. And if it can manipulate our thoughts, our desires... it could take control."

The chill in his voice made Evelyn's blood run cold. *Take control.* The very idea that the Heart, the cursed force that had already claimed so many lives, could overtake her—that it could twist her into something she didn't recognize—was the most terrifying thought she had ever entertained.

"No," she whispered, almost to herself. "It won't. I won't let it."

Victor met her gaze, his eyes filled with concern, but his tone was urgent. "Evelyn, we can't be too sure of that. We can't risk it. The longer we wait, the more dangerous it becomes."

She nodded silently, her gaze shifting to the stone once more. She could feel it, the weight of its power pressing against her chest. Every time she closed her eyes, she saw flashes of images—unfamiliar faces, fragmented memories, and the overwhelming sensation of something *watching* her. The Heart was still there, lurking just beneath the surface.

"I'll fight it," she said, her voice steady, though her mind screamed with doubt. "I won't let it consume me."

Victor stood and moved across the cabin, his footsteps soft but deliberate. He retrieved his pack and began to rummage through it, though his actions seemed mechanical, as if his mind was elsewhere. He had always been the practical one, the one who focused on survival when everything else seemed to crumble. But now, even he seemed lost in thought.

"We need to figure out what the next step is," he said, not looking up from his pack. "We can't stay here long. The longer we're in one place, the more vulnerable we become."

Evelyn didn't answer. She had been thinking the same thing. They couldn't afford to remain stagnant. If they were to find answers, if they were to free themselves from the Heart's hold, they had to keep moving. But the road ahead was uncertain, and Evelyn wasn't sure how much longer she could keep going, not with the stone burning a hole in her mind.

Victor seemed to sense her unease. He paused, turning to face her, his expression softening. "We'll figure it out," he said, though the doubt in his voice was clear. "We have to."

Evelyn nodded once more, though she couldn't quite bring herself to meet his eyes. Her own thoughts were spinning, a whirlwind of uncertainty and fear. The Heart had been bound within them, but how much control did they really have? How much time before it began to take over completely?

The door to the cabin creaked, and Evelyn's head jerked toward the sound. She hadn't heard anyone approach. Her heart skipped a beat, and for a moment, she thought she could feel the presence of something—someone—just outside the door. Her breath quickened, and she grasped the stone more tightly, as if it could somehow protect her.

Victor was already moving toward the door, his body tense, prepared for whatever might be on the other side. He reached for the handle slowly, cautiously. But before he could open it, the door burst inward with a force that nearly threw him back.

A figure stood in the doorway, silhouetted by the storm outside, drenched from head to toe. The figure was tall, thin, with long, dripping hair that obscured most of their face. A hooded cloak clung to their frame, the edges frayed and torn, as if it had been through much worse than the rain.

For a moment, neither Victor nor Evelyn moved, both of them startled by the sudden appearance. But then, as the figure stepped further into the cabin, the dim light from the fire illuminated their features. The stranger's face was pale, their eyes wide and bright in the shadows—eyes that gleamed with a strange, unsettling intensity.

"Who are you?" Evelyn demanded, her hand instinctively reaching for the dagger at her side.

The figure didn't answer at first. They simply stepped further into the cabin, their gaze shifting between Evelyn and Victor, as though measuring them both.

"You've come for it," the figure said, their voice low, but unmistakable. "You've come for the Heart."

Evelyn's heart skipped in her chest. Her grip on the stone tightened, her knuckles white as she stepped back. "What do you know about the Heart?" she demanded.

The figure's lips curled into a thin smile. "I know more than you could ever imagine. But it's not the Heart that's important. It's the stone you carry—the one that binds it to you."

Victor's hand went to the hilt of his sword, his posture defensive. "We didn't ask for your help," he said, his voice edged with suspicion.

The stranger chuckled softly, a sound that seemed too hollow, too knowing. "You can't outrun what's inside of you. And it's already too late for both of you."

Evelyn's pulse quickened, a cold chill creeping up her spine. The stranger's words seemed to cut through the cabin like a blade. *It's already too late.* The very idea made her blood run cold. Could it be true? Had the Heart already started its insidious work, binding them so deeply to its will that escape was impossible?

The stranger took a step closer, their gaze locked on Evelyn's.

"You can try to fight it," they said. "But there's no running from the Heart. It owns you now. And soon, it will claim you completely."

Victor stepped in front of Evelyn, his hand resting on the hilt of his sword. "Get out," he said coldly. "We don't need your cryptic warnings."

The figure smiled once more, their eyes glinting with something almost... predatory. "You'll need more than swords to survive what's coming. You've made a dangerous choice. And I'm afraid there's no turning back now."

With that, the figure turned and melted back into the storm, leaving the door wide open behind them.

Evelyn and Victor stood there, hearts pounding, staring at the now-empty doorway. The storm raged outside, the wind howling through the trees. But inside the cabin, the silence was suffocating.

For the first time since they had taken the stone, Evelyn felt the full weight of their choice.

It was too late. They were already tethered to the Heart.

Chapter 19: The Weights of Fate

The storm continued to rage outside, howling through the trees with a ferocity that rattled the wooden frame of the cabin. The fire flickered in the hearth, its warmth almost mocking the cold dread that had settled into Evelyn's chest. The stranger had come and gone, leaving behind nothing but a cryptic warning that gnawed at her thoughts, sinking into her like a stone into water.

It's too late.

The words echoed in her mind, relentless, like the pounding rain on the roof. There was no escape, no going back. The Heart—the thing they had thought they could destroy, the thing they had bound themselves to—was no longer just a distant threat. It was here, with them, inside them.

Evelyn stared into the fire, her hands trembling despite the warmth. The stone, still clutched in her palm, seemed to thrum with a life of its own, sending pulses of cold through her body, as though it were reaching out to her. She could feel it—an insidious presence, like a shadow in the corner of her vision, waiting for the right moment to pounce.

She wanted to scream, to throw the stone into the fire and watch it burn. But she couldn't. It was a part of her now, a tether she could never sever. She was bound to it, just as Victor was.

Victor.

She turned toward him. He was sitting near the door, his back against the cold, wooden wall, staring out into the night. His face was shadowed, his eyes distant. His silence, once comforting, was now suffocating. She had seen the change in him over the past few days—the same change that was creeping through her. The stone was pulling them both in, twisting them slowly, inexorably.

Evelyn opened her mouth to speak, but the words didn't come. What could she say? What was there to say when everything felt like it was slipping through her fingers?

"I don't trust them," Victor's voice cut through the stillness, low and tense.

Evelyn blinked, startled by the sudden break in the silence. She hadn't realized how much time had passed since the stranger had left. Her thoughts had become so tangled, so overwhelming, that time itself seemed to stretch and distort.

"Who?" she asked quietly.

"The ones who sent that... *thing* to us," Victor muttered, his voice rough with a mixture of anger and fear. "Whoever they are, whatever they want—they know about the stone. They know what it does to us."

Evelyn nodded, though her mind was still racing. "Do you think they're the reason we found the stone in the first place?"

Victor didn't answer right away. He rubbed a hand over his face, as if trying to shake off the exhaustion that had settled deep in his bones. "I don't know. I don't know anything anymore. All I know is that we can't trust anyone. And if we don't find a way to destroy the stone, we're both doomed."

Evelyn's stomach tightened at the word. *Doomed.* It wasn't a word she liked to entertain. They had made mistakes, yes. But it wasn't too late to fix things, was it?

The fire crackled and popped, sending sparks dancing up the chimney. But the warmth from the fire couldn't chase away the chill in the air, the growing unease that tightened in her chest. The walls of the cabin, once a safe refuge, now felt like a cage. No matter how far they ran, how many miles they traveled, they couldn't escape the stone. The Heart was always there, watching, waiting.

She glanced down at the stone again. Its surface was black, smooth, and unyielding. It was impossible to tell how much power it truly held, or what it wanted from them. But she could feel its weight, both physically and mentally. It was inside her, changing her, turning her into something she couldn't recognize.

"You're not the only one who's scared," Evelyn finally said, her voice trembling with a mixture of vulnerability and resolve. "I feel it too. But I won't let it take me. We can't let it take us."

Victor met her gaze then, his eyes heavy with emotion, dark with the burden of their shared curse. He pushed himself off the wall, walking toward her slowly, his expression softening. He stopped just short of reaching her, his breath coming fast, as if he, too, had been holding something back.

"How?" he asked, his voice thick with frustration. "How do we fight something we don't even understand? We've spent so long running from the Heart, but now... now we *are* the Heart. I feel it, Evelyn. It's inside me too. I can hear it. I can feel it clawing at the edges of my mind."

Evelyn stood up abruptly, her heart pounding. His words struck her harder than she expected. She had felt the changes in herself, of course—*but him?* She hadn't realized just how much the stone was consuming him as well.

Victor was a warrior, always calm and collected in the face of danger. But now, she saw the cracks in his armor, the fear in his eyes, the way his hand subconsciously brushed against the dagger at his side as if it were an anchor, grounding him to reality. The same fear that had gnawed at her now consumed him too.

"You're not alone in this," she whispered, her voice thick with emotion. "I'm here. We'll find a way."

Victor's lips parted, but he didn't speak. Instead, he reached out, his fingers brushing against the stone in her hand. For a moment, they simply stood there, the weight of the world pressing down on them.

"What if it's already too late?" he murmured, almost to himself.

Evelyn swallowed the lump in her throat. "It's never too late."

But even as she spoke the words, a cold knot of doubt twisted deep inside her. What if they were running out of time? What if they were already lost?

The fire crackled again, louder this time, the heat from the flames warming their faces but doing nothing to ease the cold that had settled in their hearts. The storm outside seemed to intensify, the wind howling like some kind of ancient beast. It was as if the earth itself were mourning their fate, and Evelyn couldn't help but wonder if the Heart had already claimed them in some small, subtle way.

She closed her eyes, forcing herself to focus. *Think. You can't give in to fear.*

"There's got to be a way," she said, her voice firm. "We just need more information. The stranger—the one who came earlier—he knew something. He said we were already tethered to the Heart. But that means there's a connection, a link, something we can use."

Victor's gaze shifted to the door, his brow furrowing. "And what if the stranger is right? What if there's no undoing it?"

Evelyn shook her head. "We have to try."

She turned toward the table in the center of the room, where the remnants of their last meal lay half-eaten, untouched. Her mind raced, trying to latch onto any fragment of hope, anything that could get them out of this mess. The stone was more than just a curse—it was a puzzle, a weapon, a key to something much greater than either of them could understand.

She picked up the stone, turning it over in her hand. The faint, almost imperceptible pulse seemed to grow stronger as her fingers brushed its surface, sending a shiver up her spine. Was this it? Was this the answer? Was the stone trying to communicate with her?

Victor, watching her, took a deep breath. "What are you thinking?"

"I think..." Evelyn hesitated, her eyes narrowing as a thought crystallized in her mind. "We need to understand the stone. We need to know where it came from, what it wants. Only then can we figure out how to stop it."

Victor nodded slowly, but there was no mistaking the unease in his gaze. "And how do you propose we do that? We don't exactly have a guidebook for dealing with ancient cursed artifacts."

Evelyn's lips pressed into a thin line. "There has to be someone who knows more. A scholar, a priestess, someone who's dealt with this kind of magic before. We can't do this alone. If we're going to survive this, we need help."

Victor took a step toward the door, his face grim. "Then let's go. We'll find them."

But even as he said the words, Evelyn felt the weight of their decision settle over her like a heavy cloak. She wasn't sure where they would find this scholar or how they would even begin to unravel the mysteries of the stone. But she knew one thing: they were running out of time. The Heart was waiting. And it wasn't going to let them go so easily.

The wind howled louder as the storm raged outside, the sound of it like some ancient creature pounding at the walls, trying to get in. Inside the cabin, the flickering fire did little to dispel the unease that had settled like a cold, unshakable fog around Evelyn and Victor. The stone in Evelyn's hand pulsed softly, and she could feel its energy working its way into her bones, filling the gaps where fear had once been, replacing it with something colder, sharper.

Victor, standing by the door, was equally lost in his thoughts. His hand rested on the hilt of his sword, but it was more a habit now, a reflex born of years spent in dangerous places. He hadn't slept properly in days, and the constant pressure of knowing that something was watching, something was *waiting* for them to slip up, gnawed at him. His body was taut, alert, every muscle ready to spring into action should they be attacked, though in truth, the greatest threat was the one they carried with them—the Heart.

"So, what now?" he asked, his voice rough from disuse, his eyes still focused on the darkened landscape outside. "We're not getting any closer to finding the answers we need by sitting here. We've got to go. We've got to move."

Evelyn raised her eyes from the stone in her hands, looking at him with a quiet intensity. She had already made up her mind. Their only option, their only chance of survival, was to seek out the answers they needed, no matter how dangerous it might be.

"We find the scholar," she said firmly. "The one who can tell us what this is. Where it came from. What it wants."

Victor glanced over at her, his expression unreadable. He'd been thinking the same thing, of course. He'd known for days now that they couldn't keep running without understanding what they were dealing with. But part of him was reluctant, unwilling to admit just how deep in they were. What if the scholar, or whoever they found, didn't have answers? What if they made things worse?

"We don't even know where to start," he muttered, dragging his hand through his hair in frustration. "We're two people with a cursed stone and nothing else. The world's big, and there are far more dangerous things out there than just a relic. Who's going to help us?"

Evelyn stood up, her jaw tight, her body drawn like a bowstring ready to snap. She had no answers, not yet. But she couldn't just sit there and let their fate consume them. They were still alive. That meant something. That meant they had a chance.

"We start by asking the right questions," she said, walking to the fire and adding another log to the flames. The crackling heat washed over her, but the cold in her chest didn't go away. *What is this?* she asked herself again, her mind spinning. "There's got to be someone who knows. Maybe not all the answers, but at least some."

Victor sighed, shaking his head, his hand still resting on the doorframe as if unwilling to let the outside world in. He didn't like the idea of venturing out into the unknown, but they didn't have many choices left. The Heart had been with them too long now. It had wormed its way into their minds, their hearts, feeding off their every fear and insecurity.

"We'll leave at first light," he said after a long pause. "Where do you think we should go?"

Evelyn's eyes flashed as she considered the possibilities. They couldn't waste time. They needed to move quickly. The longer they waited, the harder it would be to escape the grip of the Heart.

"I don't know yet," she admitted, her voice raw. "But we'll figure it out. I've heard rumors—whispers of people who can see the future, people who know ancient magic. There's a place in the mountains, a monastery. The monks there are said to understand the old ways. They might know something. We'll head there."

Victor nodded, though the tension in his shoulders remained. "We'll need supplies. We can't survive another week like this."

Evelyn agreed, though the thought of leaving the relative safety of the cabin made her uneasy. The Heart was inside them now. It would never let them rest. Every step they took from here would be a step deeper into a world of darkness they might never escape.

"I'll pack," she said. "We'll leave at dawn. No more waiting."

The next morning came far too soon. Evelyn awoke to the dim light of dawn creeping through the cracks in the cabin's wooden walls. The storm had passed, though the air remained thick and heavy with humidity. She could hear the chirping of birds in the distance, but it felt hollow—too calm after the storm that had raged both outside and within her.

Victor was already up, packing the few belongings they had left into his rucksack, checking his weapons with mechanical precision.

His brow was furrowed, his movements stiff, but at least they were moving. At least they were doing something.

"I've gathered what we need," he said when Evelyn appeared at the doorway, her own pack slung over her shoulder. "We're as ready as we'll ever be."

Evelyn nodded, glancing down at the stone in her hand. She had thought about leaving it behind, tossing it into the river, burying it somewhere far away. But she knew that would be pointless. The stone wasn't just an object; it was a part of her now, connected to her in ways she didn't understand. If she ran from it, it would only follow.

She took a deep breath, steeling herself. "Let's go."

As they stepped out into the morning light, the first rays of sun were breaking through the clouds, casting a pale golden light over the landscape. The world outside felt different, as though the storm had washed away the past, leaving behind only the road ahead. But that didn't bring her comfort. No amount of sunlight could chase away the shadows that clung to her, the whispers that came with each passing second, reminding her of the Heart's influence.

Victor led the way, his hand never far from his sword. Evelyn stayed close, her senses alert, her mind still racing. Every rustle in the trees, every crack in the earth beneath her boots, felt like a warning. Something was coming for them. And no matter how far they ran, they wouldn't be able to outrun it forever.

By midday, they had crossed through the dense forest, pushing through thick underbrush and over rocks, until the land opened up into a wide, sweeping plain. In the distance, the jagged peaks of the mountains rose against the sky, their snow-capped tips gleaming like a beacon.

The journey would be long, and the path treacherous. But Evelyn could see the monastery in her mind's eye, an ancient structure hidden away in the mountains, where monks had lived for centuries.

If anyone could help them understand the stone, it would be the people there.

"I don't like this," Victor said suddenly, breaking the silence. His voice was low, his expression troubled.

Evelyn didn't look at him. She had learned by now that when Victor spoke like that, it meant something serious. "What's wrong?"

"Something's not right," he said, his eyes scanning the horizon. "I don't know how to explain it, but we're being watched."

Evelyn's heart skipped a beat. She instinctively reached for her dagger, though she knew it wouldn't help much against whatever was out there. They were already too deep into this—into the Heart's grip—for mere weapons to make a difference.

"We keep moving," she said, her voice firm. "We'll be fine. Just keep your eyes open."

Victor nodded, but his gaze never wavered from the landscape ahead. The air felt heavier now, thick with an unseen presence that was beginning to suffocate them.

For the next few hours, they walked in tense silence, each step bringing them closer to the mountains, but also closer to something darker, more dangerous. The road ahead was long, and they would have to fight for every inch.

As dusk began to settle, they reached the base of the mountains. The last rays of sunlight were slipping behind the peaks, casting long shadows over the landscape. In the distance, they could see the outline of a small village—perhaps a day's travel away from the monastery.

But Evelyn's eyes were drawn elsewhere—toward a shape moving swiftly among the trees. A shadow, almost human in form, but unmistakably not. Something was watching them, something they couldn't see clearly.

She turned to Victor, her face pale. "We're not alone."

He nodded grimly. "I know."

The chill of fear settled deeper into Evelyn's bones, but she refused to let it show. The stone, still pulsing in her hand, seemed to thrash against her palm, as if it, too, knew that something was coming. And it wasn't just the Heart.

The true danger was only just beginning.

Chapter 20: The Edge of Darkness

The sun had vanished behind the mountains, leaving behind only a dull, fading glow that lit the darkening sky in muted shades of violet and orange. Evelyn felt the oppressive weight of the evening pressing down on her, but she wasn't sure if it was the atmosphere or the sense of something lurking in the shadows that caused the unease deep in her chest. The stone in her pocket pulsed faintly, as though it was aware of the growing darkness.

Victor led the way, his form silhouetted against the rugged outline of the mountains that stretched endlessly before them. They had reached the base of the peaks, but the road ahead was steep and treacherous. The narrow path they had followed thus far had turned into a winding, rocky trail that twisted upward, cutting through sharp outcroppings and dense thickets of trees that seemed to press in from all sides.

The silence between them was thick—Evelyn's thoughts too tangled, too heavy to voice. She could hear Victor's boots crunching softly on the ground, his movements sure and methodical, but there was an edge to his demeanor that spoke volumes.

They hadn't spoken much since the unsettling realization that they were being watched. Every glance over her shoulder seemed to reveal nothing but the dark, shadowed landscape. But Evelyn had learned not to trust the stillness, not with the stone so close to her. Not with the Heart breathing through her veins.

"Do you feel it?" Victor's voice, low and taut with caution, broke through her thoughts.

She glanced at him, noticing how his posture had stiffened, how his hand was never far from his sword. "I do," she said softly, feeling the weight of his words. "But I don't know what it is. It's like... like something's just out of reach."

Victor gave a short nod, his eyes scanning the terrain ahead. "It's watching us. I can feel it too. Whatever it is, it's patient. But it's not natural. It's waiting for the right moment."

Evelyn swallowed, forcing herself to breathe deeply. The stone in her pocket shifted slightly, as if reacting to the rising tension between them. She couldn't tell if it was her imagination, but the presence of the stone seemed to have intensified since they'd set out that morning. The deeper they ventured, the more attuned to it she became.

A strange sensation curled in her stomach as if the earth beneath her feet were somehow different now. Not solid. Not dependable. Her eyes flicked to the mountains around them. The rocks felt cold, foreboding, like ancient bones jutting out from the earth. Something was buried here—something old and forgotten. Something that called to the Heart, like a flame draws the moth.

Her thoughts were interrupted by a rustling sound ahead of them. She stiffened, instinctively reaching for the dagger at her side. The noise came again, louder this time. Her pulse quickened. There was something there, something moving in the shadows.

Victor stopped, turning to her with a quiet urgency. His expression was unreadable, but she could see the tension in the way he held himself. "Stay close."

Evelyn nodded, though she had no intention of falling behind. She moved to his side, both of them scanning the dense thicket ahead.

For a moment, there was nothing but the wind and the soft murmur of leaves. Then—there it was again. A shape, darting between the trees. Something humanoid, but wrong. Its movements were jerky, unnatural. Evelyn's grip tightened on her dagger.

Without warning, the figure lunged from the underbrush, too fast for her to react. But Victor was ready. With one swift motion, he drew his sword and swung it in a wide arc. The figure recoiled, but not before its sharp claws scraped across his forearm, drawing blood.

Victor gritted his teeth, swinging again, this time landing a blow that sent the creature crashing to the ground. Evelyn's breath caught in her throat as she saw it clearly for the first time—a creature of nightmares, its face a contorted mess of angles and teeth, its skin pale and almost translucent, like the remains of a drowned corpse.

It hissed, its mouth opening wide in a grotesque display of fangs. But it wasn't the creature that held Evelyn's attention—it was what it was carrying. A bundle of dark cloth, wrapped tightly and stained with something dark and thick. She could see the faint outline of something embedded inside the cloth—a shape. A form.

"Victor—" she gasped, taking a step forward. "What is that?"

Victor turned, his face pale but his eyes hard with the weight of battle. "Get back!" he barked. "It's not over yet."

The creature, though injured, wasn't finished. It surged forward again, but this time, it didn't focus on Victor. It turned toward Evelyn, its hollow, empty eyes locking onto her with an unsettling intensity. Its clawed hands reached for her, its movements faster now, desperate.

In that moment, Evelyn's world narrowed to a single instinct: survival.

She drew her dagger, bringing it up in a swift, practiced motion. But before she could strike, a sharp, high-pitched scream filled the air, and the creature suddenly froze. Its face contorted, its body twitching, as if it was caught in the grip of something far stronger than fear.

Evelyn's heart pounded in her chest. She saw it—*the stone.*

The black stone, still nestled in her pocket, had begun to thrum, vibrating violently as if it were pulling something from the air itself. Her fingers clenched around it instinctively. The creature jerked back, its claws trembling as though it were being pulled by an unseen force.

And then, as quickly as it had attacked, the creature crumpled to the ground, its body convulsing before going limp. The air grew still.

Victor, breathless from the fight, stood over the creature's corpse, his sword still raised. His eyes flicked between Evelyn and the dark stone in her hand, his expression one of confusion and dread.

"What the hell just happened?" he demanded, his voice ragged.

Evelyn couldn't answer right away. Her mind was racing, her pulse still erratic as she looked down at the stone in her palm. It was glowing, a faint, eerie light pulsing from within its depths, as if it were feeding off the energy in the air.

"I don't know," she whispered, the weight of her words sinking in. "But I think the stone did that. I think... it controlled the creature."

Victor's gaze was fixed on the stone, and Evelyn could see the shift in him—the dawning realization that the stone, and everything tied to it, was far more powerful than either of them had imagined. Whatever they had unleashed, whatever they had brought with them, was not simply a relic. It was an anchor to something far more ancient, far more dangerous.

"We need to move," he said grimly, sheathing his sword. "Whatever this is, it's not just here. It's... *following* us."

Evelyn nodded, though her fingers still lingered on the stone, reluctant to let it go. The pulse of energy beneath her skin was undeniable. The stone was *alive*—and it was not about to let them forget that.

The rest of the evening passed in strained silence. The trail grew steeper, the night darker, and the shadows between the trees longer. But Evelyn couldn't shake the feeling that they were being hunted, not by a creature or a monster, but by the very thing they were carrying.

They made camp by the side of the path as the last rays of light disappeared behind the peaks. Victor gathered firewood, his movements tense, quick. Evelyn watched him, her thoughts distant, unsure of what they had unleashed. The stone seemed to hum in her pocket, sending subtle vibrations up her arm.

The flickering fire did little to chase away the unease that had settled in her bones. For the first time since they had set out on this journey, Evelyn wondered if they would make it to the monastery at all. And if they did, what then? What awaited them there?

"Victor," she said quietly, her voice breaking the silence, "do you think we can stop it? The Heart, I mean?"

Victor didn't look at her immediately. He continued to stoke the fire, his jaw clenched. "I don't know," he said after a long pause. "But I don't think we have a choice. We can't go back now."

Evelyn looked down at the stone in her hand, feeling its weight more than ever. It wasn't just an object. It was part of them. And perhaps, in some twisted way, it had always been.

The fire crackled between them, its warmth pushing back the growing chill of the night, but the unease was palpable. Evelyn sat on the edge of a large boulder, her eyes fixed on the flickering flames, though her mind was far from calm. The stone she carried—no, *the Heart*—rested heavily in her pocket, its presence a constant, buzzing reminder of the ancient force they were entangled with.

Victor, sitting across from her, tended to the fire with deliberate movements, but his thoughts were clearly elsewhere. Every now and then, he glanced over at her, his eyes narrowing in that way that suggested he was thinking about more than just the fire. He was trying to make sense of the creature they had encountered, trying to understand how it had been controlled by the Heart.

Finally, he broke the silence. "We can't keep going like this. Not with whatever that thing was trailing us."

Evelyn's gaze flicked to him. "What do you mean?"

"The creature... it wasn't just a random attack. It was targeting us. And whatever the stone did to it," Victor said, his voice low, "isn't something we can ignore. We need answers. We can't keep running blindly into this."

She nodded, chewing over his words. "I know," she said quietly. "But I don't know where to turn for those answers. We have to reach the monastery. The monks there—they're the only ones who might know how to break the curse. Or at least understand what we're dealing with."

Victor's eyes darkened at the mention of the monks. "And if they don't have answers?" He shifted his weight, clearly restless. "If they don't know what we're up against, then we're on our own. No more safe places. No more places to hide."

A tense silence stretched between them. Evelyn could feel the truth of his words sinking in. The monastery was their last hope, the last place that could provide any kind of clarity. But the further they moved from the village, the less certain she was of anything.

"We have no choice," she said finally, her voice steady despite the turmoil inside her. "We have to keep going. The monastery is the only place that might have any answers."

Victor didn't answer immediately, his expression unreadable as he looked out over the darkening landscape. The mountains loomed ahead, their jagged peaks like teeth against the sky. It felt as though the world around them was closing in. The path was getting steeper, the air thinner, the weight of their journey more oppressive with every step.

"We'll need to be careful," Victor said at last, his voice quiet but firm. "We can't afford another encounter like that. We're not equipped to fight whatever's out there."

Evelyn met his gaze, her heart pounding in her chest. She could see the fear in his eyes, the same fear that gripped her. But beneath it was something else—something darker. They were running out of time. The further they went, the more she felt the Heart reaching for her, pulling her toward something she couldn't understand.

"I'll keep my guard up," she promised, though the words felt hollow. How could they keep their guard up against something they didn't even understand?

The night passed uneventfully, but Evelyn found little rest. Every creak of the trees, every snap of a twig, made her heart race, but each time she forced herself to remain calm. They hadn't been followed, at least not immediately. But the fear that gnawed at her gut, the strange sense of being watched, was ever-present.

At dawn, they packed their things quickly, ready to move on. Victor had insisted on starting the day early, despite the fatigue that lined his features. "The sooner we get to the monastery, the sooner we can figure out what the hell's going on," he had said with a grim determination.

Evelyn didn't argue. She was just as eager to reach the monastery, but the thought of what they might find there—the answers, or worse, the lack of them—kept her on edge.

As they began their ascent into the mountains, the landscape became more treacherous. The trail was barely more than a narrow ledge winding between sheer drops and jagged rocks. The air grew colder, the wind biting at their exposed skin, and the trees thinned as they climbed higher. Evelyn wrapped her cloak tighter around herself, but it did little to stave off the growing sense of unease.

The mountain pass seemed endless, stretching on for hours as they moved higher and higher. The silence of the wilderness was oppressive, the only sounds being the crunch of their boots on the rocky path and the occasional gust of wind that whistled through the trees. It felt as though the world around them had gone still—waiting.

They came across a few scattered footprints, too small to be human but still distinct enough to unsettle Evelyn. Were they being watched again? Were the creatures still tracking them? Or was it something else—something older?

By midday, they reached a small plateau, a flat stretch of ground where the trail forked. To the right, the path continued upward toward the monastery. To the left, a narrow, winding path led toward a cluster of small caves. Evelyn stopped at the fork, glancing at Victor.

"We should check the caves," she said softly. "It might be safer to rest there for a while. We're too exposed out in the open."

Victor hesitated but then nodded. "You're right. It's too quiet here. Let's take a look."

They made their way toward the caves cautiously, stepping lightly over the uneven ground. The first cave they came to was small, the entrance barely large enough for a person to squeeze through. It was dark inside, but not completely empty. There were remnants of a fire—charred sticks and the faint smell of burned wood—and a few broken tools scattered on the floor.

Evelyn crouched down, her eyes scanning the area. "Someone was here," she murmured, her voice barely above a whisper.

Victor was already standing near the back of the cave, his sword out, scanning the shadows. "Not just someone," he said grimly. "They're recent. Whoever was here didn't leave long ago."

Evelyn felt a flicker of unease. "Do you think they saw us?"

Victor shook his head. "No way to tell. But we can't afford to stay here too long. We need to keep moving."

Reluctantly, Evelyn agreed. The feeling of being watched had only grown stronger since they entered the caves, as though the darkness itself was closing in around them. With a last glance at the abandoned camp, they continued along the trail.

The air grew thinner as they ascended. Every breath felt more labored, more strained, but they pushed forward. It wasn't until late in the afternoon that they finally saw it—a structure silhouetted against the fading light of the setting sun. The monastery, high on the mountainside, was just ahead.

It was an ancient building, its stone walls weathered by centuries of exposure to the elements. The roof was slanted and lined with moss, and the surrounding area was dotted with smaller buildings—cells, perhaps, or shrines. The path that led up to it was worn from years of use, but it was clear that not many had come here recently.

Evelyn's heart quickened in her chest. She could feel the Heart stirring in her pocket, as if it knew they were close, as if it could sense the answers that might be waiting for them inside. She looked at Victor, but he was already moving forward, his eyes scanning the monastery with a sharp focus.

"This is it," he said quietly, though his voice held a note of uncertainty. "This is where we find out what we're really up against."

Evelyn nodded, though a part of her—some dark, buried part—wondered if they were walking into a trap. She wasn't sure what the monks would say, or if they would even *want* to help them. What if the monks knew about the Heart? What if they were waiting for them, too?

The wind shifted, a sudden gust blowing through the mountain pass and rattling the trees. Evelyn's skin prickled as the world around them seemed to go still once more. The silence was deafening.

Victor reached the entrance of the monastery first. The heavy wooden doors were closed, but they looked old, as though they hadn't been used in ages. He pushed on the door gently, and it creaked open, revealing the darkened interior.

"Let's go," he said, his voice barely a whisper.

Evelyn followed him, her breath catching in her throat as she stepped across the threshold. The monastery's interior was dim, lit only by the faint glow of candles in the corners. The air inside was thick, stale with the scent of dust and incense. The walls were adorned with tapestries and symbols, strange runes and sigils she didn't recognize.

They were not alone.

A figure moved toward them from the shadows.

Chapter 21: The Secrets of the Mountain

Evelyn stepped cautiously into the dim interior of the monastery, her heart hammering in her chest. The heavy doors creaked shut behind her with a finality that sent a chill down her spine. The atmosphere within the ancient structure was thick with history—centuries of whispered prayers and forgotten rituals echoing through the stone walls. The air was stale, infused with the scent of incense and something... *older*.

Her fingers brushed against the rough-hewn stone as she moved forward, her steps quiet against the cold floor. Victor had already moved ahead, his expression grim, his hand resting on the hilt of his sword. It was clear that he, too, felt the weight of this place. They had come seeking answers, but Evelyn had no illusions anymore. She wasn't sure they'd like what they found.

The figure who had moved toward them from the shadows had halted just a few paces away. He was tall, thin, with an angular face that looked as though it had been chiseled from stone. His long white robes were worn but immaculate, a stark contrast to the worn, crumbling walls of the monastery. His eyes were sharp, piercing, and Evelyn could sense the age in him—both in his features and the quiet authority that radiated from his every movement. There was a calmness to him, but beneath that serenity, Evelyn detected something ancient, something unsettling.

"I see you have come," the figure said, his voice soft but commanding, with an accent that made his words sound both foreign and timeless.

Victor stepped forward, eyes narrowing, his hand tightening around his sword's hilt, but Evelyn laid a hand on his arm. She could feel his tension, the readiness in him to strike first and ask questions later. But they were not here to fight. They were here to find answers. She hoped.

"We've come seeking knowledge," Evelyn said, her voice steady despite the growing sense of dread. "We were told the monks here could help us understand something... ancient. Something that's been following us."

The monk did not respond immediately. His eyes flicked to the stone in Evelyn's pocket—the Heart—and then back to her face. For a moment, it seemed as though he was looking through her, seeing something deeper, something hidden. Evelyn felt a shiver of unease crawl up her spine.

"You've brought it with you," he said finally, his voice softer now, almost as if he were speaking to himself. "The Heart. I felt its presence the moment you crossed the threshold."

Evelyn's fingers instinctively tightened around the stone in her pocket, though she didn't take it out. "What is it?" she asked. "What is this thing? Why is it... connected to me?"

The monk studied her for a long moment, then gave a small, almost imperceptible nod. "You don't know, do you?" He spoke with the kind of knowingness that made her skin prickle. "The Heart is not just a relic, a simple artifact of power. It is a part of you now. And you have been chosen to carry it."

Victor's jaw clenched, but he didn't speak. Evelyn, however, couldn't contain her curiosity. "Chosen by who? For what?"

The monk took a deep breath and began to walk slowly around them, his footsteps echoing in the empty halls. The silence that followed was heavy, oppressive. He stopped in front of an ornate stone pillar that had been carved with strange, unfamiliar symbols. He placed one hand upon it, as if drawing energy from the ancient relic.

"The Heart was never meant to be wielded by human hands. It is a force of nature—a fragment of something much older than humanity itself. A force that predates even the first of your kind. Long ago, it was sealed away by those who understood its power. But even now, it calls to the weak, the ambitious, the desperate." He turned to face them, his eyes unwavering. "And it has called to you."

Evelyn felt a chill seep into her bones at the monk's words. A fragment of something older? A force that predates humanity? She could barely comprehend the enormity of what he was saying.

"You've already felt its pull, haven't you?" the monk continued. "That constant hum beneath your skin, the sense that it is *alive*, that it is not simply an object. It is an extension of the very earth itself, an anchor to something primal, something dark. And now it has chosen you."

Evelyn opened her mouth to speak, but no words came out. Instead, a flood of images flashed in her mind—visions of the Heart glowing in her palm, of the creatures that had attacked them, of the way the stone had reacted to her touch, to the very presence of danger. The stone *had* chosen her. She had felt it.

"Why me?" she whispered. "Why was I chosen?"

The monk's eyes softened. "It is not a matter of choice, but of necessity. You are a vessel for the Heart. You bear its power, whether you wish it or not. And it is pulling you toward something. Something that must not be allowed to come to fruition."

Victor finally spoke, his voice low with suspicion. "What are you talking about? What's coming?"

The monk raised a hand, signaling for silence. "The Heart was part of an ancient pact, one made long before the first kingdoms rose, before the first battles were fought. It was sealed away in the deepest chambers of the earth to prevent a cataclysm—a cataclysm that could undo the balance of this world. And now... it is waking."

Evelyn felt her breath catch in her throat. "A cataclysm? What do you mean? What does the Heart have to do with it?"

"The Heart is a key," the monk replied, his voice grave. "It is the key to the door that binds an ancient, malevolent force—a power so great that it could tear the very fabric of reality itself. The Heart was created to keep that door closed. But over time, it was forgotten. The pact was lost. And now, as the Heart awakens, so too does that power."

Evelyn's mind raced. A door? A malevolent force? She looked down at the stone in her hand, feeling its weight once again. She had never asked for this power, but it was hers now, whether she understood it or not.

"So what do we do?" Victor asked. "How do we stop this... this *thing*?"

The monk looked at them both, his eyes heavy with the weight of his knowledge. "You must take the Heart to the place where it was forged. To the Temple of the First Seals. Only there can the Heart be re-sealed, before it destroys everything. Before the door opens."

Evelyn swallowed. "The Temple of the First Seals... Where is that?"

The monk didn't answer immediately. He walked over to a stone table in the center of the room and spread out a large, ancient map. The ink was faded, the edges tattered, but the symbols were clear to him. He traced a line with his finger, moving it across the map until it stopped at a spot in the farthest reaches of the mountains.

"It lies beyond the known world, hidden in the deepest corner of the earth," he said. "To reach it, you will have to pass through the Shadow Vale—the heart of the storm. It is a place of great peril, and many have lost their lives trying to find it. But you must. There is no other way."

Evelyn stared at the map, trying to process everything he had just said. The Temple of the First Seals. A place lost to time. And beyond it, the Shadow Vale—a place that seemed to hold nothing but death.

"Why didn't you go?" Victor asked, his voice tight with disbelief. "Why haven't the monks stopped this before?"

The monk's expression darkened. "We were not meant to stop it. We were meant to *guard* it. For centuries, we have watched, waited, and maintained the seals. But the Heart... it calls to those who are weak, who cannot resist its pull. It has chosen you, Evelyn. You and you alone can prevent the destruction that is coming."

Evelyn felt her breath quicken. "So I have to go? I have to take the Heart to this temple, to this place... and re-seal it?"

"Yes," the monk said. "But be warned: The closer you get to the door, the more powerful the Heart will become. It will not let you go easily. And there will be those who seek to stop you. There are others who wish to use the Heart for their own purposes. They will come for you."

Evelyn felt a cold knot form in her stomach. It wasn't enough that the Heart was pulling her toward a fate she didn't understand. Now she had to contend with those who would seek to take it from her. And time was running out. She could feel it—feel the darkness that was gathering, both around them and within her.

"We will go," Evelyn said, her voice firm despite the terror that churned in her gut. "We will stop this. We have no choice."

Victor looked at her, his eyes dark but filled with determination. "We'll go together," he said. "We'll finish this. No matter what it takes."

The monk gave a slow nod, his gaze lingering on them both. "Then go quickly. The Heart's power grows stronger with each passing day. The longer you wait, the more difficult it will be to control."

As the monk turned to leave, Evelyn caught his arm. "One last thing," she said urgently. "How do we stop this force? Once we reach the temple, how do we *seal* the door?"

The monk's eyes were haunted when he looked back at her. "You'll know when the time comes. But remember—some doors are never meant to be opened. And some things are far better left locked away."

Evelyn's mind was a whirl of thoughts, each more impossible than the last. As she stood in the monk's presence, staring at the ancient map, the weight of his words pressed down on her like a physical force. The Heart was not just an object of power, it was the key to something far darker, something that had been locked away for centuries. And now, she was the one chosen to bear that key, to carry the weight of that terrible responsibility.

Victor stood beside her, his expression tense, his brow furrowed in deep thought. She could see the confusion and frustration in his eyes, the same emotions that swirled within her own chest. The temple, the Shadow Vale, the door—they all sounded like stories from the edges of myth, like legends too old to be real. But the monk's certainty was undeniable.

"This is insane," Victor muttered under his breath, as if speaking to no one in particular. "We've been through hell just to get here, and now you're telling me we have to cross *that*?"

Evelyn's gaze drifted back to the map. The Temple of the First Seals wasn't some distant landmark—it was a journey through the heart of the unknown, through places that no living soul had ventured for hundreds of years. The Shadow Vale was marked on the map with an ominous, jagged symbol, a place where even the sun feared to shine. The more she stared at it, the more she could feel the pull of something terrible, something waiting just beyond the horizon.

"We don't have a choice," Evelyn said quietly, though she wasn't sure if she was trying to convince Victor or herself. "The monks said the Heart is waking. If we don't stop it, then..."

She trailed off, unable to voice the nightmare she imagined. If the Heart's power truly was a key to something so ancient and malevolent, something so destructive, then the world as they knew it might very well end. The monastery's ancient walls, the sagging tapestries, and the dark corners of the sacred place seemed to whisper with the knowledge of it, as if the entire mountain had once known the horrors that might be unleashed.

Victor took a deep breath, his hand instinctively reaching for his sword as if to reassure himself. "We'll go," he said, his voice steady now. "But we do it on our terms. We don't let the Heart control us. We control it."

Evelyn nodded. "I can't promise we'll be able to control it. But I'll do everything I can."

The monk, who had been silent during their exchange, finally spoke again, his voice low and somber. "The Heart doesn't care about your control. It will consume you, body and soul, if you let it. The only way to prevent that is to reach the Temple before it is too late. And even then..."

His voice trailed off, and Evelyn caught a flicker of something in his eyes—something that suggested he knew all too well the dangers they faced, perhaps better than he cared to admit. But he didn't say more.

"The journey is long," the monk continued, turning toward them with a finality that seemed to cut through the thick silence. "And the Shadow Vale is not the only danger you will face. There are forces far older than you, older than even the Heart itself, who will seek to stop you."

Evelyn's throat tightened at his words. *Forces older than the Heart?* What could be worse than the power that they already knew was lurking just beneath the surface? But there was no time to dwell on the monk's cryptic warnings. They had a journey ahead of them, one that would require everything they had—and more.

As the monk turned toward the inner sanctum of the monastery, Evelyn felt a sense of finality settle over her. She glanced at Victor, his face determined but shadowed with uncertainty. They had no choice but to go forward. Their lives, their fates, and the fate of the world itself were tied to the Heart now. They had to follow this path, no matter where it led.

The Journey Begins

The monastery's courtyard was silent as they made their way out, the sun setting behind the distant mountains. The monk had offered them supplies—basic rations and a few weapons—before disappearing into the depths of the monastery. Evelyn and Victor packed their belongings, the tension between them palpable as they prepared for the journey ahead.

They had little more than a vague map, a few cryptic words, and the ancient stone that had brought them to this moment. Evelyn's fingers brushed against the Heart, still nestled in her pack. It was a constant reminder of everything they stood to lose, and everything they might already have lost.

Victor broke the silence. "Do you really think we can make it through the Shadow Vale?"

Evelyn looked at him, her brow furrowing. "I don't know. But I don't think we have much of a choice."

They set out at first light, the path ahead winding through the jagged mountains. The journey was slow, treacherous, and fraught with uncertainty. The further they moved into the mountains, the less familiar the world around them became. The trees grew sparse, the air thinner, and the weather grew colder.

Each step they took seemed to draw them closer to the darkness that the monk had warned about. Evelyn's instincts told her to turn back, but there was no turning back. The Heart wouldn't let her.

On the third day, they reached the edge of the Shadow Vale.

The vale was a valley nestled between two towering cliffs, the sky above choked with dark, swirling clouds. The air felt thick, heavy, and oppressive, like the weight of the earth itself was pressing down on them. The sunlight barely broke through the clouds, casting everything in an eerie twilight.

"This is it," Victor murmured, his voice barely a whisper. He seemed unnerved, his usual confidence fading as they stood on the precipice of the vale. "There's something wrong here."

Evelyn looked ahead, her heart pounding in her chest. The valley below was shrouded in mist, the trees twisted and gnarled, their branches like skeletal fingers reaching toward the sky. The ground was uneven and cracked, and the air seemed to hum with a low, vibrating energy that made her skin prickle.

"We have to go through it," Evelyn said, trying to push aside her own fear. "There's no other way."

Victor nodded grimly, but he did not take his eyes off the vale. There was something about the place—something ancient and foreboding—that made the hairs on the back of his neck stand up.

They began their descent into the vale, moving carefully over the rocky terrain. As they made their way deeper into the shadowy expanse, the sounds of the world seemed to fade away. The wind no longer howled through the trees. The birds had stopped singing. The silence here was suffocating.

Evelyn couldn't shake the feeling that something was watching them. The Heart, which had been eerily silent in her pack since they had begun their journey, seemed to pulse faintly now, as though it was aware of their surroundings, aware of the danger that lurked within the vale.

Victor, too, was on edge. His hand was never far from his sword, and he kept glancing over his shoulder, as though expecting something—or someone—to emerge from the shadows.

Suddenly, a faint sound broke the eerie silence—a whisper, so soft that it could have been the wind. Evelyn froze, her heart racing.

"Did you hear that?" she whispered to Victor.

He nodded, his grip tightening on his sword. "I heard it."

It was a low, guttural sound, a voice carried on the wind, but no words Evelyn could understand. The whispers seemed to grow louder, more urgent, as they moved deeper into the vale.

"Stay close," Victor muttered, his eyes scanning the darkness around them. "We're not alone."

They pushed forward, their pace quickening as the atmosphere grew more oppressive, more unnatural. The air felt thick with tension, and Evelyn could hear the faintest scraping sound behind them, as though something was following.

The path narrowed as they moved deeper into the vale, and the trees seemed to close in around them. Evelyn's hand instinctively went to her pocket, her fingers brushing against the Heart once more. The stone seemed to be drawing energy from the darkness around them, its faint pulse quickening.

Suddenly, the ground beneath them gave way, and Evelyn let out a startled cry as she slipped, tumbling down into a narrow crevasse. She scrambled to catch herself, but the stones beneath her hands were slick with moss, and she slid further down.

"Evelyn!" Victor shouted, reaching for her. But she was too far below.

She landed hard, her body crashing against the jagged rocks. For a moment, everything was black. When her vision cleared, she saw only darkness around her. The shadows pressed in from all sides.

The Heart in her pocket throbbed, its pulse erratic, as though it were reacting to something deeper, something hidden within the vale.

"Victor!" Evelyn shouted, her voice echoing off the rocks. She struggled to her feet, trying to get her bearings. Her breath was shallow, her heart racing.

But there was no answer.

Chapter 22: Into the Abyss

The world spun in a whirl of darkness, light, and pain. Evelyn's breath came in sharp, ragged gasps as she lay sprawled on the jagged rocks. Her vision flickered, and for a moment, she thought she might slip into unconsciousness. But the pulse in her pocket—the beat of the Heart—reminded her that she couldn't afford to lose herself now. Not when everything was at stake.

She pushed herself up with a grunt, her limbs trembling with the effort. Her right arm screamed in protest, the pain of the fall settling into her bones like a cold weight. She winced, touching her forehead. Blood. A trickle of it. But it was nothing compared to the pain that radiated from the deep crevasse in which she now found herself trapped.

Victor.

The thought cut through the fog in her mind like a knife. She couldn't lose him—not here, not now. But her heart thudded in her chest as she looked around, trying to make sense of her surroundings. All she saw was a canyon of blackness and jagged rock, the air thick with a musty scent. The shadows pressed in, whispering, swirling around her like living things.

"Evelyn!" Victor's voice broke through the haze, a frantic shout echoing from above.

Her head snapped up, her eyes straining to see him. She caught a glimpse of his silhouette at the top of the crevasse, his face twisted with worry.

"I'm here!" she called back, her voice hoarse. "I'm alright!"

But she wasn't alright. Not by a long shot. The fall had shaken her, and her head still swam with dizziness. The ground around her was slick, and as she tried to push herself to her feet, she slipped again, her feet skidding on the loose stones. Panic gripped her, but she fought it down, clenching her jaw as she steadied herself.

She had to focus. She had to survive.

"Can you climb down?" Victor asked, his voice tight with urgency. "I'll find a way to help you—just stay where you are!"

Evelyn looked up at him, trying to gauge the height. It was too far to climb, even for someone as nimble as Victor. She'd never make it. The walls of the crevasse were too steep, the rocks too unstable.

"No, don't try it," she called back, the words a sharp command. "Find another way. There has to be another way down."

Victor paused, and for a moment, Evelyn thought he might argue, might try to make some impossible leap to reach her. But then he cursed under his breath, the sound echoing faintly down into the depths. "Alright, hold tight. I'll be right back."

She could hear him moving above her, the sound of boots crunching against stone. She breathed in deeply, her eyes scanning the dark crevasse for any sign of movement, any clue as to what lay ahead. The deep shadows seemed to pulse around her, the air growing colder with every passing second.

But then, as her gaze moved across the canyon walls, something caught her eye—something unnatural, something that shouldn't have been there.

At first, she thought it was a trick of the light, some shadow playing with her mind. But then she saw it again—*movement*. A faint ripple in the darkness, like a figure sliding in and out of the crevasse's walls.

She froze.

Her instincts screamed at her to run, but she couldn't. Her legs were too weak. Her heart was hammering in her chest. The Heart—*it* was what kept her tethered to this place, to this nightmare. It pulsed again, stronger this time, as though calling to something in the dark.

She twisted, scanning the shadows, but saw nothing. No person, no creature. Just the oppressive blackness.

"Victor!" she shouted, her voice rising in panic. "Victor, get down here, now!"

Her words hung in the air, swallowed by the cavernous silence that followed. The shadows pressed closer around her, as though closing in, tightening, narrowing.

The heartbeat in her chest—a rhythm she had come to understand as a part of her, as much a signal as a warning—was growing faster, more erratic. It throbbed with urgency. *Something was coming.*

She stumbled backward, her boots slipping on the loose stone as she moved further into the crevasse. Her eyes darted around, seeking refuge, seeking escape, but there was no safe haven. The air was too thick. The walls of the crevasse too steep.

And then she saw it. The movement again.

This time, it wasn't in the shadows. It was on the rocks, right before her eyes.

A figure emerged from the darkness—a tall, skeletal form draped in dark rags that fluttered like tattered sails in the windless air. Its face was obscured by the hood of its cloak, but Evelyn could feel its gaze, like ice, crawling over her skin. The creature was hunched, its body angular and bony, and it moved with a predatory grace that set her nerves on edge.

Her pulse quickened, her body frozen with fear.

The thing took a step forward. And then another.

Evelyn's breath hitched. She took a step back, her heart thumping against her ribs.

The creature's long fingers reached out toward her, its clawed hands scraping against the stone as it advanced.

And then, as if from nowhere, the air seemed to shimmer with an unnatural energy. A crackling noise filled the space—*the sound of an electric charge building in the air.* The stone beneath her feet trembled, and the Heart pulsed again, its power responding to the creature's presence.

It's here.

Evelyn's mind raced. The Heart wasn't just a key—it was a *beacon*. The creatures that lurked in the shadows of the vale were drawn to it, to her. She was the magnet, and they were the steel.

Her thoughts became a blur, but one thing was clear: She couldn't face this alone. Not here. Not now.

"Victor!" she screamed again, her voice rising in desperation.

From above, she could hear his voice—his tone filled with panic. "Evelyn! Hold on!"

But the creature didn't stop. It was closing in, its sharp claws clicking against the rocks like the ticking of an inevitable clock. Evelyn couldn't move fast enough. She could barely breathe, let alone fight.

In an instant, the creature was upon her. It reached out with its claws, its long fingers brushing against her shoulder.

Evelyn recoiled in terror, but as she did, the Heart in her pocket surged with energy. The pulse was overwhelming—so strong it felt like the very air was vibrating with power. The creature paused for a moment, its head tilting slightly, as though confused by the sudden onslaught of energy. Then, it lunged.

Time slowed.

Evelyn reacted instinctively, her body moving before her mind could even process the danger. She ripped the Heart from her pocket, clutching it tightly in her hands as a surge of energy erupted from it—an explosion of raw power.

The creature recoiled, its screech of pain and fury filling the air. The light from the Heart flared, illuminating the dark recesses of the crevasse for just a moment before it dimmed again.

The creature staggered back, but it wasn't done. Its movements were jerky, as though the energy from the Heart had wounded it, but it wasn't enough to stop it. It was relentless. And so was Evelyn.

Desperation gripped her as she raised the Heart higher, focusing on the force it radiated. She could feel its power flowing through her, coursing in her veins. The Heart wasn't just an object. It was a part of her now. Its will was her will. And its energy was her energy.

For the briefest of moments, she felt something strange—a flicker of control, an understanding of the creature's presence. She felt its malice, its hunger. And she realized something else. This wasn't just any creature. This was *one of them*.

The *Others*.

The beings who had once roamed the earth, twisted by the Heart's power, creatures born of darkness and suffering. They had been sealed away—trapped beneath the earth—but the Heart had awoken them. And now, they were coming for her.

The realization struck her like a bolt of lightning. She couldn't stop them. Not without something far stronger than the Heart's raw power.

Suddenly, the darkness above her seemed to shift. She looked up, her heart racing, and saw Victor descending the walls of the crevasse, his face grim and determined.

"Hold on!" he shouted.

Evelyn's mind screamed at her to run, to get away. But she couldn't. The creature was too close now. And she could already feel the others coming—more shadows, more creatures hungry for the Heart's power.

And then, through the confusion, she heard it.

A whisper.

Not from the creature. Not from the vale.

But from the Heart.

A voice, soft but clear: *Run.*

The Heart pulsed in Evelyn's hand with a raw, aching energy. It was both a blessing and a curse, a tool she wasn't fully equipped to control. As the creature continued its slow, predatory advance, the glowing stone in her hand seemed to call to it—a beacon in the darkness. She could feel the tendrils of its malevolence tugging at her mind, whispering promises of destruction, of eternal night. She was drowning in the weight of it, struggling to keep her head above the water.

The air crackled with power, but Evelyn wasn't sure if it was coming from the Heart or from the creature itself. The thing before her was still, its clawed fingers flexing slowly in anticipation, as if it was savoring the moment. Its pale, leathery skin was stretched tight over bone, the faintest traces of shadows clinging to its form like the remnants of a nightmare. Its eyes, glowing with a sickly yellow light, locked onto hers, burning with an ancient, hunger-driven malice.

Evelyn's heart pounded in her chest, her breath shallow and quick. The darkness seemed to close in around her, the silence almost deafening. The only sound was the rhythmic thumping of her heart and the occasional scrape of the creature's claws against the stone.

The Heart pulsed again, and she realized—too late—that it wasn't just reacting to the creature's presence. It was feeding off her fear, amplifying it. Every second she spent in the creature's gaze, every second she hesitated, made the power of the Heart grow stronger, but it wasn't the strength she needed. She needed to find a way out. She needed to think, to act—before the creature reached her.

Suddenly, the creature lunged. It moved with lightning speed, its claws reaching for her throat. She had no time to think, no time to react.

But then—**Victor.**

His shout reached her in the same instant the creature moved. A split second. He was *here*.

"Evelyn!" Victor's voice rang through the air, filled with raw desperation.

Without thinking, Evelyn acted. She threw the Heart forward, holding it out like a weapon—an extension of herself. The glow intensified, blindingly bright, filling the crevasse with a white-hot light that pushed against the surrounding darkness. The creature hissed, its form jerking back as if the light was a physical force. The Heart's power surged out of her like a shockwave, but it wasn't enough to stop it.

The creature growled low in its throat, its glowing eyes narrowing as it shook off the light, like a shadow trying to shrug off the sun. It advanced again, its movements more erratic, as though it was feeling the effects of the Heart's energy, but it didn't stop.

Run. RUN.

The voice returned, stronger now—faint but unmistakable. A whisper from the Heart, a command. Evelyn's heart thudded with the sudden realization that the Heart wasn't merely guiding her; it was driving her. It wanted something. And if she didn't move now, if she didn't do something, the creature would take it—and her—before she had a chance to fully understand what was happening.

Victor's voice was closer now. She could hear him climbing down the rocks, his movements hurried and frantic. But the crevasse was wide, and the distance between them seemed like miles.

The creature snarled, its claws flashing as it reached for her once again. Evelyn took a deep breath, every muscle in her body coiling with anticipation. She needed more. She needed more power.

The Heart in her hand seemed to pulse in response to her will. She focused everything—her fear, her desperation, her rage—into it. The Heart was connected to her now, bound to her as much as she was bound to it. She didn't need to control it. She needed to *surrender* to it.

The next moment, she felt it.

A surge of energy, far stronger than anything she had felt before, erupted from the Heart. It was pure, raw power—wild, untamed, and chaotic. It filled the crevasse with an unbearable light, pushing back against the darkness that clung to the walls, making the shadows retreat.

The creature recoiled, screeching as the light burned into it. It tried to shield its face, but it was no use. The Heart's energy surged outward in all directions, overwhelming the creature's senses, flooding its very being with a force it wasn't prepared to withstand.

Evelyn gasped, feeling the power coursing through her body, through her very soul. It was *too much*. She couldn't control it. She could barely stand under the weight of it.

But just as the creature shrieked again, flailing in the light, Evelyn felt a sharp tug—a pull deep within her. The Heart was calling to something. It wanted her to finish it. To end this.

With a final, desperate cry, she thrust the Heart forward, focusing all of her remaining energy on the stone. A jagged bolt of light shot from it, piercing the creature's chest.

The creature howled, its body writhing as the energy burned through it like a flame. The air around them vibrated with the force of the Heart's power. And then, with a final, agonized scream, the creature collapsed to the ground, its form disintegrating into nothingness as the light from the Heart faded.

For a moment, everything was still.

The silence that followed was almost deafening. Evelyn's hands were trembling as she lowered the Heart, her breath coming in ragged gasps. The power of the Heart still hummed beneath her skin, still thrumming in the air, but now it was a dull pulse, a reminder of the destruction it could unleash.

"Evelyn!" Victor's voice came again, closer this time, and suddenly, he was there, scrambling down the last few feet of the crevasse, reaching out to her.

She barely had the strength to lift her hand to him as he pulled her into his arms, holding her tight.

"We need to go," Victor said urgently, glancing over his shoulder as if expecting something to emerge from the shadows.

Evelyn's mind was still foggy, the rush of adrenaline starting to wear off. She could barely process what had just happened. The creature. The Heart's power. The way it had surged through her like a flood.

But Victor was right. They couldn't stay here. Not now.

With great effort, she pushed herself to her feet, swaying slightly as the last remnants of the energy from the Heart pulsed through her. Victor steadied her, his arm around her waist. "Are you alright?" he asked, his voice filled with concern, but there was an edge to it now—an urgency.

"I'm fine," she replied, though the words felt hollow. She wasn't fine. But she didn't have the strength to argue. "We need to move. The creatures—more are coming. And the Heart—" She stopped herself, the memory of the power she had just unleashed still too fresh in her mind. She wasn't sure she fully understood what had happened. How had she done it? How had she controlled the Heart?

But Victor didn't wait for her to explain. He was already helping her climb back to the surface, his movements swift and sure. He didn't question her. He didn't ask what had just happened. He simply helped her, his eyes scanning the darkness above them, his posture tense.

Once they reached the edge of the crevasse, Evelyn could hear the faintest sounds from below—scraping, dragging noises that sent a chill through her. The creatures weren't dead. Not all of them. They were regrouping.

"We can't stay here," Victor said, pulling her toward the next path, which led deeper into the vale. "We need to move. Now."

Evelyn didn't argue. Her mind was still spinning, and the fear was still there, coiling in her gut. The Heart. The creatures. The thing inside her that she didn't understand. But one thing was clear: they were not safe yet.

With Victor leading the way, they moved quickly, pushing through the dense mist and gnarled trees of the Shadow Vale. The path was treacherous, winding and narrow, but it didn't matter. They had to keep moving. They had to find the Temple before the Heart could draw more of the creatures to them.

The thought of what lay ahead—the Temple, the door, the Heart's true purpose—kept her moving forward, even though every instinct told her to turn back. The road ahead was dangerous, but Evelyn knew one thing for sure: she couldn't stop now.

Not when they were this close.

And as the shadows grew darker around them, as the winds howled through the trees, Evelyn could feel it. The pull of the Heart. The *urgency*.

The time was coming. She could feel it in her bones.

Chapter 23: The Darkening Path

The wind howled through the trees, carrying with it a chill that cut through Evelyn's skin, burrowing deep into her bones. Every step she took felt heavier than the last, each footfall dragging her deeper into the heart of the Shadow Vale. The dense mist, which had been ever-present since they first entered this cursed place, clung to the air like a suffocating shroud. It wrapped around them, damp and cold, obscuring their path and disorienting them at every turn.

Victor was still at her side, but the silence between them had grown thick with unspoken tension. She could feel the weight of his gaze on her from time to time, as if he were studying her. Watching her. And why wouldn't he? She had almost gotten them both killed back in the crevasse. The Heart's power had surged through her like a tidal wave, and in the aftermath, she had felt both triumphant and terrified. What had she unleashed? And what else would it demand of her?

She gripped the Heart tightly in her hand, its pulse steady but unnervingly strong. It was as if it was alive, calling to her, urging her forward. Its glow, though dimmer now, still pulsed softly in the dim light, lighting her way as they moved through the vale. But with every step, the feeling of being watched only grew stronger. The creatures they had left behind were not the only threat here. Something else—something far older and far more insidious—was waiting.

"You alright?" Victor's voice broke through her spiraling thoughts, his words gentle but edged with concern.

Evelyn nodded quickly, not trusting herself to speak. She could feel the weariness settling in, her body aching from the fall, the fight, and the strain of the last few hours. But there was something else, something she couldn't shake. The Heart's presence was a constant hum in her chest, and though it wasn't *calling* to her in the same way it had before, there was a deep, lingering pull—a gravity that was slowly increasing. The closer they got to the Temple, the more she felt it. The weight of destiny.

Victor glanced at her again, his brow furrowed in quiet worry. "We're close. The Temple should be just up ahead." His voice had an edge to it, a sharpness that Evelyn hadn't missed. He was worried. And why wouldn't he be?

The last few days had taken their toll on both of them. She knew Victor was feeling the strain of the journey, the danger, the weight of everything they were carrying—the Heart, their mission, their survival. But what worried her more than his physical exhaustion was the question that lingered between them: *Why did I feel that surge of power?*

Victor had barely spoken since the encounter with the creature in the crevasse, and Evelyn hadn't pushed him. She wasn't ready to talk about it either. But the silence was becoming unbearable. She wanted to ask him—*Do you think we can control this?* The Heart. The creatures. The shadows.

Instead, she kept her thoughts to herself. They needed to focus on reaching the Temple. They needed to get there before the vale consumed them.

A low growl rumbled in the distance, a warning. Evelyn froze, her senses heightening. She had learned not to ignore such sounds. The creatures were close. But these weren't the same creatures that had attacked them earlier. These were different—more numerous, more dangerous.

Victor reached for his blade, his grip tightening around the hilt, and without a word, he gestured for Evelyn to follow him off the main path. There was no time to waste. The creatures, whatever they were, were getting closer. The air around them had shifted, growing colder, sharper, as if the vale itself was preparing to strike.

Evelyn followed him, keeping the Heart pressed tightly against her chest. The air smelled of wet earth and decay. She tried to focus, to push aside the fear that threatened to overwhelm her. But every sense she had was alert. There was no hiding from what was coming.

The trees around them creaked and groaned as though in pain, their twisted branches reaching out like skeletal hands. The shadows deepened as the mist thickened, and Evelyn found herself wondering if the vale itself was alive. Was it watching them? Was it controlling the creatures that hunted them? And what of the Heart? Was it leading them here for a reason?

Victor stopped suddenly, his hand outstretched. Evelyn stumbled into him, her heart racing.

"What is it?" she whispered, trying to peer into the darkened forest ahead.

Victor's eyes narrowed, his body tense. "There's something in there. Something that doesn't want us passing."

Evelyn strained her ears. At first, she heard nothing but the wind and the distant rustling of leaves. But then—*a faint whispering*—like voices, carried by the breeze. And with it, a low, rumbling growl.

Her throat tightened. *Not again.*

But this time, it wasn't a creature she could see. This time, it was something more subtle—more insidious. The mist seemed to grow thicker, coiling around the trees like tendrils. The whispering grew louder, more distinct, as if the forest itself was speaking in a language she couldn't understand.

Victor's grip tightened on her wrist, pulling her away from the growing disturbance. "We need to move. Fast."

Evelyn followed, but her eyes lingered behind them, where the shadows seemed to grow darker and deeper. The voices continued to murmur, now louder, now in sync with the rhythm of the Heart.

The Heart's pulse had begun to change. It wasn't steady anymore. It was erratic, thumping in her chest like the beat of a drum—wild, chaotic. And then, as if in answer to the call, the shadows seemed to *shift*, like living things, reaching toward her.

She was running now, her legs carrying her faster than she thought possible, but it wasn't enough. The creatures were everywhere. She could feel their eyes on her, their presence closing in from all sides.

Victor glanced over his shoulder. "Evelyn, we need to make it to the Temple—now!"

She didn't need any more encouragement. The Temple was their only hope. The Heart's power had been increasing since they'd entered the vale. She could feel it, could sense its overwhelming force, but it was a power she didn't understand—one she wasn't sure she could control.

They reached a clearing, and there it was—a massive structure rising out of the mist like a ghost from the past. The Temple. Its towering stone walls loomed above them, covered in ivy and moss, its weathered stones darkened by centuries of neglect. The entrance was a massive archway, almost completely overgrown, with intricate carvings that spiraled around the door. There were symbols on the door—symbols Evelyn didn't recognize, but they felt familiar. The Heart had drawn them here. She could feel it in the air, in the pulse of the stone.

Victor reached the base of the steps first, his boots scraping against the stone as he stopped to look back at her. "Go! I'll cover you!"

Evelyn's breath came in short bursts, her body aching from the exertion. She didn't look back. She couldn't. All that mattered was the Temple. Reaching it. Getting inside.

She sprinted toward the entrance, her fingers brushing the ancient stone of the archway. It was cold, rough, and strangely comforting under her touch. The Heart in her chest began to thrum, its energy growing stronger as if it sensed the proximity to its resting place.

The moment her fingers made contact with the stone, the ground beneath her feet trembled. A low rumble, like the beginning of an earthquake, rolled through the air. Evelyn gasped, pulling her hand back, but before she could move, the door began to shift.

The sound of grinding stone filled the air, and before she could fully comprehend what was happening, the massive door began to open, inch by inch.

"Victor!" Evelyn shouted, turning back toward him, but he was already there, moving toward her.

"We're not safe yet," he muttered under his breath, his hand on her arm, guiding her into the Temple.

Inside, the air was heavy, the silence absolute. The darkness here was deeper than anything they had encountered in the Vale. It swallowed them whole, making it impossible to see more than a few feet ahead. But Evelyn could feel it—*something* waiting in the deep shadows, something ancient.

And then, as the door closed behind them with a resounding thud, the silence was broken. The Heart pulsed, its glow flickering as though it were reacting to the very presence of the Temple. The sound echoed through the vast, empty halls—an ancient sound, a calling, an awakening.

The Temple wasn't empty. Not at all.

They were not alone.

The door closed behind them with a final, deafening thud, sealing them inside the Temple. Evelyn's breath caught in her throat, the echo of the heavy stone reverberating through the vast, oppressive hall. The darkness around them was so thick it almost seemed to have substance, like a living thing that swallowed everything whole.

Evelyn took a tentative step forward, her boots making a soft scrape against the cold stone floor. The air inside the Temple was heavy with dust, ancient and untouched by time. There was no light, no source of illumination except for the faint pulse of the Heart, which continued to glow softly in her hand. It felt like a beacon, its gentle radiance cutting through the oppressive blackness. But it wasn't enough. The shadows seemed to deepen with every breath she took, as though the very walls of the Temple were pushing back against the light.

Victor's hand rested firmly on her shoulder, grounding her. "Stay close," he said, his voice low and steady. But there was a hint of something else in his tone, something that told her he wasn't entirely calm himself.

Evelyn nodded, not trusting herself to speak. She could feel the pulse of the Heart growing stronger with each passing moment. It was as if the stone was alive, feeding off the Temple's ancient energy. But that was not the only sensation she felt. There was something else—a presence—lurking just beyond the reach of the Heart's glow. It was a weight in the air, a sense of being watched. The hairs on the back of her neck stood on end, and her skin prickled with the sharp edge of fear. She wasn't alone in this place.

Her pulse quickened, and for a moment, she felt like she might suffocate under the weight of the darkness. She looked at Victor, who was already scanning the surroundings, his hand on the hilt of his sword, ready for anything. His eyes flickered toward her, a silent reassurance that they would face this together.

They had no choice. They were trapped here.

Victor stepped forward, his boots echoing softly against the stone, and Evelyn followed, her steps lighter, though her heart beat like a drum in her chest. The deeper they went, the more oppressive the atmosphere became. Every corner they turned, every new hall they entered, seemed to stretch the boundaries of the Temple into infinity. The walls were lined with carvings—symbols and runes that Evelyn couldn't understand, but they seemed to pulse in time with the Heart. It was like the very stone of the Temple was alive, responding to the ancient power inside the Heart.

They moved through what felt like endless corridors, the silence between them broken only by the echo of their footsteps and the occasional creak of the ancient stone settling. There was no sign of life, no movement—yet Evelyn couldn't shake the feeling that something was watching them from the darkness. Her mind raced, a thousand questions filling her thoughts. What was this place? Why had the Heart brought them here? And who—or *what*—was waiting for them?

Victor stopped suddenly, his hand raised. Evelyn froze beside him. He didn't speak, but his eyes were locked on something ahead of them.

Evelyn followed his gaze, her stomach sinking. At the far end of the hallway, partially obscured by the shadows, there was a large, stone door, carved with intricate designs. The symbols on it were more elaborate than anything they had seen before, ancient and foreboding. The moment Evelyn looked at it, she felt a chill crawl up her spine, as though the very air had become heavier.

"Do you feel that?" Victor asked, his voice tight.

Evelyn nodded slowly. She could feel the change in the air, the pressure building, like the calm before a storm. The Heart pulsed again, louder this time, almost as though it were answering something. Something in the dark.

"We need to go through that door," she whispered, her voice barely audible, though it sounded loud in the heavy silence of the Temple. The Heart was pushing her toward it, urging her forward.

Victor hesitated, his eyes narrowing, but he didn't argue. "We don't have a choice. If we want answers, we have to go through."

They both moved toward the door, and as they drew closer, the temperature in the hall seemed to drop. The walls, once covered in ancient runes, were now slick with condensation, and the faint glow from the Heart didn't seem to penetrate the oppressive darkness ahead. The air grew thick with a strange, almost metallic scent—like blood, but old, tainted with time.

Evelyn's heartbeat accelerated, and she reached out to touch the door. The moment her fingers brushed the stone, the door *moved*.

The grinding of stone against stone was loud, breaking the silence like thunder. It slid open with a slow, deliberate creak, revealing what lay beyond.

What they found in the room beyond the door was not what Evelyn had expected. It was a vast, circular chamber, its walls lined with shelves filled with ancient books and artifacts. But what truly caught her attention was the large pedestal in the center of the room, covered in strange, twisting symbols and runes. And on the pedestal, resting in the center, was another Heart.

This one was different. It was darker than the one Evelyn held—a deep, shadowy black, with faint veins of crimson pulsing through it. It was larger, its edges jagged, and there was something about it that felt... wrong. It hummed with a dark, malevolent energy, an energy that was so powerful Evelyn could feel it vibrating in her bones.

Her hand trembled as she reached for the Heart at her chest, almost as if the two were connected. The Heart in her hand responded, pulsing rapidly, its glow flickering erratically, as though recognizing the presence of its counterpart. But Evelyn couldn't take her eyes off the blackened Heart. It was like a magnet, pulling her in, calling to her in a language she couldn't understand.

Victor stood behind her, silent, his hand hovering near his sword as he surveyed the room. "This... this is what we've been looking for," he said, his voice barely more than a whisper. But there was no joy in his words, only a sense of dread.

Evelyn stepped forward, her legs feeling like they were made of stone. Every instinct screamed at her to turn and run, to escape this place, but something inside her—*the Heart*—drove her forward. She couldn't stop herself. The urge to reach out, to touch the dark Heart, was overwhelming.

As her fingers brushed against the pedestal, a surge of energy shot through her like a lightning bolt. Her body seized, and the Heart in her hand flared to life, its light growing blindingly bright. The air around them seemed to hum with power, and Evelyn felt herself falling, her mind spinning, her vision blurring.

"Evelyn!" Victor's voice broke through the haze, but it sounded distant, muffled, as if she were underwater.

Her grip on the Heart tightened as she fought to stay conscious. She could feel something else—something pulling at her, drawing her closer to the dark Heart. It was as if the room itself was alive, a sentient force that knew her, that knew the Heart she held.

And then, with a violent shock, she was thrown backward, slamming into the cold stone wall with a force that stole the breath from her lungs. The world spun, and for a moment, she couldn't remember where she was or what had just happened.

"Evelyn?" Victor's voice again, sharp with fear. She blinked rapidly, trying to clear the fog from her mind.

She slowly lifted her head and saw Victor kneeling beside her, his hand on her shoulder. His eyes were wide, filled with concern and something else—*fear*.

"What... what happened?" she asked, her voice hoarse.

"You touched it," Victor replied, his voice low and strained. "When you touched the other Heart, something... something happened. You... you vanished for a moment. I couldn't see you. Couldn't hear you. Then you came back. Just like that."

Evelyn looked down at her hand, still clutching the Heart that had once again grown cold. She could feel the faintest tremor in her fingers. "I... I don't understand. It's like—"

The Heart in her chest pulsed once more, and suddenly, the walls of the Temple began to tremble. A low rumble filled the air, and the ground beneath them began to shake. The room was alive, reacting to her touch.

"No," Victor hissed, pulling her to her feet. "We need to leave. Now."

Evelyn barely had time to process his words before the rumbling grew louder. The ceiling above them cracked, dust and debris falling like a shower of ash. The pedestal began to shake, and the dark Heart on it started to glow, its black veins pulsing with a sickly light.

Something was awakening—something ancient, something terrifying.

And they were right in its path.

Chapter 24: The Awakening

The ground beneath Evelyn's feet shuddered again, the vibrations creeping up her legs like an ominous warning. She could feel the walls of the Temple groaning in protest as the dark Heart pulsed in rhythm with the tremors. The room seemed to be alive, throbbing with the energy of something ancient, something powerful. The air grew thick with the scent of decay, of time itself unraveling. And it wasn't just the Temple that was stirring—something far darker was awakening, something that had been dormant for centuries.

Victor's hand tightened around her wrist, pulling her away from the pedestal, his face pale with fear. "We need to go. Now!"

Evelyn barely heard him. Her eyes were fixed on the dark Heart, which was growing brighter, its jagged black edges now pulsing with a crimson light. The light wasn't steady, but erratic, like a heartbeat in overdrive. It called to her, beckoned her, a familiar pull that echoed deep inside her chest. She could feel it in her blood, in her soul—the Heart was calling to her, and it was demanding something from her, something she couldn't understand.

"Evelyn!" Victor's voice broke through her haze of confusion and desire. He tugged harder on her arm, but she resisted, her gaze locked on the Heart.

"Wait," she murmured, her voice barely a whisper. She didn't know why she couldn't look away, why she couldn't break free of the pull. But she couldn't. The dark Heart was alive, responding to her. *It needs me,* she thought. *It wants me to do something.*

"No," Victor said urgently. "This isn't you. It's controlling you. You have to fight it."

Evelyn blinked, but the words didn't seem to register. All she could think about was the dark Heart. The pulse in her chest was growing louder, and with it, the sound of the Temple's rumbling increased. The walls cracked again, the air thickening with the smell of dust and something far more pungent, like rotten earth. The room was coming alive, shaking with energy. Whatever was happening, it wasn't just the Heart—it was everything. The Temple, the land, the Vale itself—it was all stirring.

"Get away from it!" Victor shouted, his voice now desperate. He grabbed her shoulders, shaking her, but Evelyn's mind was clouded. The Heart was calling her, and she couldn't fight it.

But then, something inside her stirred—a small spark of clarity, of resistance. She had felt this before, hadn't she? The surge of power, the strange desire to let go. It had come when she first touched the Heart, back in the Vale, back in that cursed forest. But this was different. This wasn't just a call. This was a command.

She turned slowly toward Victor, blinking as if waking from a dream. The haze in her mind was lifting, and for the first time since entering the Temple, she felt *present* again.

"Victor," she gasped, her voice shaking. "I... I don't know what's happening. The Heart—it's doing something to me."

Victor's expression softened with a mixture of fear and relief. He quickly wrapped his arms around her, pulling her away from the pedestal. "It's manipulating you. We need to get out. We need to leave before—"

A deafening crack split the air, followed by a guttural growl that seemed to come from the very depths of the Earth. The walls trembled again, and this time, the floor beneath them cracked open. Stones fell from the ceiling, showering the floor around them like debris from a collapsing building. The rumbling grew louder, a roar that sounded like the Temple itself was coming to life.

Evelyn felt her heart race as she stumbled backward, her hand instinctively clutching the Heart at her chest. The dark Heart, now fully awake, was glowing brightly, casting long shadows against the walls of the chamber. She could feel its power surging, a violent pull that threatened to swallow her whole.

The ground cracked open beneath their feet, and before Evelyn could react, a sharp pain lanced through her chest—a burning, agonizing pain that spread like wildfire. She gasped, clutching her heart in agony. Her breath caught in her throat, and for a moment, everything around her seemed to spin out of control.

"Evelyn!" Victor shouted again, but his voice sounded distant, muffled by the agony radiating from her chest. "You have to fight it! You have to stop it!"

She tried to speak, but the words were lost in the scream of pain tearing through her. Her vision blurred, and she sank to her knees, her body trembling. The Heart's pulse had become unbearable, its thrum vibrating through every fiber of her being. It felt like it was merging with her, like she and the Heart were one. She could feel the power coursing through her, filling every inch of her soul, her body—filling her with a desire she couldn't understand, a hunger she couldn't satisfy.

The darkness in the Temple was closing in, the shadows becoming tangible, like creatures made of nothing but the air itself. They crawled along the walls, whispering, their voices low and guttural. Evelyn could hear them now—*voices in the dark*, laughing, mocking, taunting her.

"You're too late," one voice rasped, its words so low that Evelyn could barely hear them. "The power has been awakened. You cannot stop it now."

Another voice joined in, a voice that sounded almost familiar. "You *think* you're in control? The Heart is far beyond your understanding."

Victor's voice broke through the chorus of whispers. "Don't listen to them, Evelyn! This isn't real! You *can* fight it!"

Evelyn looked up at him, her vision swimming with black and red. He was beside her, kneeling, his face contorted with worry. She tried to speak, but all that escaped her lips was a choked gasp. The dark Heart *wanted* her. It wanted her to surrender, to let it consume her entirely.

But deep inside, she knew something was wrong. She could hear the whispers in her mind now, each word wrapping around her thoughts like a vine, twisting, pulling. They weren't real. The power they offered was a lie. She could feel it, *sense* it—the darkness was nothing but a trick. She had fought too hard, too long, to let this take her now.

Victor's hand on her shoulder was a lifeline. "Evelyn! *Focus!* You have the power to stop it. You always have."

Her breath hitched, the agony in her chest intensifying. But his words cut through the fog of the Heart's influence. *I have the power.* She realized it then. The Heart didn't control her. It couldn't. She was the one in control. It was her will, her determination, that gave the Heart its power. She could *choose.*

With all the strength she had left, Evelyn reached for the dark Heart on the pedestal. The moment her fingers brushed against its cold surface, the room trembled violently, and a high-pitched wail filled the air. The whispers grew louder, more frantic, as though they were fighting to stop her.

But Evelyn was resolute.

She gripped the dark Heart, and as she did, a surge of energy unlike anything she had ever felt ripped through her. The world spun, the shadows around her flickering and twisting, but she held firm. She wasn't going to let it control her. She wasn't going to let it consume her. Not now. Not ever.

The Heart in her hand flared with a brilliant light, its darkness fading, burning away in the pure white glow of her own will. The darkness around them screamed, a guttural wail that shook the very foundation of the Temple, but it couldn't fight her. The darkness was not stronger than her will.

With a final, forceful cry, Evelyn willed the Heart to cease its pull. And it did.

The room fell silent. The trembling stopped. The shadows that had once seemed so alive vanished, retreating into the far corners of the Temple, leaving nothing but the stillness of the stone walls behind.

Evelyn collapsed onto the cold floor, gasping for breath, her body shaking with exhaustion. She could feel the Heart's energy slowly ebbing, the pulse in her chest returning to a steady rhythm. She had done it. She had stopped it.

Victor was beside her in an instant, his hands hovering over her but unsure where to touch. "Evelyn... are you okay?"

She nodded slowly, still struggling to catch her breath. "I think so," she whispered. But she knew the fight wasn't over. The Heart may have been silenced for now, but its influence still lingered. And somewhere deep in the bowels of the Temple, something ancient had awoken. They were far from finished.

Victor helped her to her feet, his hand steady on her back. "We can't stay here. We've only just begun to scratch the surface of whatever is going on."

Evelyn nodded, wiping the sweat from her brow. The darkness may have been momentarily quelled, but the true battle was just beginning. The Temple had not given up its secrets. Not yet.

"We need to move," she said, her voice firm, her resolve sharpening. "We're not done yet."

And as they turned, the rumbling began again.

Chapter 25: A Moment of Reflection

The silence after the battle felt unreal. It was as if the Temple itself had exhaled, its ancient, crumbling walls finally still after centuries of tense waiting. Yet, as the dust settled, a sense of dread clung to the air like a damp fog. Evelyn's heart thudded in her chest as the echoes of their struggle reverberated through the chamber, the distant rumbling a reminder that something *far* larger than they could understand had stirred beneath them.

Victor kept his hand on her back, his grip firm but gentle, as if afraid that if he loosened it for a moment, she might fall into the abyss once more. But Evelyn didn't need his touch to stay grounded. Something inside her had shifted—something in her mind had snapped into place. For the first time in what felt like an eternity, she understood the stakes. They weren't just fighting for their survival. They were fighting for the *world*.

She stood up slowly, shaking off the remnants of dizziness from her earlier struggle. The last flickers of the dark Heart's influence were fading, but she could still feel its pull, like a distant whisper in the back of her mind.

"We can't let our guard down," Victor murmured, eyes scanning the room as he took a step back toward the large stone door through which they'd entered. He was right—Evelyn could sense it too. The sense of urgency that had been pressing on them since the moment they set foot in this accursed Temple hadn't abated. The power they had disturbed was far from vanquished. They were still very much in the heart of something dangerous.

"What was that thing?" Evelyn asked, her voice hoarse, still reeling from the surge of energy that had nearly consumed her.

Victor's jaw tightened, his gaze focused ahead. "I don't know. But it's tied to the Heart. That much is clear." He glanced at her, eyes narrowing. "And the fact that you were able to hold it back—*stop*

242

it—that's something. We need to figure out how to use that power. It's the only thing that's kept us alive so far."

Evelyn didn't respond immediately. The words hung in the air between them, heavy with implication. She had no idea how she'd done it—how she'd managed to exert control over the Heart in that moment. It had felt almost instinctual, as if something inside her *clicked*, aligning her with the ancient force. But there had been a cost—her body still ached, her chest burned, and the aftershock of that battle left her feeling fragile, vulnerable.

She swallowed hard, trying to push the fear down. "How do we move forward from here? We know what we're up against now. But we don't have the full picture."

Victor gave her a grim look. "We don't have time to piece the whole puzzle together. We have to get to the source of this—whatever it is—and destroy it before it consumes everything. The Heart is a key, Evelyn. A key to unlocking something much bigger. And we're running out of time."

He was right. The rumbling had intensified again, a low growl that reverberated through the floor beneath them. The Temple itself was shifting, reacting to the disturbance they had caused. And it was not about to let them leave without paying the price.

Evelyn's mind raced. The Heart had led them here for a reason, and though she feared what that reason might be, she also knew they couldn't afford to turn back. They had come too far to abandon this mission now.

The symbols carved into the walls—those intricate, swirling patterns that seemed to pulse with a life of their own—were growing brighter again. It was as if the Temple had come alive, reacting to their presence, and perhaps even to the dark Heart they had disturbed. She could feel the atmosphere shifting around them, the air growing thicker, like something was watching them, waiting for them to make their next move.

With a final glance at Victor, Evelyn nodded. "Let's keep moving. We can't stop now."

Victor gave a small nod of agreement, his gaze steely. "Stay close. We don't know what lies ahead."

They moved through the room quickly, taking in the space around them. The walls were lined with bookshelves filled with dust-covered tomes, their spines ancient and worn. There was an eerie sense of stillness, as though the books had been untouched for centuries. A large, raised platform dominated the far end of the chamber, its surface etched with more of the same runic symbols that decorated the walls.

The pulsing light from the Heart in Evelyn's hand cast flickering shadows against the room, making the already oppressive space seem even more claustrophobic. The further they moved, the more the air grew thick with an unseen weight, pressing down on them like a physical force. It was as if the Temple itself was alive, and it did not want them here.

"This place," Evelyn murmured, looking around with a shiver running down her spine, "It feels... wrong. Like it was built to trap something."

Victor nodded, his eyes scanning the room. "I think you're right. There's a darkness here that goes beyond just the Heart. The Temple was meant to contain something. But it's been disturbed, and now whatever was sealed inside it is fighting to break free."

Evelyn glanced down at the Heart in her hand, now pulsing erratically, as if echoing the unease she felt. It was almost as if it were trying to communicate with her, urging her forward. The pulsing felt familiar in a strange way—like it was calling to her, reminding her of the bond they shared.

Suddenly, the ground beneath their feet shuddered again, a violent tremor that sent dust and debris falling from the walls. The rumbling intensified, and the once still air now felt alive with movement. A high-pitched screech rang out, like a thousand voices screaming in unison.

"What the hell was that?" Evelyn gasped, instinctively reaching for Victor's arm.

Victor's face had gone pale. His hand instinctively went to the hilt of his sword, his grip tight. "We're not alone."

Before Evelyn could respond, the screeching noise grew louder, more deafening, until the very walls seemed to vibrate with it. The temperature in the room dropped suddenly, a chilling cold that made her breath freeze in her chest. A dark, shadowy figure appeared at the far end of the room, emerging from the darkness like a phantom.

It was tall—towering, even—and cloaked in shadows that seemed to crawl and writhe around it, as if the darkness itself had given it form. Its eyes, glowing an unnatural red, fixed on them, burning with an ancient, malevolent rage. The thing moved forward, its steps slow and deliberate, as though savoring the moment.

Evelyn's heart raced, her body tensing. She instinctively stepped closer to Victor, who unsheathed his sword with a fluid motion, ready for whatever was about to come.

"What is that thing?" Evelyn breathed, her voice a whisper.

Victor's eyes narrowed. "Whatever it is, it's connected to the Heart. It's *feeding* off the disturbance we caused. We have to stop it."

The creature stopped in the center of the room, its glowing eyes flicking between the two of them. For a moment, there was an eerie silence—an unsettling stillness that seemed to press in from all sides. And then, in a voice like a thousand whispers, it spoke.

"You have awoken *me*."

Evelyn froze, her blood turning to ice. She had heard that voice before—not in the real world, but deep in the recesses of her mind. It was *familiar*, like a memory she couldn't place. The words echoed with a terrifying certainty: *this thing had been waiting for them.*

Victor's grip tightened around his sword, his eyes flicking to Evelyn. "Whatever it is, we need to fight."

The creature tilted its head, and its voice grew louder, more commanding, resonating deep in her bones. "You *cannot* escape. You are already too late."

With a horrifying screech, the creature lunged forward, and the very air around them seemed to crackle with energy.

Evelyn barely had time to react before it was upon them.

The creature's form seemed to stretch and warp, as if the shadows themselves were bending to its will. Its movement was unnaturally fast—blurring with speed that Evelyn could scarcely comprehend. The air around them seemed to bend, warping the very fabric of space as it neared. A low growl reverberated from deep within its chest, an unnatural sound that seemed to reverberate through the very stone beneath their feet.

Victor moved with practiced precision, his sword raised in a defensive stance. His eyes never left the creature, his muscles coiled in anticipation. Evelyn didn't hesitate, though fear gnawed at her insides. She had faced danger before, but this was unlike anything she'd ever seen. The pulse in her chest, the one that had subsided after she'd forced the Heart to quiet down, surged back with renewed force. The dark Heart, still in her hand, hummed with a low, vibrating energy, almost as if it were alive once more.

"Stay close," Victor muttered to her through gritted teeth, his gaze flicking from the creature to the shadows around them. He didn't have to say more; his every movement was a clear instruction.

Without a word, Evelyn nodded, clutching the Heart tightly in her hand, feeling the strange power surge within her. She could feel the echo of its dark energy in her veins, and though it terrified her, there was also something intoxicating about it. A part of her wanted to give in, to surrender to the pull and allow the Heart's influence to take over, but she knew better. If she did, there was no telling what would happen next.

The creature lunged again, its clawed hands swiping through the air with blinding speed. Victor blocked with his sword, but the sheer force of the blow sent him stumbling back. Evelyn's heart leapt into her throat as she watched him falter for a split second, the beast's claws grazing his side. He grunted in pain but recovered quickly, his sword flashing as he parried the next blow.

"Get ready!" he shouted to Evelyn. His voice was hoarse, tight with strain.

Evelyn wasn't sure what he meant, but instinct kicked in. She raised her arm, focusing on the Heart, trying to feel its power course through her as it had done before. Her mind connected to it, threading through the dark energy like a lifeline. She could feel it beckoning her, urging her to *embrace* its power, to become one with it.

Her breath quickened. The Heart was alive, and it was not only feeding off her fear and confusion—it was *calling* to her, demanding she use its power. Evelyn closed her eyes for a moment, shaking off the panic. This wasn't the time to hesitate.

The beast lunged again, but this time Evelyn was ready. She thrust the Heart forward, focusing all the energy it had given her into a single point of release. The moment she did, an explosion of light erupted from the Heart, blinding in its intensity. The power pulsed outward in a shockwave, crashing into the creature like a thunderclap.

The thing shrieked, a high-pitched wail that cut through the air, and staggered back, momentarily stunned by the blast. It staggered but didn't fall, its shadowy form twisting and contorting as though the blast had done little more than irritate it. The creature snarled and then charged, more ferocious than before, its movements becoming erratic, wild.

Victor swung his sword with a roar, slashing toward the creature's glowing red eyes, but it moved too fast, twisting around him. The beast's claws caught him on the shoulder, the impact driving him to the ground with a grunt of pain.

"No!" Evelyn screamed.

The panic that surged through her body was almost overwhelming, but it was also the spark she needed. Her fingers tightened around the Heart. She could feel its pulse—erratic and angry. As the creature moved in for another strike, Evelyn's mind raced. She couldn't let it win. They were close. So close.

With a guttural cry, Evelyn focused all her will on the Heart. *You can control it. You can stop it. You have to stop it.*

The Heart thrummed louder, its energy filling her chest, rushing through her veins. It was more than just the power to destroy; it was power to *control*, to *command*. The more she embraced it, the more she realized—this was the Heart's true nature. It wasn't just an artifact of destruction; it was a force of *dominion*.

The creature, sensing the change in the air, hesitated for a moment. The shadows around it began to ripple, as if it, too, could feel the shift in power. Evelyn's eyes snapped open, and she saw it clearly now—the Heart's power was *calling to the creature*. It wasn't just an attack; it was a *summon*. The Heart had awakened something deep within the Temple—something that had been bound to it, waiting for centuries.

It wasn't enough to just push the creature back; she had to *bind* it.

Evelyn extended her other hand toward the creature, her fingers splayed wide. A thin stream of glowing light shot from her hand and connected to the beast's shadowy form. The creature roared, its body writhing against the glowing thread. The light was burning into the shadow, searing the darkness like a wound.

The creature's movements became erratic, desperate, as it fought to escape. Its glowing red eyes were locked onto Evelyn's, filled with a mixture of hatred and fear. Evelyn gritted her teeth, feeling the strain of holding the creature in place. Sweat beaded on her forehead as she concentrated, pushing every ounce of energy she could summon into maintaining the binding.

Victor, having regained his footing, rushed toward her. He didn't speak, but there was a silent understanding between them. They had to finish this now.

Victor lunged at the creature, sword raised. He slashed at its limbs, but the creature's form was still shifting, twisting in ways that defied reality. Its body was like smoke, unable to be pinned down. Yet, the creature's struggle to escape Evelyn's binding weakened it. It was becoming more material, more *solid*.

With another cry, Evelyn forced more energy into the Heart, pushing back harder. The glow from her hand intensified, as did the pulse of the Heart. The creature let out one final screech before its body exploded in a burst of light, dissipating into smoke and shadows. The air cleared in an instant, leaving nothing behind but the faint smell of sulfur and burning earth.

For a moment, there was only silence. Evelyn's breathing was ragged, her heart pounding in her chest. The Heart, still glowing faintly, hummed in her hand as if responding to the final struggle. Her body was shaking with the aftershock, the weight of the power she had wielded settling in.

Victor stood beside her, his breathing just as labored, but his eyes were filled with relief. "We did it," he said, though his voice was tinged with disbelief. "We actually did it."

Evelyn didn't answer right away. Her mind was still spinning, still processing what had just happened. The Heart had been more than just an artifact. It had been an ancient force, a force tied to the very structure of the Temple itself. And that force had responded to her—had obeyed her. But there was something unsettling about that.

What had she just done? What had she *become* in that moment?

A low groan echoed through the chamber, and she snapped out of her thoughts. The Temple was far from done with them.

Victor turned toward the sound, his sword still in his hand. "We need to move. Now."

Evelyn nodded, her eyes still scanning the room. The shadows were still thick, but they seemed to be retreating now, unwilling to stand against the Heart's power. She didn't trust it, though. There was too much left to uncover, and the echoes of that battle—the sense that something far darker had been awakened—hung heavy in the air.

Together, they moved, step by step, into the heart of the Temple, where deeper darkness awaited.

Chapter 26: The Heart of Darkness

The air in the Temple had thickened, now nearly suffocating, with an oppressive weight that clung to Evelyn's skin like a shroud. The faint glow from the Heart in her palm was the only thing that seemed to pierce the gloom, casting eerie shadows that stretched and swirled across the stone walls. It felt like the entire structure was alive—alive with something ancient, something *hungry*.

Victor was ahead of her, his steps deliberate, as though he were scanning every inch of the darkened chamber. She could see the strain on his face, his jaw clenched, his muscles tense. He was waiting for something—waiting for another attack, another ambush. He was on edge, and Evelyn understood why. After the confrontation with the shadow creature, they both knew they were far from safe. The true nature of the Temple was still hidden, and it had a way of shifting, of *hiding* its secrets, like a sentient thing playing with them.

"What is this place?" Evelyn whispered, her voice echoing unnervingly in the silence. She didn't mean to ask it aloud, but the words tumbled out before she could stop them.

Victor didn't answer immediately, as if the question was too heavy to bear. But then he glanced back at her, his eyes full of something akin to sorrow. "This was never meant to be found. Not by any living soul. Whatever is locked here..." His voice trailed off, and Evelyn could see the weight of his words pressing on him, as if he were reliving something from his past. Something he didn't want to face.

But Evelyn pressed on. She needed answers, more than she needed air. "What happened here, Victor? Why was it sealed away? Why are *we* the ones meant to stop it?"

Victor turned fully toward her, his face softening for the briefest moment. But it was only a flicker before his hardened resolve returned. He stepped closer to her, lowering his voice, almost as if

251

afraid of the walls themselves listening. "I don't know. But I have a feeling we're about to find out."

And that was the truth of it. They were walking in the footsteps of forgotten gods, treading the very path that had been sealed for centuries. Every inch of the Temple seemed to be a warning, every stone etched with secrets they could barely comprehend.

The rumble from beneath them had grown louder, like the heartbeat of some slumbering beast awakening from a long, deep slumber. It was almost as though the Temple itself was *breathing*—the floors trembled beneath their feet, the walls groaned and shifted as if adjusting to their presence. The deeper they went, the closer they got to the heart of the darkness that had been sealed away.

They reached another large chamber, this one even more imposing than the last. The architecture was different here—less decorative, more functional. The stone here was raw, almost jagged, as though it had been hewn from the earth itself. There were no carvings or symbols on the walls, no relics or remnants of previous worship. Just emptiness. A vast, hollow emptiness that sent a chill down Evelyn's spine.

In the center of the room was a large stone altar, its surface cracked and weathered, as though it had borne the weight of ages. There were no torches in this room, no lights to break the dark, but even so, Evelyn could see the strange, shifting shadows near the altar. It felt as if something was waiting for them there. Something that had been waiting for centuries.

Evelyn's breath caught in her throat as she approached. The Heart in her palm seemed to thrum louder with each step, as though it was *calling* to whatever lay ahead. She could feel it, deep within her chest—a resonance, a pull that matched the beat of her own heart.

Victor was a few steps behind, his sword still drawn, but there was something in his eyes that told her he was thinking about the past. About his family. About why they were here.

He didn't speak. But Evelyn didn't need him to.

There was a presence in this room, something *alive*, something that seemed to stretch its fingers through the cracks in the stone, reaching for them.

And then she saw it.

The altar—barely noticeable beneath the shifting shadows—held an object, a long, cylindrical shape wrapped in tattered cloth. It seemed ancient, even older than the Temple itself. The faintest, flickering light glowed from underneath the fabric, casting strange reflections on the walls. A low hum filled the air, like the sound of distant thunder, vibrating through the floor and up into Evelyn's very bones.

"That's it," Evelyn murmured, almost in a trance. "That's what we've been looking for."

Victor's grip on his sword tightened. "The Heart's calling to it," he said, his voice grave.

Evelyn nodded. She had felt it too—the pull. The *urgency*.

Without another word, she stepped forward, drawn toward the altar. Every instinct screamed at her to turn away, to leave this place, to *run*. But her hand moved of its own accord, reaching for the cloth that covered the object.

As her fingers brushed the fabric, the hum of energy in the room surged, as though the very air was reacting to her touch. The cloth began to unravel, disintegrating into dust with a gust of wind that blew through the chamber, though there were no visible openings.

The object beneath it was revealed in full.

It was a crystal, long and jagged, glowing with a pale, sickly light. It was embedded in a base of blackened stone, as though it were part of the very altar. The crystal itself was a deep, almost inky purple, but within it, veins of crimson ran like lightning strikes. The energy from the Heart seemed to *merge* with the crystal, as if they were connected by an invisible thread.

Evelyn stared at it, transfixed. She had seen nothing like it in her travels, and nothing in all the texts and artifacts she had studied had prepared her for the sensation of *pure power* radiating from it. This was something ancient. Something beyond comprehension.

"This is the source," Victor said softly, his voice filled with reverence. "The *key* to the Heart's power. And if we don't destroy it now..." He didn't finish the sentence, but Evelyn didn't need him to. The weight of what he was saying was clear.

The crystal was a *nexus*, the focal point of all the darkness that had been festering here, feeding the power of the Heart. And if they didn't destroy it, the cycle would continue—*forever*.

Evelyn could feel the pull intensifying as her hand hovered over the crystal. It wanted her to take it. It wanted to *bind* with her.

"No," she whispered to herself. "I won't let it."

But the moment the words left her mouth, the ground beneath them trembled again, more violently than before. The walls cracked and groaned, and the air filled with a deafening roar, as though the entire Temple was in pain. Evelyn stumbled, her hand jerking back from the crystal as the Heart in her palm throbbed in response.

Victor staggered toward her, his face twisted in pain. "Evelyn!" he shouted, but his voice was drowned out by the increasing intensity of the sound.

The room was collapsing.

Evelyn couldn't think. Her mind was racing as the stone began to crumble beneath their feet, large sections of the ceiling falling like boulders. But through the chaos, she heard it—another voice, a voice that had been silent until now.

You can't escape.

It was a whisper in her mind, a cold, malicious whisper that *fed* on her fear. The darkness surrounding the altar seemed to grow, the shadows crawling like living things, reaching for her, for them.

She could feel it, the presence, the entity that had been awakened. And it wasn't just the Heart. It was something far older, something far darker. The true enemy was about to make itself known.

Victor grabbed her arm, pulling her toward the exit. "We have to go. Now!"

But Evelyn couldn't move. She couldn't look away. The crystal was calling to her. *It* was the answer to everything. It was the way forward.

But Evelyn wasn't so sure she could trust it anymore.

As the ground trembled beneath them, Evelyn's heart raced, a cold sweat spreading across her skin. The pulse of the Heart in her hand had grown erratic, as though it, too, was reacting to the dark force that was now unravelling around them. The walls of the chamber seemed to shrink, and the shadows twisted, becoming something far more sinister. The air was thick with the scent of sulfur, and the oppressive weight of the Temple pressed in on them from every direction.

Victor's grip on her arm tightened, yanking her from the trance-like state she had been in. He was shouting something, his voice harsh and urgent, but the words didn't register in her mind. All she could hear was the low, eerie hum emanating from the crystal, a sound that vibrated deep within her bones, that seemed to echo in the very core of the Temple.

You can't escape.

The voice, cold and ancient, wrapped itself around her thoughts, each word a dagger of fear, and she could feel its influence tugging at her, pulling her in. It was *calling* to her. No—*compelling* her. Evelyn stumbled backward, her breath coming in shallow gasps. The Heart in her hand pulsed with a strange rhythm, as if it were reacting to the voice, responding to the presence that had risen in the shadows.

Victor's voice broke through the haze, this time more forceful, more desperate. "Evelyn, we have to leave, now!" He pulled her harder, shaking her from her stupor, and this time, she allowed him to drag her back toward the doorway. But it was no use.

Something was holding them in place, some unseen force that made every step forward feel like wading through quicksand. The stone beneath their feet shifted, the ground groaning like it was alive, and the darkness around them thickened, pressing in like a vice.

Evelyn fought the rising terror in her chest, the cold, creeping fear that threatened to freeze her to the spot. But she couldn't ignore the truth. They were not alone anymore. The entity, the one that had been whispering to her, was closer now. It had awakened, its presence radiating from the crystal, from the altar.

She tried to shake her head, but the words kept coming, louder now, more insistent. *You cannot leave. You belong to me now.*

Victor reached for her again, his face twisted with concern, but she couldn't look away from the altar. The crystal was glowing brighter now, the veins of crimson running through its core pulsing like the beat of a heart. The light was unbearable, and Evelyn could feel it tugging at the very fabric of her being, calling to something deep inside her.

Her fingers tightened around the Heart, and for a fleeting moment, it felt as though her body was being pulled into the altar. The weight of the power that coursed through her was overwhelming. She could feel her connection to it growing, could feel the overwhelming temptation to let go, to give in. She could wield this power. She could control the darkness.

"No," she whispered to herself, shaking her head as though she could physically dislodge the thoughts from her mind.

Victor's hand shot out and grabbed her shoulder, spinning her around to face him. His eyes, usually sharp with command, were filled with raw desperation. "Evelyn—*listen* to me!" he shouted. "We're not strong enough to fight this. It's not just the Heart. *It's the Temple*—it's alive!"

Her mind spun. Alive? She could feel it now—*yes*, the Temple itself was reacting, as though it had come to life, an ancient sentience that had been dormant for centuries and now, with the awakening of the crystal, was coming into being.

It was drawing power from the Heart, feeding off the dark energies that had been contained within the Temple's walls. The same dark energy that had twisted everything in its wake—the same energy that had created the shadow beast they had encountered earlier.

And now, it was reaching out for her. For both of them.

The shadows around them thickened, swirling in tendrils like smoke, shifting and writhing as though alive. Evelyn could see them moving closer, creeping toward her and Victor, the space between them narrowing with each passing second. The walls of the chamber seemed to pulse with energy, as though the Temple was breathing in time with the force rising from the altar.

Victor was pulling her harder now, urging her to move, to *run*. "We have to get out of here, Evelyn. Now!"

But Evelyn couldn't bring herself to move. Her eyes were locked onto the crystal, the eerie light from it filling her vision. The Heart, still warm in her palm, seemed to hum in agreement with the power coming from the altar, and she could feel it—*could feel it deep inside her, calling to her.*

Her pulse quickened, her body betraying her as she took a step closer to the altar. The darkness in the room seemed to press in around her, the shadows now forming shapes, twisted and indistinct but full of malice. They were moving toward her like a living nightmare.

Evelyn could feel it. The darkness was hungry.

Victor noticed the change in her, the shift in her stance, the way her body was leaning toward the altar as though it were a magnet pulling her in. "Evelyn, *no!*" he cried out in panic.

But Evelyn's mind was no longer fully her own. The voice, the presence in her mind, was growing stronger. The pull of the crystal was irresistible now. She could feel herself slipping, could feel herself becoming *one* with it, with the Temple, with the darkness itself.

You were always meant to be here. You were always mine. The voice caressed her thoughts, sweet and cold, wrapping itself around her like a lover's embrace. *Now, take it. Take your place.*

Victor's grip on her arm tightened, but she hardly noticed it. She could feel her heart beating erratically in her chest, but it was no longer her heartbeat she heard. It was the pulse of the crystal. The pulse of the *Temple*.

And then, something broke through the fog in her mind. A memory. A flash of her father's voice. His warnings. His words before she had left for the Temple.

"The Heart is not just power, Evelyn. It's a curse. A prison. It's alive, and it feeds on those who wield it."

Her eyes snapped open. The realization hit her like a punch to the gut. She wasn't just a *vessel* for the Heart. She wasn't just an innocent bystander in this ancient drama. She was part of the curse. She was the key.

The power in her hand surged again, filling her entire body with a burning, unbearable heat. She could feel the Heart calling, but she could also feel the walls of the Temple pushing back, *fighting* to reclaim her.

Victor yanked on her arm again, harder this time. "Evelyn, snap out of it! You have to fight it!"

His voice reached her, barely. She blinked, shaking her head, as if trying to break free of the pull. But the Heart was relentless. It whispered promises of power, of control. It fed on her fears, on her doubts.

Victor was still pulling her, his hand strong and steady. She felt herself slipping again, but then she heard something—*someone*. A voice, soft and distant, like a whisper on the wind.

It was her father's voice again. *You have to choose, Evelyn. You have to choose the light, or you'll become a part of the darkness. Choose wisely.*

Her breath hitched. The weight of his words crashed down on her. She *had* to choose. She *could* choose.

With all the strength she could summon, Evelyn forced her hand away from the Heart. The power in her veins screamed in protest, but she clenched her fist, fighting it. It *hurt*, more than anything she had ever felt before, but she fought through it.

And then, with a final scream of effort, she *let go*.

Victor stumbled backward as she tore herself away from the altar. The Heart in her hand pulsed once, then went silent, the glow fading. The shadows that had been pressing in around them began to dissipate, as though the very essence of the Temple was pulling back.

The room seemed to exhale, the pressure lifting, the humming of the crystal slowly fading into nothingness.

Evelyn's knees buckled, and she collapsed onto the stone floor, gasping for breath. Her body was trembling, every muscle sore from the struggle, but she had done it. She had broken free.

Victor was beside her in an instant, his hand on her shoulder. "You're okay," he murmured, though his voice was filled with concern. "You're okay. You made it."

Evelyn didn't answer immediately. Her mind was still reeling, trying to process what had just happened, trying to understand the weight of the decision she had just made. But one thing was clear now.

The Heart was not done with her. Not yet.

Chapter 27: Unmasking the Killer

The storm had settled into a sullen quiet. Outside, the night sky churned with the remnants of a thunderstorm, heavy clouds hanging low in the distance, barely allowing the moon to break through. Inside the walls of the decrepit mansion, the air was thick with the tension of unspoken words and buried secrets. The investigation was reaching its boiling point. The killer was close—closer than ever—and Evelyn felt a cold certainty in her gut: the moment of reckoning was near.

Victor stood by the fireplace, his back to her, staring into the dying embers. His face was set in grim lines, the weight of the past few days heavy on his shoulders. She had never seen him so withdrawn, so unsure. But Evelyn couldn't afford to dwell on his silent turmoil. There was a job to finish. She could feel it, the way the puzzle pieces were beginning to fall into place, all the fragments of truth coming together in a singular, undeniable realization.

The murder had been brutal, its aftermath even more so, but the deeper she dug into the lives of the people connected to the victim, the more she felt like she was peeling back the layers of a twisted game. Every piece of evidence—every odd detail—pointed toward someone close to her. Someone who had been playing a dangerous game, and now, it seemed, they were ready to expose the final card.

"Victor," Evelyn said, her voice breaking the silence like a stone dropped into water. "I think I know who the killer is."

He didn't turn around at first. Instead, he took a long breath, his hands tightening into fists as he faced the fire. She could feel the intensity of his presence, even without him saying a word. He was on edge. She knew he wouldn't believe her so easily—not without evidence. They had been down this road before, chasing shadows, running in circles. But this time felt different. This time, the killer was no longer a ghost hiding in the dark. The truth was within reach.

Victor turned slowly, his eyes locking with hers. "Who? Don't tell me you're jumping to conclusions again, Evelyn. We've been down this road before." There was a warning edge to his voice, a sharpness that made her hesitate for a split second.

"I'm not jumping to conclusions," she replied, her voice steady. "I've been watching the others. Analyzing the behavior. The victim wasn't just killed out of rage or fear. This was calculated. Carefully executed. And there's one person who fits the profile."

Victor stepped forward, crossing his arms over his chest. "And who's that?"

For a moment, Evelyn allowed herself to look away, her gaze drifting toward the small group of people who had gathered in the mansion's sitting room. They were all suspects in their own right, their faces shadowed with uncertainty, fear, or guilt. Each of them had their own reasons for being here. Each of them had their own secrets. But Evelyn was certain that one of them was hiding the truth.

"Elena Rourke," Evelyn said, her voice barely above a whisper. "She's the one. She's the killer."

Victor's eyebrows shot up in disbelief. "Elena? *Rourke*? You're sure about this?"

Evelyn nodded, her pulse steady despite the rush of adrenaline. "I didn't want to believe it either, but the pieces fit. She's been manipulating the others. Watching us, pulling strings. She's not just a bystander in this. She's been at the center of it all."

Victor paced across the room, the heavy thud of his boots on the floor loud in the silence. "What makes you so sure? She's been—what—cooperative? Nervous, maybe, but she's been part of the group. She's—"

"I know," Evelyn cut in. "But that's the thing. She's been playing us, Victor. She's been hiding in plain sight. The way she reacts to certain questions, the way she's always one step ahead of the investigation, the way she *looks* at the others. It's all a front. And I think she's been waiting for the right moment to strike again."

Victor shook his head slowly, a flicker of doubt crossing his face. "I don't know, Evelyn. Elena's been here the whole time. She's been with the group since the beginning. She has no reason to—"

"Exactly," Evelyn interrupted, her voice firm now. "She *has no reason*. That's the key. It's the perfect cover—being part of the group, blending in, making us all think she's just another victim of circumstance. But the truth is, she's the one pulling the strings behind the scenes. She's playing a long con."

Victor seemed to be processing her words, but the doubt still lingered in his eyes. "I want to believe you, Evelyn. But we've seen this before. Where's the evidence? We can't just accuse someone without—"

"I don't need evidence," Evelyn said, her voice cold and certain. "I've seen enough. Elena is the one who killed them. And we need to confront her. Before it's too late."

Victor's lips pressed into a thin line as he nodded. There was something unspoken between them, a shared understanding of what needed to be done next. They couldn't just sit back and wait for the next victim. They had to act now. No more games. No more waiting.

As they moved toward the door to the sitting room, Evelyn's thoughts raced. Elena had been carefully constructing her alibi, positioning herself as an innocent, distraught victim, but Evelyn had seen through the act. Elena's subtle manipulations—the way she played on people's sympathies, her careful probing of each person's vulnerabilities—had all been too well-rehearsed. She was orchestrating something, and it was only a matter of time before her mask slipped.

When they entered the sitting room, Elena looked up from where she sat by the window, her fingers delicately tracing the rim of a glass. She seemed almost serene, too composed for someone who had been through the same traumatic events as the others. The moment her eyes met Evelyn's, a flicker of something cold crossed her face, but it was gone as quickly as it appeared.

"Ah, Evelyn. Victor," Elena said, her voice smooth, almost too smooth. "I was wondering when you two would come to join the rest of us." She smiled, but it didn't reach her eyes.

Evelyn could feel it now—the tension hanging between them. Elena knew that Evelyn was onto her. But she wasn't going to give up without a fight.

"We need to talk," Evelyn said, her voice firm. "We need to talk about the murders. *Your* murders."

Elena's smile faltered, just a fraction. "My murders? I think you've been under a lot of stress, Evelyn. We've all been through hell, but I'm sure you don't mean that."

"Oh, but I do," Evelyn replied, her gaze unwavering. "I know it was you, Elena. I know you're the one pulling the strings here. You've been playing us all, setting the pieces in motion. The victim wasn't just some random casualty. They were part of your plan. Your *game*."

Elena stood, her movement deliberate, controlled. "You're delusional if you think that. What *game*? What are you talking about?"

Evelyn didn't flinch. "The game you've been playing. The one where you decide who lives and who dies. You've been manipulating us all—everyone here. You knew exactly how to stay in the background, how to make sure we didn't look too closely at you. But I've been watching, and I know what you've been doing. The way you've been pushing people to their breaking point, making sure the tension builds until it reaches a climax."

Victor stepped forward now, his eyes cold, his voice hard. "You won't get away with this, Elena. We have enough on you. Your time is up."

Elena's mask finally cracked. For the briefest moment, her composure faltered, her eyes narrowing in cold fury. But it was only a moment before she regained control, her lips curling into a twisted smile.

"You really think you've figured it out, don't you?" she said, her voice now laced with venom. "You think you know who I am? But you have no idea what you're dealing with. You never did. And now it's too late."

The room seemed to close in on them, the air thick with the weight of impending danger. Evelyn could feel it now, that familiar tension—the sense that they were on the edge of something far darker than either of them had imagined. Elena was playing her final hand, and Evelyn knew that the killer wasn't done yet.

The game was just beginning.

Elena's smile twisted into something darker, more sinister, like a mask that had finally shattered, revealing the true face beneath. Evelyn stood motionless, her pulse quickening with each word that Elena spoke. The weight of the moment pressed down on her, the anticipation of what was to come almost unbearable.

"You're right about one thing," Elena said, her voice low and dangerous now, stripped of any pretense. "You don't know who you're dealing with. None of you do. I've been playing you all like pawns in a game you don't even realize you're a part of. And you," she pointed at Evelyn, "you were never meant to figure it out. But you did. And that's the problem."

Victor moved slightly closer to Evelyn, his eyes narrowing as he kept his focus on Elena. He could sense the shift in the air, the growing tension in the room. Whatever Elena had planned, whatever she was about to do, they had to stop her now. They couldn't let her play out whatever final move she had in mind.

"Stop talking in riddles, Elena," Victor growled. "What are you really after? Why are you doing this?"

Elena let out a short, cruel laugh, and Evelyn could see the malice in her eyes. "You still don't get it, do you? It's never been about money. Or revenge. It's never been personal. This—" She gestured widely around the room, as though encompassing everything—her surroundings, the mansion, the people in it—"this is about power. About control. I've been in the shadows for too long. But I've learned how to manipulate situations, how to push people into places they don't want to go. And now, Evelyn, the game is over. You've reached the final move, and you still don't know how it ends."

Evelyn's mind raced, trying to piece together the final moments of their investigation. She had always suspected Elena was hiding something, but the truth—this truth—was beyond anything she had prepared for. There was a darkness in Elena that stretched far beyond the killings themselves. It wasn't just about murder. It was about orchestrating a twisted symphony of destruction.

"What do you want?" Evelyn asked, her voice a mixture of frustration and determination. "What are you trying to accomplish? You've already killed two people—what do you gain by killing us?"

Elena's eyes glinted with something cold, calculating. "You think I'm trying to kill you?" she scoffed. "I'm not the one who's been killing anyone. But I do know who is. And it's not just about revenge or greed. It's about control—control over all of you. I've been setting you up, pushing you all toward the same endgame. The killings weren't random. They were all part of a plan, a test, really. To see who would crack first. Who would become a threat."

Victor stepped forward, his voice gaining strength. "You're not making sense, Elena. Who's been doing the killing, then? If it wasn't you, then who? And why—"

"The killer?" Elena cut him off. "You're looking at her. *I* am the killer. But you've been so blinded by your investigation, so sure that it's someone else, that you didn't see the most obvious truth. It was all part of the plan."

Evelyn's heart pounded. The words twisted in her mind, but it took a moment for them to sink in. "Wait... You're saying you've been the one doing it all along?"

Elena's smile never faltered, though now it seemed to have a touch of madness. "Yes. Yes, Evelyn, I've been the one. And I've done it for one simple reason: to make you see. To make all of you see what's right in front of your eyes. You've all been so focused on finding the killer, on trying to stop the murders, that you never stopped to think about *why* they were happening. What was really going on."

Victor clenched his fists. "You're insane."

"You think so?" Elena's tone was soft, almost sympathetic, as if she were explaining a difficult concept to a child. "The real insanity is in how you've all been playing along. How easily you fell into my hands. You see, I didn't need to kill anyone. I just needed to make you believe it. To make you trust the wrong people, push you into corners where you had no choice but to fight back. And once you started looking for a killer, once you thought you had someone to blame... that's when I knew it was time to pull the strings."

Evelyn took a step forward, narrowing her gaze. "So you've been controlling everything. The killings. The fear. The paranoia. The trust between us... that's all been part of your game."

Elena nodded slowly, her eyes gleaming with something akin to satisfaction. "Exactly. All part of the plan. You're smart, Evelyn. But even you couldn't see the bigger picture. You're a detective, sure. But you're too close to it. You couldn't see what was happening right under your nose."

The room felt suffocating now, the weight of her words pressing in on them like a physical force. Evelyn felt a chill run down her spine. If Elena had been the killer all along, then every conversation, every moment of tension, every clue they'd uncovered had all been manipulated. They had been mere players in a game she had orchestrated from the very beginning.

Evelyn's thoughts raced as she tried to piece together the logistics of Elena's plan. How had Elena managed to kill without leaving a trace, without suspicion falling on her? There had to be something more, some other layer to her deception. And then it hit her.

"Wait—if you were the killer all along, why didn't we find any evidence pointing to you?" Evelyn demanded. "You've been here with us this entire time. How did you pull it off?"

Elena's grin widened, the kind of smile one might give an unruly child who had just figured out a difficult puzzle. "That's the thing, Evelyn. I didn't have to do anything at all. I never killed anyone directly. I just made sure the *right* people did the killing for me."

Victor blinked, confusion washing over his face. "What are you saying? You didn't kill anyone?"

Evelyn's eyes widened. "You... you manipulated the others?"

"Yes," Elena purred. "I manipulated their fears. Their paranoia. I watched them, learned their weaknesses, and carefully nudged them into committing the crimes. You see, the mind is an incredibly fragile thing. All you have to do is plant the right seed, and watch it grow. In this case, the seed was the fear of being found out. The fear of being caught."

Evelyn took a slow step back, her mind reeling. The others in the room—their confusion, their terror, their suspicion—none of it had been real. They hadn't been reacting to genuine fear. They had been reacting to Elena's carefully planted ideas, reacting to a game that she had designed.

"But why?" Victor asked. "Why go through all this trouble? Why go this far?"

Elena's smile turned cold, her eyes darkening with a dangerous gleam. "Because I could. Because you all needed to be taught a lesson. I've been underestimated my entire life. Just another woman in the shadows, always seen as a *victim*. But I knew. I knew I could use that to my advantage. I've been watching, waiting for the right moment to take control. To show you all that I am the one who decides who lives and who dies. No one else."

Evelyn's heart pounded in her chest, her instincts screaming that she was on the brink of something even darker. "This isn't over, Elena," she said, her voice steady. "The people you've manipulated—they'll see the truth. They'll know what you've done."

"Oh, I'm counting on that," Elena said, her smile sharpening. "Because when they do... when they realize what I've turned them into, that's when the real game begins."

Victor's face hardened as he stepped forward. "You've made a huge mistake, Elena. You're not going to get away with this."

"I already have," she replied, her tone flat. "You're just too late."

Evelyn and Victor exchanged a glance, their minds working in tandem. This wasn't just about catching a killer anymore. This was about stopping someone who had already set a far more dangerous plan into motion. They needed to stop Elena, and they needed to do it now.

Evelyn reached into her coat, pulling out the gun she had kept hidden. "Elena... this ends tonight."

Elena raised an eyebrow, clearly unfazed. "You think a gun will stop me? You think *you're* the ones in control here?"

"No," Evelyn said, her voice cold. "But it'll stop you from controlling anyone else."

As the tension in the room peaked, the weight of the decision settled heavily on her shoulders. The game was finally over, but in the end, there was only one thing left to do.

Chapter 28: The Price of Truth

The sound of the clock ticking filled the oppressive silence in the room. Evelyn could feel the tension curling around her, coiling tighter with each breath she took. Her fingers tightened around the grip of the gun, the cold metal almost a comfort in the midst of the storm that raged in her chest. She could see Elena standing there, so calm, so composed, even in the face of imminent defeat. It was like she had been expecting this moment all along, and in a way, Evelyn realized, maybe she had.

Victor was watching Elena carefully, his jaw clenched. The adrenaline coursing through him was palpable, but there was something else there too—something darker. For a split second, Evelyn thought he might act on his own impulses, might charge at Elena, but he held back. They both knew what was at stake now.

Elena's smirk never wavered, but there was a flicker of something—fear, perhaps? Or maybe it was realization that her perfect game was coming to an end. For the first time, there was uncertainty in her eyes, though she tried to mask it behind the veneer of confidence.

"You really think you can stop me?" Elena's voice broke the silence, thick with disbelief. Her eyes were wide, almost laughing, but Evelyn could see the strain beneath the mask. "You think one gun, one moment, will make everything go away? You've been chasing ghosts, Evelyn. You've been playing right into my hands the whole time."

Evelyn didn't flinch. Her focus was clear. "You've been playing all of us, Elena. But the game's over. You're not getting away with it."

"You don't get it," Elena said, her voice low and steady. She took a small step forward, like a lioness sizing up its prey, testing the boundaries. "You think you're the hero in this story? The one who's going to save the day? But you're not. You're just a part of it. You always have been. The question is—do you want to know the truth? The real truth?"

The air grew thick with the weight of her words. Evelyn could feel the uncertainty creeping in again, threatening to shake her resolve. She had already seen the depths of Elena's manipulation. She had already uncovered the lies. But this—the truth Elena was offering—was something far more dangerous. Evelyn didn't need to hear it. She didn't want to.

But Elena pressed on, sensing the hesitation.

"The truth, Evelyn, is that the people who died, the ones you've been chasing, they weren't the victims. Not really. They were part of a much bigger picture. A much darker one. They were casualties in a war you didn't even know existed."

Evelyn's grip on the gun tightened, and she fought to keep her voice steady. "I'm done with your games, Elena. I'm not listening to you anymore."

But Elena's smile widened, twisted with a dark pleasure. "No, you *need* to listen. Because the truth isn't just about who kills whom. It's about power. The kind of power you can't even begin to comprehend. You see, I'm not the only one with blood on my hands, Evelyn. You're part of this, too. And when you know the truth, when you finally see it for yourself, there will be no going back."

Evelyn shook her head, her mind racing. "You're lying. You're trying to manipulate me again, but it's over. You've lost."

Elena's laughter echoed in the room, hollow and mocking. "Lost? No. You don't understand. This was never about winning or losing. This was about survival. You think you can just walk away from this? You think you can just kill me and go back to your normal life? No, Evelyn. You're in this now. You've crossed the line."

For a moment, everything stopped. Evelyn's thoughts came to a screeching halt. What Elena was saying, the way she was speaking—it wasn't just about the murders. There was something bigger here, something Evelyn hadn't fully understood until now. It wasn't just about stopping a killer. It was about the ripple effect, the consequences that would unfold the moment Elena fell.

Evelyn took a deep breath, trying to steady herself, but there was something deep in her gut telling her she wasn't prepared for what was coming next. Something darker was lurking, waiting to pull her under.

Victor, sensing the shift in the air, stepped forward, his voice calm but resolute. "Enough, Elena. We don't need to hear your twisted philosophy. You've killed people. You've manipulated us. And now it ends."

But Elena wasn't finished. Her eyes locked with Evelyn's, and for a moment, the room felt suffocating. Her gaze was piercing, almost hypnotic. "You think you can stop it? You think one bullet will change anything? The damage is already done. You're already part of this story, Evelyn. And so is Victor. So are all of you. The real game was never about finding a killer. It was about control, about knowing who will break, who will crack under pressure. You're too far in now to just walk away. You've all played your part. And you don't even realize it."

Evelyn felt her heart rate spike. Every word Elena spoke seemed to sink deeper, gnawing away at the very foundations of everything she believed. She had always been driven by the pursuit of truth, by the idea of justice. But what if the truth Elena spoke of was something she couldn't handle? What if there was a price she wasn't willing to pay?

"I'm done listening," Evelyn said through gritted teeth. "I'm ending this now."

She took a step forward, her eyes locked on Elena's, unwavering. Elena's expression faltered for a brief moment, but only for a fraction of a second. Then, just as quickly, her composure returned, the smirk creeping back onto her face.

"You think killing me will fix things? That you'll walk away, your conscience clear?" Elena's voice was almost a whisper now, filled with dark satisfaction. "No, Evelyn. This isn't about me. It's about you. And when you pull that trigger, you'll be making a choice. A choice you can never take back. The price of truth is high. It always is. But you're not ready for the cost."

Evelyn hesitated. For just a moment, she wavered. The weight of the gun in her hand seemed to grow heavier with each passing second, as if the weapon itself had become a burden she could no longer carry.

Victor's voice cut through the tension. "Don't listen to her, Evelyn. She's trying to manipulate you again. Don't let her."

But it wasn't Elena's words that were trapping Evelyn now. It was the realization that, deep down, she knew Elena was right. The truth always came at a cost. And no matter what happened next, she would never be the same.

Evelyn's gaze never left Elena. She could feel the storm of emotions swirling inside her—anger, fear, uncertainty—but she also felt something else: clarity. She couldn't undo what had been done. She couldn't take back the lives that had been lost. But she could stop Elena. She could put an end to the madness, even if it meant facing the darkness within herself.

With a deep, steadying breath, Evelyn raised the gun.

"Goodbye, Elena," she said, her voice steady, even as the world around her seemed to spin.

The echo of the shot filled the room.

The deafening crack of the gunshot split the air, leaving an eerie silence in its wake. Evelyn's heart hammered in her chest, and for a fleeting moment, the world seemed to slow down. The gun's recoil had sent a shudder through her arm, but the target—Elena—stood perfectly still.

The seconds stretched on like hours.

Evelyn's breath came in shallow gasps as she stared at the woman who had orchestrated everything—the death, the manipulation, the twisted game they had all been part of. There, on the floor before her, Elena crumpled slightly, her eyes wide in shock. Blood began to seep from the wound in her chest, staining the pristine carpet beneath her.

But Elena wasn't dead.

Not yet.

For a moment, there was no sound in the room except for the faint drip of blood hitting the floor, the soft, sickening rhythm of it falling in time with Evelyn's racing heartbeat. She could barely process what had just happened. She had pulled the trigger. The shot had landed, and Elena was still alive—barely—but alive. How could that be?

Victor was the first to move. He rushed forward, kneeling beside Elena's prone form, his face a mask of confusion and disbelief. The blood was pouring from her chest now, seeping into the rug like dark ink staining paper.

"Elena..." Victor's voice was a mixture of disbelief and desperation, but there was something else there too—something Evelyn couldn't place. "Why... why didn't you fall?"

Elena's eyes flickered as she tried to focus on him, a thin, twisted smile curling at the corner of her lips despite the blood spilling from her mouth. "You thought... that was it?" she rasped, her voice weak but still dripping with malicious amusement. "You thought that killing me would stop everything?"

Evelyn took a step back, her pulse pounding in her ears. She had heard that line before—*the truth always has a price*. Elena was trying to manipulate them again, wasn't she? Trying to make them doubt everything they thought they knew.

Victor's face twisted in horror. "You planned this, didn't you? This was all part of it. You wanted me to shoot you. To believe I could end this with one bullet."

Elena's chest heaved as she struggled to breathe, her laugh coming out in shallow, rattling gasps. "Of course, I did. I had to make sure you *believed* you had control. That was always the game. You had to think you could stop me. But you can't, Victor. You never could."

Evelyn's hand shook, the gun still in her grip. She could feel the cold sweat trickling down the back of her neck, but her focus was unwavering. She had to stop this. They had to finish it. This madness, this endless game, needed to end. But as she looked at Elena, her resolve faltered once again.

What if Elena was right? What if the truth was something far darker than either of them could understand?

"Elena, stop," Evelyn said, her voice shaking but firm. "You're not going to manipulate us anymore. Tell us what the hell is going on."

Elena's smile flickered again, more genuine now, as if she were amused by Evelyn's desperation. Her breathing had become shallow, erratic, but her eyes still gleamed with that same unsettling light.

"You really don't get it, do you?" Elena whispered, her voice hoarse. "You think this is about *me*? About killing me and ending the game? No. It's about the people behind all of this. It's about the ones who *made* me, the ones who molded me into this..." She coughed violently, more blood spilling from her mouth. "I was just the instrument. The one who did the dirty work. But there's a bigger picture. And you, Evelyn... you're in it."

Evelyn's mind raced, but she couldn't stop the creeping sense of dread that began to settle in her gut. She had suspected something much larger was at play here, something beyond Elena. But this? What was Elena talking about? Who was behind her?

Victor's eyes widened. "What do you mean? Who? Who's behind you?"

Elena's lips parted in a grim, knowing smile. She couldn't answer right away—her body was failing her, the blood loss taking its toll—but she managed to gasp out a single word, a name that felt like a shot to the chest, more piercing than any bullet could ever be.

"*Corvus.*"

The name landed like a weight in the room, suffocating the air and freezing both Evelyn and Victor in place. Evelyn's heart skipped a beat, and Victor's face drained of color.

"Corvus?" Victor repeated, his voice hoarse with disbelief. "But... but that's impossible. That was... that was a myth."

"No," Elena whispered, her eyes glazing over, "it's not. Corvus is very real. And they've been watching... waiting for this moment. The moment when everything *shattered*. When the pieces fell into place. When the world you know, the world you *think* you understand, is no longer the same. *Corvus* is the shadow behind everything. The organization that's been pulling strings for years."

Victor shook his head, his voice trembling with a mixture of anger and confusion. "You're lying. There's no organization like that. This is just some sick manipulation. You're trying to pull us into another trap."

But Elena's eyes didn't waver. "It's not a trap, Victor. It's the truth. And now you're both part of it. Whether you like it or not."

Evelyn stepped forward, her fingers trembling as she lowered the gun. She felt her grip loosening, her thoughts scattering like leaves in the wind. Corvus. The word resonated deep inside her, like an echo from a past life she had never known. An organization? A shadow group pulling strings in the dark? The idea seemed so absurd, so far beyond anything she had ever encountered. Yet Elena's bloodied smile made it feel terrifyingly real.

"You're saying *Corvus* is real. That they've been behind this all along?" Evelyn asked, her voice barely more than a whisper.

Elena's smile faltered, but only for a moment. "They've been behind everything you've seen. The deaths, the fear, the chaos. They orchestrated it all. And you, Evelyn, were their final piece. You were always meant to find out. But the moment you did... you sealed your fate. Corvus doesn't *lose*, Evelyn. You were never going to walk away from this."

Victor's face was drawn in lines of frustration, his mind obviously trying to piece together the puzzle. "But what does that mean for us? For me? You said we're 'part of it.' What the hell are we supposed to do with that?"

Elena's gaze darkened, and her lips parted with a final, breathless laugh. "That, my dear Victor, is the real price of truth. You think you've been playing this game, that you've been in control? But in reality, you've been pawns, too. And Corvus always gets its way. Always."

Her voice trailed off into a wheeze, her eyes fluttering as if she were drifting in and out of consciousness. Evelyn couldn't take her eyes off the woman who had, in her final moments, revealed the most devastating secret of all.

Corvus.

A shadow. A hidden organization. The true puppeteers of this entire nightmare. But what did it mean for them now? For Evelyn, for Victor? Could they even stop what was coming?

The room seemed to close in around her. The weight of Elena's words hung heavily, thick with the promise of danger. There was a bigger game at play, something far more dangerous than anything Evelyn could have imagined. And now, she had no choice but to confront it.

Evelyn finally looked at Victor, her voice barely above a whisper. "We need to find them. We need to find Corvus."

Victor nodded grimly, his face hardening with resolve. "We do. And when we do, we'll make them pay for everything they've done. Starting with Elena."

But deep down, Evelyn knew the battle they were about to face would be unlike anything they had ever imagined. The truth had come at a cost—now it was time to pay the price.

The weight of Elena's final words seemed to hang over them like a storm cloud that wouldn't dissipate. Evelyn could feel the darkness of it creeping into her bones, the air thick with the oppressive weight of truth and the heavy burden of what they had learned. Corvus. An unseen force that had shaped the very fabric of their lives without them even knowing. Their names had been written on a list somewhere, their roles preordained by the twisted hands of those in the shadows.

Evelyn glanced at Victor, her eyes searching for some semblance of reassurance, but all she found in his face was grim determination. He was as lost as she was—lost, but resolute. They couldn't run anymore. There were no more choices that would lead them to safety. The only way forward was through the heart of the storm. And that meant confronting Corvus head-on.

Victor had been right when he said that Corvus was no myth, no boogeyman to scare children. It was very real—and it was hunting them now, whether they were ready for it or not.

They stood in the room for what felt like hours, the only sound the low hum of the city outside and their quiet breaths filling the silence. The files on the table were a maze of information—clippings, photos, names, dates. At first glance, it all looked like a random collection of documents, but Evelyn knew better now. Every piece was connected. Every name, every photograph, every date—each one was a piece of the puzzle, and she and Victor were the ones tasked with putting it all together.

Evelyn shuffled through the papers, her fingers trembling as she flipped from one document to the next. She didn't need to understand all of it right now. But there was one thing she had to confirm. One person's name had to be on the list. And if it was, that would be the thread that could unravel everything.

"Victor," she said quietly, her voice barely above a whisper. "What if... what if Elena wasn't just a pawn, but a piece in a bigger game? She said we were part of it. But what if she wasn't talking about us, specifically? What if we were just..." She trailed off, unsure how to finish the thought. "What if we were just the next pieces?"

Victor stepped closer, scanning the documents she was holding. His brow furrowed in concentration as he read over the names, his hand resting on the back of the chair. "You're thinking too much, Evelyn. She was trying to mess with your head. But I get it. She played us all. She wanted us to question our every move. But that's exactly what Corvus wants—to keep us in the dark. To make us second-guess every decision."

Evelyn stared at the photo she had found earlier—the figure with the shadowed face. Her fingers hovered over it again, feeling the pulse of connection. This wasn't just some random shot. This was deliberate. This person had been in the room, behind the curtain, orchestrating everything. But how did he fit into the puzzle?

Before she could voice her thoughts, the sound of footsteps echoed from the hallway outside the room. Instinctively, she dropped the papers and grabbed the gun that had been tucked into her waistband. Her pulse quickened, the threat of discovery hanging heavy in the air.

Victor reached for his phone, checking the screen. He let out a frustrated sigh. "We're not alone anymore. Someone's coming. We need to move."

Evelyn nodded sharply, taking one last look around the room before grabbing the flash drive from the table. She shoved it into her pocket and motioned for Victor to follow her. Their time was running out.

As they moved to the back exit, their footsteps were muffled against the worn carpet. The narrow hallway outside was dim, the flickering fluorescent lights casting long, uncertain shadows. Evelyn's mind raced as she mentally mapped out their escape. They couldn't leave the building the way they'd come. Whoever was on their way in would be expecting that.

"Let's head through the basement," Victor whispered, pulling her closer. "We can use the service tunnels to get out. No one will expect us down there."

Evelyn nodded, feeling the familiar tension in her chest rise as they hurried through the maze of corridors. The urgency of their situation was palpable, but beneath that, there was a deeper feeling. It was a fear that had been building since they had first learned the name *Corvus*. A fear that they might be too late to stop it. That the dark forces they were chasing were always one step ahead.

The basement was even darker than the rest of the building, the air thick with the smell of mildew and decay. They moved quickly, their footsteps echoing against the cold concrete floor. It didn't take long before they reached the service door, the heavy metal handle cold under Evelyn's fingers. She turned it, and the door swung open with a groan of protest.

"Stay close," Victor muttered, his eyes scanning the darkness ahead. "We'll take the tunnels to the old subway station. From there, we can figure out where we go next."

They slipped into the tunnel, the door shutting softly behind them. As they walked deeper into the underground labyrinth, Evelyn's thoughts kept circling back to the files they had left behind. To the names. To the photo of the man whose face they couldn't yet fully see.

Corvus wasn't just a shadow anymore. It was a reflection of everything they had been running from.

She didn't realize how much time had passed until they reached the subway station. It was a hidden, almost forgotten part of the city, like everything else they had encountered. The silence of the underground was a stark contrast to the city above, as if they had entered another world entirely. The flickering lights cast long shadows over the walls, the sound of distant trains rumbling somewhere far away.

Victor turned to her, his expression unreadable. He had been quiet since they entered the tunnels, his mind clearly focused on the task at hand. But Evelyn could feel the weight of the questions between them—the same questions they had both been avoiding. What now? What did Corvus want? And how could they possibly stop it?

She was the one who spoke first.

"We have to find the source," she said. Her voice was steady, but inside, she felt a gnawing emptiness. She had been walking in the dark for so long, and every step seemed to bring them further into a maze with no way out. "Elena was right. We're part of something bigger. And if Corvus is really behind all of this... then the people who are running it are too dangerous to ignore. They've been pulling strings for years. They've watched us, studied us, and they've always known exactly what we would do."

Victor stopped walking, his gaze fixed on the far end of the tunnel, as if trying to look through the concrete and steel to the world beyond. "And if we're right, if Corvus is everywhere... then where do we go from here? What happens when we bring them to light?"

Evelyn let the question hang in the air. She didn't have an answer. She didn't know if they could bring down an organization like Corvus. They were too small, too outmatched. But what she did know was this:

They had to try. They had to go deeper into the heart of it. No matter the cost.

"I don't know," she admitted. "But we won't stop until we find the answers. And when we do, we'll expose them. All of it."

Victor's face softened slightly, his eyes darkening with a mix of determination and something deeper—perhaps a shared understanding of the risks they were taking.

"Let's go," he said. And together, they stepped into the shadows of the unknown once more.

Chapter 29: Into the Light

The silence of the underground tunnel seemed to swallow them whole as Evelyn and Victor continued their trek through the forgotten pathways beneath the city. The dim flickering lights above cast uneven shadows that danced across the walls, creating a labyrinthine effect that made it seem as though they were walking in circles. The air was thick with the smell of rust, dampness, and stale earth, a stark reminder that they were far from the clean, sterile world they once knew. The grime on the walls seemed to mirror the grime that had built up in their lives since the day they learned the name Corvus.

Evelyn's mind raced, as it had for hours now. They had discovered the truth—the horrifying reality that Corvus wasn't just an isolated criminal organization, but an all-encompassing, insidious force, with tendrils that reached into every corner of the world. She had once thought that knowing the truth would bring some kind of relief. But the more she uncovered, the more she realized that knowledge alone wasn't enough. It was a curse. It put a target on her back. And Victor's.

Every step deeper into the bowels of the city felt like a step closer to something inevitable, like they were walking toward an end they couldn't quite understand yet.

"We're getting close," Victor said, breaking the silence. His voice was quieter than usual, more measured. There was a tension in his words, a weight that Evelyn could feel in her chest. It mirrored her own fears.

Evelyn glanced at him, noticing how tense his shoulders were, how his jaw was clenched. She could tell he was as exhausted as she was, but neither of them could afford to stop now. They had no choice but to keep moving. To get to the heart of this nightmare before it consumed them whole.

The flash drive they had stolen from the hidden room in the building felt like a live wire in her pocket. The weight of it reminded her constantly of the price they had paid for this information. Elena had died to give them the key. And now, they were risking everything to unlock the truth—no matter what it cost.

"Do you think we're ready for this?" Evelyn asked, her voice barely above a whisper as she slowed her pace. Her breath came in uneven bursts. The silence around them was deafening, and yet she felt like every sound, every breath, was a signal that they were being watched. That Corvus was closing in.

Victor didn't answer immediately. He was looking ahead, his expression unreadable. He was calculating. Thinking. Evelyn knew him too well. He didn't show fear. He didn't show doubt. But she could see it now—flickering behind his eyes, the same doubt that had plagued her.

"I don't know if we'll ever be ready," he said finally, his voice rough. "But I do know this: If we don't do this, no one will."

His words hung in the air as they walked deeper into the tunnels. They passed an abandoned maintenance room, its door slightly ajar, a draft of cool air drifting out. The further they moved, the quieter the tunnel seemed to become. Until it was just the two of them—alone in the dark with only the echoes of their footsteps.

"We should be close," Victor said, turning to a narrow passage that led downward. "This should take us to an old service entrance near the core of the station."

Evelyn nodded, and without a word, followed him down the steep staircase. It wasn't long before the narrow passage opened up into a larger, more expansive space. A vast underground chamber stretched out before them, filled with the sound of distant rumblings—an old subway track long abandoned, a skeleton of the city's former transit system.

There was something eerie about it. The air felt different here—thick, almost electric. They had crossed into a place forgotten by the world above, a place where the past and present collided in a way that left no room for light.

In the distance, barely visible through the gloom, stood a door. A door that, to Evelyn's surprise, was not locked. The handle was cold beneath her fingers as she pushed it open slowly.

Beyond it was a room that looked like it had been untouched for decades. A control room, from the looks of it—rusted consoles lined the walls, wires hanging from the ceilings, and old monitors blinked with static. There was an odd familiarity to the room, an unsettling feeling that gnawed at Evelyn's mind as she stepped inside.

"This place... it's part of the old Corvus network," Victor muttered, his voice reverberating in the stillness. "They've been running operations out of here for years. It's a hub—a base of operations."

Evelyn nodded. "So this is it, then. This is where everything starts."

She stepped forward, feeling a surge of anticipation and dread. Her hand reached for the nearest console. She could almost feel the pulse of something hidden beneath the surface, a waiting energy, as if the room itself was a dormant beast ready to be awakened. The flash drive in her pocket seemed to hum in sync with the feeling.

Victor had already begun rifling through the papers scattered across a nearby desk. Most were unreadable—old files, half-crumpled documents, faded photographs—but he quickly found something of interest.

"Look at this," he said, holding up a photo that made Evelyn's blood run cold. It was a picture of the man from the files they found earlier—the blurred figure whose face had eluded them for so long. Only now, the image was clearer. His face was still obscured by shadows, but there was something undeniably familiar about him.

Evelyn took the photo, examining it closely. She didn't know why it felt like a blow to the gut, but it did. It was as if she had seen him before, though she couldn't place where or when. The mystery of who this man was—who was behind everything—seemed to swirl just out of her reach.

"Who is he?" she asked, her voice hoarse.

Victor stared at the photo for a long moment, his face unreadable. "I don't know. But I'm starting to think this isn't just a random figure. He's the key. He's been pulling the strings all along."

Evelyn felt her pulse quicken. "If he's the one behind it all, then we have to find him. Before Corvus can do more damage."

Victor agreed, but there was something in his eyes that told Evelyn they were both afraid of what that might mean. They had already come so far, uncovered so much, but the closer they got to the truth, the more dangerous everything became.

The sound of a door creaking open behind them made both of them freeze.

Someone was there.

Before they could react, a voice called out in the darkness. A voice that sent a chill down Evelyn's spine. It was deep, authoritative, and yet there was an unmistakable calm to it—a man who wasn't worried about being discovered. He had been waiting for them.

"Well, well... I see you've made it this far," the voice said, smooth and cold. "I must admit, I'm impressed."

Evelyn's hand immediately went to her gun, but Victor placed a hand on her arm, shaking his head. He was trying to read the situation, trying to figure out who was behind the voice.

The man stepped forward into the dim light.

And Evelyn's heart dropped into her stomach.

It was him.

The man from the photograph.

He was taller than she had imagined, his face sharply angular, the kind of face that belonged to someone who had spent years in the shadows, crafting his power with cold precision. His eyes were piercing, like daggers that could see through her soul. He wore a dark suit, his hands folded neatly in front of him, as if he had all the time in the world. And perhaps, in that moment, he did.

"Who are you?" Evelyn demanded, her voice trembling despite herself. She wasn't sure if it was fear or fury that made her heart race. Either way, it didn't matter. She needed answers.

The man smiled, but there was no warmth in it. "I am the one who's been pulling the strings. The one you've been running from. And now... I believe it's time for you to understand the full extent of your situation."

The man stepped fully into the light, his features becoming clearer with every step. Evelyn's grip tightened on her gun, but she didn't raise it yet. Something about him made her freeze—a calmness in his demeanor that unsettled her more than anything else. She felt as if she were facing a force much greater than mere physical danger. This man wasn't just a threat. He was a symbol of everything that had been unraveling around her for the last few months.

Victor stood slightly in front of her, his own posture rigid but ready. She could sense his readiness to act, his instincts finely tuned, but even he seemed unnerved by the man's presence.

The stranger didn't seem to be in a hurry. He moved deliberately, his polished shoes clicking against the concrete floor. His suit was immaculate, perfectly tailored, the kind of suit that made you think of power—of men who made decisions that altered the course of history without anyone realizing. The kind of man who made *you* feel small, even when you were standing on the same ground.

Evelyn's mouth went dry as she studied his face. There was no recognition, no familiarity. And yet... the feeling that this man had been watching her for a long time, had known her every move, made the hairs on the back of her neck stand on end.

Finally, he spoke.

"I've been waiting for you," he said smoothly, his voice a rich baritone that seemed to reverberate through the room. His words were both an invitation and a warning, like a door slowly opening to an inevitable truth.

Victor didn't flinch. "Who are you?"

The man's lips curled into a smile, though it didn't reach his cold eyes. "You've already met me, in a way. My name is Samuel Corvus."

The words struck Evelyn like a punch to the gut. Samuel Corvus. The name that had been a shadow hanging over everything. The name that had haunted her dreams. The name that, until now, had felt like a myth—a legend spoken of in whispers. But now, standing before them, was the man himself. And he wasn't some distant figure. He was real. He was tangible. And he had orchestrated everything that had led them to this moment.

Evelyn could hardly breathe. It felt like the world had tilted on its axis. The name that had seemed so distant now echoed in her mind, tying together all the pieces of the puzzle. Corvus wasn't just some faceless organization; it was him. The man standing in front of her.

"I see you're surprised," Corvus continued, his voice soft but full of command. "I've been watching you, Evelyn. I've watched you for a long time. All your moves, all your questions, your determination. You've been clever, but I'm afraid it's too late."

Evelyn's mind raced, trying to make sense of the flood of emotions crashing over her. Fear. Anger. Confusion. Betrayal. She had known Corvus was powerful, but she had never imagined he was this close—this *personal*. He had been in their lives in ways they couldn't have understood. But now that she saw him, she realized there had been hints all along. The careful orchestration of events, the way her life had become a puzzle piece in a much larger game.

"What do you want?" she forced herself to ask, her voice shaking only slightly.

Corvus didn't respond immediately. Instead, he glanced at the control panel behind him, where old monitors still flickered with static. "What do I want?" he repeated, as if savoring the question. His eyes glinted with amusement. "What I want is simple. I want control. Power. And the ability to shape the world in my image."

Evelyn felt a surge of disgust. "You've done all of this for power?"

Corvus' smile deepened, but it was cold, calculating. "Not just for power. For the future. You see, the world is chaotic. It's a system on the brink of collapse. People like you, people who believe in ideals and the greater good, think that you can fix it. But you can't. The world needs order. It needs direction. And I intend to provide that direction."

Victor's voice broke in, sharp and defiant. "By controlling everything? By manipulating people's lives like puppets on strings? That's not order. That's tyranny."

Corvus' gaze flickered toward Victor, assessing him with a cold, almost detached curiosity. "You think I'm a tyrant? No, Victor, you're mistaken. I'm a visionary. A man who understands the nature of true power. The system is broken, and I'm the one who will fix it. The old ways—the so-called ideals of democracy, liberty, and equality—they're weak. They've failed. And in their place, I will build something far more efficient. Far more lasting."

Evelyn took a step forward, her hands clenched into fists. "And how do you plan to do that? By destroying everything?"

Corvus' smile never wavered. "By rebuilding it from the ground up. By removing the obstacles that keep this world in chaos. You, for example." He motioned to Evelyn, then to Victor. "You've been in my way for far too long. But I suppose that's to be expected. People like you can never see the bigger picture. You always think your actions are righteous. But in the end, you're just blind children."

Evelyn's stomach churned. "What happens to the rest of the world when you get what you want? What about the people you've destroyed to get here?"

Corvus didn't respond immediately. He simply watched her with that same unblinking gaze, as though sizing her up. "The weak will fall, Evelyn. That's the price of progress. Every revolution has casualties. But in the end, the world will be better for it. A new order will rise, one where strength and intelligence are rewarded, not blind loyalty to outdated ideals."

Victor stepped forward, his eyes flashing with a mixture of anger and determination. "You're delusional if you think you can control everything. People don't bend that easily."

Corvus chuckled softly. "Oh, I don't need to control everyone. I just need to control the ones who matter—the ones with the power to change things. You, Evelyn, for example. You and your little crusade. Your pursuit of truth. It's admirable, in a naïve way. But in the end, you'll understand. You'll see that I'm right. You'll see that this world needs a guiding hand."

Evelyn felt a knot form in her stomach. He was trying to manipulate her, to break her will. But she wouldn't let him. Not now, not when she was so close to the truth.

"You won't get away with this," she said, her voice steady, despite the anger rising in her chest. "We'll stop you. We'll expose you for what you are."

Corvus' eyes darkened, and for the first time, there was a flicker of something dangerous in them. "You think you can stop me? You're already too late. I've already won. It's just a matter of time before the rest of the world sees things my way."

His words hung in the air like a weight that pressed down on them both. The cold certainty in his voice made Evelyn's blood run cold. He was right about one thing—he had been waiting for them. He had anticipated their every move. And now, they were standing in his lair, cornered by the very man who had been orchestrating everything.

But Evelyn wasn't ready to give up. Not yet.

"You haven't won yet," she said, her voice low but fierce. "You may have the power, but you'll never have the truth. And that, Samuel Corvus, is something you'll never control."

For a long moment, there was nothing but silence. Then, Corvus leaned in slightly, his gaze narrowing. "We'll see about that."

The tension in the room reached a boiling point. Evelyn knew they were at a crossroads—this was it. The moment they either stepped into the light or fell into the shadows forever.

Chapter 30: The Vanishing Point

The air was thick with the tension of finality. The hum of the failing generators, the flickering lights, the distant groan of the facility—all these sounds seemed to blend into a single, ominous symphony. For Evelyn, standing at the center of it all, it felt as though time itself had slowed. Every second stretched out, every decision, every action weighed heavy with the knowledge that they were on the precipice of something monumental.

The truth was about to come to light. And Samuel Corvus, the man who had orchestrated so much of the chaos, was standing just a few feet away, as calm as ever, watching them with that cold, unblinking gaze.

Evelyn had always known this moment would come. She'd spent years chasing the truth, following a trail of blood and lies that led her to this dark corner of the world. And now, here she was. The final confrontation. The culmination of all their efforts, their sacrifices, their losses. She had no illusions about what it would mean—this was no victory march. This was the end of something, and the beginning of something else entirely.

Behind her, Victor was tense, his hand resting on the gun at his side, ready for anything. But Evelyn could feel the weight of his uncertainty. Even he knew that Corvus wasn't the kind of man you could simply shoot and be done with. There was something deeper at work here—something far more dangerous than a single individual. Corvus was a symbol. A representation of everything that had gone wrong in their world.

Samuel Corvus took a step forward, his polished shoes clicking against the floor in the otherwise quiet room. His presence filled the space like a dark cloud, suffocating and all-encompassing. He had orchestrated everything—the corruption, the manipulation, the destruction. He was both the mastermind and the machine, and Evelyn knew he would not be easily defeated.

"You're wasting your time," Corvus said, his voice low and smooth, like honey sliding over steel. "You've made your choices. But in the end, it doesn't matter. The system is already in motion. The pieces are already set in place. There's nothing you can do to stop it."

Evelyn's chest tightened, but she didn't back down. "I'm not here to stop you. I'm here to make sure the truth gets out."

Corvus raised an eyebrow, his expression a mix of amusement and condescension. "The truth? You really think that matters in the end? You think the world will care about the truth? People don't care about the truth. They care about power. They care about survival."

Evelyn shook her head. "You're wrong. People care about what's real. They care about what's right."

The words sounded hollow even to her own ears. She *wanted* to believe them. But in the cold, unforgiving world she was facing, she wasn't so sure. Could truth really change anything? Could it stop a man like Corvus, who had spent his life building an empire of control and deception?

Victor stepped closer, his voice low but determined. "You think you've won, Corvus? You think this is the end of the line for us? It's just beginning. The truth is already out there. People are already listening."

For the first time, Corvus' smile faltered. There was a flicker of something in his eyes—something like frustration, or perhaps disbelief. He wasn't used to people challenging him. He wasn't used to losing control.

"You think some files, some documents, will stop what's coming?" Corvus sneered. "You think a few leaks will bring down everything I've built? You're naive. The world doesn't care about some vague notion of justice. It cares about power, and I've already ensured that it's on my side."

But Evelyn, despite the gnawing fear in her gut, didn't flinch. She knew better. She knew that even in a world dominated by men like Corvus, there were cracks. There were people who would rise up, who would hear the truth and demand accountability. The fight wasn't over. It had only just begun.

"You're wrong," she said, her voice steady. "People will rise. And when they do, your empire of lies will crumble."

Corvus stared at her, silent for a moment, as though weighing her words. Then, with a small, almost pitying laugh, he turned away, his gaze scanning the darkened room, the control panels, the monitors that were slowly flickering back to life. It was almost as if the man didn't care anymore. As if he had already written them off as irrelevant.

"Do you honestly think I'll just let you walk away from this?" he said, his voice sharp, cutting through the silence. "You're here, at my mercy, in the heart of my world. And yet you still believe there's something to fight for. It's pathetic, really."

Evelyn took a deep breath. This was it. The final moment. The culmination of all her work. She had one last chance to make sure Corvus didn't disappear into the shadows again. One last opportunity to expose him to the world, to take him down for good.

Her fingers hovered over the console. She had only moments before the facility's security system would reactivate, before Corvus could implement his countermeasures. She couldn't waste any more time. The documents, the evidence—they were all uploading now, out of Corvus' reach. The data would be transmitted to the world, the truth about his empire, his manipulation, his crimes. But only if she acted fast.

"Victor, cover me," Evelyn muttered, her eyes never leaving Corvus.

Victor nodded once, his hand instinctively reaching for his weapon. But he didn't need to act yet. They were close. So close.

The final confirmation from the network was almost there. Once the transmission was complete, Corvus would be exposed. The world would finally know the depth of his corruption.

Corvus, still seemingly unaware of the impending threat, turned back to face her. There was something in his eyes now, something almost imperceptible—a shift, a hint of understanding that he was losing control. It was a momentary lapse, but it was enough.

"You think you've won," Corvus said slowly, his words deliberate. *"But the truth is like a wave. It comes, and it goes. It washes over everything, and then it disappears into the sea of forgetfulness."*

Evelyn didn't reply. She didn't have to. The truth would not disappear—not this time. She knew that even if Corvus believed he could silence her, the data she had uploaded was already out of his grasp. The files were moving fast, faster than he could possibly comprehend. His empire was collapsing from the inside, piece by piece.

And yet, as she watched him standing there, so sure of himself, so unshakable in his belief that the world would never change, Evelyn couldn't help but wonder: Was Corvus right? Was this just another fleeting moment of hope that would vanish as quickly as it had arrived?

But then, she thought of the people—the families, the victims, the countless lives that had been torn apart by his machinations. She thought of the truth, the power that it held, and the ripple it would send across the world. This was it. There was no going back. She had done what she came here to do.

The countdown on the console flashed. **100%.**

The transmission was complete.

The light in the room flickered as if in acknowledgement, and Evelyn knew—deep in her bones—that this was the moment. This was the vanishing point. The end of everything Corvus had built. The truth had finally been unleashed.

Corvus turned toward her, his face a mask of fury and disbelief. "You... you think this changes anything?"

Evelyn didn't respond. She didn't need to.

The room was silent once again, but this time, the silence felt different. It wasn't the calm before the storm. It was the storm itself. And this time, the storm wasn't going to pass.

Evelyn had brought the truth to light. Corvus' empire of lies was crumbling, and there was nothing he could do to stop it.

The silence was deafening, the moment suspended in a heavy, thick air. Evelyn's fingers hovered over the controls of the console, her mind still processing the enormity of what had just transpired. The files had uploaded. The world was about to know. And for the first time in a long time, Evelyn allowed herself to breathe. It felt like the weight of the world had lifted, even if just for a brief, fragile moment.

But Samuel Corvus, the architect of it all, was still standing there. His face, once calm and confident, was now a twisted mask of anger. His eyes locked on hers, an almost predatory gleam in their depths. He was silent, but she could feel his thoughts swirling in the air, could see his mind working through the implications of what had just happened.

Victor, standing at her side, took a step closer, his presence a shield behind her. His body was taut, ready for action. The room was dark now, the only illumination coming from the dim red emergency lights overhead. The hum of the cooling systems echoed off the walls, an ever-present reminder of the ticking clock. Evelyn knew they didn't have long before Corvus would activate whatever fail-safes he had left. But there was one thing he hadn't accounted for.

Evelyn's heart pounded in her chest as she turned back to the control panel. Her fingers moved quickly, rapidly cycling through the security systems. Corvus had assumed he was invincible, that his empire could never be brought down by a handful of people. But the truth was, he had underestimated one thing: the power of the people.

"The world will know," Evelyn said, her voice steady, cutting through the tension. "Your lies, your manipulation—it's all over."

Corvus' lips curled into a tight, cruel smile. But this time, it didn't reach his eyes. "You really think this changes anything? You think the world will rise up against me because of some files you've managed to leak? You're so naive, Evelyn. So very naive."

Evelyn didn't reply. She didn't need to. She had already done the one thing that would ensure Corvus' downfall. The data was out. The truth would be impossible to suppress. It wasn't about what Corvus could control. It was about what the world could no longer ignore.

Victor stepped forward, his voice hard. "You're right about one thing, Corvus. It's not just about the files. It's about what comes next. The world is waking up. And when they do, you'll have nowhere to hide."

Corvus scoffed, taking a step toward them. "You think they'll care? People are weak, easily distracted. This—" he gestured vaguely at the walls of the control room, "—this is all that matters. Power. Control. You think the truth is going to bring me down? You think it will change anything?"

Victor's jaw clenched. He was done talking. "It's already changing. People will hear this. They'll know exactly what you've done, who you are. You won't control the narrative anymore."

Corvus' smile vanished. For a moment, his eyes flickered with something dangerous. Something Evelyn had seen before in powerful men who had lost control. Fear. A flicker of panic, buried under layers of confidence and arrogance.

It was fleeting, but it was enough. Evelyn seized the moment, stepping forward and positioning herself between Victor and Corvus, her voice unwavering. "You've already lost, Corvus. This game is over."

The words were simple, but they carried a weight far heavier than anything Corvus had expected. He recoiled as if struck, his eyes narrowing as his mind processed what was happening. But before he could speak, the emergency lights above them flickered, the monitors that had once shown his empire's strength now blank. The system was shutting down. Evelyn had overridden it. The countdown was running out.

"You think this is it?" Corvus spat, his voice rising with a fury that shook the still air. "You've made a huge mistake, Evelyn. You've exposed me, but you have no idea what's coming. You have no idea what I've built."

But the anger in his voice felt hollow, a desperate act to maintain some illusion of control. The data, the files—*the truth*—was out there now. It was already spreading across encrypted channels, reaching journalists, activists, whistleblowers, anyone who could help expose the heart of Corvus' empire.

Evelyn felt the satisfaction of the moment, but it was tempered with something else—dread, anticipation. The battle wasn't over. Corvus was a dangerous man, and if there was one thing she knew, it was that cornered animals were the most dangerous. He was calculating, still dangerous, and that made him unpredictable.

Victor shifted, his hand now fully gripping the weapon at his side. "You may have been right about one thing, Corvus. It's not about the truth. It's about power." He took a breath, then added, "But now, we're the ones with the power. And that's something you can't stop."

For a long moment, Corvus said nothing. He simply stared at them, his face unreadable. But Evelyn could feel the shift. He was no longer the confident leader, the puppet master. He was a man realizing that the walls were closing in. The power he'd spent years building was slipping away, and he couldn't control it.

Then, without warning, Corvus turned away, walking toward the far end of the control room. Evelyn tensed, her instincts screaming at her to act. But she held back. This was not a man who surrendered quietly. And if there was one thing Corvus wasn't, it was predictable.

"I'll never be taken down by the likes of you," Corvus muttered, almost to himself. "I'll make sure the world stays the way it is. You'll see. The system always wins."

Evelyn moved toward the center of the room, her eyes on him, calculating, waiting for him to make his next move. She wasn't going to let him slip away again. Not after everything they'd been through, everything they'd sacrificed. She could feel the rush of adrenaline building in her chest as the final confrontation neared.

Victor raised his weapon slightly, eyes locked on Corvus' every move. There was no turning back now.

Just as Corvus reached a terminal at the far end of the room, the door to the control room opened, the heavy metal creaking on its hinges. A figure stepped inside, shrouded in the dark, tall and imposing.

"Don't make another move," the figure said, their voice low and dangerous.

Evelyn's heart skipped a beat. She knew that voice.

"Luke?" she whispered, almost in disbelief.

Luke Bennett, the man who had once been her ally—before everything went sideways—now stood in the doorway, his gun trained on Samuel Corvus. His face was grim, unreadable. There was no warmth, no recognition in his eyes. Only cold, hard focus.

Corvus, for the first time, looked uncertain. He glanced between Luke and Evelyn, then back to the monitors. He could see it now—the trap closing in around him. He had no escape. The truth had spread too far, too fast. He had been cornered. And yet, he still refused to give up.

"Luke, what are you doing here?" Evelyn asked, her voice almost a whisper. She couldn't quite process the situation.

Luke didn't answer immediately. He only gave her a tight nod, his gaze locked on Corvus. "I'm here to finish what we started."

The weight of his words hit Evelyn harder than she expected. There had been so much history between them—betrayal, trust broken, secrets uncovered. But now, it all seemed to fall away in the face of the bigger picture. They were no longer working for their own purposes. They were here to end Corvus' reign once and for all.

Victor's gaze flicked between Luke and Corvus, his grip on his weapon tightening. "What happens now?" he asked, his voice steady but tinged with uncertainty.

Luke glanced back at Victor, then to Evelyn. His face softened for just a moment. "Now we finish it. We make sure he never hurts anyone again."

For a moment, the room was still. The air was thick with tension, the realization of their victory hanging like a weight. The system Corvus had built—the web of lies, the manipulation—was crumbling. And there was nothing he could do to stop it.

Evelyn stepped forward, her eyes meeting Corvus' one last time. "You won't escape this, Corvus. You've lost."

Corvus stood still, his fists clenched, his breath ragged. But there was no fight left in him. Not anymore.

He was finished.

And with that, the walls of his empire began to fall. The vanishing point had arrived.

The room was silent, save for the heavy breaths of those who stood at its center. Samuel Corvus, the man who had masterminded a sprawling empire built on lies, deception, and manipulation, was standing at the precipice of his own destruction. The harsh glow of the emergency lights cast long shadows across the cold concrete floor, and the hum of the cooling systems, once so soothing in their consistency, now seemed like a countdown to an inevitable end.

Evelyn stood just a few feet away from Corvus, her hand still resting on the console where the final transmission had just been completed. The files were out. The truth had been exposed. She had given everything to bring this moment about. She had sacrificed her career, her safety, and her sense of self—all for the chance to dismantle Corvus' empire.

Victor stood at her side, still tense, his hand on the weapon at his side. But for now, there was no need for force. No need for violence. The battle had already been won. The truth had already shattered Corvus' carefully constructed world.

And then, from the shadows, another figure stepped forward. Evelyn's heart skipped a beat as she recognized the tall, dark figure in the doorway.

"Luke?" she breathed, her voice barely a whisper.

Luke Bennett—once her partner, the man who had disappeared without a trace—was standing there, gun raised, but there was no malice in his eyes. Instead, there was something else—determination. Steely resolve.

"Don't make another move," Luke commanded, his voice low and commanding. There was no warmth in his gaze, only focus. He wasn't here to negotiate. He was here to finish what they had started.

Corvus turned toward him, his eyes narrowing in suspicion and fear. For the first time, his cool, confident demeanor faltered. Luke had always been a wildcard—someone who never quite fit into the polished world Corvus had built. But now, Luke's sudden reappearance in the middle of this final confrontation had thrown everything off balance.

Evelyn's mind raced. She had never anticipated Luke's return, not after everything that had happened. Not after the betrayal, the lies, the silence. But in that moment, she understood. Luke had come to finish the job—just as they had promised, back when they first set out to uncover the truth.

"What are you doing here?" Evelyn asked, almost incredulously, though her eyes were locked on Corvus.

Luke didn't take his eyes off Corvus as he answered, his voice measured, like a man who had been waiting for this moment his whole life. "I'm here to make sure Corvus doesn't escape this. This ends now, Evelyn. No more running. No more hiding. He won't have another chance."

Victor, his eyes still suspicious, shifted his weight, positioning himself slightly in front of Evelyn. "What happens now?" he asked Luke, his voice quiet but tense.

Luke met his gaze, his expression hardening. "Now, we make sure Corvus faces justice. All of it. He won't just disappear into the shadows again. Not after what he's done."

Corvus, for the first time in what seemed like years, seemed to lose his composure. He looked between Luke, Evelyn, and Victor, then back at the control panel, the terminal where he had once held the power to manipulate entire systems. His eyes flickered with panic, and for a moment, it was clear that he understood the gravity of his situation. He was cornered. There was nowhere to run.

"You don't understand," Corvus said suddenly, his voice rising in an almost desperate plea. "You think you've won, but you have no idea what you're dealing with. You can't just expose me and expect everything to fall apart. There are forces at work, people who will protect me. The system is too strong."

Evelyn felt her chest tighten, but she didn't flinch. "The system only works as long as people believe in it. And the people—" she said, her voice growing stronger— "will no longer believe in you. They'll see you for what you really are."

Luke gave a tight nod, his gaze never leaving Corvus. "The truth will set them free. And it will bring you down."

Corvus' gaze flickered to the monitors, the terminal now displaying the evidence of his fall from power. Files, data, proof of his corruption, his manipulation, all of it was now out there, spreading across the world. Activists, journalists, and even law enforcement were already picking up the pieces, uncovering the sprawling network of lies that had supported his reign.

Corvus turned back to face Evelyn, his eyes cold and calculating once more. "You think this is over? You think exposing me will change anything?" His laugh was bitter. "I'll rebuild. I'll always rebuild. The world needs people like me. Power always finds a way. Always."

Evelyn shook her head. "Not this time. You're not going to rebuild. You're finished."

Victor moved forward slowly, his voice steady. "Your empire crumbles from within, Corvus. You can't escape it. No matter how much power you have, the truth is stronger than any of your lies."

For a moment, it felt like the world had stopped. The room, once full of the hum of machinery and the oppressive presence of Corvus, was now filled with the hum of victory. The light, though dim, seemed brighter somehow. The walls—so long the stronghold of corruption—seemed to shrink.

But then, something unexpected happened.

A loud noise rang out, echoing through the chamber. Corvus, ever the master of control, had managed to activate one final contingency. The floor beneath them trembled, and the emergency alarms screamed to life. The monitors blinked back to life, displaying a new set of codes. The security system was rebooting, faster than Evelyn could process.

Luke's hand was already at his side, pulling out his gun in one swift motion. "He's trying to escape," he warned, his voice urgent. "We have to act now."

Evelyn's heart skipped a beat. "What is he doing?"

Corvus was already moving, his hands working at the terminal with a frantic urgency. He was trying to trigger a reset, to wipe the evidence. But it was too late.

Before Corvus could finish, the heavy doors to the control room suddenly slammed shut, locking from the outside. The lights flickered, then went out completely. The hum of the cooling systems went silent. The room descended into pitch blackness.

"**No!**" Corvus shouted in frustration, his voice full of rage.

Evelyn and Victor moved instinctively, their eyes adjusting to the dark. "We can't let him destroy the evidence!" Evelyn shouted. "We need to stop him!"

The door behind them was sealed, and there was no way out.

The sound of Corvus' frantic typing echoed in the dark, followed by the violent clattering of the terminal keys. The desperation in his movements was palpable. He wasn't just trying to reset the system—he was trying to burn everything. To erase the truth.

"Stop him!" Luke yelled. "Get to the terminal!"

Evelyn bolted toward the control panel, but before she could reach it, a sudden flash of light illuminated the room, revealing Corvus standing by the terminal, a wild look in his eyes.

"*You don't understand,*" he growled. "This is just the beginning. You think you can take everything from me, but you can't. It's already too late!"

Evelyn sprinted forward, her heart racing as she dove for the terminal. She slammed her hand on the override button just as Corvus reached for the emergency shutdown. A deafening screech filled the room as the data that had been uploaded was finally secured.

The terminal went dark. The systems, once so powerful, were now powerless. The evidence of Corvus' crimes had been scattered, saved, and protected from his grasp.

There was a finality to the moment. No more running. No more secrets. The truth had triumphed.

As the lights flickered back to life, the silence that followed was heavy with the weight of their victory.

Corvus stood there, his face pale and crumpled, defeated for the first time in years. His empire was gone. His influence had evaporated. His name—his legacy—was now an echo, fading in the aftermath of the truth.

And in that moment, Evelyn realized that this wasn't just about taking down Corvus. This was about taking back control. About reclaiming the power that had been stolen from the people. The fight had been long, but it was worth it.

Luke's voice broke the silence. "It's over," he said, his tone firm.

Evelyn nodded, her heart heavy but her resolve clear. "Yes. It's over."

Corvus was done. The system was already shifting, and though it would take time for the full scope of the fallout to be realized, Evelyn knew that nothing would be the same again. The truth had come to light, and there was no turning back.

Don't miss out!

Visit the website below and you can sign up to receive emails whenever J.D Rivers publishes a new book. There's no charge and no obligation.

https://books2read.com/r/B-A-DZGWC-NPXIF

BOOKS 2 READ

Connecting independent readers to independent writers.

About the Author

J.D. Rivers, the pen name of Jerald D'Souza, is a new and emerging author in the world of mystery, thriller, and suspense fiction. With a passion for crafting gripping narratives and intricate plots, J.D. Rivers aims to captivate readers with thrilling stories that keep them on the edge of their seats. Drawing inspiration from the complexities of human nature and the dark twists of life, Rivers creates immersive tales that blend suspense, intrigue, and unexpected turns.

Milton Keynes UK
Ingram Content Group UK Ltd.
UKHW030146051224
452010UK00001B/87

9 798230 075448